D0481709

VAIL LIBRARY
1 16 0002309213

DREAM HOUSE

DREAM HOUSE

A NOVEL

VALERIE LAKEN

HARPER
An Imprint of HarperCollins*Publishers*
www.harpercollins.com

HarperCollins books may be purchased for educational, business, or sales promotional use. For information, please write: Special Markets Department, HarperCollins Publishers, 10 East 53rd Street, New York, NY 10022.

FIRST EDITION

Designed by Susan Yang

Interior Art © Jim Ferguson, Sandlapper Studio
http://www.sandlapperstudio.com

Library of Congress Cataloging-in-Publication Data is available upon request.

ISBN: 978-0-06-084092-1

09 10 11 12 13 OV/RRD 10 9 8 7 6 5 4 3 2 1

For Rodney,

who makes everything possible

Imagine that Noah knocked his house apart and used the planks to build an ark, while his neighbors looked on, full of doubt. A house, he must have told them, should be daubed with pitch and built to float cloud high, if need be. A lettuce patch was of no use at all, and a good foundation was worse than useless. A house should have a compass and a keel. The neighbors would have put their hands in their pockets and chewed their lips and strolled home to houses they now found wanting in ways they could not understand.

—MARILYNNE ROBINSON, *Housekeeping*

DREAM HOUSE

PROLOGUE

JULY 1987

If you took away the police tape and the squad cars and the neighbors murmuring in a cluster on the sidewalk, it would look like the kind of house little kids draw: a wooden, two-story box topped with the steep triangle of a full attic, and a chimney tilting slightly from the ridge line of the roof. The blistered paint was the gray-blue of dishwater, and there were no dormers or bay windows or Victorian details—just that blunt, workman's box and triangle, fronted by a wooden porch that sagged toward the street. Some kids might scribble coils of smoke above the chimney or plant flowers near the windows, but these windows were bare and dusty, reflectionless, and the chimney was quiet. It was ninety degrees and humid, even at twilight. Jay opened the door of his work van to let in more air.

The house was only eight blocks away from his one-room apartment over in Ann Arbor's student ghettos, which meant he had probably gone past the place lots of times without noticing it. These old clapboard houses all looked alike, crowded on their lots in orderly rows. But now this one, cordoned off, had gone and distinguished itself.

The neighbors on the sidewalk glanced up at Jay's open door, at his foot kicked out on the running board. He adjusted his side mirror to take them in.

Always, the rubberneckers. They crowded around every job site, outraged that catastrophe dared strike so close to home, in a house so like theirs. Tonight it was an old white guy with a collie, two obese women squinting and gasping, and a bony, bug-eyed black girl who kept crumpling over into tears. What they wanted to know was how he was connected to the house, and whether, unlike the police or the ambulance guys, he would tell them about the murder.

He stayed put, kept his mouth shut, checked his watch. It was after nine, and still, no Mack.

It didn't make sense to waste the night waiting for him, but stepping over the threshold was the hardest part of the gore jobs, and Jay didn't want to do it alone, surrounded by a bunch of boneheaded cops and spectators. Their regular, bread-and-butter cleanup jobs were disgusting but emotionally neutral: basements soaked with rain or sewer backup, the occasional aftermath of a fire or caved-in roof. No problem. Then there were the croaks—old folks found dead and decomposing at home, sometimes days after the fact. These still gave Jay the shivers. He tried to tell himself that such scenes were just the natural end of a lonely life, and there was nothing unjust or cruel about a body working its way back toward dust, however messy the process might be. But it didn't always work.

As often as not the old croaks and some of the other jobs, too, involved wretched, reeking messes that ordinary people would call gore. But in Mack's lingo the word referred only to blood, death by violence, and the pay was double time. Gore calls came at odd hours once or twice a month, mostly from Ypsilanti, the failing town five miles east. Mack lived in the other direction, west of town, in Dexter, so they covered any catastrophe within a twenty-mile radius of Ann Arbor. Every once in a while Mack would talk about expanding farther east, into Detroit, where there would surely be more gore jobs but less money. Jay always shrugged and said, *Sure, why not?* It wasn't his investment, and he needed the work. He had rent, food, books, art supplies to pay for, sometimes even tuition when his dad got behind. But every time the idea of expanding the business came up, Mack would shy away two sentences in, saying he was too old to get enterprising. *And it's a special service we do,* he liked to say. *Not some corporate hustle.*

A uniformed cop came out on the porch and squinted at Jay in the driveway. "You the cleanup guys?" The work van was a plain white number, no advertising.

"We'll be in in a minute." Jay tried to sound resolute, as if the delay were a matter of protocol, not fear. The cop stared at him a few more seconds, which Jay got a lot. He kept his hair dyed black and gelled up in long, spiky tufts that stood out around his head, like that guy from the Cure, Robert Smith. Evidently the world believed that if you did such things, if you wore black shirts and big boots and junkyard belts, if you occasionally let your girlfriend draw up your eyes with thick black eyeliner or force her earrings through your eyebrows, you were inviting stares and should be glad to get them. Jay understood that logic, but the fact was he didn't like eyes on him, especially cop eyes, especially at these jobs. He could feel them imagining the worst: that these punks were death-crazed sickos, liable to do just about anything once the doors were closed. He pulled his work cap from under the windshield visor and tugged it down over his hair till it crunched and gave way.

"I've got to wait for my boss," he said to the cop.

On the sidewalk another old geezer joined the cluster,

and Jay heard one of the women say, *Had it comin'.* The cop fired them a menacing look, but the rubberneckers just stared back in a silent standoff. It was their street, after all, where they borrowed shovels and sugar and hollered at one another's kids. And when someone got wheeled out under a police blanket—slowly, in no paramedic hurry—after a rash of gunshots that interrupted all their dinners, they had a right to ask questions, didn't they?

Finally the old man with the collie whistled up at the house and shrugged. "You're a little late *now*, ain't you, Officer?"

The cop made a shallow grunt, digesting the insult, and went back into the house.

At her apartment Jay's girlfriend Claire would be on her back in the bedroom, the only room with air-conditioning, waiting for him to call. Like everyone else she had heard the sirens earlier and wanted the scoop. She lived just four blocks away, up Madison Street, toward the UM campus. But it wasn't plain fear or gossip-mongering that moved her. Lately she'd developed a peculiar fascination with his job.

Earlier tonight, she was at Jay's tiny apartment when he played back the message Mack had left on his machine, and her eyes flared open when the word *gore* came up. He turned off the machine midmessage, wrote down the address—Macon Street—and checked his watch. Ignoring Claire, he opened the refrigerator to see what they could eat before he had to go. Claire slithered in between him and the open refrigerator shelves.

"Well, what do you know?" She smiled. "An opportunity."

In the nights, these past weeks, she'd begun grilling him for stories. "Do you get to, like, see the bodies?" she had asked him last week, her voice thrilled, her hands moving over him. He did not.

"It's not going to happen, Claire," he stopped her. "You can't come over there." Among the other things he regretted telling her was the fact that on some jobs, when it got very late and there was just basic painting or disposal left to do, Mack sometimes left him alone in those newly sterile, haunting spaces.

Now she was pressing herself against him, kneeling down. A cool cloud of vapor came up from the fridge behind her and whispered over him.

"Come on, Jay." Her cheek was against his jeans, her fingers working the top button. She was his first real, full-time, adult-life girlfriend, and he had hardly any defenses against her. As she pulled down his jeans and took him in her mouth, Jay stared dimly at the condiment jars and beer bottles that were lit up on the top shelf. Then he lowered his eyelids and saw only the top of her head, the blurry mass of her white, spiky hair.

"Really, Claire," he struggled to say. "You're not going over there."

A few seconds more and she stopped. "Are you sure?"

He stared at her, at himself there, wanting her. "It's just wrong."

She shrugged and stood up, then turned from him and started poking through the refrigerator. "I guess we should eat something then. What have you got?"

"You're a bad influence." He grasped at her, smiling.

"Let's just eat." She shrugged him off. "I mean, it's just *wrong*."

Jay leaned back against the counter. Pulled up his boxers. Every day with her and their art-major friends was a game of Truth or Dare, rebellion or convention, and he never won. It was all beginning to feel paralyzing, predictable, teenaged.

Jay felt himself outgrowing it, though this was anything but reassuring: they were still his friends, after all. They were what he had. When he couldn't live up to their schemes and adventures, Claire had a way of making him feel like a worthless little fraud. Already he understood that maybe not today but someday, before too long, this would be how he would lose her.

"I have an idea," she said, turning around.

Jay forced himself to hold still. He was cool, he was elsewhere, he could live without her, he could.

"How about if you just call me tonight? From there?" She sidled up to him and put her chin over his shoulder without bringing her arms up to actually hold him. "We can just talk on the phone. Use your powers of description."

Jay slipped his hands around her, feeling light and lucky. He was human, after all, just human, not quite twenty. "That I can do."

Mack showed up just before nine-thirty and slapped his hand against the back of the van. "Let's hit it," he called, and Jay got out and tried to act steady, though a shiver of what he was about to see was working its way from his intestines to his throat.

The cluster of people on the sidewalk had dwindled. Porch lights were coming on along the street. He and Mack lit cigarettes and went up on the porch to meet the cops on the scene. Jay had found, in the past, it helped to focus on the details of architecture, woodwork, design. The essentials of a house were always innocent, no matter what twisted damage people had done to each other inside. This particular porch was held up by three wooden columns that had rotted out near the bottoms and were teeming with carpenter ants. The wooden decking was tongue-and-groove, painted gray, except for a traffic pattern near the door that was worn down to bare wood. There were three metal folding chairs, a broom, a broken stroller, a shower curtain coiled on its rod.

"It's about time, Mack." An old cop came out and shook Mack's hand.

"Sorry. Sorry. Couldn't be helped. What are we looking at?"

"Come on in." The old cop opened the door. "I'll show you."

But just then two younger cops shuffled out, telling the old one they were leaving. They did their *See you tomorrow* routine and drove off in a squad car. The cop stood waiting for Mack and Jay to enter. Mack lifted his hat, smoothed back his white hair, and knocked on the door frame as he did at every job—it was some kind of superstition. Jay touched the spot Mack had rapped on and, keeping his gaze tight on Mack's thick, rounded shoulders, followed him in.

It was a large but simple house inside, with none of the elaborate detail work Jay expected from old houses. The wooden newel post at the foot of the staircase was blunt and squatty, coated in sloppy layers of brown paint, and stood uncomfortably close to the swing of the front door. An acrid, baby-puke, cat-litter stench tightened Jay's nostrils. A narrow hallway stretched alongside the staircase, leading from the front door to a large, fluorescent-lit kitchen in the back. To the right of the front door was a dark living room, with matted orange carpeting and disco lounge decor that suggested parties and cocktails and freewheeling—but in a different era. Now the sagging, creased cushions and stains only gave proof of a family that had peaked five or six years ago and slid downward ever since.

They almost never got called to houses that looked like magazine spreads.

The old cop led them up the stairs, pointing his walkie-talkie idly toward the smears of blood on the banister and wall. "You got some mess here." He pointed at a puddle on the landing. "Don't want to track it around." Mack nodded and surveyed the walls and ceiling, flipping on the light switch casually. The cop led them into a bedroom at the top of the stairs. The sheets and blankets had been stripped off the mattress, which was studded with brown, bloody patches that looked like countries drawn on a map.

"The main issue is in here," the cop said, opening the door to the walk-in closet. "Victim was shot first in here, then again here."

There was what you would expect, a large splash of blood and debris on one wall, splatters all around, a smaller smear on the wall outside the closet, and a series of congealed puddles spread along the floor.

"Yup," Mack said. "Terrible thing."

Mack and the cop stepped out of the closet and started back toward the staircase, talking about the crime, the family, the neighborhood and how it had gone to shit. Jay stood still, inhaling, exhaling. He closed his eyes. Something was rising up in his chest, and he had to hold on to himself inside to squeeze it back down into place.

There. He opened his eyes.

The finish on the wood floor had been worn away almost to nothing, which meant that the blood was liable to have stained the wood. He might have to try bleaching it. There were faint spatters across the ceiling that he would have to get on a stepladder to scrub away. Then it hit him: the clothes. The outside sleeve of each shirt was splattered, maybe ruined. He foresaw her, the dark, heavy woman of the house, walking around from now on with one reddish-brown arm, wearing the remains of this victim wherever she went.

He rushed into the bathroom, locked the door, spat into

the toilet. His mouth overflowed with saliva; a bubble of acid clung to the back of his throat. He swayed over the toilet, which was filthy with someone else's hair and dust. He breathed in and out, in and out, didn't want Mack or anyone to hear him up here doing anything but pissing. He spat again. It was going away, would go away. He could stay outside himself, let the machine of his hands and limbs do these things that were asked of him. He could keep his mind, his insides, out of it. It was only a few hours, only work, only for the money. He wretched and flushed. On the floor just behind the toilet, he noticed, somebody had carefully painted three little brown cockroaches. They gave him a shiver. What kind of people did that?

Though it wasn't his job, Jay picked up their toilet brush and Lysol and scrubbed out this poor filthy family's toilet for them.

"Mack," he said, once he was back on the driveway, digging into the truck for supplies. "The clothes in there? Are we going to wash them, or what?"

Mack took his hat off and rubbed at the back of his head. "Shit, I don't know," he said. "What do you think, Ed?"

The cop squinted up at the house. "How should I know? What's your norm?"

Mack made a half smile, half grimace. "Well, we don't usually do laundry, no."

"But all their things," Jay said. "The stains."

Mack nodded.

The cop said, "It's probably out of your domain."

"Yeah. Just let it go, Jay."

"Lady's coming back in the morning." The cop held out a piece of paper for Mack. "This is the number they gave, her minister's number, I think." Jay thought of this woman being hand-patted in the basement room of some church.

While Mack chatted with the cop, Jay got some gloves and shop towels and cleaners and took them into the house. He started with the small things, trying to ease into it. He sprayed down the blood on the banister and wiped his way up the stairs, stopping at the landing to clean up the small, sticky puddles there. He put the dripping rags into a plastic bag, then wiped the floor again, scrubbing at the cracks between each floorboard. At the top of the stairs he turned on the lights in every room and glanced around to see if there was anything to clean in them.

They were kids' rooms.

On the right was a very small room with no furniture except a twin-bed mattress on a box spring in the center of the floor. The walls and ceiling were a deep twilight blue, and on top of that color someone had painted several rocket ships—as big as punching bags—blasting off over orange flames along the walls. The ceiling was dotted with strange, multicolored moons and planets. On the other side of the hallway was a yellow room with a Big Bird bedspread and a child's red plastic desk-and-chair set. Stuffed animals covered the bed and floor, as if they'd been rifled through in a big hurry, and Jay got a terrible idea about it suddenly. He stepped closer to check, and sure enough, there were bits of dried blood on the stuffed animals, too. He didn't want to think about it. He closed the door for now, went back to the main bedroom, where at least he had seen everything there was to see.

From the front bedroom he could hear Mack out on the porch, still talking with the cop, and a low chuckle broke through the air and drifted up to him. If he went out there he'd have to act casual about it all, have to find out what had happened, how, to whom. Like it was business, like it was TV drama. The house, he could deal with. The mess of the house was a physical thing, concrete, anonymous. Fixable.

The picture frames had been swept off the dresser. Jay picked them up, pulled away the glass shards, rubbed them with his rag and rearranged them. Mostly they were school pictures of kids, black kids, each new year's photo tucked into one edge of the frame, on top of the glass and the pictures from previous years. There were two steely-eyed teenage boys, and a little boy in a ball cap—maybe seven or eight—who smiled through a number of missing teeth. Last was the smallest, a little girl with thick black pigtails sticking out all over her head. All of them had clear, mocha skin and something about their mouths that made them look congenitally frightened. A pair of men's underwear was sticking out of one of the dresser drawers, and before wondering whether it was his domain or not, Jay opened the drawer and stuffed the underwear back in. That much was easy.

What was hard was not wondering who had died in here today. Jay walked over to the splashes on the wall and gauged their height. The first one, at least, seemed too tall to have involved the littlest kids.

He pressed a towel against the stained mattress for a long time, seeing whether any of the blood would come up, but not much did. It was just about dry. He shook out the blanket, watching it drift down and cover up the spots to make the bed look normal, almost like anyone's. He thought about Claire and her masterful feet, about those hands and lips of hers, the pale powdery breasts. He wanted to call her and say, *This is a special service we provide.* It had nothing to do with desire or daring, nothing to do with him, much less her.

If he was lucky, the phone here would be disconnected. If he was lucky, Mack wouldn't leave him alone tonight anyway.

After a while Mack came upstairs and they worked together quietly in the stuffy closet, scraping the walls with putty knives, then scrubbing them down.

Whenever Mack started to chat about what the cops had told him, Jay would go empty a bucket or run off for more supplies. He didn't trust himself with the story, didn't trust himself to withhold it from Claire, and if he couldn't keep from telling it, then his only choice was not to know it at all. Part of the story was written all over the house, anyway. Obviously, the shooting had been followed, and maybe preceded, by panic: people running everywhere, towels soaked through in an effort to stop the bleeding, little kids' shoeprints in the puddles, different-sized brownish-red handprints on the walls. Obviously, the shooter had either been justified or confessed right away, because otherwise the cops would still be here, measuring and searching and deducing. Obviously, it was a terrible story, sad like them all, and what was the use of knowing much more than that?

"What's going on with you tonight?" Mack asked the third time Jay tried to walk out on him. "It's like you're spooked."

Jay shrugged. Under his shirt, sweat was trickling down the middle of his back.

"Don't tell me it's getting to your head now."

What good would he be to Mack if he said yes?

"Because here's the thing, kiddo. There's nothing wrong with talking about it. It's normal."

Jay put his bucket of spackle back on the floor. "I know." He knelt down to face a bullet hole in the plaster. "I know."

So, like a priest in confession, he stayed in that closet, listening. And Mack went on about the mother, Loretta Price, who was already a widow two years, and didn't need more trouble like this, and so of course had gravitated right to it. "Never should have put herself in that *circumstance*," Mack said, stabbing his finger at the air. And then he moved on to the boy, her oldest son, Walker, who he said was a "stupid fuckin' hero." He was sitting in county jail right now, waiting. Had walked to the corner ice-cream shop with the gun, put it down on the counter, and said, "Call the police, please." Like that, *please*.

"He's only eighteen," Mack said. "Practically like you."

Jay smoothed a sponge across the rough edges of the spackle. There. The hole was gone now. "Will he go to prison?"

Mack shrugged and raised his eyebrows. "Black kid in Michigan?"

Jay squeezed his sponge in the milky water, envisioning himself in a cell, with the voices of thousands of others around him echoing off metal and concrete. Mack said, "Town isn't supposed to be like this. Ann Arbor." It wasn't Detroit or Ypsilanti, it was the sleepy yuppie playground of a top-twenty university. The streets were perfectly paved, the cars new and foreign, the schools and teachers and researchers winning everybody's awards. The only poor people this close to campus were supposed to be grad students and aging hippies holding out for their romantic ideals. But here, in the middle of everything, one of the town's oldest neighborhoods had gone to seed. "Fuckin' Reagan," Mack said, spitting into his handkerchief.

In Ann Arbor, even old people said things like this. In Port Huron, where Jay grew up, you'd get your ass kicked for such talk. With his hair and his clothes, Jay had been a constant target. He'd learned to live with his mouth shut, his eyes perpetually averted.

"It's the malls," Jay offered, thinking of a chapter from his American Culture class. When Mack stared back blankly, Jay explained, "The malls that are killing these downtown neighborhoods."

"Shit," Mack grunted, "it's a lot more than the malls."

When they finished it was late, after midnight, and they went out on the porch for one last smoke. Across the street Jay thought he saw something moving between the cars parked along the curb, and it spooked him, but when he looked harder, it seemed to have vanished.

They went back into the house to make sure they hadn't missed anything. Up in the closet again they turned the lights on and off, smoothed their hands over the wall, where a wide stain was still faintly visible.

"You know, I could paint that, Mack."

"Aw, Jay," Mack said. "You gotta let some things go."

Jay nodded and they collected the last of the tools, turned off the lights, and went back outside, with Mack walking ahead. This time, Jay saw what he'd only suspected before: between two parked cars across the street, Claire was sitting in the shadows on the curb, with her pale, unmuscular legs sprawled in front of her. This time she didn't hide. She was wearing cutoff shorts and a white tank top that glowed, like her hair and her skin, in the streetlight. Jay's instinct, after this long night, was to rush over and throw himself at this girl, press his face in her hair and roll her through the grass and be nineteen and safe and drunk on something, anything.

She stared up at him without moving: he hadn't called. There were things she would tolerate and things she wouldn't, and he had come up on the boundary.

"You know, Mack." He saw his next choice laid out, stupid and unavoidable. "Maybe I should just go paint that spot. It won't take more than ten minutes."

Mack rolled his eyes at him. "My wife used to say perfection is a vice."

"So I've heard."

"Suit yourself. But be quick, okay?"

When Mack drove off Jay put the tools away in the work truck and pretended to root around for a paintbrush while he waited for Claire to approach.

"Here I am," she said, sounding somewhere between coy and guilty. "I remembered the address."

"Here you are." Jay turned around. She had put on makeup, hard-spiked her hair—she looked like one of those Victorian fairy paintings they'd studied, the way she glowed so pale in the streetlight, with all the creepy details of the neighborhood doodling around in the dark behind her.

She reached up and pulled off his work hat, ran her fingers through his sweaty hair to try to stand it up again. "Oh, you're soaked," she said, but instead of pulling away she nuzzled right into his wet, filthy shirt, pressing her cheek to his sternum.

Instead of that family's smells and Mack's sweat and the cleaning products and the blood, he just smelled her, Claire. In that moment he just wanted what she wanted.

"I can take you inside," he said. "But only for a minute."

So many strangers had gone through the house today, anyway. What harm could one more possibly do?

He took her in through the back door, in case anyone was looking, and followed her up the staircase, watching her careful, artist's way of turning around and around to take everything in. It was like a slow-motion dance she did. And when he showed her the places where there had been puddles, trauma, she knelt right down and touched them: "Here? Here?

"What are you afraid of, Jay? It's so clean now anyway, it's like nothing ever happened."

He straightened up, pleased. But she was disappointed at the lack of blood and evidence. She asked after this family's story again and again. "It'll all be in the paper tomorrow anyway," she said.

He pressed his lips together. The real stories never made it into the paper. The facts—time, place, weapon, victim, accused—never explained anything about what had really gone wrong.

"Fine." She shrugged. She stepped through each room, running her fingers along every trinket, looking for a souvenir.

"Please don't do that," Jay said, pushing her hands away from this family's things. She giggled and slapped at him—"Oh, come on, what is this worth, anyway?"—holding up a tiny stuffed frog from the little girl's bed. It was as small as Claire's palm, a bean bag, a piece of nothing in a pile of cheap, bright things. It had the brown flecks that she wanted. "I think I'll put this in some kind of art project somehow." She smelled it. "I think all of this will go into some project someday."

"Just, whatever," Jay said. "Fucking take it, let's go."

He wanted to blame her for the way he was feeling, hollowed out and criminal. But there, in the little girl's yellow room, she flopped down on that Big Bird bedspread and reached up to him.

"Nuh-uh." He shook his head. "Let's go."

Her hand clamped down on his wrist. She didn't let go.

It had been such a long night, already filled with mistakes. His throat was corroded with bile. He wanted to gargle and spit, to go home to bed. Clouds suddenly blanked out his vision—a head rush—he was starving, blurry, weak to the bone. But when this weakness passed, there she was, this luminous girl among toys. He could almost see the little girl she must have been just a few years ago. He sensed that he could just disintegrate.

"The guy," Jay gave in. "It looked like he staggered around. For a while. Like someone tried to help him or something. His blood was puddled up all over the house."

Claire drew his head onto her chest, and the words tumbled out of him. He felt his brain, with all its dark knowledge, seceding from his body, which just went about its business, making its crude demands. Claire tightened her legs around him, rose and fell with each new fact. In huffs and whispers, in muffled groans he told her about the Price family. The father dead two years already. The kids spread out, from eighteen to four. Walker, Jerome, Martin, Natasha. He knew their names and faces now, their smell. He went on about the fight and the gun, and about D. B. Chenille, who didn't survive the trip to the hospital. Claire clutched at and rewarded him, she thrived.

When they were finished and she rolled out from under him, he opened his eyes and found a picture painted right onto the wall behind where the pillows had been. It was primitive as a child's drawing but more beautiful. It was a green and red chicken in an Easter basket, with the name TASHA spelled out in big letters underneath. He felt a sort of soul-hangover coming on. "Let's get out of here," he said, smelling his own sweat.

Once she pulled on her shorts, Claire dug into her bag, producing a camera. In a daze he watched her lining up and focusing a shot of the little girl's bed, the stuffed animals, and by the time her act registered with him, she had flashed the photo and turned the lens toward Jay. He rushed at her, needing to stop her, but at the last second she turned.

Instead of knocking the camera away, he slapped it hard into her face. It rattled his palm and flipped something over in his stomach. Then she was holding her nose, there was blood seeping through; he was bending to scoop up the camera, and the red drops hit the floor. More of them. So this was how these things happened.

"Fuck you!" she screamed. "Fuck you!" And as they glared at each other Jay felt his hand rising up again, felt the muscles of his forearm and biceps clenching in preparation. It was as if the spirit of the house was surging through him.

He gasped and pulled back. Claire raced down the stairs, out the door, and she was gone.

He would have lost her anyway. But maybe not so soon. And once she was gone and wounded by him, it was easy to forget how she'd ridiculed the fat girl in Studio Art, how she shoved things in his coat pockets whenever they went in a store, how she said to him once, in a disgusted jeer, "You're just so totally *harmless*." Instead, all he saw and remembered was her pale girlish form moving across the campus Diag, chin down, toward the library. He'd never seen her so stripped of confidence, so shaken. When she looked up, he could see it: the swollen nose, the gray-blue arc around one eye, the black spider legs of stitches on her cheekbone. It would scar.

She wouldn't take his calls, wouldn't even take back the camera. So he was left with it and the film, which yielded two black-and-white pictures, eerie and artful. One of the little girl's ravaged bed, one of his crazed face bearing down, eclipsed in part by his own blurry hand: hard evidence.

On his jobs with Mack, it didn't take long before Jay saw things worse than what he had seen in that house on Macon Street. And what he had done there with Claire, *to* Claire, wasn't the worst thing a person could do. He'd seen proof. The night, the house, even Claire should have faded from his memories, over the years. Instead, they hung there, clumped together—the sneaking in, the sex, the hit, the desire for another. And what happened to her later, in the months that followed, when she vanished. All of it got knotted up somehow with the murder. He assumed part of it, swallowed it, carried it with him. All this time.

1

2005

Eighteen years later. In an apartment in Ann Arbor. In a bedroom hardly bigger than the full bed it contained, Kate Kinzler was waking up. Pinned down by the sandbags of her husband's limbs, she closed her eyes again, but the dream came back: she was barreling through a grocery-store parking lot, inexplicably fast—45, 50 mph. She was stomping on the brakes to no effect when a sleek brown Thoroughbred stepped into the aisle, in front of her. A smash of glass and metal, and his body flew through the air. She saw it through the sunroof, impossibly high and falling toward her fast. When she managed to wrestle the car to a stop, he had cracked the pavement, and was writhing and heaving, staring at her. Kate blinked at the dim ceiling. If she fell back asleep, it would go on, get worse. Her dreams often ended in catastrophes of her own making. She woke up most mornings wound tight and careful, trying not to live out any of her dreams.

It was a Sunday, six a.m. Late March, though through the window it still looked like February—lead gray and barren, with sparse piles of snow lining the streets. The trees were budless and black. Next to her, Stuart was giving off a faint snore, huffing out traces of rum. They'd thrown a party last night, and now the tiny bedroom was littered with dirty clothes and half-empty beer bottles. Stale smoke wafted in from the living room, which was a mess of spills and dirty dishes. They were twenty-nine, full grown, seven years out of college. And still living like this.

She peeled herself out from under Stuart, trying not to look at him. His snoring stopped for a second, and she held still until it resumed. From the pile of clothes she put on a sweatshirt and a pair of socks, and pulled her long, frizzy red curls into a knot on the top of her head. Muscling open the window, she crawled out onto the porch roof, a mild slope of black tar with cigarette butts scattered around, dropped from the window above by the three college guys who rented the attic apartment. She kicked them toward the gutters and sat down against the wall, drawing her arms and knees up into the sweatshirt.

They lived on Packard Street, at the edge of the student neighborhood strewn with plastic cups and abandoned couches. It was just a few blocks from the dorms they'd lived in as undergrads, and just thirty miles from the Detroit suburb where she'd grown up.

"Hey." Stuart stuck his head out the window.

His sandy, curly hair was mussed, his brown eyes still half-lidded with sleep. He had their blue comforter wrapped around his shoulders, like a boy with a cape. He smiled, locking his eyes on hers as if performing a magic trick in which everything except her disappeared from the world.

This was how he got her. Suddenly she thought of Bloody Marys and breakfast, a shower and sex and a morning in bed.

But then it took him two tries to squeeze through the window—he was thin, but clumsy and tall, and plainly still drunk. He dragged their new blanket across the damp, dirty tar and plopped down next to her with a thud that shook the porch. She pulled away. This was how it went lately: her rushes of feeling for him were so brief, so fragile.

"What time did you come to bed?" she said.

"I don't know. After three? Oh, you missed it—Billy told this story about when he was studying abroad in St. Petersburg—"

"And got beat up by the cops?"

"How'd you know that?"

"And had to sneak out of the hospital in his underwear?"

Stuart nodded incredulously.

Billy had been telling that story for years. They'd been hanging out with the same friends—mostly Stuart's—since college. They got drunk and had the same conversations over and over.

"*I* never heard it," Stuart said, mystified.

Kate sat quietly, watching the cars move up and down along Packard Street, a 30 mph zone that never cleared out. To the Laundromat. The food co-op. To church, to breakfast, to Kinko's. Each car probably filled with pairs of mad, wild lovers.

"Do I have to go to your folks' today?" he said after a while.

It was her dad's birthday. "Nah. If you do the laundry?"

"Deal."

"Deal."

He fell sideways in relief until his head landed in her lap, heavy as a bowling ball.

"What's the matter?"

"Nothing," she said.

He reached one hand up to her jaw. "What did you dream?"

She tilted her head away as politely as possible.

She had tried drinking, exercising, pills from her doctor—for anxiety, for depression, for sleep. She had tried buying things, cooking, reading books. She had tried telling herself everyone probably felt this way about their partner sooner or later. But she didn't believe it. No one had ever admitted such a thing to her.

They watched a college-age couple carrying duffel bags into the Laundromat across the street. The girl gave the guy a bump on the ass with her bag, and he stumbled and laughed, then held the door for her. The cars hissed past on the street, a white noise that you forgot about inside, though it was always there, if you listened.

"You should just skip your parents'," he said. "You always get this way when you go there. And then depressed after. Always."

Kate came from strivers. Stuart had been a break from all that. The first time she met him, she was hiding out at her usual corner table in the basement of the library, studying for a calculus midterm and twirling a strand of hair from the base of her skull around her index finger. Whenever her mind got soft or sleepy, she snapped off a single hair at the root and felt herself spring to attention. She'd lined up an almost perfect column of A's on her transcript. And whenever she got scared about her lack of a plan for life after graduation, she pulled out her transcript and felt her heart slow down.

"Is it really worth all that?" was what Stuart had said that day, pointing at the nest of rust-colored hair on the floor just behind her chair. There were others down the back of her sweater, she knew: she brushed them off each night before heading home to her roommates.

She slammed her books together and into her bag, keeping her hot face tucked into her chest. She'd been destroyed by two boyfriends in a row and couldn't bear to give herself over again to anyone, even for a minute.

"Hey," his voice got quieter, and he touched her arm. What had he seen in her? What had her face just done? "Hey, I'm sorry, man. It doesn't matter." He was wearing a choker of beads and one of those coarse woven pullovers from Guatemala that even total potheads had stopped wearing years ago. Probably in that front pocket was a Hackey Sack and some Visine.

"It's just hair," he said, his hand still holding her arm. He was scruffy, but his eyes were a light, bright brown. He had the slender, stooped posture of someone who could never hurt you.

He said, "Who cares? Some people shave their hair, like, every day."

For months she'd been palpating her growing bald spot, dreading the day when it got so big everyone would see it and know: she was crazy. But now, with his eyes on her, all she felt was relief. It was just hair. Exactly.

Two weeks later they were already in bed, and he turned her over and with his knobby fingers pushed up the frizzy hair at the back of her head and kissed her there, where the hair was gone, as if he knew it would be her most vulnerable spot. This was the single touch of her life, the one she replayed, the one that surpassed all others.

From then on, though it happened gradually, she earned B minuses and incompletes, learned how to type fake doctors' excuses, how to play pool and quarters and beer pong. She learned to disdain the aspirations her family had seeded in her. She sank into the waterbed of Stuart's life. His friends became hers, and her old friends—who seemed so dull suddenly—drifted away.

Instead of becoming an architect, as she'd once hoped, she

was a teacher now, high-school math, with summers off and days that ended at 3:05. Stuart was a computer programmer—not one of those cutting-edge, stock-optioned kinds, just a calm eight-to-sixer getting off on the code lines and quiet.

"I better get to work on the cake," she said, getting up from her spot on the porch roof.

"Oh, Kate, for once, just fuck the cake. Fuck the cake." But she was already climbing her way back in the window.

She went to work in the kitchen, dumping out bowls of dip and chips and filling the sink to wash them. Stuart spent a long time crouched in front of their stereo, searching through the radio stations until, finding nothing, he settled on the Mexican station, which was playing the Spanish version of "Hotel California." He started moving through the apartment in a half dance, half shuffle, trying to sing along in a quiet, scratchy falsetto. But the only Spanish he knew was profanity from a dishwashing job he'd had in college, so he filled in the blanks with nonsense murmurs and *pinche cochino* or *chupame la verga.*

And every time Kate turned around, there he was, blocking her way out of the kitchen or into the bathroom, reaching around her at the sink, grabbing her waist and coercing her into a dance.

Their apartment was a scant five hundred square feet. Brown shag living room with water-stained ceilings; tiny bath; tiny bedroom; and a kitchen that tilted southward so that half the cabinets hung open. And now, tortilla chips crunching underfoot through stale smoke while mariachi horns filled the air. "Here," she said finally, thrusting a Hefty bag at him. "Want to pick up the garbage?" He took the trash bag and went around chucking things in indiscriminately, each beer bottle crashing into the others, splitting the airwaves.

"Can you just—" She reached for the bag, then pulled back, trying not to snap. "Why don't you go back to sleep? You must be tired."

Stuart threw up a hand and headed back to the bedroom. "Whatever."

She finished the dishes and set them out to dry. She scrubbed dried puddles of salsa off the coffee table, wiped down the sticky chairs and counters, put the CDs in their cases and the video games on their shelf. Took out the garbage. Scraped candle wax off the floor and got out their iron and some paper towels to melt away the remains. There. It was soothing. It put her apart from the chaos.

From the lower shelves of the refrigerator she pulled out the trays of cakes she had baked and frosted yesterday. This time it was a miniature version of the clubhouse of a golf course her dad was developing. He had started out building houses, as a frame carpenter, a high-school dropout. Then he moved on to general contracting, building house after house, then entire neighborhoods, and now he was altering landscapes, creating property value where before there had only been cornfields.

There wasn't much Kate could do for her family, but she could make cakes. She had started at age twelve, enthralled by a TV special on wedding cakes, and worked her way up to bigger and more elaborate models: her brother's car or her dad's fishing boat, a two- by three-foot replica of her parents' house for their anniversary. Each cake raised everyone's expectations for the next. When relatives and guests asked if she wanted to be a baker when she grew up, Kate stood wide-eyed and silent, waiting for her dad's answer, which made her swell up: "She can do better than that."

Her mom had sent her copies of the architects' drawings for the clubhouse, which Kate tacked to the wall like a recipe. She leaned over the cake, plunging the dowels into the first layer, topping them with a piece of cardboard and the second layer, then attaching the angular shapes of cake she had cut to simulate the A-frame entry and the hipped rooflines. She built the stone façade and chimney out of slivered almonds and walnuts; she painted the windows a cool gray and framed them with icing. The more she worked, the more the dim walls of their apartment fell away. She saw only the cake in front of her, which seemed to grow, to turn life-size, as if she could stand in the doorway or lean close to see her reflection in the windows. From parchment-papered trays she plucked the rosebushes she had built yesterday and set them into the mulch of chocolate shavings spread around the edges of the building.

"Voilà," Stuart said, and she jumped, gasping. He'd been leaning in the doorway, watching, for who knew how long. She hadn't seen or heard him, hadn't even noticed how the light had shifted into late afternoon and she had only forty-five minutes left to shower and dress and get the cake to the party. "It's really something."

She shrugged. "Something retarded."

"Developmentally disabled, I think you mean."

"Exactly. Hey, you showered."

"Decided I'd go with," he said magnanimously.

Stuart stopped the car at the gate to punch in the code. Down the long driveway Kate's parents' glass-and-stone house was spread out on its acreage under the low gray Michigan sky. Her father had built the whole subdivision on eighty acres of marshland he'd bought decades ago for next to nothing. She still remembered the land as she'd first seen it at age five: rotting trees tilting over, up to their ankles in swamp. A wasteland, it frightened her. But her dad and his men set to work, hauling away brush and lumber, carving out a good-size lake in the middle to collect all the water, and building up mounds of dry land along the banks and planting new trees everywhere. He kept ten acres for himself and parceled off the rest in one-acre lots around the circumference of the lake, and then built their house and sixteen others, carefully arranging the sites and landscaping so that the homes were hidden from one another. Kate had seen them go up brick by brick; she knew the floor plan of every house. They were all unique, two or three stories tall, with complex rooflines and vaulted great rooms and stone terraces stepping down to the lake. In between them stretched lush mounds of perennial gardens and tracts of fast-growing trees: cypress, poplar, weeping willows. He could have cut corners, could have packed in smaller, cheaper houses for more profit, but that wouldn't have lived up to the dream that controlled him. Kate's mother was Catholic; her father's religion was houses.

"Are you ready for this?" Stuart said. Kate glanced back to check the big cake hulking on the floor of the hatchback behind them. It was unharmed by the car ride but looked suddenly ridiculous. She nodded, but Stuart just squinted ahead, chewing his lower lip.

"They mean well, my family," she said without much conviction.

"Nobody has seen us yet. We could still blow it off, go get some burgers."

"It's tempting." The automated gates began to close, and Stuart raised his eyebrows, daring her.

"Go, go!" She laughed, and he hit the gas to get through before they closed. He didn't say, "Coward." He never criticized her at all.

The garage door opened and out came her mother, a tall,

slender brunette in a charcoal-gray sweater and flannel pants, with a cream-colored scarf tied around her long neck. It flapped once in the wind, making her look like an aviator as she stood in the open garage door and moved one arm in the suggestion of a wave telling them to pull in. Kate straightened her posture and pushed at the mess of her hair.

As she got out of the car her mom leaned in to kiss her on the cheek but missed and bumped her nose into Kate's ear. "Hey, Katy-eight," she said. She smelled of oranges.

Kate and Stuart maneuvered the cake in through the back entrance, setting it down in the big, walk-in pantry. From the other rooms they could hear laughter and voices bouncing off the stone floors and panels of windows that looked out on the frozen lake. Theirs had been the model home for the development, and was outfitted with the best options available at the time: black walnut floors and woodwork, Italian chandeliers, a kitchen fit for a catering company. It was a good strategy for selling luxuries, her dad said, because "Nobody wants a shittier house than their *builder* has." As kids they'd lived in a state of constant preparedness for client walk-throughs: beds made before breakfast, drawings and toys hidden away in cupboards, family photos kept in albums, never on the walls.

Kate's younger sister, Julia, came rushing at them through the kitchen and enfolded Kate in a hug. She was wearing heels and stockings and a sleek, chocolate-colored dress that made Kate regret her sweater and corduroys. Julia and Kate's brother, Derrick, took after their mother, with elegant long limbs and broad shoulders, dark, straight hair and wide-set eyes. They looked and moved like purebreds, sleek and fearless. Though their dad had once had red hair like Kate's, for years now it had been mostly gray and cropped close as he went bald. Kate alone had the full, ruddy cheeks, the stocky legs, the eyes such an odd, translucent light green that people often double-took her in an unsettled way, as if she were an exotic but off-putting cat.

"Look at this amazing cake. I'm telling you, you should start your own company. Don't you think, Stuart? *Kate's Cakes.* Think of the money."

"No way, José," Kate said.

Julia took a step back and cocked her head at them, smiling. "Guess what?"

Kate turned her hands up. Her hangover hadn't fully retreated, and in this commotion she felt a headache burning its way up from the back of her neck.

Stuart said, "He did it. You're engaged."

Julia made a quick squeal and hugged him.

"How did you guess that?" Kate said, baffled. The last time she'd talked to Julia on the phone, she'd gotten the distinct sense Julia was losing interest in her boyfriend, Alex, not getting ready to marry him.

"Did Alex tell you he was doing it?" Julia squinted at Stuart suspiciously.

"No," Stuart said. He shrugged. "It's all over your face."

Julia thrust out her hand, grinning. "He came through, didn't he?"

The diamond was huge, set in a plain platinum band.

"I'm hiding it for today, okay?" She slipped the ring onto her right hand, turning the diamond in toward her palm. "I don't want to steal the King's thunder on his birthday."

"I'm sure he'd be happy," Kate said.

"Sure." Julia shrugged as if she wasn't certain of this. "I'll tell them later, you know? Tomorrow. But I was dying to tell someone. Thank God you showed up."

Stuart had already gone off for drinks and was shaking Alex's hand across the room. Alex was a quiet and muscular former Michigan baseball player who now worked as some kind of lawyer for the Detroit Tigers. He was devoted and smart, though a little bit dull. He often stood mutely on Julia's sidelines, watching her fluttering monologues as if relieved that he might never again have to speak. He didn't quite seem up to the task of Julia.

"You guys don't waste any time, do you?" Kate teased. Julia had met Alex only a year ago.

"Hey, I'm not getting any younger," Julia said.

Kate laughed, then realized her sister—age twenty-four—was being serious.

"We have to talk dresses," Julia whispered, then someone called out for a toast, and she disappeared into the living room.

"Well, hello, Big Red." Kate's dad grinned, throwing one of his thick, hairy forearms around her neck and giving it a squeeze. "How's the teaching going? You failing any of 'em?"

Kate shook her head. "It's fine."

"So where's the cake?"

"I thought the cake was a surprise."

"Ha!" He shook his head, as if nothing she did could surprise him.

When Kate was little, he was heavier and wore quilted flannels and T-shirts and jeans every day, and came home from work with smashed black fingernails and scabbed knuckles. Even after a shower back then he still smelled of sawdust and engine oil. But now he wore pressed slacks and sleek, tailored shirts. His hands were impeccable, and he didn't smell like anything anymore.

"How's the golf course project coming?"

"The goddamn zoning board is going to give me a stroke." He shook his head. "I got a joke for you." He collected teacher jokes. "What's the difference between a teacher and a prison guard?"

She shook her head.

"The union." He slugged her on the shoulder. "When are they going to make you principal?"

"Never, Dad."

"Vice principal?"

"Nope."

He whistled through his teeth. "You should come work for me. We've got plenty of math you can do. Look how good Jules is doing." Julia and Derrick both worked for their dad—Julia in accounting, Derrick as a project manager.

When Kate was five or six and Derrick was ten or so, they sometimes got to hang around their dad's job sites on weekends. He worked so many hours they would hardly have seen him otherwise. Derrick would play in the big holes and gravel piles, or pretend to drive the backhoe or skid steer, but Kate would just follow her dad around silently, watching him pour cement or build brick pillars, rough-frame a house, mark up blueprints. The number of things he knew how to do seemed infinite, and she wanted to learn all of them. Back then, under cover of her brother, if she was quiet enough and tough enough, she could sneak her way into her dad's world, into his focus. Then Julia was born—Julia, Jules, Jewels: even her name oozed femininity—and Kate became one of "the girls" who had to stay home with their mother. "You can help me out with the baby," her mother said, but this was just consolation: her mother had never needed anyone's help with anything.

Julia was over near the windows, dancing with Derrick, who spun her forward and laughed, then pulled her back. They were so at home here. Kate gazed past them out the window at the lake. At Christmas it had been covered in a pristine, dreamy snow, but now the ice was melting in dark, swelling patches that looked like wounds seeping through white fabric.

She moved through the loud crowd of elbows and eyes and cocktails. Her breath quickening, she flinched at the scrape of heels on tile, the tinny bounce of music off the windows. She dizzied her way down the hall to the study. There he was, finally, Stuart.

He was on all fours, laughing, with both Derrick's kids riding on his back. Sadie was six and Sammy was four, and Stuart was trying to buck them both off his back like a bull. But they clung to his sweater, stretching it out into a series of handprints. When he finally shook them off, he stood up and did a victory dance, then knelt back down and let them climb on again. He glanced up and grinned at Kate. "You want to take a turn at this?"

She leaned against the door frame, breathing deeply, taking him in.

"Well, I'll be damned," her dad said when they brought the cake out to him. They had dimmed the lights and sung the birthday song. The room glowed with candles Kate had stuck in the grass surrounding the clubhouse. He walked around the table slowly, forcing everyone to make way as he surveyed the cake from every angle. The room cooed.

"It's flawless," her mom said, beaming at Kate.

"Wait, can we do this?" her dad said, carefully turning the tray around so that the north wall of the clubhouse lined up with true north. Then he blew out the candles in a rush, as if they were a nuisance, and turned on the lights. He reached up, taking the hanging light fixture in one hand, and angled it in slow motion from east to west, trying to catch how the light and shadows would shift with the sun's movement over the building.

"Look at that!" he said, bobbing his head. "You did this straight from the blueprints?"

Something surged in Kate.

"How did you make the chimney like that?" someone said.

"Hey, though," her dad said. "This window . . ." He poked his finger right into it, then looked with odd surprise at the frosting that came away on his finger.

"What is it, John?" her mother said nervously.

He cocked his head. "That hack architect left out the south windows that I wanted. There were supposed to be four here, and look, there's only two."

Kate's mom glanced apologetically around the room. "Oh, nonsense."

"Honey, why don't you go get those blueprints out of my office," he said, crouching down and scrutinizing the cake.

"We'll do it later, John." Kate's mom flashed a grim smile at their guests. "Let's cut it. Doesn't it look good? Is it chocolate, Kate?"

Her dad just stared at those little buttercream windows.

"I'm sure Kate just . . . adapted it a little. I'm sure it's just fine on the plans. Right, Katy?"

Kate and her dad locked eyes, knowing a mistake like that just wasn't in her. "Yeah," she lied. She smiled. She nodded vigorously. "I probably messed up."

There was a room under the basement stairs where Kate used to hide as a kid. Her mother used the space as a storeroom for all the old papers, gifts, and mementos that no longer fit the decor but were too personal to throw away. Kate had found incredible things here in the past: old baby pictures and school photos, report cards, handprints and valentines from their childhood, teapots and vases that had been broken and glued back together. Kate tried to imagine her mom sitting in here for hours on end, rifling through all the sentimental things that didn't suit her house. But she'd never seen her mom in here in this dusty, stuffed room, and there was really no place to sit.

Someone knocked. The door opened a crack, then some more, until a head poked through. It was Stuart. He had two beer bottles swaying in his hand, and held one out to her.

"Your parents are looking for you."

She scrunched up her face. "What for?"

"Apparently there's an extra rosebush on the side of the clubhouse that's got your dad all in a quandary."

She laughed and took the beer. He sat down next to her on the carpet.

"You know, you should stop making cakes for them."

"Ah, it doesn't matter." Kate thought about it. "They didn't mean anything by it."

"Yeah, but he can't just say, 'Wow, a huge monster cake. How nice. Let's eat'? Why do you even bother?"

The big basement dehumidifier cranked into motion and filled up the room with noise. She knew why she bothered. If she walked in behind a cake, no one even looked at her. It was such a relief. And if they liked the cake, maybe they would like her. Maybe they would overlook all the imperfect parts of her.

"So they're really looking for me?"

"It seemed like they were excited about something."

Upstairs, all the guests were gone, even Julia and Derrick.

The house was scattered with cocktail napkins and crumbs and half-eaten pieces of cake, which Kate collected as she walked past. Her mom was loading dishes into the dishwasher, and her dad was sitting at the kitchen table with a serious look on his face. There seemed to be some strange gravity in the air. *Oh God*, Kate thought, *one of them is sick. Cancer or heart disease, a blood clot. They've told everyone else, and now I'm the last to know.*

"Good party," she said tentatively.

"That cake, Katy," her mom said. "I had so many compliments on it."

Her parents looked at each other, as if wondering who would begin.

"Is everything okay?" Kate said.

"Oh!" Her dad laughed. "Yeah. Hell yeah. Your mother and I just . . . we wanted to give you something." There was a greeting-card-size envelope in the middle of the table.

Kate cocked her head and glanced at Stuart, but he just gave a slight shrug.

"It's just a little something, some money," her dad said. "No big deal."

But her dad didn't believe in giving away money. It had taken their mom years to talk him into paying their college tuition, and even still he made them work and take loans to pay for their room and board. *So you'll appreciate it*, was all he ever said. He believed in being "self-made," saw college and big checks as a crutch for the wealthy. That they'd become well-off themselves didn't seem to occur to him.

"We just thought you two could use a little extra help," her mom said apologetically. "Maybe get you out of that apartment or something."

Kate raised her eyebrows. How much were they talking? She reached out and took the envelope, but it seemed in poor taste to open it. They never talked about money. They pretended it didn't exist.

"When I think of what you two must spend on rent." Her dad made a birdlike motion with his hands and whistled. "It's like throwing money out the window." Kate recognized this: it was his sales hustle from back in the days when he sold the first houses he'd built, little starter homes for people who could barely afford them.

"So you're doing this for Julia and Derrick, too?" Kate asked.

A funny look flashed on her mother's face. "Well," her dad said. "Not exactly."

"Just us? Won't Jules and Derrick get mad?"

"Shoot," her dad said. "They make plenty all on their own."

Kate watched Stuart's reflection in the dark windows, which were so clean they shimmered like two-way mirrors.

Her mother changed the subject. "We'd just be so happy to see the two of you with a home of your own, you know? We want you to have that."

"That apartment of yours." Her dad made an exaggerated shiver. When Kate didn't smile, he clapped her on the shoulder. "I'm sorry. It's fine. Just, you know, a little small, right?"

"Well." Kate looked over to Stuart, waiting for him to say something, but he wouldn't. "We appreciate it. You really don't have to do this."

Stuart was sitting very stiffly, his hands on the tabletop. "What if?" he said finally, his face a blank, innocent page. "What if we don't want a house?"

Her parents looked from Stuart to each other, before finally settling their awkward gazes on Kate. What he'd said was incomprehensible.

She blushed.

2

Twenty-one hundred square feet," Kate said. "Can you imagine?"

"A thousand fifty apiece." Stuart let go of her thrilled, squeezing hand, feeling his mouth go dry. "You could almost pretend you're single."

They were on the third floor of an old house on Macon Street, in a bedroom someone had converted from an attic by shoddily Sheetrocking the walls and installing a coarse black floor covering that appeared to be indoor-outdoor carpeting. It was the sort of stuff Stuart had only seen on motorboats, and the floorboards beneath it shifted underfoot. This was the nicest room in the house.

It was the thirty-first house they'd looked at in a month, and he didn't want to live in any of them.

"The windows are nice," he offered quietly. Large blanks of light at each end of the long room, they were connected by two long, sloping ceilings that stretched from the shoulder-high walls to a peak fifteen feet overhead, giving the room the feeling of a chapel. The window on the back wall of the house looked out over the trees and colorful clapboard houses of the Old West Side, Ann Arbor's modest historic district. The houses were simple, built by and for German brewery workers at the turn of the century, but now the neighborhood was being gentrified by yuppies looking for anything exploitable this close to campus and to the trendy downtown restaurants. The window at the front, where Kate was standing, gave a good view of the redbrick office buildings and shops just a few blocks away, where those kinds of people toiled and shopped so they could toil and shop some more. But peeking out beyond those buildings, in the distance, stood the old stone bell tower of campus, looking harmless and uncorrupted in its solid lack of purpose.

"We could walk to everything," Kate said. "Sell one of the cars, even."

"That'd bring in a whopping twelve hundred."

"Come here." She waved him over.

The house must have stood higher than all the others nearby, because when he went to her at the front window, he could see down on the rooftops of all the other houses along Macon Street. They were a motley bunch, a handful of impeccably restored Victorians interspersed with neglected bungalows and a mechanic's garage and an aging ice-cream and doughnuts shop that drew a steady stream of old men. Next door stood a small, box-shaped apartment building left over from the sixties. Just a block from the railroad tracks and five blocks from the bus station and homeless shelter, the house was probably too close to downtown to be what her dad or any of those types would ever consider a secure investment. In a way, though, that appealed to him.

"I feel like the Pope on his balcony," he said, waving one hand stiffly at the window. The couple pushing their stroller along the sidewalk down there looked like dolls, distant and powerless. Kate folded her arms around his middle and leaned in.

"We could get a dog," she murmured into his chest.

He had gone so many months without feeling her need him like this.

"A barbecue grill." She squeezed him. "Lawn furniture." So many months without her even seeming happy.

"I think you're using *lawn* a little liberally." He pointed down at the front yard, which was nothing but knee-high weeds.

"Two full bathrooms," she said. "Four bedrooms. Just think about it."

And now here it was: the tentative, searching look she gave him whenever the idea of kids came up. When Stuart imagined having a kid, it came out looking like his brother, Danny, who was autistic and rarely spoke. He just walked around with a pained, puzzled look in his eyes, like he'd been locked in the wrong body and couldn't even find a way to say so.

"Maybe we should just buy this window." He turned away. "Just the view."

The rest of the house was devastated. For some reason the original woodwork in most rooms had been torn away and replaced with thin plastic molding, and the plaster everywhere was either crumbling or covered in fake wood paneling. The first floor had revolting orange shag carpeting, and most of the second floor was covered with the same black AstroTurf as the attic. The owner had been renting the house out room by room to college students and dropouts, so each of the old, five-panel bedroom doors had been ruined by a series of deadbolt locks. It looked as if no one had cleaned the kitchen or bathrooms in years.

"I mean, be reasonable, Katy. It's practically uninhabitable." He went on for a while, trying to scare her with hazards like lead paint and mold and asbestos. He noted the shoddy little house next door that looked like it could be condemned any day. He took her to the back window and pointed at the giant rotting elm tree that began in the neighbor's yard and leaned far over the roof above them, ready to break apart in the next storm and do some spectacular damage.

Kate leaned her cheek against the window and sighed, "I know, I know," until her breath fogged up the pane. "But think what we could do for this place, for this neighborhood."

She had a weak spot for improvement projects—old tables she found in the garbage and repainted, thrift-store jackets that just needed new linings, friends who were new in town, broke or broken. She believed in the power and responsibility of humans to fix what was wrong with the world. Before, these had mostly been risk-free endeavors, but this house, it was something different. Like picking up hitchhikers or taking home drifters, there were attempts at charity that could end in your own ruin. "It's no better than our apartment," he said.

She turned her hands up. "So? I mean, what's the difference then?"

He shook his head, unable to explain. He ran his hand along the windowsill, came away with its pale gray dust on all his fingers.

"Think what a great *project* it would be," she said. Then she adopted her father's voice to quote him: "'With big risks come big rewards.'"

"Yeah, don't do that."

She put her hands on his chest, searched his eyes. First she was smiling, like this was all a fun performance, but then the mask fell away, and in her real-life voice she said, "I need this. I'm sorry. I really need this."

He shivered a little but managed to come out with it: "Why?"

She slinked away from him, doing a shuffle that looked like the start of a dance. The show was back on. "Oh, just *because*, Stuart. Come on. Just because." She spun back into his arms.

Something was so far from right between them. She had been sliding away from him for so long, and no house was going to fix that. But he squeezed her waist and smelled her neck, her shampoo, her fabric softener. He liked what she was believing. He wanted to believe it, too.

Back in their apartment that night, Stuart turned over and over in bed. His heart rate was up, then went even higher when he realized he was incapable of calming it. He tried deep breaths, tried relaxing his muscles from his forehead to his feet, but no use. He was sweating now, and threw off the covers. Kate, for once, was in a deep sleep, free of her usual tossing and nightmares. This plan that so fulfilled her was shutting him down.

He thought about the first time she'd ever invited him out to her parents' house, how the whole way there his skin sort of buzzed with the seriousness of this outing, with the thrill of how it suggested that this skittish, distant girl might actually let him into her life for real. And how bad he'd *wanted* that. He had totally fallen. She pulled her car up to the automated gate and he caught sight of the big house behind it, and a great, heavy dread settled over him. He said to himself, Relax, it'll be okay. People liked him; people were basically good; everybody had their own little flaws. But everywhere he turned that day he confronted perfection: orderly, monochrome beds of flowers and spotless, magazine-style rooms filled with people who looked like they'd never so much as spilled on themselves. They were nice enough—perfect manners—but he spent the day in a panic, suspecting that any minute someone would pop up with a snapshot of his past: the cluttered and tiny house he grew up in, his shadow of a brother, his dead father, depressed mother, the hundreds of nights he had spent shitfaced and sloppy with despair. His affinity for drugs, his terrible grades, the fact that he was nearly flunking out—and not for lack of smarts but out of sheer laziness. These people of Kate's were optimists, opportunists. They brought success on themselves because they couldn't *conceive* of failure. Failure as a whole way of life was beyond their ken. "What's wrong?" Kate had said on the drive back to Ann Arbor at the end of the day. "I know, they're insane. I'm sorry. I have no idea how I came from all that." She looked genuinely lost and shaken, and she clung to his hand the whole way back, as if he were her ticket out of there. It felt so good to be needed like that, he almost believed they could do this. But something inside him knew that day that it was only a matter of time before Kate would discover his true nature and get scared or revolted and flee. Or try to remake him. He had waited for it all these years, and now here it was.

In his sleeplessness, the calm, rhythmic huff of her breathing grew increasingly loathsome. He sat up and opened his eyes. What she had told him was true: in the dark, despairing hours, the four walls of their tiny bedroom did seem to be closing in.

He went out into the living room, and suddenly it, too, looked awfully small. Over the past weeks, Kate had enlightened him to a miserable new view of their life: the carpeting was worn down to a drab, nubby mess, the walls were uneven and dingy, the ceilings had bulges and smoke stains.

He got a beer from the fridge and sat down in his underwear on their sagging little futon couch and picked up his video camera, holding it at arm's length and pointing it toward his own face. He said, "News flash, Danny. April twentieth." In the night like this he often made videos to send to his brother. He liked the idea of Danny falling asleep to his own insomniac ramblings.

"Our apartment is degrading us. Turns out, we're worthless. People *our age* need assets, room to *expand*. We're supposed to have matching furniture, a guest bed. A dishwasher." He sipped at his beer, played with its label. "Connection between big houses and American obesity? Will we swell and swell till we fill up all that square footage?"

It didn't really matter what he rambled about, because Danny rarely seemed to understand conversation and generally watched the videos on mute. Though he didn't really talk, he would nod or cringe in response to simple questions about what he wanted. He made his feelings known, and he kept secrets. Occasionally, though, after a particularly complicated remark, Danny's eyes seemed to glint with a mischievous comprehension; he would smile and nod and point, leaving Stuart wondering if maybe his brother understood the world much better than they realized—maybe even much better than anyone else. And *that* was how he knew enough to forgo striving and keep quiet.

Stuart took a long swig of beer, then smacked his lips and did the "ah" sound Danny always made after drinking something.

He squinted into the little lens and made the palms-out gesture that he and their mom always showed Danny before breaking bad news. "So it looks like we're thinking about—"

Moving was a word Danny knew and didn't like. *Moving* was a word like doctor or school or airport, a word that could send Danny into screaming fits that sometimes went on for so long he began to hyperventilate. Stuart's family had moved only once in their lives, when Stuart was seven and Danny was four, because it was becoming apparent that with all Danny's problems, particularly the fits he threw in the nights, it wasn't fair to ask Stuart to go on sharing a bedroom with him. They moved to a three-bedroom house just a mile away from their previous home, in the same school district, on a similar street, even with a similar ranch-style floor plan. Despite all their efforts, Danny was so traumatized that he hid in his closet all week, coming out only briefly, when they could coerce him with food or the prospect of baths, which he adored. To ease the transition, they painted the walls the same colors as their old house, arranged the furniture in the same way and hung the same curtains, but this seemed only to confuse Danny more. It was as if their home, their essence, had shape-shifted.

For the first year Stuart slept in Danny's room anyway.

But the word *moving* came to mean something like death to Danny—a change that took away everything you knew. Years later, when their family cat wandered off once, Danny stood by the door all day and then asked with clinical, emotionless curiosity, "Cat move?" Their mom inhaled with such force Stuart could hear it across the room. Her eyes, her sudden, terrific, rare smile. That was still in the years when she saw every new development as evidence Danny might *get better.* "That's *good*, Danny," she enunciated. "Freddy moved away. That's very good. Yes, the cat *moved.*"

Danny's face blanched. It was as if he thought a black hole had opened up somewhere beyond the front door and sucked Freddy up. He went back in the closet for days; he panicked whenever anyone tried to go outside. Stuart stayed inside, watching for Freddy, but Danny was right: he was gone.

When their dad died, Danny murmured, "Move, moved, moving," in puzzled incantations for weeks. This was hard enough on its own but made worse by the fact that Stuart was scheduled to move away for real, to college—all the way from Omaha to Michigan—within the year. He was going to abandon them.

The videotapes came like a brainstorm. They didn't make it possible for Stuart to live in two places at once, to be his own self as well as the one they needed, but Stuart's mom said they helped. Whenever Stuart went home to visit, the first thing Danny did was lead him by the arm back into his bedroom, where he would make Stuart sit by his side on the bed—not touching, but close—watching one tape after another. "I'm right here," Stuart would say, poking at his own chest. "We don't have to watch this." But Danny would hold up a hand to silence him, pointing toward the screen, as if an unmissable moment was coming up.

Stuart paused the video recorder and went to the kitchen for another beer. He set it on the floor next to the futon and then poured a short glass of whiskey. He settled back in with the camera and started again.

"Imagine a really big place, Danny. A room just for you, just like yours at home, with a TV, so if you and Mom want to come visit, you can." This was impossible. Danny never traveled at all, had never seen any place Stuart had lived. "I'll videotape it for you, I'll show you. And if you see it enough, if you see it enough . . . You'll recognize it."

To show Danny what he meant, Stuart flashed the camera down at the coffee table covered in all the magazines Kate had started buying. The oversize, thick, glossy pages showed houses that looked like museums, with vast, columned rooms and cantilevered balconies with views of oceans and deserts.

The photo spreads were absurd, depressing. "*These* are the things that belittle us, right? I mean, even if you had the money, let's say—but who would, really? Anyway, the minute you lived in it, it wouldn't look anything like this."

Stuart stabbed at the pictures, rattling and tearing the pages. "There'd be, like, mail on the counter here in the hallway and a matted-down part in the carpet by the door, and like, shit stuck all over the fridge, stupid reminders to get your teeth cleaned, your hair cut. There'd be at *least* one coffee mug in the sink. If you're lucky, right? Otherwise, man, you're dead." The liquor was cheering him up. He felt like dancing, felt like throwing her things out the window. He picked up the entire stack of magazines and carried them into the kitchen, holding the camera at his shoulder so that Danny could witness it all, and he dropped them with a great thud into the metal garbage can. A few of them wouldn't fit, so he opened the window, leaned out, and tossed them like Frisbees toward the Dumpster below. "Fuck your magazines," he said to the night. He would have liked to shout it, but Danny couldn't stand for anyone to raise their voice.

A creaking in the hallway interrupted him—a footstep. Stuart sucked his breath in and listened, but there was nothing. He held still in the kitchen, waiting, heart thumping, wondering what he would say to her. Maybe her approach was the right one: maybe if they just kept quiet about what was broken between them, it would heal.

Then he heard it again, the faint creak of loose floorboards underneath their cheap carpeting. This time they were moving away from him, back to the bedroom as if they had never happened.

Stuart rubbed his hand over his mouth. He drank down the rest of his Jameson's and put down the video camera. He tiptoed into the hallway, and sure enough: a faint light was bleeding out from under the door. As he stood watching, it went black. That was his wife in there, his wife, the woman he was tangled up with. And no matter what she was feeling for him these days, he loved her. People didn't always have to love you back. Sometimes they didn't have it in them.

He knew that when he opened the door she would be stretched along her edge of the bed, as far away from him as possible. She'd be trying to breathe evenly, and if he said her name, she wouldn't respond. If he touched her shoulder, she'd draw away, like one of those cringing mimosa plants. And if he asked her tomorrow if she'd woken up in the night, she would say, *No, I don't think so,* and they would go on as if nothing had happened.

3

It was Tasha who picked Walker up the day they released him. He had spent years trying not to imagine the day, the exact minute when he'd finally get the hell out and stay out, but always it came crawling into his dreams, getting more elaborate as his years inside piled up. Usually, the way he saw it, he'd be wearing some crap-ass secondhand suit they would give him, clouded with mothball stink, and his mother would be over on the other side of the room, dressed up in something fruity—pink or yellow—nervous, watching the door so she wouldn't miss a beat when he came through. And when he did, the air would be different, dry and sweat-free, packed full of unrecycled oxygen. He would hear that heavy steel *ga-chink* for the last time in his natural life. His mother's face, when she saw him, would flutter and seize up with something way beyond a smile, and she wouldn't just walk but run at him: teary-eyed, hooting, bobbling from side to side the way older women did. Everything forgiven. Sometimes, in the dark, when he let himself go too far, he even imagined her first words as she clutched him to her chest right there in the prison parking lot or waiting room: *Thank you.* It was a lot to ask, and in eighteen years she hadn't managed it, but maybe, coming to pick him up here, seeing all he'd given up for her, maybe she'd say it then. Maybe just once, in a whisper, if it was understood she'd never have to say it again.

Her letters over the years didn't give Walker any reason to expect this. They were dry and meaningless, as if she was afraid some prison censor would go scanning them for emotion. Her handwriting, her words, were brittle, tilting things that got bigger and bigger toward the bottom of the page, as if she couldn't wait to fill up the space and sign off. "We had fried sausages last night," she once wrote, filling a whole paragraph about that. And even about mundane shit like that, it seemed obvious she was stopping between each word, struggling to pick the next one: *bracelet, gas bill.* Still, Walker read them over and over, ran his fingers across them, smelled them, wished they hid some kind of secret message. If they did, though, he never figured out what it was.

In his letters to Tasha, once she got old enough to understand, Walker would always ask about their mom, but she found lots of ways to avoid the questions, until eventually, when he pressed her, she would just write, "Mom's hanging in there." The idea that their mother might never be the same again had occurred to him. What had also occurred to him, and this bothered him more, was that Tasha might not be able to remember the way their mother really used to be.

But it was Tasha there to pick him up, not his mother, when he got out. He saw her through the window in the wall, standing there, jiggling her key chain, glancing around out the corners of her eyes like she half expected to be mugged. She'd sent him pictures like crazy over the years, but still it was hard not to always imagine her the way he last saw her, as a little kid, hair all braided up in pigtails that stuck out all over her head. Beads and plastic clips everywhere, rainbow colors. But here she was, grown up—tall and skinny—the only curve on her body the good strong shelf of an ass at the top of her long legs. No more braids. Her hair was all glossy black ringlets: how did she do that? She had Pops's big high cheekbones, he realized suddenly, her face broad and flat and smooth and pretty. His sister. He huffed through his smile, trying to get control.

And they didn't give him a suit, just Wranglers and an itchy flannel shirt—in June—and eighty dollars gate money for his eighteen years of work. He didn't want any of the things he'd had on him when they brought him in, didn't want the letters he'd collected over the years, didn't want a single reminder of this place or how he got here. "Just throw it away," he said, not even looking at the personal-effects package they made him sign for.

"Baby," he said, coming through the door, and because he'd never let her come visit, she double-glanced at him now to make sure his face matched up with the old pictures she'd seen. Two hundred fifteen months spread out like a swollen river between them.

"Look at you," she said. "I can't believe it." She didn't squeal or lunge at him, but she held her arms out and let him walk right into them. Almost as tall as he was. And there, round the back of his neck, he felt her cheek shift as she kissed him behind the ear. So she was like that.

"Let's get out of here."

And there it was, Pops's old truck in the parking lot, baby blue and white, 1978 Ford, with those goofy-looking puffed-up body panels and the hint of fins at the back. There wasn't even much rust on the thing. Pops would have been happy. Walker stood and smiled at it, remembering too many things at once to hold any of it still.

She was standing apart from him in the sunshine, watching him take it all in. "You want to drive?"

"Shit," he said. "No. You better."

The doors creaked and slammed, and from inside, high up on the big woven bench seat, he felt like he could just about see the whole world. Cars and trees and the blue, blue sky of summer. The colors of everything brighter than he remembered, bright like on TV. They made their way out of the parking lot, leaving the sprawling mess of Jackson Men's Facility behind them without saying a word about it, then moved through the gray streets of Jackson till they found the highway and got on, heading east, toward all the signs saying Detroit, Ann Arbor, Ypsilanti in big white letters.

"Can't believe you still driving Pops's old truck."

"Well, I don't usually take it very far."

"But you're *driving*. You got a *driver's* license, girl."

She shoved her hand against his knee. "And the Cold War is over."

"All right, shit. You just got to give me a little time. Adjust."

Tasha was a good writer, wrote him almost every week, all her life. Even back before she knew cursive, when mostly all she did was draw pictures and pencil out scrappy bits of sentences that didn't fit together, still she wrote to him like he was Santa Claus at the North Pole or Donald Duck down in Disneyland—invisible, harmless, larger than life. DEAR WALKER, I AM FINE. MOM AND ME GOT A KITTY TODAY BUT SHE THINKS I MAYBE ALERGIC SO WE LET IT GO. NEXT WEEK WE ARE GOING TO THE FORD MUSEEM WITH SCHOOL BUT I DONT WANT SEE NO OLD CARS. After that she had printed HOW ARE YOU? and then erased it—*erased* it—and crossed a thick pencil line through the remains of the words. MOM SAYS YOU BETTER BE EATING ENOUGH DON'T GET SKINNY. BE TUFF. LOVE TASHA.

He saw her grow up in the letters. Every little thing—spelling tests and bus routes and shopping and track team, chemistry exams she barely passed, the prom date who puked down the back of her dress, the regulars at Josie's where she did dishes and bused and finally waitressed, her Eastern Michigan college applications and loans—until he started to think he had never known so much about another person in his whole life. Not even about Jerome, his brother, way back when they shared that attic bedroom and almost couldn't get twenty minutes apart. Not even his longest cell mate, Fowler. And Fowler could talk bullshit all through the night.

Walker figured Tasha would be chattery like that in person, but she didn't say much, at least not now. That was okay. He didn't know what to say either. Once they got up to speed on the highway, the truck rattled and shook so much they would've had to shout at each other anyway, and Tasha seemed to be concentrating real hard on the driving. Her knuckles were tight on the big wobbly steering wheel, and she kept leaning forward to squint in the rearview mirror. He let her be. He had learned everything in the world about keeping quiet.

"So," she said after a while. "How's it feel?"

"What, this?" He shrugged. "No big deal."

She gave a big genuine laugh at this, and he felt a little bit of the awkwardness chipping away. Outside the car, the fields and trees and weeds moved in the wind like he'd only sometimes seen in movies. They passed a field of horses standing and chewing in the afternoon heat. Then there were patches of new subdivisions cut out of the farm fields, with two-story pale-colored houses that all looked alike.

The thought of driving past the old house had occurred to him. It wasn't really out of the way—they had to pass by or through Ann Arbor to get to Ypsilanti anyway. But still he hesitated. Didn't want to seem *fixated.* It wasn't like he didn't know his mother had lost the place, moved on. He knew it. Still, even though Tasha had described their new house, sent him little-kid drawings and, later on, real pictures, when he settled into his bunk at night to imagine what they were up to at home, how big Tasha and Martin had probably gotten, Walker just couldn't picture them anyplace but back there on Macon Street. How could he imagine them having birthday parties, putting up Christmas trees in a place he'd never seen? What *he* had in his head wasn't that scrappy little joint in Ypsilanti, where only half his family was left, crowded around a rickety metal pine tree for a Polaroid flash, their faces all frozen and ruined. In his head Christmas was still back in that big old living room in Ann Arbor, with Detroit Junior on the hi-fi and Pops dancing around with little Martin up in his arms, pointing his baby fingers at the big fat glowing tree. A real tree. Lights everywhere, all colors. The house all clean and ready for Santa. And his mother there on the couch, still pretty and slim and happy, stroking her hand along Walker's skinny boy shoulder. Humming. She had a good deep humming voice she brought out only sometimes. Those were the years, all right, Pops working hard to make it happen.

'Course there were those two or three years in between, after Pops died and Mom went all to seed. But Walker didn't want to think about those years.

"You ever go by the old house?" he asked Tasha, looking out the window to try to make it seem casual.

She didn't say anything, so after a little while he sucked in some air and repeated it, not really much louder but slower, turning to face her. She twisted her mouth up before he even finished. "Mom's waiting for us," she said.

"Really?"

"What do you mean, really? What'd you think we'd do? We got to have a little party."

He raised his eyebrows at her.

"Okay, well, it *is* little," she said, braving a speedy glance at him before turning back to the highway. "But there's cake."

"You make the cake?"

She snorted and shook her head. "Not exactly."

"Not exactly."

"You know what they say about beggars, Walker?"

This line pleased him. It was something Pops used to say. And since there was really no way Tasha could remember their father, being barely two when he died, it meant that somebody—Mom, Martin—was keeping a little of Pops alive for her. And that was something.

"Fuck beggars," Walker recited, the set response.

So they didn't go by the house. They bypassed Ann Arbor, staying on the interstate all the way to Ypsilanti. He could still see some of the outskirts of Ann Arbor anyway from the highway. The mall was still standing, bigger than ever, surrounded by new hotels and apartment complexes and what looked maybe like condos. In between the thick clusters of trees there were big signs for Audi dealers and sushi restaurants and all the new chain places he had seen on TV but not yet in real life. It was like he was one of those space travelers dropped back to Earth so many years in the future. But where had he been off to, which planet had he seen?

They took the Michigan Avenue exit and drove through the empty downtown streets, past overgrown gas stations and barbecue joints and liquor stores. Tasha turned down a residential street right off the downtown area and pulled the truck to a stop in front of a little-bitty one-story place with wide white aluminum siding and a tilting cement front stoop.

No garage, no flowers, not much of a yard to speak of. It was no Ann Arbor, they were not moving up, they were not getting ahead of anybody. All of Pops's work was for nothing, less than nothing. Jerome was in the ground, next to Pops, and Martin, they said, was living with some guys from EMU, though he'd dropped out and was training to work at the new casino in Greektown. And Walker himself, fresh out of prison, ought to be ashamed. All of Pops's sweating and dreaming just wiped away.

"So this is it?"

"This is it."

They didn't even own it. They were renting.

His mother didn't come out to the front yard. She wasn't standing in the window or the doorway. Tasha got out of the truck first, and Walker stayed in the front seat. He could still back out. He could ask Tasha to just drive him over to the room he'd be renting. He could promise to come back and see Mom and Martin some other day.

The last time he saw his mother, the thing she said, he remembered it, he hadn't been able to forget it all these years.

"Well, come on," Tasha said.

Reluctantly, he followed Tasha up the sidewalk, up the cracked and sagging stoop, feeling the rust of the black metal railing like acid under his hand. *A wire brush*, he thought, *a little Rust-Oleum*. He might be able to hammer it back into shape.

The front door opened into a living room dominated by a big TV in a fake wood console that covered one whole wall. When they walked in, a little piss-and-shake curly white dog came yapping at his ankles first thing. As he crouched down to make the thing shut up, he set one fist on the carpet to balance, and it felt sort of greasy and sticky and pretty much like the dog itself. The air inside was cool and stuffy and stank.

"Mama?" Tasha called. "Martin?"

His mother was still nowhere in sight, but Martin came stepping out from the hallway shyly. His little brother, just a skinny little thing, as always. Must be twenty-five by now. He cast a closed-lip smile at Walker, and Walker stood up from the dog and grinned back. "Little man," he said, and went over. Martin thrust out a hand to shake, no hug, and Walker nodded and shook it, leaning awkwardly in toward Martin's shoulder. Martin allowed him that much. "Good to see you, man," Martin measured out in a flat voice, hardly more than a whisper.

And then his mother made her way out of the kitchen, wearing a twitching, unsure smile. "Well, come on in, Walk. Don't just stand there like a salesman."

He stepped forward, and she leaned in to hug him. It was a polite hug, though, just at the shoulders and neck. Her big warm hand landed between his shoulder blades for a few seconds, went back and forth, then flew away. It was like being in some stranger's house, not home. And his mother was different, vacant-like around the eyes, and fat. Really fat, over-the-edge kind of fat. She had sometimes looked heavy in the pictures over the years, but he hadn't expected to see her this big. Walker stood there stupidly, wanting this party over. The way she and Martin looked at him, he could see it: they were afraid of him.

After they sat together a while Walker started to smell barbecued ribs. He couldn't believe it. His mouth got all wet, just smelling it. She always was a first-rate, knockout cook, mixing up flavors nobody could ever guess, and never giving away her recipes. Pops used to say she should start a restaurant once the babies were all in school, that folks would line up to pay for food like this. But she'd just say, "In this town? Ann Arbor? Ain't enough of us. By a long ways."

"They'd come all right," he would say, and start mapping

out his elaborate business plan for her. "First we'll get you a cart—do the farmers' market on Saturdays and lunch hours downtown till folks develop a taste for your stuff, a little Loretta Price *addiction*, like I've got. Then we'll get ourselves a little storefront." Walker never knew if Pops really believed one day he'd talk her into it, or if they just liked acting out the conversation over and over. He'd say, "Ain't fair, keeping this food all to ourselves." And she'd say, "Ain't nobody else I can cook for like you." Pops would smile and move one of his big hands around from the small of her back to her belly. "You do cook, Retta. You really do."

But now, when Moms pulled the tray from the oven, he could see it was store-bought, a big tinfoil tray just like what they'd filled with slop inside, in Jackson. His stomach turned over a little, tricked. But then he remembered how she'd actually stopped cooking long ago, when Pops died. Maybe it was true: she couldn't cook for anyone else. Not even her kids, not even D. B. Chenille. So much of her went away when Pops went. It was like losing both of them, but one still walked around.

The kitchen counters and table were covered with piles of magazines and old mail, so they had to eat in the living room, from paper plates balanced on their knees. The TV played the Tigers game in the background, so they followed the game, not saying much, just sucking their fingers and wiping at their faces. Tasha worked hard to include Walker in the conversation, but everything he said came out stupid, and the sight of his mother sitting there, so distant and empty, was making him madder and madder. Martin kept his mouth sealed like a can, just stared into that baseball game all day like he expected the ball to fly out of the screen any minute. After they finished with the ribs and the cake and there was nothing else to do, their mother said, "Now, Martin, take him down to the basement for some clothes." Martin rolled his eyes back, then waited till a commercial to get up. They went down in the moldy little basement, where a trickle of water moved across the middle of the floor, and started rooting through old boxes.

"So, you still painting?"

Martin was the artist of the family, back then. Even as a little kid, he was good. Couldn't stop him from drawing on anything near him—place mats and napkins, magazines, phone books. Twice Pops caught him painting the basement walls when he was little, maybe five. The first time, Pops took the belt to him. The second time, he just went pale with fury that Martin would defy him like that not two weeks later. First week after Pops died, Walker caught Martin painting spaceships on his bedroom walls and dragged the kid up by his collar, threw the paintbrush across the room. But Moms just leaned in the doorway, arms crossed, and said, "You go right ahead, Martin baby. Make it pretty. Do what you do." From there on out every wall was fair game, and the house grew pictures on every surface. Two purple lizards crawled right across the countertops; a big black bear looked out from behind the fridge.

"Painting?" Martin shrugged like he'd forgotten what the word meant. "Not really. Here." He pulled down a box from an overloaded shelf. "This is some of Jerome's old stuff. It ought to fit."

The way he said it was casual, and after all, Jerome had been dead almost nine years. But still, the words left a dent in Walker's chest. He'd have to go visit that brother, too. He'd have to go talk to the grave.

Walker stood staring at the boxes. "What about my stuff?"

Martin chewed the inside of his cheek. Looked away. Shuffled.

"You didn't save anything of mine?" Walker said. His books, his music, his baseball cards Pops paid for. "Nothing?"

"I was seven, Walk," Martin said. "What do you want from me?"

Walker rubbed at his ear, where a sound like water or wind was starting to rush in.

"She got a boyfriend these days?" Walker asked, angling his jaw up toward the ceiling, toward their mother upstairs in the room above them.

"Who, Tasha?"

"Mom."

Martin scoffed. "Don't start with that. Shit."

"What, does she?" Walker went and stood over him to wait for his respect.

Martin shook his head slowly, exaggeratedly. Not to answer the question. To show his disgust with Walker.

"You know, you can stop looking at me like that. Boy."

"Here." Martin shoved a box into Walker's chest. "You can take it from here."

That's it, Walker thought. He was ready to go now. He carried two boxes of Jerome's things upstairs and set them down in the kitchen, where his mother was standing, all ready to say good-bye.

"Now, Walker," she said. "I'm sure sorry you can't stay here with us."

"Really?" he said. She let this go, staring down at her little fat feet.

He couldn't help it. He had to ask. "You remember the last thing you said to me, Mom?"

She turned away from him and busied herself at the sink with the dishes. "Why you want to talk about that now?"

"I just do."

She shrugged.

He came up close to her and saw the fear flame up again in her face. He should have stopped, but somehow he couldn't hold himself back. Eighteen years was a long time to wait for one simple thing from her.

"You said I was like an animal—" That last word stuck in his throat, didn't come out right. "Like an animal that had *turned*."

She was trembling now, and cowering away from him, tucking her chin to her chest so he couldn't get to her face or hurt her.

"And I just wanted to tell you—" Here he stopped and breathed for a while, trying to calm down. There were times, inside, when he'd wished for that animal quality, shit, if he was a praying man he'd have prayed for it. Because people like that, the animals, didn't suffer, didn't have any fear at all for folks to sniff out. Animals, he had met them, shit-brained logic-less motherfucks who screwed up everything for everybody inside. And she, his mother, had a knack for bringing them home. "You were wrong," he said, wanting to spit. "You were wrong when you said that."

She nodded, real fast, like she just wanted rid of him. Her head was all hunched up in her shoulders, her face hidden, but he had the sick sensation he'd made her cry. Tasha came in from the other room to see what the commotion was.

Walker stared at his mom, waiting. "There's nothing you want to say?"

She just shivered.

"I'm gonna go then," Walker said. He would never say he was sorry for what happened, not to his mother, not to the parole board. This thing they all wanted from him, this thing that would have made his life so much easier, would've bought his freedom years ago, he couldn't give it. "Thank you for the party," he said, too loud.

Tasha made a strange face but didn't say anything, and she helped him carry the boxes out to the street. When they got to the truck, she set down a box and started trying to pull apart her key chain.

"Here," she said after a few minutes. She put a key in his hand, squeezing down and holding his palm for a second. "The truck. You oughta have it."

He protested, but she wouldn't hear it. "Pops'd want you to have it. Anyway, it's a serious piece of shit. Scares me. You gotta add oil constantly. Don't forget."

"I don't guess I even got a license anymore," he said.

"Well, you better get one. Pronto."

"Okay." He smiled. "Okay then." There was something in her, something a little bit like home. She hugged him and then stood watching him from the curb. He could see her back there in the mirror as he turned the big steering wheel and drove off toward Ann Arbor.

4

You gotta be kidding me," Kate's dad said. "You didn't really put in an offer on this place."

"John," her mom said in a low voice, touching his arm.

"Seriously," he said. "You're serious?"

Kate shifted and avoided his gaze. It had been a mistake to bring her parents here. But her parents had asked, and she couldn't refuse, and by using her dad as the inspector they could save hundreds of dollars. The plan was they would all go out to dinner afterward—to celebrate, Kate had hoped. But now they'd spent three hours following her father around the house inside and out, from the basement all the way to the attic, hearing him point out every flaw. The crack in the foundation, the basement's corroded plumbing, the bow in the wall of the front porch and the rotting windowsills and the lack of insulation and the ungrounded electrical outlets. For a start.

"I don't want to tell you what to do," her dad said, "but you've got to get out of the contract." They were up in the attic room, and he hunched and looked over his head, as if the roof might crumble down on them any minute. "Places like this can ruin a person, bankrupt you."

"We signed the offer," Stuart said.

"So what? Back out. Tell them you want sixty, eighty grand off the price to fix everything, and they'll tear up the papers themselves. That's how it works."

Kate cast Stuart an apologetic glance, but he was elsewhere, his face a mask of blankness. He had such skill in tuning things out when he wanted to.

Kate's mom nodded. "No dishwasher, no garbage disposal. Honey, what kind of relationship can you have with a house like this?"

"No AC even," her dad said. "I mean, be realistic."

The reality was that these houses on the Old West Side were being snapped up left and right, and when they were remodeled, they sold for at least double this price. She had tried to explain this to them; she had thought they'd be impressed.

"Haven't you ever just fallen in love with a house?" she said feebly.

Her dad huffed. "That's the worst thing you could do."

"Isn't that what you want your customers to do?"

"Sure. Then they overlook all the flaws. But it's not what *you* want to do, Katy."

It is, Kate thought. I want to stare hard at something flawed and love it anyway. "You don't understand how hard it is. How expensive Ann Arbor is."

"You don't have to live right in Ann Arbor. There's some great new developments in Pittsfield and Saline." Her mother put one understanding hand on Kate's arm, and Kate felt herself shrinking. "With houses not that different from, say, Derrick's, even." Derrick lived in a 3,500-square-foot box in a field, with a professionally landscaped half acre complete with automated sprinklers. It had a huge granite kitchen, a gas fireplace that burned only fake logs, and a garage that could probably fit a school bus. After her wedding, Julia would probably move into one just like it: floor plan B.

"They're just so alike, those houses," Kate said.

Her dad rubbed the sole of one shoe across the plasticine indoor-outdoor carpeting, making a *vvvt vvvt* sound. "I can show you fifty houses in this neighborhood exactly like this one. And another seventy-five like the one next door. Originality has never exactly been big in architecture."

"A house across the street just sold for twice this amount, remodeled," Kate said.

Her dad sighed and looked at Stuart. "Are *you* sold on this house?"

Kate thought, *This is it.* It was obvious Stuart wasn't crazy about this plan and would jump at the chance to avoid going through with this.

"The thing is, John." Stuart woke up suddenly and stepped forward, wearing his most open, excited smile, or a very good fake of it. "I *am* sold on it. I just *like* it!" He clapped Kate's dad on the shoulder casually, a gesture her dad himself used to dismiss people.

It was a lie, a beautiful, sweethearted lie. Stuart took her hand and turned, leading them all back downstairs, case closed, conversation over. Behind her she heard her dad quietly groan and knew her mom was shooting him glances, but they stayed silent. One thing her parents wouldn't dispute was the right of a man to make decisions for his wife.

"It's got character, John," Kate's mother said. "And she's right about the neighborhood. I've seen the listings." They were downstairs now, in the foyer that smelled of cat pee, next to the cheap laminated front door with all its hodgepodge deadbolt locks. "Couldn't you send over some of your guys to help them fix it up?"

Her dad lifted his eyebrows. "Sure, we're just sitting around idle all day. I was thinking I'd turn my whole operation over to the goddamn Habitat for Humanity." Two beads of sweat clung to his forehead. He was breathing heavily. Kate thought of his heart, of all his narrowing arteries. She thought of the way he'd once teased her for swinging a hammer wrong when she was little, how he had shown her how a *man* swings a hammer, the heel of his hand curving off the end of the handle. And how she'd swiped a box of his ten-penny nails and hammered them all day long into a two-by-four, trying to mimic the way he could sink a nail in just one strike. She never managed, and came away with crushed, bleeding thumbnails. But for a girl, she swung a hammer pretty well.

"Look, it's your money now. Do whatever you want. What do I know?" He pushed through the screen door, which slammed back too fast, since it had no spring. Then he paused on the front porch and turned back. "You asked for my advice. *You* asked." He put his hands up as if she had hurt him somehow.

Kate shriveled. She could do nothing but nod. He stepped off the porch and got into the car.

Her mom was still there, kneading Kate's shoulder in a supportive way that Kate felt sure would leave bruises. "Don't let him get to you, honey. You know how he is."

"I thought he would . . ." Kate shrugged, getting out from under her mom's hand. "I don't know. I thought he'd be impressed."

They stared at each other in a rare silence. "Well," her mom said, patting her purse and scarf, doing her inventory before leaving. "Just, you know. Just, I don't know . . . prove him wrong." She fluttered a hand through the air as if this were easy.

"Just like that?" Kate snapped her fingers.

Her mom smiled. "*I* couldn't. But you can." She locked eyes with Kate for a moment, as if daring her. Kate's dad started the car, and her mom rolled her eyes and hugged Kate, then hurried off the porch.

He was the kind of man people followed, without knowing why. People rarely defied him. She'd never seen her mom or siblings do it. When his workers did it, he fired them.

5

They closed the deal in the first week of June, just as Kate was finishing her last days of school. The day before her semester ended, Stuart and his friends moved boxes and furniture from one place to the other in a borrowed truck, and she stayed up late cleaning the old apartment so they could get back their security deposit in full. He came home after two in the morning, a little drunk, his T-shirt torn and misshapen with sweat. "Mission accomplished," he said, then stumbled toward their all-but-empty bedroom for one last night.

Kate stayed in the kitchen, wiping out cabinets and washing the floors, and collecting their last forgotten items in a big box by the door. By three-thirty the place was clean, but she was wired on NoDoz and couldn't imagine sleeping. She had only a half day of school today anyway: she could make it. She crawled out on the porch roof and sat watching a few remaining college kids stumble home from their bars and parties, and she thought, *This is it. I'm graduating.* The house faced west, so she couldn't see the sunrise, but she watched the sky around her turn a peachy then bluish gray. When they finished their showers, she packed the last of their toiletries and cleaning products, and together they broke apart the bed and hauled it down to the parking lot, where they leaned the mattresses against the filthy, overloaded Dumpster.

"What about the sheets?" Stuart said, looking dazed and hungover in the harsh morning sunlight. "Don't we want the sheets?"

Their new bed, barring complications, would be delivered to the new house this afternoon. It would be firm and stain-free and massive, and Kate was planning to buy new sheets for it right after work. *New sheets, new mattress cover, detergent, new blanket?* Like a receipt clattering out line by line, a great to-do list rolled forth in her head.

"Wouldn't it feel good to make a clean break?" she said.

Stuart nodded. They headed for their cars, but as Kate sped off she caught a glimpse of him in her rearview, wrestling the mattress to peel off the old brown sheets.

Even on ordinary mornings the parking lot of Frontier High resembled an anthill, a vortex of savage bustling that drew in more bodies every second. The last day of the year was always an electrified version of this, as students raced in the driveways and over the speed bumps on bikes and skateboards, or packed into junkyard Frankensedans and sports cars and SUVs. Once out of their vehicles, they tackled and high-fived one another, rode piggyback into the building they were so eager to leave behind. It wasn't one of those sleek, finely angled, free-form high schools, like the newer one on the wealthier northeast side of town. Frontier High was an ordinary, three-story, red-brick building, built in the fifties and augmented each decade with a series of botched additions and rickety annex buildings. Despite the additions, the school was still overcrowded by four hundred students, which gave the hallways the feel of a Japanese subway. *New sheets, mattress cover, detergent, new blanket, groceries, grill, charcoal, shower curtain, bug spray.* Kate tucked in her arms and her aching head and moved through the mass of students, trying to keep her body compact but malleable. When a water balloon sailed past her ear, she knew she was supposed to exert authority, protect the general welfare, but instead she just ducked into her trigonometry classroom and pressed herself against the closed door.

The students stopped chattering immediately. They stared at her there, clinging to the door, until she feigned a smile and moved toward her desk. Sometimes the front of the classroom, the pairs of eyes on her, all the authority they expected her to wield, all the knowledge they thought was locked up in her head, made her want to crawl behind something and hide. By the end of each day she hated the sound of her own droning voice. Like a sports highlight reel showing nothing but fumbles, her brain replayed each inaccurate, bumbling comment that she'd made.

But this was the last day. Her students took their seats and quieted down, suspecting nothing. She was a force, the same one they'd come to know—the one they'd in part constructed out of her fear, which they took for aloofness, and out of her shyness, which they took for strict condescension. Some of the other teachers brought in last-day treats, threw parties, or gave the students a free hour to sign yearbooks and say good-byes. Kate had never done this. It seemed sycophantic, pathetic. She didn't suppose she'd ever be anyone's favorite teacher, though sometimes they did say she was their favorite *math* teacher, by which she supposed—if they weren't lying—they meant she was fair and patient and rarely humiliated them, and she could explain the alchemy of angles and equations in ways they finally, for the first time, understood. This was no mean feat, and even the students knew that.

What they were scheduled to do was go over the correct answers to the final exam they'd taken Monday. Kate could do this on autopilot, even with her NoDoz jitters and bleary vision. Slowly she walked through the aisles handing back the tests without making eye contact. *Steaks, bread, broccoli, butter, brownie mix, lettuce, vinegar, tomatoes, toilet paper.* She was planning a special night for Stuart, something to make up for . . . for everything. She was difficult, she knew it, and he wasn't crazy about this house business, and from time to time she had to reward his tolerance. If she could just get through this hour, this morning, she'd have the new house and summer vacation, and she would make everything right again.

While she gave them a few minutes to look over the corrections, Kate pulled up the blinds and stood blinking out at the bright day. *Garden hose*, she thought. *Garden hose, sprinkler.* Those kids behind her, with their hopes and hormones, she wished that they would vanish. Still her mouth formed the words, "Does anybody have any questions about the exam?"

The room breathed quietly. The walls on either side of them bustled with laughter and celebration.

She turned and faced them. "No questions?"

They squirmed, torn between the deeply conditioned desire to please her and their suspicion that if no one voiced any questions she'd have no choice but to give them free time, after all. Kate imagined releasing them, like fireflies from a mason jar: they might hesitate near the door in their half-dead disbelief, but if she shook them and shook them, they would have to flutter forth. It was a beautiful day, she could say, and life was short, and each year she heard rumors of teachers who did this sort of thing without suffering any consequences.

More practically: she could send them next door for study hall and make her way down to the nurse's office to plead some sort of flu. In six years here she had called in sick only twice. Who could doubt her?

"Mrs. Kinzler?" A boy in the back waved his hand. A low but unmistakable groan sounded from the rest of the room.

It was Robbie Bergran, a wild card, a B+, a chess club acolyte and yearbook photographer who also played football and headed the LGBT committee. None of his signals lined up; when his hand went up, he was liable to ask anything.

"I was just wondering if we could just, like, call it a day?"

Laughter erupted, was swallowed back down, and the kids eyed Kate anxiously.

Just do it, she thought. *Liberate yourself.*

"Wait." From the back of the room Sarah Morgenson, A-, was waving her arm. It swung like a mast in a violent storm, tipping the great, rounded boat of her body from side to side. Next to her, Ronda and Leanne, the room's only black students, rolled their eyes in unison. They were all supposed to be postracial in this progressive blue town, where almost everyone was white anyway. But at Frontier the black kids still ate with the black kids, the Asians with the Asians, and so on. The janitors were almost all Hispanic, and black girls had to drive to Ypsilanti or Detroit if they wanted to get their hair done.

Kate nodded and pointed, and Sarah, steady Sarah, launched into a three-part attack on problem #24. It had lowered her grade by the critical two points required for a solid A. Robbie Bergran caught Kate's eye, telecommunicating the word *coward*.

One question bled into another, one class filed out and another came in, and even when the last bell of the semester rang out, Kate was too polite to rush off, interrupting the good-byes and well wishes of her coworkers. She got stuck in the classroom, the hallways, the stairwell, until nearly one o'clock.

Flowers, lighter fluid, matches, vacuum cleaner bags. By the time Kate had packed up and started heading out, the halls were ghosted and strangely quiet. From the bulletin board in the teachers' lounge a lone Polaroid stared at her. It was a picture of a dog, an enormous, white and black spotted hound with a face that encompassed all the world's suffering. For a few blissful seconds the ticker tape of her thoughts held still while he stared at her. From his drooping, wet jowls and eyelids, from the lazy way his back paws were flopped into the easiest tangle under his haunches, it was clear that haste and anxiety would be impossible in the presence of this animal. If he could talk to her, she believed he would say, *Relax.*

FREE TO A GOOD HOME, someone had written in the soothing blue sky over his left ear. In the white space under his paws there was a phone number. Kate started to jot it down on her shopping list but stopped. She checked the empty room around her, then plucked out the thumbtack and swiped the picture itself.

There was no time to browse through the mall for high-thread-count sheets, then make her way over to Kerrytown for fresh flowers and grass-fed beef. If she wanted to meet the mattress men on time she would have to take daring steps. She'd have to go to LeMar's.

LeMar's was a giant superstore near the interstate. It was as big as the Michigan stadium inside, and sold everything from groceries and prescription drugs to furniture, cheese fries, batting gloves, lawn mowers, and underwear. Open around the clock, the place was like a self-contained, fluorescent-lit kingdom, with its own maps and flags and propaganda and uniformed police.

The store was laid out like a labyrinth, with each aisle

leading into a different but related section, so that just as she stepped away from the butcher counter Kate emerged before charcoal and a long row of grills, which blended into tiki torches and lawn furniture, which very soon became grass seed and shovels. At every turn, as if someone were reading her mind, Kate found more things they needed: their own set of outdoor garbage cans, a wheelbarrow, a rake, fertilizer, doormats, several boxes of lightbulbs. In the plant and garden section, in every slow-shuffling elderly couple and each mother irritably corralling her kids, Kate saw *her people*, other homeowners, each confronting the same needs and problems. "Hello," she said to an obese man fingering the buttons on a microwave oven. "Let me help you with that," she offered to a pregnant woman reaching up for a board game. This was her domain now.

Pulling into the driveway with her car full of purchases, Kate didn't care that the lawn was thigh-high with weeds, broken glass, and garbage; she didn't mind that the little old detached garage leaned to one side precariously, or that some of the porch floorboards had rotted away, leaving holes the size of rodents. This was her house, her property. The checkout boys had called her "ma'am" today: she was a woman of substance. Unloading her car, she looked around to see if any neighbors would like to wave hello.

No one did. The small front yards and porches were empty, except for one elderly woman three houses down, who was slowly dragging her garbage can down her driveway. Kate started toward her, thinking to offer to help. Wasn't that what neighbors did? She held up one arm in a vague gesture. The woman blinked her bluish, hazed-over eyes at Kate and turned away.

Kate lowered her arm. The tree-lined street seemed strangely quiet. She gazed at each house in turn, studying their faces as she would a new group of students or strangers at a party. What went on in their hidden interiors, when they thought no one was looking? Which ones showed promise, character, pain? Which ones were bursting with trouble, discontent? Which ones might save your life?

And then she turned and looked at her own house. What would other people make of it, and of her, when they looked up at this bundle of wood? *It would take a while*, she thought. It would take a while for the place to start looking like her.

Surprise. It was showtime, Stuart realized as soon as he pulled into the driveway. The thank you, I'm sorry, and welcome home show. He got out of his car and stood warily, surveying the changes she'd made in a single afternoon. She may as well have hired a band and strung up carnival lights. She had bought flowers in pots and put them in the corners of the front porch. Between them, two new wicker chairs sat angled toward each other, as if in conversation. A garden hose was coiled up near the spigot on the side of the house. Though she had left the weeds standing, she had clearly gone through the yard and picked up the more conspicuous garbage.

She was a great fan of surprises and special occasions. She had once filled his car with helium balloons, had often made elaborate breakfasts in bed, had several times subjected him to embarrassing surprise parties. Whatever she was up to today, he dreaded it. He'd had a long night, slept badly, endured an utterly miserable day at work—he was responsible for a big flaw in a routing program that he should have noticed and fixed months ago. Now he had to rewrite thousands of lines of code, which would set back the program's launch date by weeks. He'd been hazed all day by his coworkers, in smiling, joking ways that scarcely managed to conceal how irritated everyone was with him. He felt like a first-rate loser, like a burden.

Inside, melon-scented candles were burning on top of the radiator in the hallway to the kitchen. She had reassembled their futon couch and set up the stereo on the coffee table. Jazz music bounced off the bare windows and high ceilings. It was old-people music; they'd never listened to it at their old place.

"I'm up here," Kate called from somewhere above him, in the echoing, empty halls, and her voice seemed suddenly older, all grown up. It was a house big enough for six people, eight. There were entire clans in the third world getting by on half this space.

He creaked his way up the stairs, and in the big front bedroom he found her, lying diagonally across their giant new showroom bed. She was naked. She was on her back with her hands clasped behind her head, trying to look casual, as if she'd been lying there all day just waiting for him. But her chest was thumping visibly, her breathing still heavy. She had clearly raced to the bed and stripped just as he'd pulled into the driveway.

"What's all this?"

"Your new bed," she said.

"I see that." He made his way over. They had decided to make do for now by just putting the new mattress and box spring on the floor, without any frame or headboard. The surface was firm and springy; he knelt on it and bounced. "The sheets are warm."

"I ironed them," she said, stroking the open space with one hand.

"Ironed," he said. "Ironed?"

She nodded, tugging his shirt out of his pants.

Next to the bed, on the floor, she had placed two gin and tonics, reading his mind.

"So you've been shopping." He sipped, trying to interrupt his half-conscious tally of how much money she'd spent.

"I bought you a present."

"You bought a lot of things."

"We've needed them." She teased her fingers through the short, curly hairs at the nape of his neck.

The garbage can in the corner was packed full of cellophane and plastic shopping bags. He read the labels. "LeMars? What's next, Wal-Mart?"

"Don't knock it," she said. "The prices were really good."

She peeled off his shirt and drew faint zigzags across his back with her fingernails. "Come on, honey."

He sighed. He brought his hand up to cup the back of her head, her soft hair that coiled automatically around his fingers, like the grasp of an infant. She was his pale, freckled, redheaded wife, she was the only one. He kissed her.

"So are we better now?" he said quietly. Those months of her cringing when he touched her, of her looking for any chance to be apart from him, were they over? "Will we be better, now that we've moved?" When she tried to glance away, he held her head steady like that, forcing her to face him.

"Better than what?" she said. And he was alone as ever.

She went back to kissing his chest, and he lay down and closed his eyes, trying not to think so much.

She said something, she was saying something, but somehow he had missed it. "Hmm?"

"You know what I'm going to do?" she said in an unusually sultry voice, like a phone-sex commercial. "I'm going to—"

"Let's do this without talking," he said.

So she used her body. She dug her nails into the flesh of

his back; she flipped her hair out of the way when she rolled on top of him. She moaned and moved in uncommon ways, performing an elaborate ecstasy. The candles were color-coordinated, the sheets unwrinkled, her body slender and taut. All of this had been planned for him, and yet he couldn't shake the sensation that it had nothing to do with him.

When they were finished, they lay on the sheets for a while, and Stuart noticed how far away the high ceilings seemed. As if reading his mind, Kate said, "Doesn't it just feel like there's more air in here?"

"Yeah," he said, "yeah," feeling a genuine smile coming on.

"And once we take down the dropped ceiling and fix all this plaster, think how cool—"

Stuart got up and went into the bathroom. He didn't want to hear about any more plans for change. They had changed enough. He fumbled with the doorknob, the toilet seat, too. Nothing was where he expected it; nothing worked the way it had in their old bathroom. The tension on the faucet handle was too loose; the water came spraying out too hard; the towel rack was wobbly and too far away. And there, behind the toilet, someone had painted three little cockroaches. He leaned against the sink for a long time, staring at himself in the big, newly polished mirror. On the back of the door was a different, full-length mirror angling downward, and both of them seemed slightly distorted to him—too fat, too tall, too wavy. He felt a queasy funhouse slipperiness to it all. He squeezed his eyes shut until his breathing slowed down. It was fine. He would be fine. Inside, they were the same as ever.

When he came back, Kate was lying facedown on the new bed. He said, "Hey," but she didn't move. It was as if she had passed out, crashed, let go. There was nothing left of her to be annoyed with. He stared for a minute, enjoying the quiet. When he knelt down and touched her, she didn't move away or wake up or pretend anything. She just lay there honestly sleeping, breathing. He ran his knuckles down the valley of her back, smoothed his palm over her ass, her thigh, the back of her knee, the bulge of her calf. Back up again. Her ribs were visible along the sides. She was thinner than he'd seen her in years, maybe ever. She had been working so hard. She meant well, didn't she? He would have to help her more. He pulled the clean new sheets up to her waist, and really, she was right, they were a good soothing gray color, and soft. They were nice. He laid the blanket on top, then took her ponytail holder off the floor and pulled her hair loosely into it, the way she liked it while she slept. He got up, then thought of something and went back. Kneeling next to her, he pushed the hair away from the base of her skull. There it was: she had worried her bald spot back after all these years.

Downstairs, he found the other surprises. The giant box wrapped up under an enormous bow in the middle of the dining room turned out to be a big red Weber grill, and he sat down and put it together right there in his boxer shorts. The bottle of champagne in the refrigerator was cold and expensive; he ran his fingers over the label briefly, then decided, what the fuck, to open it. Beneath it, on the bare, clean shelves of the fridge, he found lettuce and dressing and two steaks wrapped up in white paper. And suddenly, he was hungry, starving, suddenly this was exactly what he wanted. On the back porch there was lighter fluid and charcoal, which he took out to the backyard with the grill and set it all down in the corner of the small cement patio. The backyard was, he had to admit, the most interesting part of the house. It had a renegade jungle feel, like the way he imagined New Orleans courtyard gardens—small and at some point planned but now wildly overgrown, creating a sense of mysterious privacy even though the neighbors were just yards away. He breathed it in. He had no idea how to grill things, but he built a little pyramid of coals like he had seen people do at parties. When he squirted the lighter fluid over them, he felt like a father, like a real man connected to every other grown man in the country. This was what a grill did, and Kate knew it before he could realize it himself, and she gave this feeling to him. Sometimes she was right. Sometimes he got it all wrong.

While the fire flared up he went back in the house to salt and pepper the steaks and put together the salad. He poured more champagne and rubber-banded two forks together to use as tongs, and when he returned to the yard he didn't even notice the weeds or the rotted elm tree. The air prickled his skin, and though he knew he ought to go in and get dressed before the neighbors caught sight of him through the overgrowth, it was *nice* to stand alone in his underwear, in his very own private territory. It was like the sky was lighting with stars just for him.

"Jesus!" Kate came racing out the back door, shaking her arms as though they were crawling with bugs.

"What's wrong?"

"Oh, God," she said, too panicked to make sentences. She scratched at the damp hair clinging to her neck. "I had this dream." She paced the sidewalk in her loose T-shirt and shorts, turning away abruptly every time he got near her. "The house was on fire," she said, "the house—"

Stuart wrestled her into his arms, but she stood rigid against him.

"It was awful."

"It was a dream," he said. She had nightmares all the time, terrible, violent nightmares that flopped her around in bed and rattled her for hours afterward. They cast a constant fear over her days. "Just a dream. It's okay."

"Why did you put this so close to the house?" she shouted, pointing at the grill.

"The house is fine, Katy." He rubbed her back. "The house is not on fire."

"I woke up *smelling* this," she said, on the brink of tears, her chin tightening up. "The fire, the lighter fluid, all of this." She waved her arms around again, pointing out demons that remained invisible to him.

"*You* bought it." He attempted a laugh.

Her eyes flared back viciously.

"I'm sorry," he said at last. "I'm sorry. I'll move it away."

The flames were still shooting two feet into the air, and waves of heat radiated around the grill, but he grabbed the handle boldly and dragged it across the rough, pocked sidewalk until she at least pretended to be satisfied.

6

Walker woke with a shiver in his rented room, feeling himself falling, not knowing where he might land. It was light out at last. Flashing awake all through the night, he dreamed in sweats of his own pumping arms and thighs, racing, escaping, jumping low walls and scraping up high ones, his skin tearing through razor wire, falling, running again, the wet teeth of dogs at his heels. But here he was, horizontal, tangled in flowered sheets. Alone. The old-school alarm clock ticked away on the dresser, six feet away and still loud as lockdown. Six-thirty. He had a lamp. He had two dressers, a desk, a nightstand. And on the nightstand, two keys: the truck, and now, this house.

He was thirty-six, and never in his life—aside from those fourteen days in the hole—had he had a room all to himself. If he did something wrong, if he fucked something up, they would take it all back in a second.

The bathroom was just down the hall, but he stood in his doorway first, listening, not wanting to find anyone. Safe, he was safe. Now tell it to his bumping chest, his lungs, his throbbing veins, tell them to stop with their crazy state of emergency.

Moving like a burglar, he pressed his feet into the worn carpet, down the hall into and out of the bathroom, then back to his own doorknob, turning and lifting the door against its frame to keep it quiet.

He made the bed. Looked at his boxes. The cardboard was damp and soft, like old skin. He peeled the flaps back and dug his hands into those stacks of Jerome's things, trying not to think of Jerome. His brother, his dead brother, his deadbeat brother. Everything smelled so musty he half expected to find a dead animal or some mystery rot down in the bottom, but no. He picked out a shirt and some underwear and jeans, put them on, feeling the stink on himself. Traces of Jerome, little bits of skin and hair, no doubt, were on him now. Well, that fit. It wasn't the first time. In the third box, the last one, under some T-shirts and socks: a stack of tittie mags from 1989. "Well, thank you, Jerome." He sat on the edge of the bed with one, saving the rest. Mounds and curls and skin airbrushed soft. A rising rush, blood coming in. Something shifted on the floor below, the reverend moving his heavy bones around. Walker flung open a drawer, stashed the magazines, closed it tight.

When he pulled the last things from the last box, something heavy dropped through his armful of socks and thudded to the floor. He put his foot over it, looked around, listened for footsteps in the hall or down below, cursing his carelessness. No one came. He picked it up, backed himself against the door to be sure. Tucked inside a ball of socks was Jerome's old knife, six inches long, heavy and silver-plated like a ridiculous trophy, with Jerome's initials scratched in the oval design he always used to make, JTP—like the old STP logo. Walker remembered it, remembered those months near the end of his other life, life number one, when Jerome started coming home, first with a little pocketknife, dull piece of garbage that could hardly scare anyone but little Martin, and then working his way up to this flashy silver one, then later coming up to their attic room with weed and money and coke, and finally the gun. Eighteen, Walker was, a year too late, and Jerome seventeen, all his mistakes still erasable, and if it weren't for selling drugs he'd have no business at school at all. Waste of life, Jerome, a waste of everything. Walker weighed the knife in his palm, flicked it open. Still sharp. Jerome had to have sharpened it, kept on sharpening it, even down to the end of his scumbag days. Junkie in the streets of Detroit found dead of causes nobody bothered to figure out. Maybe overdose, maybe cracked in the head, maybe just frozen to death. And another funeral to pay for, and Walker locked up, no help to anybody at all. Walker closed up the knife, put it back in the sock, stuffed the sock under his mattress. It was like, all over again, Jerome was trying to supply him.

Walker checked the bed for signs of the knife, then the room for signs of himself. None. Everything tucked away like he'd never been here. Good. No Bible in the room, no crosses or Virgin Marys, good sign. Specially since he was working for this room, not taking charity like some fucking washup.

Walker'd expected the reverend to give him a sermon last night, set up some ground rules, lock off some part of the house from him, maybe put him up in the garage or cellar, but none of that happened. The old guy just shook his hand, sleepy-eyed, and said, "Well, come on in then."

It was only later, after they'd sat together a while with cookies and decaf, when Walker was starting to unclench his shoulders a little, that the reverend stood up, brushed the crumbs from his lap and shirt, held out his hand to shake, and said, "Just don't con me." And he went to bed.

Now, making his way down the stairs, carrying his shoes in his arms, Walker could smell the coffee already and knew he would have to face the old man again, and sure as shit he wouldn't go two days without making sure Walker knew his place, his limits, his rules.

The reverend was sitting at a rickety little two-person table in the corner of the kitchen. It was covered in a flowered green vinyl tablecloth and stood right up against a tall double-hung window. Behind him, through the window, leaned the little shed garage at the corner of the dried-up backyard. The old man huddled over the table, chewing, staring into his cereal.

Walker stood like a ghost in the doorway. They were only eight blocks away from Macon Street. So you couldn't go home again, but you could come close.

The room was dim, the walls papered in a mossy color with gold braids weaving through it. It peeled away at the seams and bubbled near the ceiling, like something in the walls was swollen up, trying to hatch.

The reverend's jaws creaked, a pop and a slush in every bite, with little grunts on the swallow. He was wrinkled deep, with a wide, flat face, a high thinning hairline, and brown spots all over his face and forehead and neck. He was white, but all those spots made him look awfully dark.

When he finished with the cereal, the reverend picked up his pill container, one of those long plastic seven-day ones, and with a trembling finger and long fingernail started prying at the lid for today, Saturday.

"Thought I heard you up there," he said, still working at the pillbox, not looking up. "You help yourself." He waved one arm behind him, toward the kitchen cabinets. "To the groceries. Part of the deal."

Walker nodded, setting his shoes down. His stomach was a knot, curled in on itself. Yesterday had been release, celebration, whatever, anything under the sun. Today was the real beginning, the start of what he would be and do and how the world would or wouldn't let him go forward.

He opened a cabinet timidly, and inside, more colors and cans and choices than he'd seen in years. His stomach moved. Swooning a little, to buy time, he opened a second cabinet. More. And more and more.

"I'm not going to wait on you," the reverend said. His eyes were a milky blue.

Walker settled his hand on a cereal box. It seemed to float for a second, but he waited, squeezing the thin cardboard, then picked it up and shook it to hear the reassuring clatter inside. He was fine. Exhaled, set it down. No one would take it away, no one tell him how or when to have it, come up behind and hit him for it. He pulled out a bowl, and it seemed so weirdly heavy and clean, not tin, not Styrofoam, not plastic, not throwaway.

"I have a garden." The reverend thrust one arm toward the window beside him and the yard beyond it. "Can't work it anymore. That's to you, right? You can do that?"

Walker nodded. "I can do that, Reverend."

The old man grunted again. "Howard," he said. "I'm retired. You call me Howard."

Sure, maybe the yard had had a garden once, sure. Now it was just yellowed patches of crabgrass getting eaten over by dandelions and scrub. It was obvious the reverend had grubs: you could feel the spongy turf, see how easy it was to peel back the grass, the roots all eaten out to nothing, the grass starving. "These are my cherry tomatoes." Reverend Howard pointed a rickety finger at one corner of the overgrown rectangle at the back that was enclosed in a low, mangled chicken-wire fence and was knee-high with weeds and overturned plastic pots. "And that's cucumbers over there." He waved at another spot with nothing but weeds growing in it.

"You mean—" Walker wavered. "You mean you want me to plant some there?"

"They're right there," Howard said, then bent over and took a closer look. "Little overgrown, I guess."

Walker scratched his stomach. "Well." He thought. The dirt was hard and dry, compressed from years of hot neglect, not brown but a grayish-soot color, the color of filth, not soil. Pops would've pissed on it, had it hauled away. "I'll get rid of the weeds," Walker said. "See what you've got."

Couldn't hurt anything to do that much. Lord knows he had weeded shit in his life, knew plenty about crawling around on his knees. And Pops had taught him everything anybody ever knew about work, about plants, about digging. He dug in, hacking at the thick, ropelike network of roots. When he got a good grip, pulled them up, the dirt all around broke like an earthquake and raised sister weeds three feet away. He took them, too.

The sun was moving up, it was probably eighty or so and muggy as hell. The reverend sat down in a lawn chair in the shade by the garage. He watched and sweated.

Every so often Walker looked over at him: sometimes sleeping, sometimes staring into space. Sometimes when Walker asked him questions, he seemed not to hear, so Walker just kept working, using his own best judgment. Like Pops said, there was never any trouble could come from keeping your head down and your hands moving. Sooner or later the rest of your life would work itself out around you.

'Course, in the end, lot of good it did Pops.

At first he fingered and sniffed every plant, making sure it was a weed. They were, they all were, every last one. He had done this work over on Macon Street, too, that first spring when they moved in. Pops took Walker out back first, when everyone else just ran inside the house like mice. They were a twosome. "Look at all this, Walk." Pops pushed his big hands against Walker's shoulders. "Look at all you and I can do here."

That would have been 1983, Walker was fourteen, Jerome thirteen, Martin three, Tasha not even an idea yet. The other kids went in the house with Mama. Walker my worker, Pops used to say, counting on him for everything, or so it seemed. So the two of them stood staring at the scrawny little yard, Walker trying to see what Pops was seeing.

It was just a patch of weeds, only one thin tree at the back. The houses all around had big old trees, maples and oaks and a few struggling elms, but this place had only one feeble evergreen in the back corner, its needles hanging off the limbs like the tattered clothes of a ghost.

He squinted up at Pops, whose eyes were jittering, calculating. "Gonna grow an arch over this here." He lifted his big arms to trace an arc over the passage between the house and the rickety shed garage. He'd been with the Detroit Parks eight years, and now he'd gotten taken up by the U of M—landscaping, horticulture—and that meant that Pops really could do anything green, anything he wanted. If the University of Michigan stamped you, it was true.

Then Pops pulled Walker into his hip, a hand on his shoulder, and he crouched a little and brought his voice low. "See that?" He pointed at the two little bungalows whose yards backed up to theirs. "May be white, but who's got the bigger house?"

"We do." Walker smiled, couldn't help it. But then, of course, it crept up on him: "Will they hate us?"

Pops was already loose from him, measuring the yard in

footsteps. "I'm gonna get some dirt delivered, I know a guy. And two trees." He put his arms out like an artist. "Russian olive," he said, moving his left hand in a motion toward the back corner. "And something over here, I don't know what. Red bud, saucer magnolia . . . don't know yet. Maybe you can decide."

Walker picked his way through the weeds and dog turds and shards of glass. Their place in Detroit had been a big walk-up, the first floor of a rental house, with only a gravel lot on every side.

"And at work," Pops went on. "Larry tells me I can get plants for free, ones they don't use. And this." Pops waved his arm at the back wall of the house. "We're gonna paint it. You boys and me, once your mother picks a color." The house was a pale gray-blue, its skin bubbled and peeling.

"Purple?" Walker said.

Pops shook his head. "It's for your mother to pick."

She picked blue. Hardly any different from the color it already was. She never did have much imagination, and she sure didn't help them paint it. Walker and Jerome scraped and caulked and puttied the walls, then climbed up on ladders and painted it. Jerome always taking too long going to get things, Jerome always sneaking off, hiding somewhere: in the end really it was Walker who painted the place, and Pops on the weekends. Martin, only four that summer, what could he do but get in the way, ruin his pants?

Most Fridays Pops came home a little late, with clippings and seeds and sometimes mulch or compost. Every week or two he'd get a line on some oddball piece of trash he'd go pick up on a roadside—an old wooden barrel, a bent lamppost, a homemade bird feeder. "Building a junkyard, all's you doin'," Mom used to say, but Pops would just say, "Wait and see." She never did go out back much though, never liked the weather. Too hot or too cold was all she'd ever say. Pops went on building his crazy garden anyway, always saying it was for Mama or the kids, though anybody could see it was just for him. For his pride.

Last night when Walker went down to Macon Street, he'd slipped behind the garage, through the remains of the old passage where they used to crawl through the lilacs, and he'd stood at the edge of the backyard, trying to see through the dark if any of Pops's trinkets still stood. Maybe he could take one. But there was only a shovel, a rake, a wheelbarrow leaning up against the garage, as if somebody planned on digging away at the tangled mess the yard had become. It cut at him. Whoever lived here, they didn't deserve one plant, one single blade of Pops's grass. But then that didn't feel right either. If they tore it all out, whose yard would it be then?

Pops's old yard had gone tall and bushy. It was hard to see. The lights had gone out inside, it was going on two a.m. They must have fallen asleep, he figured. He squeezed past the last lilac bush, feeling the branches scraping at him. No one, nothing. A rustle of leaves, one broken branch, and he was in.

He stood still against the bushes. It was one of the places Martin used to hide. That one a hider, too, not to avoid work but to do his own drawings, his own little work, not the kind Pops ever wanted. Walker crouched down low and stepped out into the open grassy spot. "Twenty feet of grass, all you give 'em, after we move here to the country," Moms said when Pops's plan started growing in—all bushes and ferns and small trees around all the edges and just one kidney-bean patch of grass in the middle like a little green pool. And he treated that like it was garden, too, getting down on his knees whenever he saw a weed. Now Walker rushed through the open spot to the dark thick growth at the back corner of the yard. He remembered what'd been there.

About a year after they moved in, Pops came home one Friday, backed his truck in the driveway so the tailgate came right up to that arch to the backyard. He hollered for help, and Jerome took off up the staircase. Walker had to grab him by the ankle and say, "Not this time, J." It took Moms and a neighbor guy, too, this time. Pops leaned a plywood plank against the open tailgate: inside was a log, at least two feet in diameter and four feet long. Massive deadweight. They wrestled it down the plank and flipped it over into the yard, then crouched down and rolled it across the yard till Pops wedged it into place. "A bench," he said, and Mama rolled her eyes.

It was still there.

The back corner was the spot Pops built for them, the kids. It took a long time, and Pops never saw it done, but he said, "That's okay. It'll be done for this little one," squeezing Tasha's little baby arm. It was a cave, a living cave made of rhododendrons and trumpet vines and cypress and lilacs, all hovering over that log bench like guards on duty. "Your thinking spot," Pops called it. "For when the world gives you trouble, which it will." Jerome, who never did much thinking, used to chase Martin in there and block the exit, always too dumb to realize Martin didn't mind being in there at all.

"You go in there," Pops said, "and read and think with that brain of yours, and you dream up all your plans where nobody can see or tell you no. 'Cause it's *your* spot, and I'm giving you permission. And when you come out, you write them down, you got it?" He looked at Walker, waiting for the set answer.

"Yes, sir."

"And once your plans are wrote down, you know what you do then?"

Walker stared at him. Giving the wrong answer was a terrible thing. Not because he'd hurt you, but because of how he looked at you.

"You *work* for 'em, Walker. You work for 'em."

"Work for them," Walker murmured, staring at the spot that wasn't even defined yet, that was still waiting for the plants to grow up and surround that idea of Pops's.

Walker crouched down and went inside now. Finally it had grown in, a real cave made of plants. The log was cool and damp on this warm night. It still felt firm, not rotted out, and when he pushed on it just to make sure, it didn't budge. Must've weighed four hundred pounds. How Pops had ever gotten it into the truck was a mystery, but that was just him. He could do anything.

He would be like that, Walker. He had felt it all his life.

From inside the thinking spot in the dark Walker couldn't even see the house. It was that dense. Could be that these folks didn't even know the spot existed. He'd have to come look in the daylight and see how hidden it was. But so he sat there, holding the stump down with his hands and his thighs and all his man weight. He pressed his feet against Pops's soil, and he waited for a plan to come to him.

Now, while Walker made his way on his knees through the brown patch of Reverend Howard's burned-up, empty, imaginary garden, Howard sat on a rickety metal chair by the fence, dozing. When he woke up, he stared at Walker with a puzzled squint, like he was trying to push through the clouds in his brain and remember who he was and what he was doing there.

Walker looked over, then kept back at his work. He understood now what the guys inside meant when they hazed him for being from Ann Arbor. *Fucked-up white-boy town*, no doubt about it. Back when he was a kid, the houses were all gray and brown, maybe a white or tan one here or there. Now the neighborhood was all candy colors. The whole town looked like a cartoon, like a commercial for sweet success. Pink and peach and green, yellow and burgundy, colors he didn't even know the names for, and in every driveway a BMW or Volvo wagon, and every face lily white. The whole town sanitized, made new, nothing but lofts and condos and sleek brick offices for lawyers and architects, interior decorators.

And at every house that wasn't already pristine, in the driveway: a big rusty Dumpster filling up with the past that nobody had any use for anymore.

Now he was at the corner of the yard by the sidewalk. The ladies walking past him with their expensive dogs and baby strollers, did they know he grew up here, did they know his own pops had owned the place down the street, with the same hopes that they had twenty years before it even occurred to them? Did they know Walker had shoveled their driveways and sidewalks, had gone to the schools their kids went to now, had trick-or-treated on their very own porches? Were they eyeballing him now, suspicious? Did they know he'd done eighteen years' hard time? Did they sense that?

He held the gaze of one woman as she passed.

She half smiled, murmured a hello.

Then off down the street he heard another lady calling out in long singsong notes, like birdcalls: "Nigger! Nigger!" He bristled and stepped out to the sidewalk for a better look. She advanced down her driveway, clapping and bending, craning her neck, until a giant black dog burst out of the neighbor's hedge. She grabbed his collar and leaned down to put her face against his. "Bad dog, Bigger," she said. "Bad dog."

Bigger. Jesus. *Bigger.*

He stabbed at the ground with his hand shovel, cleared every last living thing out of the dirt patch, till there was nothing left but the little line of rocks marking the borders.

So it had been a garden at some point, he guessed, if someone had planted those rocks. He stood up and raked the dirt smooth. Wasn't too late to plant some things. Maybe beans, tomatoes, if the man wanted a garden.

In the garage there were grass clippers, hedge trimmers. He found Miracle-Gro and a hose. He trimmed the grass away at the fence line. He bagged up all the weeds and garbage he had pulled up. When Walker turned on the hose and started spraying down the grass, Howard blinked awake again. He gripped the arms of his chair, stood up too fast, stumbled back into the chair.

Walker put down the hose and went to him. "You okay there? Want a hand, Reverend?"

The old man blinked at him, eyes panicked and lost.

"We're just workin' in the yard here, remember?" Walker's grandpa sometimes used to get like this, needed a little help sewing himself back into reality. "You remember me?"

Howard squinted. "I'm Howard Sparks." He stabbed at his chest. "I live here."

"Right," Walker said. "That's right. And who am I?"

Howard scowled and stalled. After a while he got a lightbulb look. "You're a criminal."

Walker took a step back and held still. Well, sure. Nice. Walker nodded, the way you nod at an animal you want to get away from. "Walker Price," he said. "My name is Walker Price."

"What did you do to my garden?" Howard wrestled his way out of the chair and went over to all that clean, turned soil. "You tore up my garden!"

"It was weeds, Mr. Reverend, Howard," Walker stammered. "There was nothing there but weeds." Walker put his hand on Howard's arm to steady him.

"My tomatoes!" Howard was actually crying. Well, old

people's eyes teared up easy like that. "I'm calling you in!" He whipped his arm away from Walker and headed back into the house.

Walker stood, dry mouthed and empty. It couldn't be happening. Then again, sure it could. What kind of crazy offers ex-cons a home, anyway? Of course it was too good. Of course he would kick Walker out, probably set him up, take his money, call parole. No. He would still have his things. The eighty dollars was his and safe in his sock, and he'd still have Pops's truck he could sleep in. Who could take that?

He walked in the back door, where he could hear the old man raving into the phone.

Walker climbed the stairs. There was no use fighting a man in his own house.

He was in the midst of putting his stacks of Jerome's old clothes back into those moldy boxes when he saw a man walking around the backyard with his arm around Howard. He had a thick, short body and a blond head that was sunburned on its bald spot.

"Well, here we go." Walker got the knife out from under the mattress, wrapped it in a shirt, stuffed it deep in the box, carried his boxes to the foot of the stairs. He took one last look at the quiet house, at its TV and rugs and books, its gauzy curtains. He had no claim on any of it. He went outside.

"That's him." Howard pointed at Walker, like he was picking out a guy in a lineup.

"Dad, calm down," the man said. "This is just Walker. Remember? He's helping you."

The man guided Howard into his lawn chair and came over with his hand out to shake. "I'm sorry about all this," he said. "I'm Dean." He led Walker over to the other side of the yard so Howard wouldn't hear them. "It looks great, what you did. I'm sorry about him. He's, you know. We're just getting used to it." He turned and stared off at the reverend, wordless. Walker waited.

"Alzheimer's?"

Dean shrugged and looked away. "He hasn't been this bad before. He's very sharp, you know. I'm sure it'll pass."

Walker chewed on his lip, tasted the salt of his sweat there. "There was nothing but weeds in that garden. I was trying to help."

"Of course," Dean said. "Of course they were all weeds. I mow the grass here. I know. It looks great." Dean rubbed his hand along the back of his neck, like he was mapping something out in his head.

"He's got an account at Home and Garden, you know, down on Macon?" Dean said, still far off and grim. "You could take him there, pick out some seeds or flowers, if you want."

"Okay," Walker said. They stood looking over at Howard, whose head was tilted down toward his knees, his shoulders hunched in. His hands were twisted in on his thighs in a way that made him look palsied, or dead. Walker looked away. "I shouldn't have let him sit out in the heat, right? It was too much?"

"Maybe that's it." Dean looked away, too, then seemed to lighten up. "I bet the heat just got to him."

"Sure. So . . . So I'll just keep him out of the sun."

Dean glanced back at Howard. A cardinal settled on a branch just above him, twitched its head back and forth at the reverend, like it was thinking about landing right on the old man's shoulder. "I can't put him in a home, Walker. This is his home. He wants to be here. You'd be helping us out to stay."

Walker dug one toe at the grass. It was a good-size yard. He tried to imagine how it might've looked once, or how it could again with some work. It wasn't too late to fix it.

"Every day isn't like this," Dean said. "He's just got to get used to you."

It was a nice house. There was work, there was the free room plus the four hundred dollars a month he'd been promised. "It's not that," Walker said. "It's . . . Do you know about me?" he said in a low voice. What kind of son set his old man up with an ex-con?

Dean stared at him. "He's done this all his life, helped out guys like you, coming out, getting back on your feet. Even when I was a kid growing up, this was what he did."

"When you were a kid, you had folks like me come stay?"

"Yeah." Dean nodded and chuckled a little. "It was weird, sometimes. Unusual. But you know, that's how he is."

"He retired, huh?"

Dean's mouth made an O shape. "He did more than retire. He gave up the church altogether."

Walker turned that over in his head. "Did something happen?"

Dean got a far-off look then and shrugged. He started watching a garbage truck move down the street.

"You should know," Walker said, "I'm not like other cons."

Dean flashed up his eyebrows, almost as if to scold him, to show he was offended.

"We've met all different kinds of people," Dean said. "No two alike."

Walker didn't know about all this, what kinds of cons these were. The guys he'd met inside, lots of them, he wouldn't even shake their hands now, much less let them in his house to stay. His own mother wouldn't let him sleep in her house now. His Pops, shit, Pops would never have taken in a convict. Not even a relative.

"Anyway, Walker, my point is, this is a rare flare-up. I think he just got a little confused, but you'll see, in a half hour he'll be sharp as a tack again. You start to see things like this, anything at all, you call me, okay? This isn't his usual."

"Okay."

"And keep him sharp. Talk to him, ask him questions. Trivia, even math tables. Watch his game shows with him. *Jeopardy*, *Wheel of Fortune*, all that. He likes that. You've got to hold him accountable, you know?"

Walker searched his face.

"I mean, if he says it's raining out today or he lives in New York City, I don't want you nodding politely and agreeing with him. You get it? He would hate that."

Walker nodded. He could do that.

Dean went on anyway, his words coming faster and louder. "I mean, it might start a fight sometimes, but that's okay. Because letting him slip away into some dreamland like that, it's *not* polite, you know? It's not dignified."

"I got it," Walker said. "I can do that."

They stood there, tensed, until Dean put his hand into Walker's and shook it. "He's got a lot of good years still. And I trust you."

Walker felt himself flush. His hand felt wrong in Dean's. He had to say it. "Does he know about me, what I did?"

"It was his idea," Dean said. "He followed your case. He knew your family."

7

Each night Stuart came home to a new improvement. While he was gone she *did* things, with an eerily magical speed and efficiency. She stripped the yard of weeds and garbage, raked out the soil, spread grass seed, ran the sprinklers. She set ant traps, planted flowers, sealed the driveway. One night the kitchen cupboards were stripped of their contents, which she stacked up neatly in boxes in the dining room; the next night they were sanded and scrubbed; by the weekend they were painted bright white, fitted with new chrome knobs. Next came the floor. She brought home a book on tiling, then boxes of big square flooring tiles and mortar, and finally a rented tile saw that made excruciating screams with every cut. The neighbors complained. But she kept at it for three days, and they had a new kitchen floor. When he walked across it the first night after work, she asked, "How does it feel?" It felt fine. It felt like a floor.

She had taken to writing on the walls, too, because apparently they would all have to be painted or torn out altogether. So sometimes he would come home to find, in red marker on the wall by the staircase, a note saying where she was, when she'd be back. In Sharpie black on the bathroom wallpaper he found each day's to-do list and strange, cryptic notes:

8′ X 6′4″ = > 3′ VANITY? ($890)—OR PEDESTAL ($360)??

It was as if she and the house had developed their own code.

Even though he was working long hours to help fix his screwup at work, most mornings Kate was up and working before his alarm even went off. From that giant new bed they could come and go without even stirring each other. He kept waiting for her to crash and burn, to lose her temper or her enthusiasm, but every night there she was, coated in paint or dirt or sweat. And smiling. He tried to remember if he'd ever made her smile like that.

Once he came back from playing Frisbee in the park, and said, "You know there's a homeless guy living in our park?" Even then she wasn't fazed. She said, "He's only there in the afternoons, just for naps. He's not really *homeless*. He's, like, between homes. I mean, he has a cell phone."

Chimney chase? Movable?
Went to Home Depot. Leftovers? Pizza?
Strip & sand. Oak or pine? Buy lead test.

Sometimes, after work and on weekends, Stuart tried to help out. He had worked construction during his summers in college, but so far everything he touched turned to shit: he didn't hold the paintbrush right and left drips; he mixed the grout too thin and it cracked; he forgot to turn off the sprinklers and washed the grass seed into the storm sewers.

"You're just messing up on purpose, to get out of work, aren't you?" Kate said once, but even then she was smiling, sounding more flirtatious than mad.

When the yard finally filled in and she had nearly finished

painting the exterior in a cheery maroon and yellow color scheme, she cooked him steaks one night and got him drunk and carefree and then pulled out their checkbook and some brochures. "I was thinking about a fence, next."

"What do we need a fence for?"

She produced a mangled photo of a dog, a drooling, cow-bodied dog. It looked as though it had ridden around in her sweaty pocket for weeks.

So that Saturday they drove out to Dexter, the next town westward, to the old farmhouse of some teacher from her school who wanted to give away his dog. Kate had called the guy and set it all up, and Stuart had gotten a firm promise from her that they would only take a look at the dog. They would make no rash decisions. He liked dogs, a dog would be nice, but you couldn't just settle on the first one you met.

"So what's the deal with this dog, that you want it?" he said. "Does it have only three legs or something?"

She smiled.

"Think you can make one grow back?"

"Exactly." Every time they passed a nice house she turned around in her seat to watch it go by, then remarked on some aspect of it that they ought to imitate. Or improve upon.

"Don't get too impressed," Stuart said as he drove. "Dexter's the capital of the Michigan militia, you know."

"I think that's a myth. I mean, look at these houses."

"They're probably loaded with guns," he went on. "Hand grenades, trench coats. This dog you found is probably trained to attack."

Kate scrutinized the photo for the hundredth time. "Yeah right," she said. "He'll bleed you dry while you sleep."

"See, look at that." Stuart pulled up close at a stop sign

behind a pickup truck that had a small but unmistakable Confederate flag sticker in the corner of its back window.

"Holy shit." She put her hand over her mouth. "Look at that. Don't tailgate him. He'll jump out and pummel you, you pinko college grad."

"Right," Stuart said wryly, but he gave the guy a wider berth anyway.

They went through the small, quaint center of town, where meticulously restored Victorian houses lined the slow, quiet streets. It wasn't at all like Ann Arbor, where people would paint their homes black and neon green or put giant abstract sculptures in their yards next to their IMPEACH BUSH signs. Here the desired illusion was more like Candyland. They even had fake old-fashioned street signs and streetlights, and a town square with a gazebo. They passed a drive-in A&W restaurant, whose parking lot held two hot rods and a Model T.

"See? It's like Mayberry," Kate said. "Where are your militiamen now?"

"Right here." They pulled off the busy road into the long gravel driveway of the teacher's dilapidated farmhouse, and Stuart pointed at three rotting barns in the backyard. "Weapons caches," he said. "Are you sure you want to do this?"

A friend of theirs had adopted an unwanted dog from a farmer once, and it bit off the ear of his cat.

Kate scanned the yard warily through the windshield. "Okay, knock it off. We've come all this way."

When they got out of the car, they were confronted by a high-pitched grinding sound coming from the sturdiest-looking barn. Eight or ten mysterious, human-size metal objects stood in a staggered row between that barn and the next.

Kate turned back to Stuart and whispered, "Okay, if it's weird, get us out of here. You be the rude one. I have to work with this guy."

"Got it."

The dog, giant and sun-sleepy, was lying in the grass. When he caught sight of them, he labored to his feet and walked to the end of his chain.

"I don't know if I've ever seen a dog this big," Stuart said.

"Hello there." Kate approached him slowly, looking around.

"Be careful. Let him sniff your hand."

She did this, and when he didn't bite her, she reached timidly over his head to pet him. Immediately he flopped onto his back and writhed around, offering up his vast, pink stomach. He was fat, he was huge, with short, soft white hair and a few large gray-black spots. He had ears like pancakes and a head the size of a ham.

"He has nipples," Kate said.

"Dogs have nipples." Stuart crouched down and patted the dog's belly.

"Male dogs?"

"Why not?" He shrugged. "I have nipples."

Neither of them had ever had a dog before, though they had always talked about how much they wanted one.

"It's sad they keep him chained up," Kate said.

The grinding sound came to a stop, and the teacher came out of the barn toward them, pulling a welder's mask off his head. The guy was in his mid-thirties or so, Stuart figured, although his hair was already fully gray and stuck out in thin spears, like a delicate brush. He was wearing faded jeans and a brownish T-shirt that hung loose from his wiry arms and shoulders. He had a sort of outlaw look about him, though with his Converse shoes and silver earrings he looked more like an aging, yoga-fiend rock star than a militiaman.

"Jay Harrison." He took off his gloves and held out a hand to shake.

"You teach shop class," Kate said, "right?"

He nodded.

They pulled some old lawn chairs into the radius of the dog's chain and sat down together. The dog paced between them, licking their hands, as if performing a taste test. He had a tremendous mouth, with long, drooping jowls and a dripping pinkish nose the size of a fist.

The dog's name was Ned. "Ned?" they said, and Jay shrugged, explaining that he had just inherited him, along with the house and an old pickup truck and two cats.

"He's a really sweet guy." Jay threw an arm around the dog in a half hug. Ned endured the embrace anxiously, turning his head around to take in all the free space he was being deprived of. "But he's been running off. I hate to keep him chained up, but I'm afraid he'll get hit by a car—or the train." He motioned toward the train tracks at the back of his property, behind the barns and the strange tall metal objects. They looked like a cross between space ghouls and melting robots. They might be anything from shooting targets to some sort of theater props.

"Well, how did he survive this long?" Kate asked.

"It's a mystery." Jay shrugged, smiling. "The last time I let him off the leash, I found him a mile away, swimming across the river like an ex-con."

They laughed.

"I think it's a new thing, since his owner died." He held his hands out, squinting skyward. "Like he's looking for the old guy or something. Or maybe he just really doesn't like me." As Jay said this, the dog rolled over at his feet, rubbing his side into Jay's shins and waiting to be petted again.

"Was it your . . . grandpa who died?" Stuart asked.

Jay shook his head. "Just this old guy I used to work for, years ago. Mack. He didn't have any family left, and we had stayed sort of friendly over the years." He got up and walked around to a few nearby dandelions, pulling them up at the roots. "But still, what a surprise. I never imagined." He waved the weeds around to encompass what looked like three or four rolling acres.

Kate nodded. "It must be worth quite a bit, with Dexter and Ann Arbor booming like this."

Jay shrugged, sitting back down. "The house needs a lot of work, obviously."

"Yeah, what a project," Kate said with admiration, the way a world-class pianist might look at a nose-picking child and say, "What a prodigy." She scooted her chair closer to Jay's. "We just got a house in Ann Arbor we're remodeling. Downtown."

Jay nodded. "Those downtown neighborhoods are really hot these days."

"We're going to have to gut the place," she boasted.

While Stuart inspected the dog's coat for fleas and scars and bulges, Kate and Jay talked about how-to books and *This Old House*, compared latex paint to oil, discussed the pros and cons of pulling permits. She was like an immigrant who'd at last found someone who spoke her little-known language.

"He appears to be deaf," Stuart interrupted. "The dog."

"Yeah. He doesn't hear too well anymore." Jay fiddled with the dandelions in his lap.

"Oh." Kate melted. "How sad."

"I mean, he's not perfect. He's a great dog, but he's not perfect." Jay rubbed the dog's ears again and leaned over him, picking little brown pieces of burrs off his fur.

"So, but, aside from the running off, and the ears," Stuart said.

Jay thought for a while. "He's an eater. Took a stick of butter off the countertop today."

Stuart nodded.

"And you ought to check him for aches every so often." Jay gave the dog what almost looked like a rubdown, clasping his hands around Ned's shoulders and squeezing, then moving down each leg, squeezing firmly and watching the dog for a reaction. "Apparently if they're in pain, they'll hide it, so you have to kind of watch for it once they're old."

"They hide it?" Stuart said.

"Pack animals. If the pack knows they're hurt, the other dogs'll turn on them or something."

"Really?" Stuart said. "Harsh."

"Makes sense, in a way," Kate said.

Stuart gave her a wry look. "In your family, maybe."

She laughed. "Exactly."

They sat admiring this obese, panting dog, and watching the sun go lower in the sky. Stuart liked him, liked the heft and imperfection of him, the thought of taking him on long, slow walks, telling him things the dog couldn't hear. But when the conversation lulled, Kate stood up abruptly, patted the seat of her pants, and said, "Well, we'll think about it." She smacked her hands together.

Jay hopped off his chair, as if embarrassed for keeping them so long.

"Of course," he said.

"Don't give him to anyone else without calling us." Stuart shook the guy's hand.

Ned remained stretched out on the ground, watching them take off, looking cheated and confused.

As they reached the car, Kate murmured into Stuart's shoulder, "Do you like him? I like him. He's sweet."

They heard clinking behind them and realized the dog had followed them. When he reached the end of his chain he started howling adamantly. Jay trotted up to Ned and put one hand on his wide back, apologizing, trying to shush him, but

Ned just sat down and angled his chin skyward, curving his great warbly mouth into an operatic O.

"He wants us," Kate said over the noise, and Stuart felt inclined to agree. They walked back to the dog and patted him some more. Jay brought out three bottles of beer, and before the sun sank below the horizon they had decided to take the dog.

"If it doesn't work out, you can always bring him back." Jay rubbed the dog's ears through the car window. "Or just visit."

The evening was hot and muggy. They rolled down the windows and Ned paced from one side of the car to the other, sniffing wildly at the racing air. He sneezed, filling the car with his rank doggy smell. They kept turning in their seats to watch him. "Let's make a video," Stuart said, thinking of how excited his brother got whenever he saw a dog. He reached across the dashboard for his minicam in the glove box. They were a threesome.

When they parked in their driveway they intended to open the dog's door only far enough to get his leash on, but as they stood fiddling with it he exploded past them and raced across the empty street.

"Jesus Christ," Stuart said. "He's like a freight train."

The man from the perfectly restored Victorian across the street was outside stretching before his evening run. He caught Ned by the collar and shuttled him across the street.

"So you're the new tenants." He was fifty or so, with a beard and a lumpen, shaved head. The guy was all bones, always running, must have been a marathoner. He had gone so far on his health craze he looked as desperate and spent as a junkie in his nylon tank shirt and short shorts, worn so thin they were grayish and see-through. "The house hasn't been this quiet in years," he added. "Always a lot of partyers here."

"We bought it," Kate said. "See, we painted it? There won't be any more renters."

"Oh, I see. I see. But . . . wow." He paused. "You *bought* it?"

They nodded dumbly.

"We're fixing it up," Kate said with some hostility. "It'll be like your house."

Stuart tried to point out that their house would never be quite like this guy's elaborate blue-and-white Victorian with its spindles and gingerbread wraparound porch. Theirs was just a simple box, like something ordered from a Sears catalog and slapped together with sledgehammers. But the guy waved off these comments, feigning modesty, and Kate shot Stuart an offended glare.

"No, that's great. Excellent." The guy seemed jazzed about something, jittery, like a kid trying to keep a secret. "So you know the history of the house then?" A university town, Ann Arbor was filled with people like this, people who always knew more than you and wanted to teach you.

Kate warmed up, suddenly smiling. She'd been talking for weeks about going down to the historic commission and doing some research. "No. I've been meaning to go look it up." She was fidgeting, nodding. "Have you done that? Do you know who I talk to?"

"No." The man shook his head, confused. "No, I just mean . . ." He glanced from his house to theirs and back again, then patted the dog on the head.

"What?"

Stuart saw something unpleasant flash across the man's face.

"There was a murder," the man said. "Didn't you know?"

8

Kate wanted to punch the neighbor guy, to knock the words from his mouth and send him off their porch, their property, out of their lives. Forget it happened.

Stuart reacted differently. He wanted details. He probed and questioned the guy with an intense, methodical calmness that Kate found eerie. All the emotion drained out of his face, and he was suddenly so cool, so blank. "So this was like, what, how long ago?" he said, putting one hand out to lean on the porch rail, then pulling it away as if it were contaminated.

"Gosh," the guy said, absently scratching at something on his shoulder blade. "I don't know. Before I moved here."

The left side of Stuart's face gave a twitch, but he huffed out a casual laugh. "Well, how long have you been here?"

They stared hungrily at the man as he squinted into the darkening sky. "Let's see . . ." He drummed his fingertips against his thigh, counting, then made a face and counted over again. "What, six, seven years?"

"1998?" Stuart said, trying to pin him down. "1999?"

"Yeah," the guy said. "Something like that."

Kate held up a hand to the neighbor guy, saying, "Good-bye . . . Thanks . . . Nice meeting you," as she wished for him to die in some awful plague.

"It could have been decades ago," she said tentatively to Stuart after the long silence that followed them inside.

He glared at her. "A Realtor would have found this out."

They hadn't used a Realtor. Kate had found the house through a tiny For Sale by Owner ad, and had considered this good fortune: a lower price, no middleman.

"I'm sorry," she said, but he didn't calm down. With his hands on top of his head he paced the kitchen floor for so long, so anxiously, that the dog started barking at him. "What can I say? I'm sorry."

He shook his head in disgust. "I had a feeling."

"Come on."

"I *knew* there was a reason I didn't want this house."

"You didn't want *any* house."

He stopped pacing and laughed a little. "Yeah. Nice of you to notice."

His eyes cut through her. The dog turned on both of them, barking his mad discontent.

"I'm taking him for a walk." Stuart stabbed his finger at Ned, who abruptly shut up. He tugged the dog toward the entryway and then slammed the door fiercely behind them, making the walls shiver.

Kate walked from room to room, scrutinizing. In every dark stain she saw blood; in every cracked bit of plaster she imagined bullet holes. She slipped her fingers into a crevice along one wall of the kitchen, feeling the sandy plaster in crumbles behind the patched skin of the surface. She tested the spot, how much it would take. Not much. With one little tug a hand-size chunk of plaster fell to the floor. It wasn't red, or brown, or black. All of it—the grains, the plaster, the area left on the wall—was just a dull gray. No blood.

She swept up her mess and moved their calendar, tacking it up over the hole. There were similar cracked or patched weak spots on the walls of every room but the attic, and the fake wood paneling in the living room and dining room could be hiding any number of evils. Alone, alone with all this new history, she decided to go outside on the porch and wait for Stuart and Ned. She leaned over the railing, looking both ways for them, but they were nowhere in sight. She sat in the dark in a LeMar's faux wicker chair, curling her knees into her chest and holding still.

That night they lay silent and open-eyed in bed. They hadn't spoken since Stuart and the dog returned. She could hear him still steaming over there, measuring out each breath before giving it back to the house.

"The guy could be lying," she said finally, to say something.

"Why would he lie about that?"

Kate shrugged in the dark. "Maybe he's just an asshole."

"Clearly he's an asshole. It doesn't make him a liar."

"I could go research the house, if you want. If you would feel better."

"If I would feel better?"

She didn't want to research it anyway. She wasn't ready to learn any more about the murder.

"I'd feel better if we were back in the apartment," he muttered. His voice was deflated, as if he had lost everything.

Kate stepped up her rehabilitation efforts. She did everything but hang an UNDER NEW MANAGEMENT sign from the eaves. She loaded the porch with more flowers, washed the windows, pulled up every weed she could find, hired men to install the fence and fix the porch wall. The dog hung around, nose to the fence slats, slobbering and howling cheerily. The dog didn't know about any murder here.

She made Stuart promise that they would tell no one—not their friends or coworkers, and definitely not her parents. They avoided the jittery, running-shorts guy; they no longer tried to wave at the neighbors. They pretended it wasn't on their minds, but every so often, in the midst of a perfectly unrelated conversation, one of them would do a double take at a dent in the floor or a missing piece of woodwork and crouch down to trace the spot with a fingertip. When she was down in the basement doing laundry, Kate would scrutinize the strange little pictures of animals someone had painted on the stone walls, trying not to imagine some victim locked up down there, painting away the hours and scheming revenge.

"I think it was on the front porch," Kate said one night while they lay awake, spooked by separate dreams. "All those holes in the floorboards, you know? And that isn't even really *in* the house. That's outside. Porches come and go. We could replace it."

Stuart shook his head. "It was in here." He had been sticking firm to this theory for several days, and it was true that their bedroom walls were more patched up than any of the others.

"No," Kate said. "At most it was on the first floor. I mean, odds are it was some kind of break-in, right? Some loser broke in. Man of the house comes to the top of the stairs, shoots him in the entryway before he gets any farther. Probably nobody even misses him."

"Nice." Stuart flopped over, away from her, facing the closet. "But it was in here. Closet floor?"

Inexplicably, someone had painted the closet floor red.

"That's nuts," she said. There were three other bedrooms to choose from, but none big enough to fit their new bed. "What would an intruder be—"

"I can't sleep in here!" He kicked the sheets off, scrambling upright.

"Okay." She sat up. "We'll start with this bedroom. We'll gut the place room by room, starting right here. Make it like new."

He stared at her with his wild, insomniac eyes.

"Okay, I screwed up. Okay? I'm sorry. We can sit here and fight about it every night, or we can do something about it."

He said nothing. The muscles of her face started to twitch. She reached through the dark where she thought his hand was but felt him pull it away in the nick of time.

"*I'll* do it," she said. "It's my mistake, right? My problem. I'll take care of it."

He ripped his pillow off the bed and headed down to the couch. And the room opened up around her. The drapes moved in the breeze and all the shadows shifted, slow dancing. She was alone in her king-size bed in her house and this was how it felt.

She ordered a Dumpster. She bought work gloves and boots. She cleared out and sealed off the second floor, putting their bed in the middle of the kitchen, their summer clothes in the small dining room, and everything else in the attic. She bought two ominous face masks and two pairs of goggles, two crowbars. By the following week, she was well into keeping her promise. She had ripped out the carpeting, the fake wood paneling, and all the plastic window trim. She hemmed and hawed but finally worked up the nerve to throw her crowbar into the plaster, pulling away the crumbling surface and the thin strips of wood lath behind it. It felt thrilling—for about ten minutes, until she realized how many more walls lay ahead of her.

She didn't ask Stuart for help. She would do this for him. She would leave him alone, and wait until he came around. He was working ten- or eleven-hour days anyway to fix his programming mistake at work, and often went out with his friends afterward. By the time he got home most nights she was passed out in bed, exhausted.

They lived shadow lives, trading pleasantries like roommates in their brief moments of interaction, slipping in and out of the big bed without touching. Eventually Stuart started dozing off on the couch to the TV each night, and after a while, she stopped coming out to get him. Every couple must go through this. It would pass. When she got the house back in order, when their bedroom was restored and the bed back in it, things would go back to normal. He would wake up one day and be grateful. He'd get over it.

And if he didn't?

If he didn't, if he didn't . . . They could—a chill moved under her skin—sell the house. She didn't like the idea, but there it was. They could take their profits and move on, put this in their past.

And if that didn't work? If nothing worked?

Other people broke up. Other people grew mean and spiteful, had affairs, ran off, bad-mouthed each other, split up their bank accounts. Started over. Other people did that. It happened. It was not a sin anymore.

By mid-July almost all the second-floor walls and ceilings were stripped down to their studs. She was hacking away at the last plaster wall of the guest room one Friday evening when she heard the front door slam. Peeling the rubber mask away from her face, she called down hello, and then stood still, listening. He didn't respond.

"Happy Friday?" she called, then waited again, rubbing at the itchy red imprint the mask left on her cheeks. Maybe he was in the bathroom.

She hated to waste the daylight standing around. If she had to work into the night, under halogen lights that felt like heat lamps, the job would grow even more disorienting and unpleasant. So she covered her face again and started shoveling the debris off the floor into a big plastic garbage can. She dragged it into the room across the hall, where she had rigged a metal chute from the open window down to the Dumpster in the driveway. Hoisting up the can, she watched as the plaster and debris sailed down the chute and landed with a thud on the other remains of their house. "Bon voyage," she said, giving it a wave.

Back in the guest room Kate surveyed the last remaining wall. Stopping the work was always a bad idea. Her stomach growled, her arms ached, and grains of plaster scratched her eyes under the lids. She was tired. How nice it would be to have a big, burly husband who was in this with her, who would come upstairs in dirty jeans and a thin white T-shirt stretched over his knotted muscles, and say, *Why don't you go take a bath, baby? I can take care of this.*

But she had once had a boyfriend who called her *baby*, and oh, how it grated on her.

She sat down on top of the Shop-Vac, pulled off her mask and goggles and work gloves, and licked her fingertip to clean it a little before rubbing it along her eyeball to clear away the grit. She was sure all the lead dust and other unknown toxins were depleting her brain cells and life span by the minute.

"Any chance you could bring me a beer, Stu?" she shouted

over her shoulder, toward the staircase. It, too, was torn apart, with half the treads pulled out for repairs and the banister in the debauched state of partial paint removal. She stepped halfway down, to the landing, and could see Ned behind the wall of plastic sheeting she had hung at the foot of the stairs to keep dust out of the first floor. He nuzzled his wrinkly face against the smudged, filthy plastic, trying to get up to her.

"In a second," Stuart called up, in a voice that betrayed some irritation of his own. But all that came upstairs in a second was the faint smooching sound of the refrigerator and freezer doors, open and shut, followed by the clink of ice cubes into a tall pint glass. He was fixing a cocktail. It would be vodka and cranberry, in a steep, sixty-forty proportion.

You couldn't drink a cocktail in the work area. You could recap a beer or pop bottle after each swig and hope for the best, but a cocktail was unthinkable. A film of industrial-strength, lead-filled dust coated every open surface within seconds.

Sudden voices from the TV downstairs confirmed it: he wasn't coming upstairs any time soon.

She clenched her jaw and glared down the staircase, but she said nothing. They had gone well beyond fighting. Fighting didn't do anything for them. Instead, she went back in the guest room and swung the claw of her crowbar at the plaster wall, then hammered the teeth in between two lath boards and pried them out. It felt extraordinary. The old, rectangular-cut nails squeaked as she wrestled them, and the blisters under her gloves fired up, but even this felt righteous and exhilarating. How easily a little pain and violence distracted her from her brooding and allowed the cease-fire between them to continue for another night.

She moved on down the wall mechanically, stepping back to let the heavy chunks of plaster drop near her feet. Within minutes the wall was down; only the old brown hand-sawn studs remained. A haze filled the room. She was ankle-deep in debris; this was the worst part. There was nothing exhilarating about stooping to shovel up the plaster and lath that covered the floor, raising a new cloud of dust with every scoop. But she went ahead and did it, as she had done for weeks. Over and over she filled the garbage can and dragged it to the chute in the other room, sending down load after load of filth. If Stuart was sitting in his usual spot on the couch by the TV, the spectacle of garbage falling from the sky outside his window might send a message.

Still he didn't come up. Kate stood staring at the ceiling, not wanting to start on it. The ceilings were the worst, most disgusting parts of the job: you couldn't step back from debris that rained down on your head. And since this ceiling supported the attic, piles of loose, ancient insulation would come down as well, in your hair, down your shirt, in your eyes. And there it went again, the smack of the refrigerator, the clink of ice: another cocktail on the lower deck for the elite.

She dragged a stepladder into the room and made her first strike at the ceiling. She closed her eyes and tucked in her head as the surface broke open like a piñata, releasing the dingy pastel bits of fuzz and old paper that had once qualified as insulation. Other things rained down, too: old nails and fuses, long-disconnected wires, shredded-up magazines, and, for some unknown reason, Monopoly money. This was new. The bills weren't ground up like the rest of the filler; they were intact, uncrumpled, and they lilted through the thick, dusty air like ribbons through snowfall. It seemed a cruel joke. She thrashed at the ceiling again, this time freeing three lath strips with their nails intact. One of them gouged her cheek on the way down and landed with a stab in the soft spot inside her collarbone. "Shit!" she cried, stung by the shock of it.

"Hey, look. Hidden treasure." Stuart said from the hallway, holding a cocktail and a beer, which he extended to her lazily. He wasn't wearing a mask or gloves; he hadn't even changed out of his office clothes. He watched the Monopoly money fall, but appeared not to notice her wounds. "I can't believe we're almost done."

Kate pulled off her gloves and probed her cheek and neck, coming away with blood on her fingers. "We?"

He leaned against one of the studs, crossed his arms over his chest, then one ankle over the other. Then he lost his balance, spilled his drink a little, and had to grab the wall and try again.

"Lovely," she said.

"How was your day, my dear?" he said in a falsetto voice.

She sighed. "Is that what you want me to say? Should I bake some cookies?"

He answered himself in a deep, TV-father's voice. "Oh, it was *wonderful.* Everyone took me out to lunch because they knew—already knew, all of them—that I was getting *fired* at the end of the day." He did a little dance move and threw his hands out at his sides in a bid for applause. "It was spectacular."

Kate stared at him.

He nodded. "Yup."

"Not fired," she said. "Laid off. Just laid off?"

"Whatever," he said. "Like it matters."

"It does matter."

"Why?" He picked up the crowbar and swung it loosely, like a batter between pitches. "Because if I say laid off you can think, Okay, my husband's not a total fuckup? It's just economics, right?" He swung at the ceiling in a sudden wild flash, sending a rock of plaster flying toward her face.

"Jesus." She blocked her face with her arms and backed

into the hallway. "Stuart, you'll get another job. We can manage." Could they? Her brain was already tallying her upcoming Visa bill.

He just kept swinging, sinking the claw of the crowbar into the plaster, then pulling down with all his weight, bringing down wide swaths of lath with the plaster still attached. He stomped through the nail-filled rubble in his thin-soled work shoes.

"Stop it," she said. "Wait a minute. Stop it. Calm down." But he moved through the room in a frenzy, ripping away every last bit of lath and plaster. From the hallway, Kate watched him, scared. She didn't want to think about where all this rage was coming from.

Then a pop and a hiss broke forth, and Stuart stopped swinging and ducked a little, holding his hands and the crowbar over his head.

He had ripped through the electric wires leading to the ceiling light. The lightbulb and socket crashed to the floor, and the frayed wire dangled, sizzling, from the joists above.

"Ta-da," he said, tossing the crowbar onto the rubble with a clang. Dust hung in the air like a toxic cloud, covering his hair and shoulders in gray. He smacked his hands together. "So. Is it dinnertime?"

"Jesus, Stuart." Kate rushed in and turned off the light switch, which stopped the wire from sparking. "What are you doing?"

He dug through the debris covering the step stool and came up with his cocktail. It was filled with plaster.

"I'd better freshen this up." He brushed past her toward the staircase.

"What's wrong with you? You could have set the place on fire."

"Now there's an idea."

This man she'd been watching didn't look anything like the boy she'd fallen for all those years ago—would he ever have been so bitter, so tightly wound? Had she turned him into this? For a second it was as if she were outside herself, watching the two of them like characters on a TV show in a foreign language. She felt nothing for them, a pure, unconfused indifference. Liberated from all the months of polite fabrication, she felt her lips peeling back to bare her teeth. She said, "Laid off, or fired?"

He moved closer to her, until the inches of courtesy between them narrowed and vanished. "Why don't you just say it? I'm a fuckup start to finish."

She was back in her skin, feeling the sick chill of it all. "That's not true."

He laughed a madman laugh. "Actually, it is." He looked from her to the window, the walls, as if surveying with pride the awful mess he'd gotten himself into. "You've been trying not to see that since the day we met."

She shook her head, backing up. "Stop it. You'll get another job."

"What if I don't want a job? What if I just want to . . ." He thrust one drunken arm out to his side. "Take a hiatus. A sabbatical. Wander the planet."

Wander the planet. "Okay, Siddhartha," she said. "We should talk about this when you're sober."

"I'm being serious. Listen, I've been thinking about this. I've got seven thousand in severance pay. You've got a month of summer left. Let's take that trip we talked about."

"Stuart." She opened and closed her mouth, speechless. She waved one arm around the room. "We're kind of in the middle of something here."

"The house isn't going anywhere, Kate. The beauty of a house is, it'll just sit here and wait for you."

But there was no way she could finish this project once school was in swing, no way she could keep up this workload. And no way she could stand living in this mess until next summer came around.

"Stuart, you can't just run away from this and make it go away."

"Asia, Africa, you name it. South America." He wasn't listening. "We can go to Machu Picchu, Angkor Wat, the Parthenon. We'll find another ruined building for you. You'll feel right at home."

She sat down on the windowsill and gazed over her shoulder at that Dumpster, at what must have been several tons of gray matter she had excavated for the sake of her stupid dream.

"If you need to go," she said quietly, lifting one arm up and letting it drop, "then, I guess, go. You can take the trip without me. I won't stop you."

He stared at her for a long time, a pained look spreading across his face. "No. You wouldn't."

"Stop it."

"You'd pick the house. Over me."

"That's ridiculous, Stuart."

"Is it?"

"You. I'd choose you." But her head was spinning as she said it.

He squinted at her. "You know, you're getting worse and worse at faking this."

Her blood throbbed through her chest, overheating her. She felt the tears rising up. She covered her face with her filthy, sore hands. "You're scaring me."

It seemed like a long time passed this way, till she felt something shift in front of her. When she pulled her hands away, he was standing there, staring into her face. "Good. Be scared." He didn't say it in a vindictive way. He said it like a guru.

"You know what? This is enough!" she shouted, then checked herself down to a whisper, glancing out the open window. "You're drunk. Which is fine. I understand. You had a shitty day. I'm sorry. But now you're just looking to pick a fight, which isn't even like you, by the way, and I'm not going to do it. Okay? Wait till tomorrow and we can talk about this all you like. But tonight? I'm done tonight."

"Tomorrow. Right, tomorrow." He whistled faintly through his teeth. "No, it's fine. I get it now. It's all clear."

She watched him recede from her, picking his way down the broken stairs. He didn't look back, didn't soften the blow or apologize or leave an open door. Something between them was turning, was breaking all their habits, all their silent courtesies.

She touched her fingers to the punctures in her cheek and neck. She pressed on the tender spots to feel the bruises blooming there so that she could concentrate on that other, surface pain, which would be gone in a week and not come back. The blood was drying. She'd had a tetanus shot last year; it would heal, it did not matter. Even if it scarred, it would not matter.

She moved through the empty room methodically, shoveling and sweeping up the mess he'd made and throwing it out the window, down the chute, and into the evening, which was growing dark around her. She flicked on the halogen lamps. In her chest something surged and contracted, the impulse to cry. She fought it. She set down her shovel and bent over, hands on her knees in a wave of weakness. "You fucking baby," she whispered, and then silenced herself again. Deep breaths. Discipline. There were people starving in the world, children dying of neglect, malaria, AIDS, whole continents plunged into poverty and war. Who was she, with her little sob story? *Keep it to yourself*, she thought.

She started gathering up the Monopoly money that had fallen from the ceiling. It didn't feel like garbage. She rooted through the rubble, unearthing the bills and stacking them. She cleared a little space on the floor and sat back, sorting the bills by denomination: $86,750. "Wouldn't that be nice?" she said to no one. For that kind of money they could pay off her bulging credit card bills and hire someone else to finish this stupid project. The surface of their lives would smooth out again; the pretending would get easier. They could go out to dinner like normal twenty-nine-year-olds and discuss work or movies or the prospect of children, and they could come home and sleep in the same bed, in a room called the master bedroom.

The light had completely faded outside, and the halogen lamps cast sharp, freak-show shadows across the floor and walls. Against her wishes, Kate felt the eeriness of the house settling into her.

The place wasn't haunted. She was over it, and she didn't see why Stuart couldn't be. She had cut the house open and pulled out its guts; she had palpated every last organ and seen that there were no spirits or skeletons anywhere. And yet, somehow, this place was exploding, throwing them in different directions.

She stood up and climbed the stepladder to check out the frayed ceiling wires. They seemed safely dormant. Warily, she started cleaning again, throwing plaster and lath out the window, but the chute was clogged with debris. She steered a flashlight into it, poked in there with her broom and shovel, but it was no use. If she wanted to keep working she would have to climb into the Dumpster and rake the debris around to even it out and clear more space. But there were ominous warnings stenciled all over the sides: DO NOT CLIMB ON OR IN. It was no normal, restaurant-alley-size Dumpster. It was almost as big as a semitrailer and filled their entire driveway.

She could go downstairs and apologize to Stuart, ask him to help her.

She could stomp through the plastic sheeting and bumble around outside noisily, and at least if she got stuck or hurt in there Stuart would hear her.

She could call it a night and sort through the Dumpster tomorrow in the daylight, when neighbors would be out and about to hear if she needed help.

"Oh, just do it," she commanded herself. How bad could it be? And maybe Stu would take pity on her and come help. Maybe he'd apologize; maybe they'd have a moment of tenderness, or at least another silent truce. It happened all the time. Armed with her flashlight and shovel, her gloves and face mask, she went downstairs.

But when she pulled back the plastic sheeting at the foot of the stairs, what she realized was that the house was empty. The TV and stereo were off; there were no lights on. The giant, spotted lump of Ned was curled up on the bed in the kitchen. Lazy and half deaf, he didn't even wag his tail or raise his head to look at her.

So Stuart had gone out without her. She knew which bars he'd be at, which friends he'd be ranting to about how much she'd let him down.

Fine, fine. Perfect. She stormed through the front door and around to the driveway on the side of the house. She scaled the metal wall of the Dumpster without giving the fear time to take hold, then waved the flashlight around to find a safe place to land inside. The lath boards, broken and laden with nails, stuck up through the plaster everywhere, like pick-up sticks. It occurred to her that this wasn't the smartest thing to do in the dark, late at night, alone, with no one around to rescue her should she get trapped inside. But in fact the debris was piled nearly to the top of the Dumpster. There was little chance of getting caught in there. It wasn't quicksand, after all, and she had her boots on.

She crouched low, feeling the crunch of plaster and wood splinters and nails giving way and sinking down under her feet. Working up her nerve, she crept over to the base of the chute to rake the debris away. She went at it frenetically, keeping her eye out for rats and raccoons.

There was nothing. No problems, no critters, no quicksand. Within fifteen minutes she had cleared out the chute and the space beneath it, had thrown the shovel and rake over the side, and had climbed down to the driveway without incident. But at the last minute she felt the creepy, too-quiet sensation of being watched. She pulled the flashlight from under her arm and waved it around the driveway and the side yard. And then she saw it. Across the street, leaning against a car parked along the curb, was a tall, thin black man in a baggy red flannel shirt and loose, drooping jeans. His arms were crossed on his chest, and though she couldn't really make out his face, it seemed clear from the set of his shoulders that he was staring at her. Kate gasped and dropped her flashlight, feeling a sudden, marrow-deep fear. *For God's sake, compose yourself*, she thought. This was a busy downtown neighborhood with lots of people out walking and parking their cars at all hours. If he was staring at her, it was only because she'd made such a ridiculous spectacle of herself. She was mortified: not only had she been caught rooting through a Dumpster at night in full face mask and goggles, but she was obviously such a racist at heart that the mere sight of a lone black man had terrified her. What sort of a person behaved like that? She raised one hand and nodded her head slightly in his direction, hoping to indicate an apology without going so far as to incite conversation. He stared back so calmly that his gaze seemed a direct challenge. Kate picked up the flashlight and hurried inside, locking the door behind her.

"You freak," she said to herself, kicking off her shoes and peeling away her mask and goggles. "Crazy racist. How embarrassing." She went to the back porch to strip off her dusty work clothes so they wouldn't make a mess on the floor.

In the kitchen, the answering machine was blinking—more messages from her sister, Kate was sure. They had been arriving in nervous flurries all month: What color bridesmaid dress did she prefer? When could she get together with the others to shop? Did she think this china pattern was too expensive? Was it too trite to have a rose bouquet? Did people prefer to pick their own seats at dinner or have them all assigned? Bracing herself, Kate stood by the phone in her underwear and hit play. Maybe it would be Stuart, saying where he was, asking her to join him. Maybe in the background would be a bar full of voices and music to sweep her up and take her back to college, to the thrill she got when he singled her out and lured her away from the neuroses at her core.

But it was Julia. She cleared her voice and just murmured, "Call me," and hung up.

It was well past eleven. *Too late*, Kate thought with guilty relief. She just couldn't fake her way through wedding talk tonight.

She ordered a pizza and got into the shower. By the time she answered the door in her bathrobe a half hour later she had nearly forgotten about the man outside in the street. But when the pizza-delivery car drove off, she saw him there again, leaning against a car, still staring at her. Jesus. Almost midnight.

She locked the doors, turned on all the lights, and went around to make sure the blinds were closed. She dialed Stuart's cell phone but hung up, too proud to make the first contact. She sat down in the middle of the bed and shoveled slice after slice of pizza in her mouth. The dog was useless, curled up beside her. The dog was no protection at all.

There was no law against staring, no law against parking in her street. Probably the guy was just waiting for someone out there.

At midnight?

The phone rang, and Kate leapt up and grabbed it, half expecting to hear that man on the other end of the line.

"Did I wake you?" Julia said.

Kate sank into the pillows and crumpled sheets.

"I know it's late," Julia went on. "I just can't seem to catch you."

"It's fine," Kate said. "I was awake. What's going on?"

"I was just up watching TV—*Titanic* is on—and I started researching vacations online. What do you think is better these days, Cabo San Lucas or Costa Rica?"

Cabo San Lucas? Costa Rica? There was never any warm-up with Julia. Everything started at full speed.

"For your honeymoon?"

"The bachelorette trip."

Bachelorette trip. A dreadful image flashed through Kate's mind: her chubby, pale self covered in remodeling bruises and scrapes, surrounded by Julia and her old sorority sisters in their size-two bikinis and spray tans. "Oh, Jules—"

"I'm going to rent a big condo. All you'll have to pay is your airfare. It'll be August, off season. It can't be more than a few hundred dollars."

"I'll think about it," Kate said grimly. She nudged the window blinds to one side. He was still out there, facing the house, just standing and staring.

"Okay, I'll pay your way, okay? It's just a long weekend. Please?"

Kate sighed. She could be dead by morning, anyone could. Last night she'd dreamed she was trapped in the basement after an earthquake, with the whole weight of the house crumbled down on top of her. "Julia, it's late. Is that all you wanted?"

An awkward silence followed. "Okay. Just think about it."

All her life Julia had wanted them to be closer than they were. She never seemed to realize how little they had in common. Kate struggled for something nicer to say. "What channel is it on?" She fiddled with the TV until she found it: Jack and Rose racing through the dark, steamy engine room of the *Titanic*. Dirty-faced men shoveled coal into the fires, stoking the engines that were carrying them all to their doom.

What Julia liked was the romance. The sappy dialogue, the crude symbolism didn't bother her at all. The only part Kate liked was the ending: the computer-enhanced scenes of those poor people falling from—*bouncing off*—the rails of the sinking ship. It was like a grand confirmation of one of her nightmares.

On-screen Jack and Rose were still running, giggling through the hot boiler room. The gauzy white folds of her dress flowed behind her like wings, like bandages unwrapping, like fabric under water, as if she were already swimming for her life.

Meanwhile, Julia was talking about vows, about how she thought it was important that they write their own vows, something original, but she wasn't very good with words and had no idea what they ought to include.

"I don't know either," Kate said. The camera cut away

from Jack and Rose to show the enormous ship moving in solitude across a huge expanse of black water, a long silvery wake flowing behind it as it sailed toward the star-packed firmament. Into oblivion, but it was a beautiful oblivion. On deck, the sailors on watch for icebergs cracked jokes in the cold, having lost their binoculars.

"What did you and Stuart do? Did you write your own vows?"

They hadn't. They had read the usual ones, though Kate couldn't even recall which version they'd used. It had seemed so beside the point back then, what exact words they used to complete the formality. The formality didn't matter at all, because they were already so obviously *bound*. Or so it had seemed.

And now Jack and Rose are pressed together in the backseat of that red sedan in the cargo hold, with its crystal vase on the side wall holding two impossibly fresh red roses. They are covered in sweat, the Vaseline of fake, movie sweat, and groping. One ecstatic lover's damp hand slaps the steamed back window, then slides down as if sinking, drowning. And after a few trembly words, it's over. The iceberg is closing in.

"Ugh," Julia said. "This is where I have to turn it off."

Back in the engine room, the giant pistons so well oiled and brand new struggle to grind to a halt, then reverse course. The idea of putting a beast this size in reverse so quickly, of having a reverse gear at all, seems ludicrous. But it is a universal human desire: to catch sight of our impending catastrophe in time, and have the vision and power to stop ourselves, turn around, go back where we came from. It wasn't happening. Jack and Rose, up on the exterior deck now, clutching each other in kisses and promises, see chunks of ice fall around them.

The first room to fill with water is the storage hold: the

walls next to that red car rupture and spray past it. Next it pours into the engine room, flooding all those aisles they've just run down. It is as if the ocean is chasing them, as if every spot the lovers touched will be destroyed, and they are bringing the ship down with them.

Kate smiled. She pulled in closer to the screen.

"You've been to a lot of weddings, right? What do other people say in their vows?"

"Why don't you just start with how it feels," she said. "Between you and Alex. Just say how it feels."

Julia hesitated. "Are you making fun of me? I know you're not crazy about him—"

"No, I'm serious," Kate said, turning away from the TV to concentrate on this. "I want to know how it feels."

Julia breathed into the phone. "It feels . . . I don't know. You're serious?"

"Yeah."

"It's like . . . I feel grown up. Like I can see the whole future laid out finally, all the questions answered."

There was something so pure in her voice, so uncorrupted.

"What are the answers?" Kate said, squeezing the phone hard to her ear.

Julia was quiet for a long time, as if debating something in her mind, then coming to a verdict. "I mean, the answers don't matter anymore. I know they'll be okay."

"But how do you know?"

"I just do. I feel like, whatever happens, if I have him, I'll be okay."

Kate muted the TV. She was alone in her living room, suddenly alone, with nothing to say or think or hear anymore.

"Have you got any advice for me?" Julia said, her voice growing weary and serious. "This will go away, won't it? This feeling."

Kate barely heard her, had to replay the question in her mind. "I don't know," Kate heard herself saying. Part of her thought, *This is your chance to warn her.* Part of her thought, *Don't you dare.* "Not necessarily, maybe." Maybe there were people out there who felt that way their whole long lives.

"You can be honest with me. I want to know. It would be better for me, I think, if I just knew. I could prepare."

"It's going to be fine," Kate heard herself saying. It was a wish.

"I just want to be good at this," Julia said.

"I know."

"And you and Stuart seem good at it. You seem so happy together."

"I know," Kate said. People always told them that.

In the morning she felt like someone coming up out of an underground storm shelter after a tornado: glad to be alive, a little suspicious that she'd made a big deal out of nothing. She looked around for signs of calamity, for windows shattered or doors bashed in, but she found none. The dog was curled up by the back door, with the remains of the pizza and its box in tatters beside him. He stretched himself mundanely, as if perfectly innocent, and waited to be let outside. Out front, the strange man was gone: she was safe. It wasn't until she went in the living room that she discovered the difference: Stuart wasn't there. He wasn't sprawled out on his couch like every morning. He hadn't come home; he hadn't come home at all.

9

Kate was taking her time, avoiding the highways, smoothing over the slow back roads to her parents' house. It should have taken thirty-five minutes from Ann Arbor, but here she was over an hour late, and well under the speed limit, and stopping at the nursery outside Plymouth to wander through the rows of flowers and shrubs, trying to put off her arrival or at least brace herself. If they asked her to explain why she was alone today, she would have no explanation. No husband, no phone call all week. No idea where he had gone.

She had spent the first day in a daze and waiting, staring at the phone in plain dumb disbelief. Fear and worry crept up on her like hiccups she couldn't shake: Stuart in ten different mangled poses, mouth gaping, forehead dented and bleeding, in a ditch, in a jail cell, in an alley outside a strip club. Eventually she could will away the worry by replacing it with anger, thinking, *Ann Arbor husbands don't just disappear*—there would be phone calls, hospitals, cops, something. This kind of vanishing had to have been done on purpose.

Of course it had. He had done what she'd asked. One little offer—*If you need to go, then, I guess, go*—and he was gone.

Africa? Asia? South America? She seethed for a while. Sure, it was a fight, a big, nasty fight, but what kind of grown man ran off without telling his wife? Not even Stuart.

And there it was, that fact. This wasn't like him. They had fought before, had been numb before. They'd exchanged lots of snide little slights over the past months, but he had never gone off and done anything like this.

So there she saw him again, bleeding, in a ditch. In a hospital bed, unconscious, with no ID, having been mugged. In the trunk of someone's car, in the swamp of a landfill. Stop it.

And how could she feel so angry with him if this was the fate he was suffering?

She called his cell phone so many times that first day that his voice mail filled up. In the afternoon she called his friends, his coworkers, his mother. She started with the blandest of questions—"Have you seen Stuart today?"—not wanting to alarm them. That was a lie. The truth was, she didn't want them to know.

"Have you reached him on his cell phone? I can't seem to get through."

"Today?" his friend Adam said. "Not today."

"Did you see him last night then?" Kate said, hearing some snag in his voice.

"Uh." His voice trailed off. He was probably shrugging on the other end of the line. "Just give him some time. I'm sure he'll come around."

Caught between the desire to grill him for information and the desire to hide in shame, Kate let the phone line fill with silence.

"Really," Adam said, his voice scratchy and playful, maybe a little high. "The guy's mad in love with you." The way he said it, he made that sound like a sad mistake. "If he could live without you, he would have done that by now, you know?"

"Thanks," Kate said.

"I mean," he started to apologize.

"It's okay. I know what you mean." She was too tired out to take offense anymore. "Will you let me know if you hear from him?"

Adam hesitated. "If I hear from him, I'll tell him to get in touch."

Most of their friends had begun as Stuart's friends. Their first loyalty would always be to him.

No one else she reached had heard anything from Stu. Or if they had, they were keeping it to themselves. She sat on the bed in the kitchen thinking, *Once it gets dark. I'll do it once it gets dark.* Then she stared out the window, watching the afternoon light fade from sunset to dusk, then twilight. Twenty-four hours had passed. She called the police.

They were calm and polite. This was their job. They sent someone over within the hour, and he sat on Stuart's futon, took coffee. "Ninety-nine percent of the time," he said, "there isn't any kind of foul play. If you know what I mean."

He meant this to be nice. He was maybe twenty-three, innocent and dim. He lowered his voice, as if someone might overhear, and said, "Have you been having any marital problems?" He made a vague gesture toward the side of her face, where she was bruised and scratched from the falling lath.

She shook her head.

"Any debts?" he went on timidly, fumbling with his notebook, glancing up toward the torn-apart staircase. "Remodeling," he said. "It adds up."

Kate narrowed her eyes at him, but then he cowered, and she felt bad. He looked like one of her ghost students, the kind who don't do well at anything—sports or books or friends—and curl into themselves, trying to get smaller and smaller until they vanish. "Is he a gambler? Any enemies?"

Suddenly, in an ice-water flash, it came to her. Her mouth watered up in a sick way. She had no idea where this thought came from. "Wait a minute." She rushed out the back door and into the driveway, heaved up the garage door. And through the harsh lines of the streetlight she saw it: Stuart had taken some things.

Not tools, not valuables that any burglar might take to pawn. What was missing, she saw, shoving through piles and ripping open boxes, was this: Stuart's backpack, Stuart's bike, Stuart's sleeping bag, hiking boots, tent. All of her things, her bike and backpack, were still there. And on a scrap of a brown paper grocery bag, next to the garbage can, a note: *Time out. I'm sorry. Stu.* She crumpled it up, threw it at the wall. Once she had moved around all the boxes like this, she could see: on the dark, rotting back wall of the garage, someone had spray-painted a giant heart in green paint. But there were cobwebs over it. It had been there for years, was intended for someone long gone.

She picked up the crumpled paper and opened the garbage can. And there, on top, were other crumpled-up scraps of the same brown bag, darkened with Stuart's harsh, sturdy capitals—I'M SORRY I NEED YOU DON'T DON'T WORRY WE CAN'T I LOVE YOU—all of them scribbled out and torn up. A catalog of efforts and failures.

Here it was now, her parents' big house, standing like a magazine spread under a picture-book blue cloudless sky. A few people were drifting in canoes across the calm, glassy lake, and dozens of cars filled the long driveway. They had come for Julia's engagement party. Kate turned off her car but couldn't muster the courage to get out and face them. She just sat watching the guests mill around, letting the heat swell up in the car around her. She thought of that thing she had heard about pack animals hiding their wounds. About the rest of the pack sniffing for weakness, ready to turn.

She shifted the rearview mirror her way and scrutinized her face, which was shiny and grim. She hadn't seen her dad since buying the house. Whenever she called her parents, all he would say to her was, "Hold on while I get your mother."

Her brother Derrick's kids, Sammy and Sadie, ran up to her car now—she was caught. They were shouting something she couldn't make out. When she opened the door, they looked her up and down, tried not to reveal the fact that they were peering past her at the empty passenger seat.

"Stuart couldn't come today," Kate admitted.

Sadie nodded somberly. Sammy turned to squint back toward the beach.

"Do you want to help me carry this stuff?" Kate said.

Sadie nodded and smiled, held out her arms. "Maybe he'll come later?" she said.

Sammy had walked off ahead of them but paused now, waiting for the answer.

"Maybe," Kate said. "Maybe."

Then there were hellos and faint kisses and hugs. There was the smell of roasting corn and chicken, citronella and DEET, old-lady perfume, and the lake, which was giving off an algae smell in the late-summer heat. There were people calling out her name and Stu's—as if a ghost of him followed her through the crowd, though all they were saying was, *Where's Stu? Where's Stu?*

Kate set her present—four crystal martini glasses—on the low brick wall among the other gifts and lifted her chin up, eyed the cocktails in everyone's hands. Her plan had worked: it was better to come late when everyone was already tipsy and too lively for prying questions. Her father was busy by the bar; her mother was surely in the kitchen cooking or tinkering; Julia and her fiancé, Alex, were introducing people around. Derrick was down by the boat pier with friends, but his voice, booming and assured of everything, carried all the way to the patio. "Forty percent return," he said. "You imagine?"

Kate squeezed through a cluster of people to get a cocktail and felt herself hovering just off the ground. I am soon to be divorced. My husband sneaked out without saying a word. I bought a house in which someone was apparently killed. I will never be able to sell it. She accepted a margarita and let herself get cornered by strangers, friends of Alex's parents who asked only the most benign of questions before launching into a detailed and slow-moving saga about their heroic, cancer-ridden dog.

Kate smiled and feigned interest, caught sight of her sister. Her hair looked like it had been professionally done. She was even thinner than usual, and her slinky white dress shimmered over her hip bones in the sunlight.

"Where's Stuart?" Julia said.

"Working. He got called in to fix something. He'll try to come later."

Julia smiled and then seemed to remember something. "Mexico!" she said. "We decided on Mexico, for the bachelorette thing. Eight of us." Kate started to resist, but Julia said, "Just think about it, please?" Someone behind Julia was trying to get her attention. She pulled away from Kate, saying, "We should talk later, okay?"

Kate nodded, watching her sister disappear in the crowd like a movie star.

"How's the house?" Her dad's business partner Al approached Kate. He was an enormously obese and good-humored man who carried his belly before him like an honor.

Kate tended to gravitate toward him. He had an easy way of holding up a genuine but risk-free conversation at these parties, and almost always had a line on the best drinks and food.

"Okay," she said. "It's a bit brutal, I guess."

"Remodeling is not for the faint of heart." He had a full pitcher of margaritas in his hand and was casually refilling the glasses of everyone around him.

"Is he mad at me?" She leaned in toward Al, whispering, "My dad?"

"Meh." Al shrugged. "He's fine. It's good for him." The pitcher looked so small in his big hands. Stirring it with a long glass rod, he made a constant ringing sound.

"So what can you tell me about drywalling?" Kate said. Al topped off her glass and started to explain how to hang drywall—with construction adhesive and a screw gun, not nails, which could pop out on you later.

"Where's your better half?" Her dad's voice and laughter came up behind her. When she turned around, he said, "Just teasing," and tousled her hair with his knuckles. She tried to read his expression: Was she forgiven or was he putting on a show for the party? "This guy's got my margarita pitcher," he said to Al, who forfeited it.

"It's good to see you," Kate said to her dad. "The lake looks so . . . clean."

"Yeah," he said absently, possibly not hearing her. "You, too." He was already moving on to the next group of people.

She raised her eyebrows at Al.

"You know how he is," Al said, and threw one of his giant soft arms around her shoulders. She leaned into his chest, his damp armpit. Ned. He was like Ned, but he could talk.

"You want me to send some guys over to drywall for you?" Al said conspiratorially.

She shook her head. "It's my mess. I'll clean it up."

He nodded and licked something off his thumb.

She could see the silhouette of her mother through the kitchen windows and headed up the terrace steps to go say hello. Inside, her mom was leaning over a tray of strawberries and cream, rearranging the berries to put the prettiest ones on top. She never had anything catered—only Kate's wedding and, hopefully, Julia's. For everything else, no matter how many people they hosted, she made all the food herself, like a mad scientist hidden in the safety of her kitchen laboratory.

"Katy. Look how thin you are." Her mom folded her into a clumsy hug. "You look great!" She must have had a little wine.

Kate looked down at her sagging, crinkled skirt. "Sorry I'm so late. Can I help?"

"Uhm . . ." Her mother scanned the kitchen counters, where all kinds of food and packages were organized in separate groupings, to be released at different hours. The kitchen itself, despite all the food, was spotless—no dishes in the sink, no dribbles on the counters. Kate, like most of the other guests, knew that no one else was allowed in the kitchen. "I think I've got it under control," her mom said. "But you can take this tray down to the patio."

Kate turned and took in the throng of people down there, feeling suddenly queasy. "Why don't you let me do this stuff, Mom? And you can go down to the party, see everyone."

Her mom emitted a single huff of laughter. "No way, José. I can see them just fine from here."

Kate smiled, and felt her mom's fingers touch her back, then fly away.

"You could help me cut these tortes," her mom said.

"Thanks." Kate took the knife and held it over the first lemon torte, calculating.

"Ten slices," her mom said, gesturing. "About this big. And oh—" She caught Kate's hand before it could make a second cut. "Wipe off the knife between." She handed Kate a damp towel.

"Right." Kate knew this; it should have been easy. These were skills and tendencies she shared with her mom. But as she hovered over the pastries, her hands started shaking. She sliced one too thin, one too big, feeling her mother's eyes catching all of this. She blinked, wiped the knife. Tried to concentrate. All her artifice was crumbling like a great ruin. If only her mom could see it, just this once.

"Stuart couldn't come today," she said, hoping for an opening.

"Oh, too bad. Working?" Her mother was busy rinsing blueberries at the sink. "Such a hard worker."

This was the highest compliment her family paid anyone. They liked him; they had always liked him, no matter what he thought.

"Yeah," Kate said. "He . . ." How could she tell her Catholic mother, who had made it through thirty-five years with that complicated man, through three kids and two grandkids, through surgeries and insults and every kind of stress, that she and Stuart couldn't even make it to their fourth anniversary?

She couldn't. She glanced at the window and said, "Do you think they'll be happy, Jules and Alex?"

"Sure. Why wouldn't they be?"

She said it so casually, as if there were no mystery or challenge to it at all. That was how she had always lived: fastened tight to the matters of fact, never showing an inkling of doubt or wonder about what she might be getting wrong. Kate envied her.

"But I mean," Kate said. "I mean, how can you know?"

"*I* don't know. How could *I* know?" Her mom laughed a little. "They seem happy enough."

How happy was that, enough? How much did it take?

"Did Stuart and I seem . . . happy enough? When we got married?"

Her mom tilted her head back. "What is this, Kate? What's going on?"

A tingle of panic spread through Kate's chest and down her arms, like a heart attack. She couldn't say it—*Stuart left me.* Not even *Stuart left.* Two little words, three syllables. Her mom's bright, innocent face couldn't take it. It would be like telling a child. And something else: right now it was her dirty secret; if he came back they could bury it together. If she said it aloud, it would be real, and permanent.

Her mother ducked her head into the freezer to get an extra bag of ice. "Listen, I know what this is. The remodeling project has got you guys all twisted up. Right? We've been through it a million times. It will blow over."

Kate gazed at her thin, pretty mother. That was the most revealing thing she'd ever said about her marriage. "Really?" Kate said.

"Oh, sure. That's just stress, honey. When your house is out of order, your whole life falls apart."

Kate stood thinking about it, waiting for more.

"Or it *feels* that way." Her mom smiled. "Hand me that, would you?"

Kate steadied herself. The conversation was over. "I'll take these outside for you," she said, and her mom said, "Good girl."

Maybe Stuart was on a flight to Asia. Maybe he was hiking up to Machu Picchu and would have a revelation there, would come back wise and content, forgive her. Be different.

She held the tray up high, near her face, to hide herself.

The scratch and bruise on her cheek from the falling lath had almost healed. She'd covered them with makeup, and no one had even noticed. She made her way through the people on the patio, smiling the distant perfect smile of a waitress, a hired hand. Stuart always complained about how much and how hard her family worked, but she understood it perfectly. It was so much easier to be a worker than to be yourself.

When she'd unloaded most of the tortes, she left the tray on a table and made her way down toward the beach, where there were no adults, just a group of boys playing with a soccer ball near the water. Apart from them, Sadie was sitting hunched up by the rowboat, her face hidden by her dark, curly hair.

"Hey, Sadie," Kate said. "What's going on?"

Sadie flashed her face up at Kate suddenly, as if caught. "Nothing." She was wearing a white linen dress with a high, empire waistline and a pale yellow sash that was tied in a loose bow that drooped down her back.

"You okay?"

"Yeah."

"Mind if I sit by you?"

Sadie squirmed a little, scrunched up her face. Usually she was a picture of courtesy, fawning over everyone for approval.

"You do?"

Sadie sighed, but finally said, "I guess not."

"How come you're not playing soccer?"

Sadie shrugged.

"Girls can play soccer, too, you know."

"I know," Sadie said. "I play soccer."

"Were the boys not playing nice?"

Sadie shrugged that off but wouldn't say anything.

So Kate sat quietly for a while, watching a blue heron carve a low arc over the lake, hunting. Beyond it, a group of

Canada geese squawked and fluttered near the island. Kate remembered when her parents first bought the land, when it was nothing but empty gray marshland. Now, in the summer like this, the lake looked like a resort, every curve and angle perfectly planned but made to look natural. The weeping willows she had helped plant as saplings now tilted thirty feet over the banks. Wildflowers bloomed in organized blocks of color off along the property line. A turtle's head emerged from the surface of the water, holding still as a stick, then ducking back down.

"Peaceful out here, don't you think?" she said in a church whisper.

Her parents had built this, had done this for the world. It wasn't nothing. All their striving, their busyness, had a tangible result, a meaning. That's what she wanted to say to Stuart. That's what she wanted to accomplish. And it looked selfish and vain, sure it did, but it could also be a thing you gave to the world, a thing that lasted.

"Can you keep a secret?" Sadie said.

"Sure."

A long silence passed. "I spilled something. Pop."

"Oh." Kate glanced over casually. Sadie had her arms wrapped around herself, but lifted one elbow up in a flash to show the pink stain of red pop down the front of her white dress.

"Sadie, you're supposed to spill things when you're a kid."

Sadie rolled her eyes.

"You know what really gets stains out?" Kate kicked off her shoes and stood up, stepping across the damp sand into the warm shallow water. "Lake water," she said. The lake was so still that the surface and shallow areas felt like bathwater after a series of hot days. But deeper down it was spring fed and got colder step-by-step.

Sadie watched incredulously as Kate stepped deeper, until her skirt caught the water and floated on the surface, then sank, tickling the backs of her knees. Kate flushed into a giggle. She glanced back at the party, but not a single person was looking this way. No one cared, she realized suddenly. What a sensation. When the water reached Kate's hips and waist, Sadie started to giggle, too. Finally Kate dunked herself under all at once, and Sadie squealed and made a break for the water.

Sadie was a good swimmer, but at six she still swam in the frantic, panting dog paddle of little kids. Kate scooped her up and Sadie straddled Kate's hips, locked her hands around her neck. Kate walked out deeper, and they bounced and danced slowly, face-to-face, splashing very little and keeping quiet, with their chins just barely rising above the surface.

They slowed down to a walk. With each step Kate's feet sank ankle-deep into the cold, silty sand along the bottom. Sadie traced her little curved fingers over Kate's ears and down her jaw, then picked up the line of those makeup-hidden scratches along her cheek and neck.

"You always look so serious," Sadie said.

A tangle of wet hair was plastered across Sadie's forehead, and Kate smoothed it over, tucked it behind her ear. Something about being in the water like this, arm in arm, made Kate feel so connected to her. That soft skin with its malleable flesh underneath, clinging to her without any sense of boundaries. Was this how it would feel to have a baby, to give yourself over? If Stuart never came back, would she never know?

"Can you keep a secret?" Kate said.

Sadie nodded.

"Stuart went—" Kate sucked her breath in, catching

herself. Where did that come from? This was not the sort of thing you told a child. And by now she was realizing, she wasn't going to tell anyone.

Sadie's eyes grew wider, urging. "What?"

"Never mind," Kate said. She bounced Sadie from side to side to distract her, but the girl's body stiffened. "What?"

Kate shook her head. Across the lake, two boys drifted idly in a rowboat, the oars dangling in the water. They were tiny in the distance.

"Sometimes being married is hard," Sadie said gravely, squinting over at the pairs of people on the lawn. "Sometimes people can't stay in the same house."

This was beyond Sadie's usual vocabulary and syntax. Kate studied the girl's face, suddenly wondering about the condition of her brother Derrick's marriage.

"Where did you hear that?" Kate said, as innocently as she could.

"Never mind." Sadie rolled her eyes and began squirming to get free of Kate.

"Did you hear that from your mom and dad?"

"Never mind."

"Okay, okay." Kate walked her toward the shallow water. "Never mind. It's okay." Sadie splashed to the shore and got out, running in her bunged-up, clinging, see-through wet dress toward where the other kids were playing up by the driveway.

Kate found a towel and walked around the shoreline for a while alone, waiting until she was dry enough to go in the house without dripping on the floors. The sun was setting, and the party was thinning out. She made her way around to the other side of the house, where only the kids would notice her, and went in through the garage, up to her old bedroom.

She looked in the closet for something to change into, but there was nothing there, just the old slip from her wedding dress and one of her dad's old fishing jackets. She went down the hall to her parents' room and found a skirt and blouse that fit, then went in their bathroom and dried her hair. In her parents' mirrors she always looked so different, so much worse. They must have been more expensive, or cleaner, or better lit. Clogged pores, a few stray eyebrow hairs, and along the part in her hair, four wiry gray hairs. She had spent an hour getting ready at home and had somehow missed all of this.

Cleaned up, she walked back downstairs and out to the patio, where only a dozen or so guests remained. The evening was warm, and someone had lit candles and torches around the yard. They flickered now, seeming to respond to the glittering lights of the other houses around the lake. Kate heard her dad saying to Al, "Now imagine if we'd done *half* acres, on cul-de-sacs." It was never enough. As his cocktails wore off he was always regretting or replanning, configuring ways he could have made or still could make more money, or create a more striking finished product.

Kate caught sight of her brother, and his wife; they were down along the waterline, walking in the slight stagger of couples who are connected by an arm thrown over a shoulder. Kate watched them closely, thinking of Sadie's vocabulary of divorce. Sadie's mother leaned in and confided something to Derrick, and then their sharp, bright laughter erupted over the lawn and the water. They seemed more connected than any other couple here, Julia and Alex included. Kate surveyed the rest of them, the ones sitting at opposite ends of tables, the ones ignoring each other who had been married many decades, the ones who had turned down their hearing aids so as not to hear the other's voice, and the ones hand in hand, the ones who smooched now and then, the ones who were bickering, the ones who sat calmly as friends. They were impossible to figure, all of them. Maybe it was just something Sadie had picked up at school.

10

When Stuart was little, seven or eight or so, and his brother, Danny, was three or four, their mother used to run away. Not often, and not for long. It lasted maybe an hour or two, Stuart figured now, though it was hard to say. It always felt like forever, like he would never see her again. This was back when Danny's signs of autism were first blooming, and the doctors had no clue about any of it, and all anyone could do was watch him and keep him from hurting himself and hope he would somehow shed this skin, break through. The slightest disturbances—an alarm clock next door, a siren in the distance, an ill-timed glance into his eyes—would set him shrieking in circles around the house. He could go on like that for hours, hitting himself, their mom, the walls.

And somewhere in the middle of it, somewhere after she'd tried distracting him, comforting him, humming to him, feeding him, somewhere in there her efforts would not just fail but make matters worse, and he would go red-faced and scream right into her face, in angry punches of sound that seemed to accuse her of something. Of not understanding. Of making him this way. Of being unable to fix it. And she would start to cry and would cover her face because Danny hated it when she cried. She would huddle on the floor or against a wall, hiding, trying to hold out a little longer. And when she couldn't, she would leave.

She never said, "I'll be back in an hour," never said, "I'm going to run some errands," never said, "Good-bye," even. If she said anything at all, it was a white-faced, "I can't take this anymore." And she was gone.

It took Stuart a long time to realize that all she did was drive around the neighborhood. She circled the house in slow, winding loops, her ruined face leaning into the steering wheel as if she were parting a strong wind with her forehead. He watched her from the front windows in the dining room. As Danny went on with his tantrum, unfazed, Stuart stood there holding the window casing and counting until she came around again.

A time-out, their dad started calling it eventually. *Mom's just taking a time-out.*

The time-outs had an interesting effect. Their mom came back calm, an alien, a variable instead of a reliable commodity. If they weren't careful, they could lose her. That was how Stuart saw it, though looking back now, he was sure his mother hadn't intended that effect. When he was eight or so, and Danny went through another awful phase, started biting them all, really biting, drawing blood, leaving bruises, one night Stuart had enough of it. Other kids didn't have to deal with this. Other kids had real lives, with vacations and trips to restaurants and movies; other kids had brothers they could play with, parents who weren't so crushed under the weight of one child that they could barely notice the other. And on that night, Stuart ran away himself. He walked around and around the neighborhood, watching the moon go higher in the sky, until the dew landed and he was damp and cold and anxious. He went back home and crawled into the back of his mom's car in the driveway and fell asleep. He woke in the middle of the night to her shaking him, waving a flashlight in his face. She was crying and squeezing him, breathing in sloppy wet sobs. He had done this to her. And—he cringed to remember this now—he had looked in her face and said in a cold, bitter voice, "I was just taking a time-out."

She never did it again. From then on, she just sat in the car in the driveway, holding the wheel, pretending.

Now he was a grown man and doing it himself. It was the first time he'd really understood it: how sometimes your only choice in life was to step out of your life altogether.

At first it was hard even to leave the neighborhood. He had a rough night that first night, woke up before dawn on his friend Adam's four-foot-long polyester love seat with a head-splitting hangover and a terrible sense of dread. There was a big swollen bruise and a gash on his forehead that he didn't remember getting. He stood in Adam's bathroom, staring in the mirror, poking at his forehead and trying to call back his memories. But the night was in fragments. Sure, he remembered the early stuff: getting fired, getting mad, saying all those bottled-up things to Kate. *You're scaring me*, she'd said. He remembered that. But when he stepped out of Adam's building he had no idea even where he had left his car. It had to be downtown, probably somewhere near the bar. He walked back that way through the quiet, empty streets, passing nobody but a homeless woman dozing on the shipping platform behind the library. She was wearing three loose cotton skirts, piled on top of one another like petticoats, and she fluttered her eyes, waking up as he passed. He thought about giving her his change, but it almost seemed rude, as if he'd be invading her privacy. Not even garbage collectors were out yet. The streets still belonged to all the invisibles, the homeless ghosts of Ann Arbor everyone pretended couldn't exist.

He found his car over on Williams, got in and started it up, but then sat stupidly: Where was he supposed to go? Hadn't he left her last night? Hadn't he told Adam and everyone they talked to that he was leaving Kate, for real and for good?

No one believed him. At first they laughed a little, then they shifted around in their seats, tried to change the subject. Even Adam said, "Come on, man. You'll shake it off."

And sure enough, here he was, parked in front of his house not six hours later. They all would have bet on it.

She was in there, in the house, dreaming her dreams, flailing around with her nightmares. The lights were all on. If Kate were up, she'd have turned them off by now. She was conscientious about things like electricity, but she hadn't waited up for him.

It would be so easy to slip through the door and do what everyone would expect of him: crawl into his blankets on the couch, pull the pillow over his head, doze off. His couch his clothes his TV his wife his dog. Kate would be asleep in her bed in the kitchen, and he could listen to the *SportsCenter* scores and highlights as he drifted off into nothing. Sleep would come, his stomach would settle itself, his forehead would heal, and when he woke up later everything would seem fine, almost fine. If he could get in that door before she woke up, they could both pretend that none of this ever happened.

He opened the car door with a creak that pierced the air on the empty street. Just then the neighbor who had broken the news about the murder stepped out of his postcard Victorian house and started his stretches for his morning run. He caught Stuart's eye and paused, giving him a nod and a smirk, as if he had just caught Stuart coming home from some all-night fling with another woman.

His look said he would keep it to himself, between men.

Scumbag. The guy turned away to stretch his other leg. What right did he have, this guy, to all their information?

You're scaring me. Yes. He had wanted to see her as scared as he was. Wanted her to wake up and see they were on the brink of ruining everything. She was always turning away from it. She could go on like this for years, for life, and they'd grow old in their separate sides of the house, with their feelings freeze-dried inside them.

If he went inside, that's what he'd be walking back into.

So he worked open the garage door, as quietly as possible, and pilfered through the boxes they'd stored in there. Camping gear and winter clothes were all he found. He took what he could and closed the door, then thought for a second: she would worry about him. He knew, though, he couldn't call her. He didn't have any of the words he would need to explain this.

He tried a note. He tore off part of a paper bag he found and stood holding it against the wall, staring at it. He tried ten different versions, but there was something either mean or dishonest about all of them.

He tried going to the airport, that first morning. He had cashed his severance check, and he stood in front of the Departures monitors, scanning the rows of flights for a destination. They kept changing. As soon as he focused on Anchorage or Beijing, the names would shift, then vanish, and he'd feel dizzy, overwhelmed. This wasn't how you were supposed to do it. You were supposed to talk to a travel agent, or buy your tickets online, in advance. You were supposed to do research, buy a guidebook, pack some bags. You were supposed to have a companion.

He walked back through the airport parking lot, got in his car, and started driving. He traced larger and larger concentric circles, taking the same roads he'd been on a dozen times before, stopping at all the same restaurants and gas stations he knew, until he ended up in northern Michigan, the Upper Peninsula, in a campground he and Kate had been to before. He'd been raised on the safety of repetition; the slightest variations in routine sent Danny into a panic. Stuart had never really thought much about it; he'd never really minded.

So now he circled back to this place they had shared, and his first week there was all blue skies and clear nights, the constellations displayed like a star map. Skies like that, pinned up over the quiet middle of nowhere, made it easy to pretend you had nothing to regret and were just living, communing with the pulsing leaves and grass, just riding the spinning planet like any dumb animal. One night he even slept on the ground outside his tent, letting his fire die out so he could see the stars better, and two deer walked right through his campsite. Even the mosquitoes left him alone that night, as if he'd stopped being human. Nights like that, he had no past or future, no thoughts, no nagging fears. He had done this big thing, he had left her, and nobody had screamed or stopped him. The world didn't shut down at all.

11

Tasha was sitting on the stoop when Walker got over to Ypsilanti. She had her purse by her feet, all ready to go, like a kid at a bus stop. When he got out of the truck he could see their mother peeking out the front window, but as soon as she saw him eyeing her, the big shadow of her body slowly drifted away from the curtains and out of sight. It was her house, had never been his, maybe never would be. Tasha met him halfway up the walk, and this was how they kept him out of the house.

"Should we go inside for a minute?" he said, just to be sure.

Tasha patted her purse. "I'm all set."

"What about Martin?" Walker said.

She turned her lips in. "I couldn't get him."

They were going to visit the graves today. "Is he around? This is important."

She got in the truck and kept quiet, stared out the windshield.

"I think we should go find him, Tash."

She breathed a long, shaky breath. "He won't go."

"Does he ever go?"

She shook her head hard.

"Maybe if I ask him myself," Walker tried.

"That's not gonna help, Walk."

"How will we know unless I try?" He stared at her and smiled, waiting.

"Okay, okay," she said. "Dang, see for yourself."

So she showed him the way over to Martin's friend Anton's apartment, which was down in the basement of a slipshod old divvied-up house off Division. There was a cement staircase outside going down to his door, and a stagnant puddle there in the sidewalk right in front of his front door. They stood on the lowest steps, not wanting to stand in it, and knocked until someone shouted something that sounded friendly enough. Tasha led the way in. It was a dark, damp space, all one room, with a bar at one end and a kitchen behind it, every surface loaded with food and dirty dishes.

Martin was sprawled on the filthy gray carpeting with three guys playing a video game on a big flat-screen TV in the corner. The air was a mix of mildew and pot smoke, and in the corner a small gray metal locker glowed through its seams and gill-like vents. Grow lights. You could smell the rich sweet smell of the plants, but it wasn't a big operation, just a hobby.

Walker sat down on the couch with Tasha.

"Little Tasha," one of the guys said. "You should come around here more often."

"Uh-huh." She rolled her eyes.

Martin looked up at Walker from the floor and said, "I ain't goin' with you guys. It's too hot."

Walker motioned Martin to come over to a corner by the door. Martin scowled and threw down his game controller.

Walker lowered his voice. "This is important to me. To all of us."

Martin just stared back and shifted. His gaze was sober enough, though his eyes were bloodshot. One of his friends jumped up on the couch with his arms raised, doing a victory thing, and shouted, "Take that, bitch," tossing the controller to a guy rolling on the floor in fake agony. Tasha threw her arms up to duck and scooted to the end of the couch.

"I want you to do this for me. For Tasha. For Jerome and Pops and this thing we call the Price family."

Martin rolled his eyes and headed back toward the TV.

Walker grabbed hold of his shoulder. He had wiped this kid's ass, held Kleenexes up to his stupid little nose to blow. He'd tucked him in and cooked him dinner and made his lunches and hid everything he could about where their mother was while he was doing it. "That man made you, Martin. Changed your diapers, bought your food, your *everything.* If you don't know who you come from, you don't know anything."

"Oh, I know who I come from, con."

Tasha got between them and pulled Martin over, murmured something in his ear. He eyed Walker for a long time, then stared back at Tasha, swallowing. She nodded.

"Shit," he said. "Fuck it. Let's get this over with."

They didn't have any flowers or anything, nothing to offer but their sorry selves. They just drove Pops's truck out to where he and Jerome kept their bones in the ground.

"Doesn't Moms ever go?" Walker asked, but nobody said anything.

The air was thick and steamy, over ninety, and the sky was a flat blue postcard, complete with two little-bitty jets inching toward each other up there. Walker was showered and buttoned down, shined, and he was trying to be glad to be here with them.

PRICE, the low flat gray stone said, with Pops's name and

years and Air Force markings on one side. On the other side, where it should have been waiting blank for their mother, was etched in the name of their brother, Jerome. Born just a year after Walker, bam bam, and buried here not six years after Pops, when they sure didn't have the money to go buy a separate plot. She saw to that, their mother, washed everything Pops had worked for to the gutter. Walker hadn't seen Jerome's name there yet. He'd already been locked up when Jerome went down.

There was nobody around the big cemetery besides a fat guy in a yellow T-shirt who was rolling over the graves at top speed on a big red lawn mower. Out of sight over a hill some kind of machinery beeped constantly, backing up. Digging new holes.

A smallish green pond festered near the entrance. The trees were all different kinds—big pines clustered along the far edges, maples and cherries and lindens sprinkled around, planted special on what was otherwise empty hillside. Maybe once it was something like prairie.

They stood there by that little gray stone, looking down, leaning over their brother and father, not saying anything. Walker had planned this much but didn't know what to do next. Then Tasha got down on her knees and clasped her hands. Walker watched her for a while, and when she got up, he waited a respectable time, then said, "So it's true? You and Mom got religion?"

She gave him a hard smile. "Got you a place to live, too, didn't we?"

He nodded. He'd seen guys saved inside, kept alive by nothing but their ignorant-ass clasped hands and cheap crosses. Whatever.

"How's that working out with the reverend, Walker?"

"Fine," he said. "But he's not religious, you know."

"He's a minister, Walk."

Walker shrugged. "He's cool, anyway." Most days Howard was just quiet and friendly. Only time he seemed to get worked up was when he watched the news, which always sent him to the dining-room table, where he wrote letters, long angry letters, to politicians, with his stiff, shaky hands. Then he wanted Walker to walk down to the corner mailbox with him to mail them right away. So they did, no matter what time of night it was. When he wasn't doing that, Howard spent his time piecing together scraps of wood to make flower boxes and birdcages, which he sanded and painted and then gave away to his son Dean every time he visited. Walker couldn't imagine what Dean was doing with all of them.

Last night Walker sat up with him, helping with the woodwork. Walker'd been working up to this for a long time, and was waiting for a clear-headed time to ask. Howard had spent the past hour telling Walker about some mission camp he'd been reading about in Zaire. He was trying to decide whether it deserved his money or a sour letter or nothing. He had a lot of ideas about the ways religion could go wrong.

"Howard," Walker said, interrupting. "Dean said you used to know my family? Is that true?"

Howard was hunched over, with his face pressed close to the two pieces of wood he was trying to glue together. "Thing is," Howard said. "If you take away a village's rituals, tell them your God's more powerful, is that a favor? Or the beginning of the end for them? So what if a little outside education and sponsorship helps a few lucky devils get out to the West? What happens to the rest of them, without their best and brightest?"

Walker nodded but didn't know what to say. He felt like maybe Howard talked to him about Africa this way because of his skin. But Walker didn't feel any more African than he felt Chinese. Didn't know the first thing. "The Price family," he said after a long silence. "Do you remember them?"

Howard wiped some glue off his hands with a damp rag that he kept in a cereal bowl. His eyes met Walker's for a second, then flashed away. "Hard to say," he said.

"My dad, he was a gardener. Scofield Price. Well-built guy, you know, big shoulders, big thick arms."

"We had an *excellent* gardener at the church," Howard said.

"Was he black? Do you think that was my pops?"

"Rosebushes this high," Howard said, gesturing two feet above the table. "Arched over trellises, climbing up. Always something blooming, always something scheduled to bloom. People used to like to get married there, by the roses."

Walker's pulse sped up. Pops was always good with roses, obsessive.

"Was he black?" Walker said. There couldn't have been that many black gardeners that good in a town this white.

"Why's his color matter so much to you?" Howard scowled.

Walker smiled but wasn't going to give up. "Well, he's gone now, you know. My dad. Died of a heart attack, long time ago."

Howard nodded uncertainly. "I never did like the weddings, you know. Worst part of the job, besides doing the budget. Those brides push you around like hired help. The weddings were worse than the funerals, that's for sure."

"Scofield Price," Walker said again. "Always wearing a Detroit Tigers cap."

"Beautiful green hands!" Howard declared. "Hard to replace him." Then he stood up and headed upstairs to his bedroom, and the conversation was over.

It was something though, it was a start.

Now Martin was wandering off from the graves toward the shade of a little wooden pavilion. Walker took out the fifty he'd been holding on to and held it out to Tasha. "I want to start helping you out. Tuition and stuff."

She backed away from him, her shoulders stiffening. "Walker, that's crazy."

"No," he said. "I want to."

"Shoot," she said. "You get yourself on your feet first."

"I am on my feet."

She shook her head. "You oughta get your*self* some things first. You can't go around in those Bobby Brown clothes forever."

He touched the loose black and red shirt over his stomach. "I got a roof, a car, all I can eat. What else I need?"

She shook her head, held her hand up. "I'm not taking that from you."

So he could see he'd have to build himself up bigger if he was going to be of any use to her.

He folded the bill carefully and put it back in his pocket.

The guy on the lawn mower came closer until it got noisy, and Tasha said, "Let's walk around a little." They headed over to collect Martin, and the three of them walked down toward the pond, nobody saying anything.

"Tell me about him," Tasha said after a while.

Martin ripped a green tree branch from a silver maple and started slapping it back and forth against the ground.

"Pops? What do you want to know?" Walker asked.

"He was a hard ass," Martin said before she could answer. "Like some other folks we know."

"Disciplined," Walker said. "He believed in things."

"Like what?"

The family, for one thing. Always wanted more. More kids, more money, more status. Moved them all the way to Ann Arbor with this dream of his kids going to the U of M, and look where they'd ended up. The man had an appetite, threw a fit if Moms ever ran out of food at dinner. *I did not come all this way to see these kids go to bed hungry.* Moms would only laugh. *Hungry. These kids don't know hungry from a hole in the ground.* Like going hungry was some kind of accomplishment.

"He was always working," Walker said. "Like, forty hours a week for the U, plus twenty or thirty on the side. Every weekend, every night after work he had some different project or sideline—mostly gardening but sometimes construction or odd jobs, in the winters. Me and Jerome used to hide from him," he laughed. "Hide out, even with Moms, in the basement, we'd all be hiding down there in the cool, and he'd be upstairs in the yard, hollering for somebody to get out there and bring him a fresh pair of gloves."

"And you'd hop right to it," Martin said. "His errand boy."

There'd been errands Walker had missed though. Requests Jerome talked him out of hearing. Like the day he and Jerome were in the attic playing Monopoly, which Jerome always won by cheating somehow, and just barely they heard Pops down in the living room yelling. He was putting up new wood paneling over the cracked plaster. They had already cleaned out the gutters and raked, had already wasted most of their Sunday with chores, and for once Walker had Jerome on the ropes, had managed to buy up almost every single property. They pretended not to hear Pops until he stopped yelling. And then—Walker remembered this part but never told it—they laughed about finally getting Pops to give up and leave them be. Their mom was out shopping with baby Tasha and little Martin. And they didn't give Pops another thought till Moms came home an hour later and they heard her start shouting, too. Martin came running up the attic stairs, crying till his nose and mouth dripped. Walker picked him up, held the back of his head, wiped his face with his own shirt, but Martin wouldn't stop crying and wouldn't say anything. So Walker carried him downstairs, reluctantly, knowing that Jerome would take this chance to steal from him or the bank.

When he got down to the living room there was Pops, on the floor, weak and contorted and moaning. Moms was just holding his hand, didn't even think to call 911. Walker had to do that. It was a heart attack, his first one, but he was okay. The doctors said he should watch his diet, slow down, but a few months later, on a hot Indian summer day, he collapsed off the big mower he was riding on campus, right in the heart of the Diag by Angell Hall. Knocked his head on the way down, but they could tell, by the way it didn't bleed much, that he was already gone, that fast. Walker thought about who it was who found him that way, thought about frat boys and rich girls glancing over at him falling, at his mower as it rolled to a stop, at his body lying there in the grass they played Frisbee on. A lot of them must have kept on walking, late for class. Walker was sixteen, Jerome fifteen, Martin six, Tasha two. And whatever little bit of strength and order their mom ever had went into the ground with Pops.

"He liked you best," Walker said to Tasha, nudging her.

"Don't believe it." Martin stopped and turned back to them. "Walker was the one he liked. The rest of us were pretty much invisible."

If you woulda helped out, Walker thought, but he didn't say it. "When you were born, Martin, I saw that man *cry.* Carried you around on the top of his head. You remember that?"

Martin smiled, then hid the smile. Tasha stood staring at him, challenging him. "You must remember something good about him."

Martin shrugged and looked all around for an answer, then his face shifted gears and he laughed. "The man danced like a . . . I don't know. Like a big drunken bird. All the damn time."

"That's right." Walker laughed. He had almost forgotten. "Do the dance."

Martin gave an embarrassed look, but he did it: let his arms float up and flap slightly, like a pelican, then he did a few bird steps forward, around, and back.

"That is one retarded dance." Tasha laughed.

"That's what I'm sayin'. I don't know where he got that," Martin said. "But every time somethin' good happened—" Martin did the dance again.

Then the silence fell around them again. What had Walker become inside that made all of this talking so hard? Finally, he spoke up. "It was better back then. Way better."

Martin walked forward in silence, making himself gone again. "Everybody has their own way of remembering," he said.

"What is it you think you remember?"

Martin threw his stick far out into the pond. The water was so thick with algae that the stick sank slowly and left an indent on the surface.

Walker wasn't going to back down on this. "You think, what, shacking up with a cokehead, getting hit, you think that's better than what Moms had with Pops?"

Martin wrestled with another tree for a branch, but they were all green, holding firm.

"Really," Walker said. "I want to know."

"It was bad all around." Martin lifted his arms up and out

to his sides, as if to encompass everything on Earth. "Before, during, after."

"You were just too little to remember it. Where we lived before you can remember? It was a shitty little rental with roaches on a garbage lot down off Gratiot. If he didn't get us outta Detroit, you'd a been going to school with crack babies, Martin. You'd a been sellin' or buyin' before you were eighteen."

"Like Jerome?"

Walker huffed. Yeah, like Jerome. "I'm sayin', he gave you *choices*. Last I heard, you graduated from a top one hundred public school."

"Choices like what you made?"

Walker pulled himself close to Martin's dumb face and said, "What I did was for you."

"Keep tellin' yourself that." Martin walked away. "I saw what you did."

Walker grabbed himself a branch and threw it at the water, too.

"Why don't you two put your dicks away," Tasha said. "This ain't gonna help anything."

"Nice mouth," Walker said.

"Look." Tasha unzipped her backpack. "I brought us some snacks. Let's just sit here and eat something. Can we do that?"

Pops never would stand for people mouthing back at him. He would've taught Martin a little respect, he would've put an end to all this mopey remembering. Nobody's dad was perfect. What did it matter?

So they sat on a rock and ate cheese curls and Pepsi. "This isn't even the point," Walker said. "I didn't come here to talk about him. What I wanted to hear about was Jerome."

"Jerome." Martin rolled his eyes. "Source of pride to us all."

He'd heard a couple of things in prison, from folks who'd known Jerome. Always a fuckup, Jerome, always headed for trouble. But there were times when Walker would get things, inside, a better job assignment or less heat from the thugs, and through the pipelines, in hints and gestures, it followed that Jerome had arranged something with someone, that Jerome was in a position somehow to make things easier for Walker. Affiliated. It made Walker both proud and ashamed. But mostly relieved, though he hated to admit it. They weren't supposed to be those kinds of kids, that kind of family, but here he was in prison, and if his brother's dealing and stealing was wrong, against the plan, he figured anyway the plan had been all shot to hell.

Those first days Walker was in county lockup, Jerome came to visit him. Jerome said, "Brother, I'm gonna owe you the rest of my life."

Walker always hated the way he said *brother*, not like what he was, his sibling, his blood, but like in some seventies jive language, the kind Pops had hated.

Walker leaned toward his brother. "Hey. It'll be like we switched places, okay? Let's say I'm payin' for whatever you've done. Let's say I wash away your mistakes. And you walk in my place. You take care of Moms, the kids. You get your shit together and graduate next year. Get yourself to college. And I'll do this other part."

Jerome nodded and teared up, like he really believed it.

"Second chance, okay? Start over. You promise me? You'll make it worth it?"

Jerome nodded down at the floor and his shoulders heaved, and Walker knew he was crying. "Man," Jerome said, "this is some fucked-up shit, blood."

Jerome had always been like that, weak. More Mom in him than Pops.

And now Jerome was over there inside that hillside. He would've been thirty-five. He was under the dirt and useless as shit, which shouldn't have surprised anyone. In the end he died like some lowlife, homeless and mindless for months, wasted up.

"Did Jerome come around much, back then, after I left?" Walker asked Tasha.

She shook her head vaguely. "Not a lot, I don't think. Mom would lose track of him for months, I remember. No calls, no way of finding him." She hesitated, looked away. "She heard he was dead once or twice before he actually was."

Jesus, the life. They sat watching Martin over by the pond, crouching down for rocks and throwing them into the water. Pulling up handfuls of perfectly good grass and throwing them to the wind.

"What do you remember about Jerome?" Walker called to Martin.

Martin turned and shook his head real slow. "Nothin'. Not a single thing." He fished another rock out of his left hand and hurled it hard into the pond. Like the water itself had done something bad to him.

"Just let him be," Tasha said in a low voice.

"He always this mad?" Walker waited, though he knew the answer.

Tasha shrugged and shook her head, and then he knew for sure.

"You know what you said, about looking for a place in the country?" she asked.

Walker nodded. He had a plan in mind, but to do it he'd need a place to work in.

"I think I got a line on a place. You want to go see it?"

He jingled the car keys in his hand.

"It's not for living in, just a barn, like you said."

"Yeah," he said. "Perfect."

So they put the cemetery behind them and drove off. Martin said he had to work, so they dropped him off and drove out south of Ypsi, down past Milan, till there was nothing but flat empty fields and dirt roads.

"Walker?" she said once Martin was gone and they'd had some quiet time on the road. "What was Mom like back then?"

"When do you mean?" Walker said.

Tasha stared and waited.

"Before Pops passed?" he said. "You know, she had her chores and he had his, and he kept everything in order. They worked good together."

"I mean after," she said.

Walker sighed. She lost her head, he wanted to say. She lost track of herself and her kids and her house, forgot how to cook and wash and stay sober, forgot how to sleep alone, how to close the door to low-life losers who had a nose for her new insurance cash. She came crumbling apart until there was nothing left of her. And that piece of garbage D. B. Chenille came along and dragged them all over the edge. They spent their afternoons drinking, their nighttimes out at the jazz club or some other dive, and sometimes late at night, after Walker and Jerome had put the kids to sleep and gone to bed themselves, they'd come home late with a fresh batch of strangers, people they picked up anywhere. Sometimes they had guitars and horns, and D.B. would take out his sax and they would make noise—it was beautiful noise. Walker listened from the landing, hating the way that music worked its way into his bones, into the rhythm of his breathing and heartbeat, which was like putting it right in his blood. Sometimes he'd sneak down a few steps and lean over the railing to watch them. D.B. played with his eyes shut, not even watching the signals of the others for changes, he just felt them coming. And Moms would gaze at D.B., feeling all the things that Walker felt, only ten times more, and willingly. Happy. She looked like a lady, not a mother, and she never once noticed Walker or Jerome there on the steps. It was never the same people twice. It was glassy-eyed noisy people, clinking bottles, cutting lines, smoking joints. The noise would get louder and louder, people shrieking and sometimes breaking things. Tasha could sleep through it all, but sometimes Martin would wake up and come out to the staircase in his fuzzy pajamas, wiping at his face and eyes and whimpering. And though Walker wanted to stay and keep watching, he knew he had to keep Martin from seeing the kinds of things they did down there. He'd pick Martin up and fly him back to his spaceship bed and do the countdown thing Pops used to do, ending with "Blast off," which was when Martin was supposed to close his eyes and not open them again till morning. He stayed there a while though, to be sure, lying back on Martin's floor, listening to his mom's blurry laughter below. He watched the glow-in-the-dark stars and moons all over the ceiling, hoping that Tasha stayed put and that all those people would leave soon and not take anything.

"She was different," was all Walker said. "She took it hard." As hard as it was to see her like that with D.B., what was worse was before D.B. came along, when all Moms did was wear her robe all day, just sleep and moan and lie around dead-eyed, not even leaving the house to get the mail off the porch. That was scarier.

But he didn't tell Tasha any of this.

The barn was a big grayed-out, leaning structure, set off from two other barns. It was clearly the oldest. There were weeds growing tall around it, and two rickety doors at either end and a couple of big empty openings without glass, one half boarded shut, one open to the weather. Tasha went to the door of the farmhouse and brought out the owner, a guy named Jeff, a big lanky guy who ran the restaurant where Tasha worked. He didn't farm, but rented out the land to a soybean and corn guy two farms over. He used the main barn for working on cars, and had no use for this other one. He leaned against one of the gray wooden walls and said, "See, it's still sturdy." Hard as he shoved it, the building didn't move.

"That fire pit back there." Walker pointed to a big charred cement circle that used to be the foundation of a silo. "Could I use that?"

Jeff nodded. "If you're careful."

"How much you asking?" Walker said.

"It's got just the two electric sources," Jeff said. "No water, but you're welcome to use my hose there on the side of the house."

Walker nodded. "How much?"

The guy shrugged, like money had never occurred to him, like he was trying to pull a number from the sky.

"Hundred and twenty?"

Walker nodded. "For a hundred I'd take it."

12

Of course it couldn't last forever. By the end of the week a minivan family moved into the campsite next to Stuart's. They brought along a boom box and the squeals of three children, and a day later: the rain.

The first night was torrential, huge drops pelting his thin nylon tent like someone throwing rocks at him. Gusts of wind pulled at the walls until Stuart got nervous and spread-eagled himself to hold down each corner of the lightweight tent, hoping his stakes would hold until morning.

By the second night over two inches of rain had fallen, and streams of water washed out enough soil to trickle under his tent and puddle up between the floor of it and the tarp he'd set it on. The floor soaked through and bled into his sleeping bag. It was like sleeping in a giant wet diaper, but by then the temperature had dropped to the low fifties and he had no choice. Starting a fire was absurd; cooking, impossible. He huddled in his cold, musty tent, picking at the thick scab on the mystery bump on his forehead, wondering when it would go down and stop throbbing like this. He made a few videos for Danny, but they were too dark, too *Blair Witch*, too pathetic.

What was Kate doing? Why couldn't he make himself call her?

Because whatever he might say would be the wrong thing, and would be final.

But the skies were opening up like a cataclysm. He had no one to talk to and no one to trust, and it wasn't much fun anymore. He hated being alone, hated the way people looked at him with pity, mistrust. In bars and in restaurants, at campgrounds, even in drive-throughs when they said, "Is that all?"—it felt like a judgment. On the third day of the storm the rain slowed to a constant heavy drizzle, and he broke down and drove to the nearest town, did his laundry, dried out his sleeping bag, then sat in a tavern all day watching reruns of the Westminster Dog Show with two old men who were so senile they asked him his name four times.

By the fourth night of rain the family next door had packed themselves into their minivan and were watching *Shrek* over and over on their DVD player. Their dog, a muddy yellow Lab, was curled up in the gravel under the minivan, staring over at Stuart with his big wet, forlorn face. Stuart's fingers and toes were deeply pruned; he had a cold and no Kleenex, and had just worn out the last of his flashlight batteries. His iPod was dead, he had no radio; his cell phone was locked in his glove box, where he'd let it die. He squinted through the tent window for a while at *Shrek*, but couldn't make out anything except the big greenish figure. He lay back, closed his eyes, tried to sleep.

If you need to go, then, I guess, go, Kate had said. It had sounded so indifferent, in the moment. But what if he'd misinterpreted? What if she was just tired, exasperated? What if she meant: *Go do what you need to do, and I'll wait here.*

He pushed the words around in his head, trying to call back the exact look on her face.

Lightning flickered in the distance, followed by thunder. *I will wait for you here while you do whatever you need.* Okay, so Kate would never put it quite that way. You had to interpret her always; words like that just didn't come out.

She had beautiful hands, Kate, thin delicate fingers that moved like artwork, like one of those hula dancers using their hands to tell stories with beautiful endings. Her eyes, too. When she wasn't tired, when she had slept well, they were piercing and clear, and they looked at people with such fierce intensity that she made them nervous. People took one look at those eyes and faltered. Most people looked away. It was because of her eyes, he thought, that people didn't ever quite see her.

Kate. He had one of those lifelike dreams then: it began at the dizzying boundary between sleep and life, and he was lying in his sleeping bag, which was soggy again, just millimeters from the cold, wet, bumpy ground; if he rolled one way, it was the big flat rock under his shoulder, and if he rolled the other way, it was the jagged stone under his hip. And the raindrops were heavying down, *plunk, slap* on the vinyl roof of his tent, which was her tent, too. They had bought it together, well before they were married, and though he'd paid for it himself and she always called it *his*, even that day, even before they'd moved in together, he had thought of it as *our* tent because he was only buying it so they could go away together and sleep in it. And they did. Two weeks of nonstop sweaty fucking in the summer after they first met. Right here by Iron River, in this forest. His cell phone rang, in his dream, and it was right there under his neck, not locked in the glove box, and it was Kate calling, of course. He was expecting her, he said, "Hello," like he already knew for sure it was her, and her response was just as routine. She said, "What road do I turn on again?" Because she was meeting him here, she was on her way, and she was always bad at remembering directions, and her night vision wasn't great, so he described the entrance to the campsite, the throng of huge pine trees opposite the turnoff, and the big sign, then to the right, past the RV section, where all the assholes went, and down to the right by the water, and then she'd see his car. "Got it," she said, sounding giggly and ten years younger. He rested his hand over his half-swollen cock. She would be here any minute. The rain, the rain. He said, "Did you bring the wine?" but she had already cut out or hung up, and so he just lay there, waiting, wondering what she'd be wearing tonight. It was like they were twenty-one and not yet used up. And then her flashlight was bobbing through the rain outside, she was slapping the side of the tent, saying, "Excuse me, excuse me?" And he scrambled up, looking for the zipper, trying to unzip it fast and get her in out of the rain, but the zipper was hiding, was missing, was on the wrong side, was tucked away, stuck, wouldn't turn up. He ripped at the opening, panicking now, and the tent was old and worn out: it came apart at the seam.

"Excuse me," the woman said.

She was crouched in the mud right in front of him, holding a little kid's pink raincoat over her head and shoulders.

"We just heard on our radio there's some kind of flood warning," she said. She bumbled her flashlight, almost dropping it in the mud, and the beam caught him in the eyes, temporarily blinding him.

"Sorry," she said. "We're not sure if this area exactly is in danger. It seems pretty high up, but we're going to head out anyway. The kids. We thought you might want to know."

"Right . . . right," he said. She was looking at him with a curious kind of urgency.

"You be okay?" she said. "You need a hand?"

Behind her, he noticed, other flashlights were moving through the woods of the campground. Car lights were firing up off in the distance.

He thanked her and waved her off, and she rushed back to her minivan and the whole family was gone within minutes. They left their aluminum and vinyl awning right where it stood.

"Shit." He flopped back on his soggy sleeping bag, listening as the rain grew harder and harder. A shock of lightning lit up the sky, followed almost immediately by a huge, jarring clap of thunder. "Christ." Why not just lie here and see what came, just let a swell of water wash you away, untie you from the last listing remains of your life?

13

Kate lurched awake, gasping. It was daylight. Late-morning sun cut through the kitchen. She was alone. The dog, her giant, half-deaf nonprotector, blinked up at her from the floor, where he was sprawled on his side by the back door. They were okay.

The dreams again. This time strangers were climbing down out of the shadowy walls and rafters of the house, wearing shaggy, gray robes, holding flowers, but they had desperate, urging eyes, and they closed in on her, clutching at her sheets and hair. She shook free.

Someone was knocking. That was what had woken her. Her muscles felt cemented in place under her skin; her hands ached in the joints from all her work. She felt like an old lady—rickety, alone. Almost always afraid.

The door again, and she got up and peeked down the hall to see who it was. She still hadn't mustered the ability to ignore the phone or the door, thinking each time, if only briefly: Stuart.

It wasn't Stuart. It was never Stuart. It was Julia. She had cupped her hands around her face and was peering through the window of the front door. Kate ducked back behind the frame of the kitchen door. Two days ago she had awoken to the sounds of her neighbors outside in the street, celebrating. They had barricaded both ends of the street: a block party. They had set up grills and tables. Kate thought back to her first few weeks in this house, how she had wanted to know all the people in these houses, wanted to weave herself into the fabric of a neighborhood. She remembered smiling and waving at them all, trying to catch their names, the names of their pets and children. But through the window, the sight of them paralyzed her now. She had gone into hiding, often leaving the shades down, staying close to the bed. Her solitude had unhinged her. What did she have to say to anybody out there? So she climbed to the hot, stuffy attic that day and watched her neighbors from the big front window: their awkward mingling, their handshakes, their kids throwing water balloons, the way they all got louder and sloppier as the day went on. She feared one of them would come ring her doorbell, urge her to come out, but no one did.

And now Julia was trying to open the front door, but it was locked, thank God.

"Katy." She knocked again, louder. She wasn't going away.

It was after eleven. Kate rubbed at her face and struggled to get her shorts and bra on. "Okay, okay," she shouted. She pulled up her hair and rubbed a finger against her front teeth.

"Hi." She opened the door, and Julia locked eyes with her.

"Hi. What the heck is going on?"

"I overslept." Kate shrugged, trudging down the hallway and into the bathroom. "I haven't been sleeping right."

On top of being totally torn apart, the house was filthy. The kitchen was cluttered with dishes and carryout trash, and she hadn't showered yesterday or today. It was all getting away from her. She didn't know what step to take next. She figured she needed an electrician at this point, though she wasn't sure who to ask or how to afford it. And then the task of drywalling everything lay before her, and she knew that was one project she just couldn't do alone.

"That's not what I'm talking about," Julia said through the bathroom door.

Kate's mind raced. What did she know? Brushing her teeth, Kate mumbled some nonsense that she hoped would buy her time. She washed her face and brushed her hair into a tight bun, trying to hide the greasy streaks. She fumbled through the hamper looking for a slightly cleaner shirt.

"Katy, come out. I want to talk to you."

Kate opened the door and stood before her sister, feeling like the younger one, feeling like a child caught at something.

"What's happened with Stuart?"

Kate gave a puzzled, noncommittal look.

"I *know*, Kate. Alex's brother saw him wasted at a bar last week, telling everyone he and you were"—she cleared her throat—"splitting up."

The water stopped dripping from the faucet. The dirty dishes vanished. The semitruck idling down the street went silent. *Splitting up. Telling everyone.*

Kate pushed past her.

"What's going on, Kate?"

Ned was dancing around by the back door. Oblivious to her dramas, he had his own daily needs. Kate opened the door for him and followed him outside. She walked over to the hidden little space in the overgrown shrubs and sat on the big log inside. She leaned forward until her head touched the leaves, and she smelled them, felt the itch of them, wished for her sister to go away, to evaporate.

But she didn't. She poked her head in.

"Go away," Kate said in a very steady voice. "I'm fine."

There was room for only one in there, but Julia pushed her way in anyway and perched herself on the edge of the log. And finally Ned squirmed in, too, shimmying his whole body against them until the leaves rustled and fell. All the vines overhead quivered, as if the whole enclosure might come apart, come crashing down.

"What happened?" Julia sounded not so much concerned as scared. "I need you to tell me."

"I wanted to tell you."

Julia inhaled sharply, as if she'd been holding out hope that the rumor was false, a misunderstanding. But Kate had just shattered the illusion. "You've got to tell Mom and Dad."

Kate shook her head. "You can't tell them. Okay?" She turned a hard stare on Julia, trying to steal back her big-sister status.

"What happened?"

"He left, you know. He left. We fought. He left. It's all very grown up."

"But not for good. Right? You're not really going to get a divorce." She hushed the last word.

Kate raised her eyebrows and shrugged.

"Come on, Kate. You're not going to do that."

"It happens, Julia."

Julia bent over, elbows on her knees, as if trying to quell a sudden wave of seasickness.

"So that night on the phone, when you were asking about Alex, about getting married?"

Kate put out her palms. "He was gone."

She knew she should feel guilty about keeping this all to herself, but all she felt was numb. Julia wrapped her arms around Kate from the side, but Kate could barely feel it. It was like some part of her had already decided to clear everyone out of her life and go it alone. She fought the urge to shrug her sister off.

"So what happened?" Julia murmured.

Kate had to get out of that claustrophobic space. She pushed through the opening and paced the yard. "If it were one explainable thing, Jules, he wouldn't be gone." She found one of Ned's toys and threw it for him—too hard, bouncing it off the fence. "Someday you'll get that."

Julia simmered for a while. Ned came bounding back to Kate, squeaking the toy with his big, indifferent jaws. "Well, just so you know, Kate? He's spiraling all out of control. Bryan said he fell down, smacked his head on the bar, and they kicked him out. Can you *imagine*? He's obviously not himself, not thinking right."

Kate cringed inside, picturing that. "Maybe. He got fired."

"See?" Julia brightened, as if this were good news. "Okay. So he's probably just having some pre-midlife crisis. Like you said, I bet this happens to—" She started to say *everyone*, then stopped herself.

Kate nodded and stayed quiet a long time, watching the dog rub his face and shoulders in something on the grass.

"This yard could be so beautiful," Julia said absently, gesturing at all the blooming orange trumpet vines and overgrown rosebushes.

"Yeah. Thanks."

"Don't take this the wrong way. I'm sure he'll come back and everything will work out. I'm *sure* of it." Julia scratched at her neck, then came over and put one hand around Kate's wrist. "But in the meantime, you should really transfer your assets. If he's going through some kind of crisis, especially, and you haven't heard from him. You should check your credit."

"Assets?" Kate laughed. "I'm a teacher."

Julia gave her a scolding look. "Whatever you have, I'm saying, you should protect it."

Kate looked around at the yard, the house. "I am."

"Where is he staying?" Julia said after a while.

"I don't know."

"Alex's brother got the sense he was maybe staying with Adam Hensen."

"Good for Adam."

"You haven't talked to him?"

Kate shook her head. She had held off crying through all of this. She was not going to do it that way.

"I'll be fine," she said. "Thanks for coming by, really. Don't tell Mom and Dad. Please? I'll tell them soon."

"I'm not *leaving*," Julia said, folding her arms across her chest. "God, what is wrong with you? I'm your sister, okay? Let me take you to lunch or something. I know, let's get massages. Whatever you want."

Kate smiled. She touched her sister's shoulder and walked away. There was a petunia plant in the corner by the fence that needed to be deadheaded. She leaned over and started plucking off the sticky, withered flowers. "I have a lot of work to do."

"Let me help you."

"No," Kate said. "Really."

Julia stepped up close, an incredulous look on her face. "You just won't let anyone in, will you?"

Kate shook her head. Stuart had been the one she let in. Whatever his faults, he had been the only one.

Once Julia was gone, Kate methodically cleaned up the kitchen. She did the dishes, took the trash out, made the bed, started some laundry. She took a shower and put on her work clothes and face mask. She stepped into the living room, which had sort of become Stuart's room. He had wanted to leave the living room and dining room intact, to give them someplace to live during all the chaos of remodeling, and then to rework those rooms later, maybe years later, in Phase II, when they redid the kitchen. It didn't make much sense to do it in phases—that would just mean two rounds of misery, two sets of Dumpsters, contractors, permits. But she had given him that. He acted as if she never compromised, but she had.

Now she folded up his blanket and pillow, gathered his magazines, and stuffed them all into a big garbage bag. She pushed his slouching futon into one corner and piled the coffee table on top of it. His stupid fucking omnipresent TV she unplugged and hefted upstairs to the attic, where all their other things were stored away. She could sell it. She could cut off their cable and save fifty dollars a month. Behind the couch she found three quarters, three balled-up socks, some used Kleenex, and a porn video. She put those in the garbage bag, too, then took it outside and heaved it up into the Dumpster. There. She piled the rest of the furniture on top of the couch in one corner and tarped it. And then, after pacing the room for a while, mumbling, "Oh, screw it," she brought out her hammer and crowbar.

The paneling made a rich tearing sound as she pulled it away from the walls, and though the plaster underneath was crumbling and ruined, there were no obvious round reddish spots, no splatters, no trace of blood or bullet holes. It was just general decay, cracked plaster, a few stains, some crayon drawings someone hadn't scrubbed away. Carefully, she carried the nail-riddled sheets of paneling out to the driveway, but the Dumpster was so full she just piled them alongside it. And back inside, she got down to the messy part, swinging her hammer and crowbar madly into the useless plaster.

For once her mind ran clear of finances and timetables and remaining vacation days; for once she didn't think of the indignities of marriage, the lies she had used to protect her ego, the pressure to uphold an image that no longer—and maybe never—resembled her. The physical work was easier than all that.

And there, in the middle of the falling dust, came one treasure after all. It lilted down from the gutted ceiling, falling slower than anything else up there. She pulled off her goggles and gloves and picked it up.

Anyone else might have mistaken it for any other worthless scrap of paper. But this was a letter, aged and burnished, folded up and sealed with a circle of thick red wax. On the front of it, in big black curly writing, was the name *Herrn F. W. Osius*. And at the top right corner: *Hanau. 18 Nov 1828*.

Kate looked up at the ceiling where it had come from. There was nothing else of its kind, nothing on the floor where it had fallen. Just this one mysterious, folded-up letter from seventy or eighty years before the house was even built. It didn't make any sense. She carried it delicately out to the kitchen, where she dusted herself off and washed her hands and the countertop before opening it.

It was one big piece of tan paper, maybe twelve by eighteen inches. The author had written in tiny frail script all over both sides, right up to the edges, with no margins, leaving only the address area clear. Kate scrutinized the penmanship, but it was no use; it was in German. She'd need a translator.

Finally, finally, something was going her way. Sure, it was only a letter, and she couldn't understand a word of it, but it was something historic and beautiful, one of a kind, something the house was giving her.

She went and stood in the middle of the living room,

doing a slow turn to take in the dark brown velvety studs through the haze of dust. If he came home, what would she tell him? He had forfeited his claim. She could say that. If he came home.

She thought about the room's potential, about how the light and the traffic pattern of the first floor would open up if she knocked a bigger opening into the wall by the front door so that the staircase was visible, climbing upward, from this room. Give the eye somewhere to go, was how her dad would put it: each view should tease the eye forward. Leave it wanting more, more, more.

Maybe she could even replace that whole wall with a half wall, with bookcases up to the waist and then a few pillars above holding up the header—she had cut out a picture of a room like that; it was probably in the attic somewhere. But how much would that cost, and who would help her with it? She had only twenty-two hundred dollars left in savings and hadn't even paid her last Visa bill.

She got on her knees in one corner and pried up the edge of the orange carpeting. She held her breath, hoping for hardwood, and peeled it back.

Tile. Linoleum tile. Chintzy, cracked, black linoleum tile. "Who does this?" she shouted. "Who puts linoleum in a living room? God, could they not do one thing right?"

But she wasn't going to quit now. With a razor and a putty knife she pried away one thin tile, scraping and scratching until she uncovered the floor beneath it: real live wood.

Not subfloor but thin oak tongue-and-groove strips. They had hardwood floors. *She* had hardwood floors. She had a letter beautiful enough to frame, and she had hardwood floors.

She scrambled to roll back the rest of the carpet, then

dragged it out the front door, her ass in the air, knuckles scraping the ground. She hustled and dragged and wrestled it into submission next to the Dumpster.

When she stood up, someone was in her driveway, looking at her. He was a tall black man, maybe mid-thirties, clean-shaven, old loose clothes, a baseball cap. He touched the cap—so old-fashioned—and said, "Hello, ma'am."

Strangers were easier than friends. They didn't know enough to judge you. Lots of old guys walked by and stopped to talk. Usually they worked in the trades or had some half-blacked-out fond memory of good old days remodeling or painting. Sometimes they had pointers, sometimes compliments.

"Wondering if you needed some garbage hauled off," he said in an oddly delicate voice, almost like he was putting it on for a role.

"Seriously?"

He nodded back at her.

To get the Dumpster emptied would cost three hundred dollars, which she couldn't really spare right now.

"How does it," she stammered. "What'll it cost?"

He shrugged and gestured toward an old pale blue pickup truck at the curb, and in that instant she felt she knew him from somewhere, had seen him before. In college, at work, in the neighborhood? But no, nothing clicked.

"Like, this construction stuff." He sized it up. "This pile here?" He shrugged again. "I could take it away for fifty bucks."

Kate hesitated. Was it wrong to haggle with a poor guy who hauled away garbage for a living?

"I have a couch I want rid of, too." What was she saying? There was nothing wrong with the futon—except for the fact that it would be in the way and that it was filthy with Stuart, his hair, his skin, his smell. The sight of it just waiting for him, she was tired of that.

The man watched her, giving a half nod, noncommittal.

"It's inside. Could you help me?"

Some kind of thrill or panic flickered through him. She saw it, and it spooked her. "Never mind," she said.

"No, I don't mind." He seemed suddenly overeager. Did she want this man in her house?

"My husband's at work," she said. "He should be home any minute. We could wait for him."

"Naw, let's just take care of it." He shrugged, casual again. What did she have to fear? She had nothing at all worth stealing, and her neighbors were ten feet away.

She let him in.

14

So he was back. He was inside, over the threshold, inside the house that would have been his if the world hadn't twisted around like that. And look what she'd done to the place. But he couldn't look. He pushed his eyes toward the floor, just looked for that couch, got his hands on it in a blur, then lifted it up and focused on the front door and moved his way fast to it, not looking at this lady's face or the brown walls stripped bare, all bones, with nothing of Pops left inside there at all. It was all buried in that Dumpster. He'd have to dig it out.

Then it was over. He was back on the porch, on top of the crawl space where he and Jerome had played strip poker with Cheryl and Lisa from the next block. On top of the crawl space where they had finally found Martin hiding that awful night, Walker's last night here.

And he wanted back in.

He kept himself quiet, collected up. He wanted back in, and he'd hurried too much. A million ways he could've stalled her, could've at least lifted his dumb-ass brown eyes and taken in what was right there in front of him before he was out the door again. A stronger man could've done that without being so scared of crumbling.

They put the couch in the back of the truck. Wasn't even anything wrong with it. He'd be glad to have it.

He set to work hauling the paneling and carpet rolls down the driveway and into his truck bed, feeling them tingling and smelling their own Price smell when he squeezed them with his hands. He didn't cry. He kept breathing and breathing, and when she looked over he smiled a bland, innocent, won't-scare-you smile, did everything he could to show her she didn't need to rush him off.

"You know, ma'am," he said when he was all loaded up. Again with his perfect and quiet voice. "If you and your husband ever need a third hand, I'm pretty handy with construction and such. I could do it for, oh, five, six dollars an hour, if it's cash."

He'd have done it for nothing, but then she'd suspect something.

She sized him up, and he tried to relax and look harmless, but still with his shoulders back, spine straight, like he was strong and useful.

"You know," she said, smiling. "You kind of just made my day."

15

In the rearview mirror, Stuart's face was shiny and stubbled, his eyes bloodshot. The bruise on his forehead had turned purplish-yellow and had a scabbed-over gouge in the middle that wasn't healing right. Maybe it was infected, maybe he should have had stitches. He was covered in mosquito bites and hadn't had a hot shower in days. He ran a hand through his hair, wiped his face with one palm. He put a little Visine in his eyes and tried to smell his armpits.

He hadn't been swept away by the rain after all. A park ranger had come around with a siren and spotlight, insisting that everyone evacuate. So Stuart pulled up his tent in the pouring rain, collapsing it with half his things still inside and stuffing it into his trunk. He plowed through the rain for an hour, looking for anyplace open all night, but found nothing. Eventually he just pulled over in an empty parking lot and crawled into the backseat for a few damp, cramped hours of sleep. At dawn he started driving again, and now here he was. He was home.

His car was cluttered with the videos he'd been making for Danny: shots of moose swimming from island to island, of deer standing calmly just fifteen feet away, of sunrises and sunsets and road signs, but mostly just of Stuart talking and talking, trying to understand what the hell he was doing. He gathered up all these movies and the trinkets he'd bought for Danny in truck stops and convenience stores. He stuffed them into a used grocery bag and headed up the sidewalk.

The front door was unlocked, but there was no one inside. The living room was littered with children's blocks and balls; there was a chart of the alphabet taped across one wall, another of the United States, hand drawn, hanging above the couch. Danny was twenty-six now, but their mother never stopped trying. Stuart walked through the kitchen, where the counters were covered with mail and catalogs, and made his way out to the backyard. It was early evening and hot. Danny and his mom were at the back of the yard, where they had set up a sprinkler. Danny's pale, chubby form was shirtless in a pair of baggy orange swim trunks, stepping in and out of the circular spray of the sprinkler. Their mother stood just out of the spray, mostly dry, holding a towel to her chest for when Danny was ready. She had a heavy, wide torso, and gray hair loosely gathered in a long, thin ponytail that rested on her back.

"Stuey," Danny shouted. He trotted over to Stuart and clamped his hand onto Stuart's shirt, leading him toward the sprinkler. Stuart submitted, as he always did, and let Danny lead him right into the spray. It would wash the smell off him, anyway. His brother considered this a boon, shrieking and clapping, jumping up and down. Stuart joined him, mimicked him, which made Danny even happier. This was what Danny did for you: he made you let go of everything that used to seem important, everything that confused you. It all went away. Stuart felt the water soak into his shirt and shorts, filling up his shoes, rinsing the mud and campfire grit off him. He crouched right down to the spray to get his hair good and wet till his head ached from the cold water, then he pretended to scrub his hair and wash his armpits. He took off his shirt and lassoed it over his head before launching it into the neighbor's yard. After this he and Danny chased their mom through the yard, trying to hug her with their big wet bodies.

When things calmed down, Danny stood for a long time looking at Stuart's scruffy, dazed face with concern. Then he reached out a hand and pressed his fingers against the big bruise.

"Ahhh," Stuart said quietly through the pain, trying to back away without upsetting Danny.

Danny smiled and pressed again. He always enjoyed provoking a reaction. This time Stuart closed his eyes and took it, made his face blank despite the throbbing. Danny pressed it just one or two times more, then gave up. "Let's get you changed," their mother said brightly, and Danny dropped his wet trunks on the patio and followed her into the house. Stuart wrung them out and hung them on a lawn chair.

They ate dinner in silence because Danny would smack his hands against his ears and pitch a fit if anyone spoke at the table. Next to Stuart was his dad's empty chair no one sat in. Before he died, during the silent meals, his dad used to look up from his plate every few minutes and make goofy faces into the windows' reflection so Stuart could see them without turning his head. And Stuart did it back. The ban on noise, on laughter, made it all funnier somehow; they were always red-faced and teary-eyed by the end of the meal, back then.

After dinner, Stuart gave Danny the grocery bag of videos and souvenirs. Danny's eyes flared, and he clutched them to his chest. "They're for you," Stuart said. "I'm not going to take them away."

Danny watched him suspiciously, inching backward out of the room and down the hall to his bedroom, where he stayed for the rest of the night.

"He'll be up all night," their mother said.

"I'm sorry. Should I have given him just one at a time?"

She smiled and shrugged. "It's okay."

Stuart and his mom stacked the dishes in the sink but didn't wash them. She got out a carton of chocolate ice cream and two spoons and set it between them at the table. "To what do we owe the honor, my dear?"

He shrugged. "I had an idea. I thought, maybe, if you wanted a vacation or something, some time to yourself, I could watch Danny for a while."

She raised her eyebrows. "I'm fine. You don't have to do that."

"You must get tired of this."

"What is this business on your head?" She waved her spoon around her forehead.

"I uh . . . I don't actually know."

"Ah," she said, processing this.

"You could take a vacation. I can watch him."

She shook her head. "Maybe I like it here. Maybe I'd like to see *you*."

He chewed his lip. "Sorry I haven't called in a while."

She kept on nodding. "You've been traveling, I take it?"

"Uh-huh."

She smoothed her hands across the table. She had been beautiful years ago, with a wide, flat face and dark hair, like an Indian princess. He remembered her that way, before the stoop came into her shoulders and her eyes went gray and slack. "Any particular reason?"

"I lost my job."

"Huh."

Other kids, when he was little, had to lie to their parents. His had never given him any reason to. They had always just seemed so grateful for him, whatever he did, however he managed to do it. Compared with Danny, he was always good enough.

"Kate didn't tell you?"

She shook her head.

Sometimes it seemed that Danny had worn all the edges off his mother. Nothing seemed to spark any reaction in her. She just took it all in, let it roll down off her back and out the door.

"She didn't call you?"

"She called last week. She asked if I'd heard from you. But I hadn't. I didn't think much of it."

His cell phone had rung all day that first day, until he turned it off and locked it in his glove box and let it die.

"I left her. I left Kate." He'd been saying it all this time, first to Adam and their friends, then to strangers he met at bars and at the campground. As if saying it would make it more real, more permanent. Irreversible.

Now his mom's face actually changed, actually registered some kind of alarm for a second, before she worked to conceal it.

"I just—I don't know, *took off.* I didn't even tell her." And now his breath came quick, his voice cracked. The weight of it was suddenly bearing down on him. "Can you imagine?"

She opened her eyes wider, and he tried to explain himself—the awful house, his screwups at work, the things he and Kate had said, but his mom said nothing. After he finished, he stared at her and waited. She poked at the ice cream with her spoon and cleared her throat. But then she didn't say anything.

Stuart moved his hands through the air, clenching and

unclenching them in the way Danny did, reaching for words that escaped him. "I don't think she's ever going to love me. Not really. Which turns out to be a pretty shitty feeling, day after day."

He squinted up at her, desperate, but she just gazed back at him. "I'm sorry."

"I couldn't stay there like that," he said.

She put a hand over his. "Sometimes I think . . ." She cast her eyes around the table. "I think sometimes we didn't . . . prepare you right. We were different, you know."

"It's not that. It's not."

She sighed. She looked so pained and guilty, it made him feel awful. But he had to ask her.

"How do you live with it?" he said. "With Danny?"

She got up and went to the sink, started shifting the dishes around, running the water. He had heard other people wonder this when she wasn't around. *God, how does she do it?* But nobody ever came out with it to her face. He thought he had blown it, that she wasn't going to answer. But finally she said, "I don't think of it like that. I just hang on for dear life."

"No matter what?" he said. "Even if it just . . . even if it messes you up?"

She rolled her eyes at him, smiling a little.

"I think you should call her, at least," she said. "Let her know you're okay."

"I have no idea what to say." He took the dish towel from her, started drying the dishes. "Indecision, you know. It's not very attractive to women."

She laughed. "Say that."

They finished the dishes, put them back in their cupboards. It was bedtime; her eyes were matted over. She would go off, and he'd be alone again. "This feels wrong," he said. "But when I'm around her, that's not right either."

She rubbed at the back of her neck for a long time. "I wish you were feeling better. Does that hurt?" She touched her fingertips gently to his forehead.

He leaned into her hand until the whole of it was against his head, warm and familiar. It felt like so long since anybody had really touched him.

"I have some painkillers," she said. "I have some really good ones."

"That'll fix everything."

"You've got to start somewhere, Stu."

They stood for a while looking at their reflections in the dark window until his mom pulled the shade down and went off to bed.

16

On weekday mornings the parking lot of Lowes home center was filled with quiet, solitary men wearing work pants and boots. They were older, mainly, with awkward haircuts and hunched-over walks and big bellies, and they kept to themselves. The aisles were broad and uncluttered; people moved slowly and rarely made eye contact, never chatted or touched. It was safe. She liked the smooth, orderly parking lot; the spare, tidy landscaping; the big blue peaked entryway angled to match the shape of her own ordinary old house. The inside was like a low-budget cathedral, with exposed metal beams thirty feet above and endless stretches of bright aisles that made her feel, though insignificant, as if she were within reach of some higher power. Anything anyone could ever need was right here on offer, at low-mark-up prices. As in church, no one pestered you except when you checked out or asked for help. No one tried to dazzle or woo you; they just left you alone to wander and help yourself to your own sheets of drywall, your own ceramic tiles, your own sink or dishwasher. The illusion was that it was all yours already, just waiting for a ride home.

Kate made her way through the sawdust and chemical smell of the entryway, past the jugs of fertilizers and pesticides, down an aisle of PVC pipes, through the electrical supplies, and on toward ductwork. She knew a faster route but took her time.

What she needed today was insulation. The man she'd met in the driveway, the garbage hauler, his name was Walker, and she figured that at six dollars an hour she'd be a fool not to use him as a drywaller. She had broken down and called her dad's partner Al, who was sending over an electrician tomorrow. Once he finished his work, she would just need to insulate the walls, and then she and this Walker could hang the drywall, and aside from woodwork and flooring, the project would be just about over. She was getting back on track. She had checked the Internet for the right kind of insulation and measured her walls to figure out how many rolls. Now she stood in the aisle sizing them up, trying to decide how to get them all home in her hatchback.

At the end of the aisle a thin, pepper-haired man had cocked his head sideways and was squinting down the long row at Kate. In front of him was a cart with one roll of ceiling insulation and two gutter extensions. She turned her head quickly to avoid his gaze, but here he was coming right up to her, pushing his stuff. This wasn't supposed to happen. There was no socializing at Lowes. "It's Kate, right?" he said.

She put on a mask of preoccupation, nodding just slightly. But when she glanced over, she remembered: the dog. "Oh yeah," she said, smiling. "You're, you're . . ."

"Jay," he said. He was wearing a black T-shirt and long tan work shorts and boots. He had the lean legs of a runner: calves bulging under compact, knobby knees. A twisting black tattoo ran up one shin and vanished around back.

"Right, Jay. The dog is hilarious. We love him." Another tattoo made a thin, black ring around his wrist.

"Oh, good. I'm glad. I miss him."

She nodded. Was she supposed to invite him to visit Ned? She wouldn't. Yet there was something about him, now as before, that soothed her. He didn't know her, she realized. To strangers, she might look innocent, harmless. They couldn't begin to fathom the mistakes she'd made.

"Insulation, huh?" he said. "You guys have already finished the demolition? That's fast."

She nodded. "Do you know anything about this? Am I supposed to put plastic sheeting over this stuff?"

"Don't need to," he said. He stood still, perfectly comfortable in the silence that followed.

"Thanks," she said. She was wearing a ratty, stained T-shirt and cutoff shorts. Her hair was dirty, her face makeup-free. Still, he just stood looking at her. Didn't he have anyplace to be?

"What are you working on?" she asked, to fill up the air.

"Oh, just some gutters. Repairs. It seems like every few days I end up back here for something or other."

"Me, too. Something about . . ." She stretched out one arm to gesture vaguely at all the stuff on the shelves, but she couldn't articulate the sensation. She blushed.

"Yeah," he said, thinking for a minute. "I like it here."

"All the little projects," she said.

"It's like everything in here might, I don't know, make your life a little better. Or that's the hope."

"Yeah. Exactly. The hope. We could write a commercial for them."

"We'd have to leave out the frustration part, of course."

She laughed. "That comes later."

"Well, if you guys ever want to bring the dog by, or whatever, you're always welcome."

"Great," she said, and this must have come out sounding final, dismissive, because he gave a little wave and walked back down the aisle.

At the car it was clear she had overestimated. She had managed to smash five packs of insulation into the car, and she had strung a rope through two more rolls and was pretty sure she had them tied tight to the roof, but there were still three more packs she couldn't fit anywhere. She was going to have to go back in with the receipt and return them when a pickup truck pulled up next to her. It was Jay.

She felt ridiculous. But he didn't laugh or tease her, didn't ask how on earth she had expected to fit all that insulation into her Civic. He just acted as though this happened to him all the time. "Throw them in my truck."

She raised her eyebrows, screwed up her face. "I could pay you?"

He made a grimace.

"Sorry," she said. "You really wouldn't mind?"

"Nah," he said. "Where do you live?"

"Well . . ." She stared at him, wondering if she could ask.

"You want to go in and buy more of it," he said.

She nodded.

He scratched his chest with one languid hand. "Hey, it's summer. I don't have much going on."

So he gave her a ride back to the entrance of the store and waited while she rushed in for another cartload of insulation. He followed her back downtown, his red pickup loaded with Pink Panther insulation. In her rearview mirror, at the stoplights, she could see him nodding his head to the beat of the radio and drumming his thumbs loosely against his steering wheel. He had a delicate face, all angles and hollows, covered with a scruff of light stubble. He didn't wear sunglasses or a hat but just squinted out from under the windshield visor.

When they got to the house, the garbage guy had already hauled away the big pile next to the Dumpster. She expected Jay to pull in and park behind her in the driveway, but he just sat idling his truck in the street, not even parking it yet. He was staring up at the house with a taut, open mouth, as if someone had shown him something gruesome.

17

They had painted it, landscaped it, put up a fence. But it was still the same house. They'd replaced the front door, washed the windows, redone the driveway—all things that, in a perfect world, someone would have done for that family all those years ago. Wiping up the blood, the broken lamps, righting the overturned furniture would never be enough. If a family was supposed to come home and restart their lives, their house needed more than two guys with buckets and mops.

"This is so nice of you," Kate called to him through his open truck window as he sat there gaping at her from the street. Jay would have to get out. There was something about her, something sad and fragile in those weird green eyes. But the house—he had gotten over the house. He didn't want it hulking in the back of his head again.

"I'm such an idiot, thinking I could get this all home in my little car." She reached into the truck bed and hauled out a roll of insulation.

"No problem." His throat went stiff around the words.

"Come and see Ned, if you want."

"You know, I remembered something I have to do."

That was all he had to say, and suddenly a mask dropped down over her face like an alarm door. She was locked up behind a bright, fake smile. She vanished. "Of course," she said way too fast, too sweet. "You must be in a hurry. I can get these myself. They're not heavy. I am possibly the toughest woman you've ever met." She grinned. She tossed the first roll in the driveway and grabbed another just as fast, and it was true, she looked like a ranch hand in that moment. He watched the lines of the muscles in her arms and legs as they flexed and shifted.

It was just a house. Cement, stone, wood, insulation, and shingles, with a bunch of pipes and wires snaked through the insides. In a small town like this, all the years he'd spent cleaning, of course it made sense he would end up in the same place twice. And actually it had happened once before, when he was still in college: he went to an after-hours party in Ypsilanti, and it was crowded and loud and he was very drunk, but he saw right away that he had been there before, on a job. He remembered the scene he had cleaned up—a burglar who'd been bashed in the face and skull with a baseball bat, right there near the fireplace, where all the cute girls were dancing. It sobered him in a terrible flash, and he had to wait outside in the cold until his ride was ready to leave.

"Maybe you can come see Ned some other time," she said, still making that twitching smile. So bright and—what was it?—brave. It was like looking at an orphan who thanked you profusely for stopping by after you said you couldn't adopt her. What had happened to make her like this? Jay reached into the truck bed and grabbed a roll of insulation. "I'll help you with these."

He could just take the insulation to the porch, stop there; maybe play with the dog outside. He could stand on the porch and talk about her remodeling plans and maybe shake her husband's hand when he came home. All of this he could do without going in.

But she was quick across the porch, and there was Ned with his nose against the front window. When he saw Jay he jumped up and scratched wildly against the glass, barking until spittle flew everywhere. Then she was inside; she'd unlocked the door and was just past the threshold. She grabbed Ned by his collar, but he strained against her to get out the door and onto the porch, maybe down the street. What could Jay do? Just two steps. Just inside the doorway.

The place was even darker than he remembered. The walls were just studs, a rich, rough, clay-colored brown, not the smooth blond of modern two-by-fours. There was nothing but the floor plan to remind him of that night here. The only real space you could even call a room was straight ahead of him, the kitchen, which was painted a pale butter color with fresh white trim, and had a giant bed staked in the middle, like an altar.

"It's a big place," he said dumbly.

She looked around, as if seeing her house for the first time. "Thanks."

A strange calm settled between them, and he realized: she was different inside these walls, suddenly not twitching, not stammering, nothing but at ease. She was like women he'd seen holding newborns: made strong and calm by their sudden and total necessity.

It calmed him, too. Just a house. Someone else's house now. On the header between the hallway and kitchen someone had marker-penned a grocery and to-do list that started with *Buy strawberries* and ended with *Get a new life.*

She blushed as he noticed it. "I'm stripping the banister." She gestured at the staircase, where the woodwork looked diseased, with patches of oak peeking out through the layers of maroon and dark brown paint. He thought for a while. Brown. It had been brown the last time he saw it. And Claire—pale, white-headed Claire—had been wandering up it, looking around and around. It seemed so long ago. They'd been barely older than his students, just kids. They had thought they'd be artists, and now she was gone, and here he was, a shop teacher. And not even hating it.

Kate was watching how he stared at the place. If he wasn't careful, she would hear his heart thumping in there. "Imagine building all this by hand. Before power tools," he said, trying to make himself think about that.

She beamed.

The furniture was gone, the carpet stripped away. The shooting, he knew without thinking, had happened upstairs, above his head, in that big front bedroom. It was okay, it was fine. It was over. He knew people who, in his shoes, might tell her the story of her house. He'd heard Mack do it to people more than once, completely oblivious to the way their faces changed afterward.

For the first few months after that night he'd spent here, Jay caught glimpses of Claire on campus and around town. She wouldn't talk to him. He would try anyway, at least just to apologize. But whenever he got within ten feet of her, she just held up one palm, shook her head. If he opened his mouth, she'd say, "Don't even talk to me." The stitches on her cheekbone had been pulled out, but he could still see the little blue-gray puncture holes where they'd gone in. Their friends asked him why they'd broken up, but by the way they asked, Jay could tell Claire hadn't told anybody anything.

Ashamed, he thought, she must have been ashamed, no matter how backward that was. So he held that secret, too, if that's what she wanted. All he said to anybody was that, whatever had happened between them, it was all his fault.

Ned was groaning and pawing at the back door. Kate moved through the kitchen to let him out, and the open door threw a gust of hot air through the rooms. Jay didn't believe in ghosts, but when it brushed past him he bristled and thought, *That's what one would feel like.* He hurried outside after Kate and the dog, slamming the back door behind him.

The yard, he had no memory of the yard. It was small but packed with overgrown perennials and trees, like some secret garden from a movie set. One strange, creepy thing after another, in this house.

Later that fall, Claire started disappearing—first from classes, then even from parties and shows. The rumor was, she was getting into things—meth. The rumor was, she'd taken up with some dealer in Ypsilanti, an older guy none of them knew. On the rare nights when they showed up at parties together, people said they didn't smell right. Their eyes were crazy, they hadn't showered, they giggled and snorted about things that weren't that funny. Then November came, the cold, rainy weeks of midterms and sleet when everyone lay low, and even her roommates stopped catching sight of her.

"So, are you going to the break-in party next weekend?" Kate was asking him.

Jay blinked at her absently, trying to bring himself back.

"Break-in. Yeah, probably. You?" Every summer, for one long, late night, the teachers and staff who could be trusted to keep the secret broke into the high school and threw a drunken, teenage-style party—usually in the windowless gym or poolroom or theater. It brought everyone back to that high-school thrill, where throwing or going to a party might actually get you into serious trouble. Anyone who didn't incriminate himself was suspect, so if you didn't go one year, you never got invited back into the loop.

"My husband likes to go to them," Kate said, but in a vague, distant way. It didn't really sound like an answer.

Ned cruised the yard, peeing on every plant he could reach, then went out of sight in the back corner of the lot, sniffing as if he'd found an intruder. Jay could hear him snorting and grunting, could see the leaves rustling around him.

"She's really gone off the deep end," Claire's roommate said to Jay one night, around Thanksgiving. "Ever since you guys broke up. It's like you were her anchor."

"Don't say that," her other roommate said. "Claire does what she wants. Nobody's ever told Claire what to do."

It was old news now. Claire had been gone so many years. He'd made peace with it.

"So, do you have any advice for me, about this project?" Kate said. She was holding open the back door for them to go inside again. He hesitated, holding the back porch railing, but she had already turned and gone in through the kitchen and down the hall back to the front entryway. He looked all around, screwed up his face. The dog glanced back at him, and Kate did, too. Okay. He followed them in.

She said, "Am I doing this right? After the electrical work and the insulation, is there anything I need to do before I drywall?"

Jay looked around at the studs, ran one hand along a few. "You should fire-block these," he said. "The inspectors will make you do that."

"Fire-block?"

The house was balloon framed. He pointed at the exterior wall next to the staircase to show her how the studs ran without a break from the floor of the first story all the way up to the attic, and how by code you had to put blocks in there between each floor. "It's sort of impressive. You'd never find lumber long enough for that anymore. It's old growth."

Her eyes followed his hands, taking it all in. "Cool. Tell me more."

By Christmas of that year Claire was on the news, or her picture was. It was also stapled up all over Ann Arbor, in every floor of every campus building, on every outdoor bulletin space, in coffee shops and bars, bookstores and gas stations. Claire's face before and after the scar he gave her. Claire with her piercings, without. Claire with long hair, short hair, head shaved. Claire was everywhere, because she was missing.

He glanced around, up the staircase, toward the second floor. Felt a shiver. It was time to get out now. "Sorry," he said. "Sorry. I've got to go."

18

I should have called." Stuart sounded frightened, as if he was bracing himself for whatever Kate would say to this.

She just squeezed the receiver until the hard plastic shell of it made the bones of her fingers smart. It was him. Calling on a sunny, windy Friday evening. Her husband.

"I'm sorry." He cleared his throat.

Kate watched a tendril of ivy slapping against the kitchen window from outside. If she left it unchecked it might keep growing, she thought, might cover the whole window in shifting green, then stretch across the clapboard to the next window and the next, and she could live nestled in this greenish cocoon, where no one could ever see her. "I probably would have screamed at you," she said after a while.

From his end of the line she heard a faint huff of surprised recognition, a laugh.

It was true. If he'd called right away, weeks ago, she would have still been under the impression that she could or should control their lives. A deadening detachment had taken over her since then.

"I was afraid I would say the wrong thing," he said.

She nodded, but of course he couldn't hear that. She lay back on the bed and gazed at the window some more. From this angle, if she squinted, it was like a big porthole, and the green leaves outside were the sea her house was drifting through.

"I feel like I'm always saying the wrong thing," he said.

They were talking very quietly, slowly, as if they would have to pay a high price for each word.

"Me, too."

"I don't know how it got this way."

She pulled the blanket over her, covered her tense bundle of bones. Outside, the neighborhood was filled with the smell of lighter fluid and charred meat. Through the quiet of her kitchen, occasional bursts of laughter bloomed like fireworks from blocks away.

"I'm at my mom's now. I went camping. The Upper Peninsula. Remember when we went up there?"

She did. It was the summer after junior year, nine years ago. They packed a canoe and some backpacks and went two weeks in the wilderness of the UP, portaging between lakes and rivers, living on granola and walleye.

"Two weeks without a shower, without buying anything, just the two of us," he said.

"Did you do that last week? Were you backpacking?" She wanted to say, *Don't do that alone. What if something happened to you?* But she stopped herself. He had revoked her right to worry about him.

"No," he said. "They turned it into a campground. There were motor homes and everything. Bathrooms, gravel. It was Wal-Mart camping."

She knew where he was headed with this. "We got older. Things change. People change."

He was quiet for a long time. She could hear him breathing, that soft, familiar whiff of life transpiring between them. For a second, under the covers like this, she felt so close to him, in bed with him. But that was an illusion. She stood up abruptly to put it out of her mind.

"I didn't want to change," he said. "I thought I would go up there, retrace our steps. I thought I'd go out in the woods and have some kind of revelation."

He made a rueful laugh that said he hadn't.

It would have been nice if one of them could have just had an affair, she thought, a brimming little secret side life that could elate one and devastate the other and make a clean, set-able break. Theirs was a stress fracture, the kind of thing you could go on living with for months, maybe years, a nagging deep wound that only an X-ray could see. Maybe people had affairs for just this reason, to make the problems obvious. But now he was gone: How much more obvious could you get?

"Kate, I don't want to wake up someday and be gone, find myself living someone else's life, someone else's idea."

My idea, she wanted to say for him. But instead she just said, "Me either."

"And I don't want to be this person who ruins your life." His voice squeaked. He was breathing hard again.

"Me either."

But that was the most they could say. No one asked, no one told. They just sat there, holding their phones, keeping quiet together.

19

Jay dimmed the lights and eased his car to a stop a few streets over from the little strip of woods that separated this ranch-house neighborhood from the four lanes of Seventh Street that ran next to Frontier High. In their dark clothes, he and his friend Marcos slipped between two boxy houses and into the woods, jogging over the mulchy path, feeling loose as kids. Probably there were other teachers and staff all around them, trying to sneak up to the side entrance of the school. It was 10:30, a full moon, hot and humid. They pushed through another patch of brush and came out at the edge of the woods, facing the wide, well-lit street. He and Marcos hesitated, waiting for a long-enough break in traffic so that no one would see them. There. An opening.

They did a hundred-yard dash over the sidewalk, curb, pavement, over the dry institution grass, across the fire lane, and up to the door. It opened. They had the right spot, the right night, they were safely in. And behind them, sure enough, in rushed three others they hadn't even seen—two women Jay didn't know, and his friend Serena, who taught Spanish. The five of them stood in the hallway for a second, letting their eyes adjust to the darkness. Marcos pulled off his dark, hooded jacket to reveal a bright red Hawaiian shirt and orange swim trunks. "Victory is ours," he said, clearly drunk already.

Serena just laughed, but the two younger women gave Marcos a strange look. "This is our first time," one of them said anxiously, as if somebody was going to ask her for a password.

"Ah, follow us." Marcos clapped an arm around each of them. The rest of them trusted his lead and followed the outline of his stocky form, his shaved head that gleamed when they approached the red EXIT signs. They turned a corner and listened, hearing the faint trace of music and a cackle of laughter on the floor below them, so they went down past the foyer, past the theater. They bypassed the administration hallway and headed for the locker rooms.

Raucous voices and the smell of chlorine: it could be a teenager's graduation party or some kind of celebration after a swim meet. But instead of the parents and teachers being gone, the kids were gone, and everyone could stop keeping order. There was an unspoken expectation that everyone who showed up tonight would do at least one immature and ill-advised thing. The history of break-in night was filled with pranks and streaking, hookups in classrooms or in dark, abandoned hallways. Very few people woke up the next day without embarrassment. The good news was, you didn't have to go back to work with these people for another five weeks. In his own adolescence Jay wouldn't have been caught dead at a party like this, but once a year now it was okay: he liked the theatricality of it, the way the teachers seemed to be acting out a fantasy of a teenage bash that maybe none of them had actually ever experienced.

The boys' locker room was booming with Van Halen music that ricocheted off the tiles. The benches were scattered with clothes—lots of dark jackets and sweatshirts that people had worn to sneak in.

In the steamy poolroom there were fifty or sixty people already, mostly the younger teachers, with a few of the older, hard-drinking types mixed in. There were two kegs of beer in a baby pool full of ice, and a big yellow Gatorade barrel of margaritas. Someone had set up a few bowls of chips on a folding table, but they had put it too close to the diving boards and everything on it was soggy now.

A cluster of beer-bellied football and wrestling coaches were milling around in their big, baggy trunks near the base of the high dive, formulating a strategy or prank of some kind. The theater teachers, Nelson and Caravaggio, were sitting on the floor blowing up inflatable rafts shaped like whales. Lots of people were still fully clothed in black. Others, like Marcos, had gone for a beach theme, wearing gaudy Hawaiian shirts, bikinis and board shorts, leis and straw hats. These were probably the ones who had brought the beach balls and inner tubes that were floating in the water.

Jay got a cup of beer and followed Marcos and Serena up to the top of the bleachers, where they could watch everything from a safe distance. Marcos fired up a joint, and they passed it around. Down on the main deck, a couple of guys came running in from the girls' locker room, carrying big red tumbling mats they'd dragged out of storage. They threw them in the pool, then jumped on top, trying to surf them. One fell over sideways, nearly cracking his head on the edge of the pool.

"How come parties never looked like this when I was in high school?" Serena said. She was what Marcos, when she wasn't around, called luscious—curvy and dark-haired, half Puerto Rican, half black, with big drooping eyes and high cheekbones. Years ago, she and Jay had dated for a while. It didn't work out, but they'd been friends ever since.

"They did, Serena. You just didn't get invited." Marcos slapped her knee. He was one of the custodians and had helped arrange the party. He was an avid organizer. On warm Sundays he put together football games on the front lawn of the school; whenever it snowed, they all got calls to go sledding with him in the Arboretum. "No shit, though. Our idea of a party in high school was some Night Train and a bonfire in a farm field. It didn't look like this."

"Yeah," Jay said, thinking back. Between this party and that day at the house on Macon Street, he felt like he was trapped on memory lane. It had taken so long to catapult Claire from his mind, and now here she was again. Today at the grocery store he'd caught sight of a woman with short, platinum hair, and he whipped around to catch her face, to check if it was Claire. He had kicked that habit years ago, and now it was back.

"Were you like one of these dudes in high school?" Marcos said, pointing at all the aging jocks who were lining up now, two by two, to climb the ladders to the high dive and jump in in pairs, while the others in line called out scores, judging their awkward, plunging acrobatics.

Jay shook his head. "Not likely."

"Oh, I know. You were what, one of those spooks, a Flock of Seagulls kid?"

Serena sputtered out smoke, laughing. "I'd bet money on that."

Jay put his hands up, guilty. "Totally Flock of Seagulls."

"I knew it. You dye your hair then? Wear those safety pins and shit?" Marcos said.

"I'm gonna take the Fifth on that one."

Marcos laughed and shoved Jay's leg. "What do you think about her?" he said, gesturing with his chin toward one of the guidance counselors. Marcos and Serena started a running commentary on who was datable and who wasn't, but Jay wasn't paying attention. He had spotted Kate down on the other side of the pool, standing near some other math teachers under the scoreboard. She was wearing a long gray skirt and a blue tank top. She had one hand tightly clasped around a red plastic cup; with her other hand she kept smoothing back her thick shock of hair, almost compulsively. Behind her was the big purple mural of the school logo: a pioneer wagon charging over rocky terrain.

Kate turned and headed toward the deep end, waving one hand tentatively at that awful woman—what was her name? Erika Fleiss—who taught German. She had struggled her way out of East Berlin just two years before the fall of the wall and was clearly still bitter about the path her life had taken. However inaccurate it was, everybody called her the Communist.

"Ooh, bikinis," Jay heard Marcos say in a low voice as two PE teachers pulled off their shirts and shorts to dive in. His eyes were half lidded by now and glassy. "I'm gonna go swimming this year," he said. "In ten minutes, the three of us are jumping in."

"Yeah, right," Serena said.

"We are. I'm gonna find us some floaties, and we're going in. Ten minutes."

Jay pretended to listen, but really he was watching Kate approach the Communist over by the diving boards. Kate hunched forward, almost bowing to Erika, making apologetic motions with her hands.

"Look at this, Marcos," Serena said, gesturing with her chin. "I think Mr. *Jay* has finally taken an interest in someone."

"Uh-oh," Marcos said, following Jay's gaze.

"The Communist?" Serena said. "Really, Jay?"

"No."

"You're staring at her."

"Nope," Marcos said, leaning over to get a better view. "He's checking out Kinzler. Who, by the way, is married, yo." Marcos was the ultimate source of information about everyone in the school. He read through the things he found in garbage cans—old discarded grade books and reference letters—and even rifled through file cabinets when he got the chance. He knew the salaries, habits, and review history of everyone at Frontier High.

"I'm not staring," Jay said. He was just thinking about how nervous she looked. He was thinking about how, at some point, somebody was going to tell her the story of her house.

"So, do you know her?" Jay asked, and Marcos and Serena burst into a fit of inebriated laughter.

"Okay, okay," Marcos said, composing himself. "I mean, aside from the obvious, right? Kind of hot, wound tight, terrified half the time. Kids like her, or would like her, 'cept they're scared. She brushes 'em off. Tough grader, man. She's next in line for department head."

"Already?"

"Hell yeah," Marcos said. "Just look at her. Wired tight."

Two football coaches went wrestling by on the wet tile, trying to throw each other in the pool, until one of them fell down and the other one decided to just dive in.

The Communist was squinting in a guarded way at Kate, holding out one hand, but Kate pulled something out of her purse, a Ziploc bag.

"Hey, now." Marcos smiled and pointed. "What's in that bag, honey?"

In the bag was some kind of paper, which Kate unfolded carefully before Erika's face. Marcos made a disappointed groan.

"So what's your story with her?" Serena said. Since they'd broken up, Serena had taken on a sort of big-sister role in his life, always trying to get him to date people, always asking why it didn't work out.

"She and her husband adopted my dog." Jay shrugged. "No story."

A beach ball came their way, and they put their hands up to keep it alive. Sammy Waters, a short, three-hundred-pound bowling ball of a physics teacher, made it to the top of the three-meter diving board and gave a whoop as he cannonballed in, splashing half the crowd. But just then the lights flickered and the music and noise were blurred by the piercing buzz of the fire alarm. "Oh, shit," Marcos said. Like the other janitors, he had pulled more strings, taken greater risks than the teachers to make this party happen. Everyone else stood looking around at the others—some nervous, some cavalier, in proportion to their seniority.

"It's got to be a fluke, right?" Serena said. The school had false fire alarms as often as rainstorms—why should tonight be any different? "But does the fire department automatically come out?"

"Not sure," Marcos said, hustling off toward the exit. "Hold on, everybody, I can handle this!" he shouted, though with his bleary eyes, flip-flops, and Hawaiian shirt, he seemed too drunk to be trusted.

"Are we screwed?"

This was what everybody was saying. They had dropped their voices, and someone turned the music off. It was like being in the basement of a teenage party while the cops circled outside.

Kate turned around just then and caught Jay staring. He felt his face go flush, but she raised one hand in a wave.

Then the lights flickered and went out entirely. The room went wholly black for a few seconds. People gasped, a few shrieked, and someone splashed into the pool. Then the red exit lights flickered on at three corners of the room.

"I think we should get out of here," someone said.

Soon everyone was pushing toward the red lights.

"Shoot. I'm out of here," Serena said. "I need this shitty job."

"Serena?" Jay called, but she was already gone.

Fifty or sixty people wasn't that many; the room hadn't seemed crowded at all before, but now the wet deck of the pool was jammed with bodies jostling this way and that, desperate not to get caught, not to get fired or arrested or whatever might happen. They were *teachers*, for Christ's sake, each of them was thinking. How embarrassing.

"Shit, calm down. They can't fire *all* of us," some man's voice called out. But it was horribly slurred and drunken, the exact opposite of reassuring.

Jay himself felt a strange lack of urgency. He pressed his body against a wall and let the others shuffle around him. People were calling out to the friends who had driven them, trying to connect and arrange meeting places, rides home. Some were planning different exit routes, analyzing the likelihood of capture in one hallway or another. And there, across the pool where Kate had been, Jay heard a woman's voice say, "My letter."

It was familiar. It was Kate.

The room was already clearing out. By the time he felt his way along the wall to her corner, there was no one left to struggle against. And he heard her again, and saw her faint form, kneeling and mumbling now, "My letter."

He heard a splash, saw the edges of her body going down into the pool.

"Kate," he said. "You okay?"

He seemed to hear no more voices, only that infernal buzzing alarm. He couldn't hear her. He felt his way to the edge of the pool and crouched down. "Kate?"

"Fuck," she said, and her voice was angry, not drowning. "Fuck." On the second word the alarm turned off suddenly, so her voice echoed and bounced around the room.

"It's me. It's Jay."

"I lost the letter," Kate said, then dove under the water again. When she came up, she gasped and said, "It's here somewhere. It must have gone in. She must have dropped it."

Though he didn't have any idea what kind of letter could be worth this, what kind of letter would have to be carried around in a plastic bag, Jay started pawing through the dark, slapping the wet tile with his hands. Kate said, "I tried that. It isn't up there."

So Jay kicked off his shoes, took off his shirt, and lowered himself into the water, wondering as he slid down whether this was the shallow end or not, and thinking how strange it was that he couldn't remember which end of the room they were in.

He was high and a little drunk, and the dark air and water gave him no sense of up or down. He kept bumping his elbows and knees into the bottom, the walls. Occasionally he bumped into a beach ball or raft and freaked out before realizing it was nothing. Above the surface a strange new silence filled the room, broken only by the sometimes distant, sometimes nearby sound of Kate's own paddling and gasping.

And suddenly a flashlight beam entered the room. He groped for Kate's arm and pulled her under. From under the surface he watched the light beam move across the room, up and down the walls. He heard a man's muffled voice calling out, and sure, it could have been anyone. It could have been

Marcos coming to find him; the whole alarm could have been an accident. Maybe a joke. There might not be cops or fire trucks out front. There might not be any reason to call off the party. But suddenly Jay cared very much about his job; suddenly he felt he had everything to lose. He held his breath until he thought he might pass out, and told himself he could hold it just five seconds more. And sure enough, the light went away, and he and Kate bounced back to the surface.

They were within a foot of each other now, and he realized he was still holding tight to her forearm. He could feel the little hairs of her skin standing on end. He let go. They stayed there silently dog-paddling, tucking their heads low under the ledge of the pool, winded but struggling to breathe quietly.

They listened and listened until Jay felt sure they were alone.

"Kate," he whispered.

"Yeah?"

It was there, between his fingers, he felt it: a melting-down flimsy piece of paper wrapping itself around his hand.

"I found it."

Their faces were suddenly blanched by fluorescence as the lights came on. They ducked under the water again in fear, before realizing that of course water wouldn't hide them in the light. They came up and looked around. No one was there. There was no trouble. At least not yet. He pulled his wrapped hand slowly out of the water, and when she saw it her face crumpled up.

She climbed out of the pool and tried to delicately peel the letter from his hands, but it tore where she touched it, so he just held still with it. She sat against the wall on that industrial tile, making him feel helpless and dim. She tucked her face into her knees, and then her shoulders started heaving up and down. She didn't make any noise. The letter draped over his hand was ruined, the ink washed out and blurred. He peeled it off his palm as carefully as possible and laid it out flat on his shirt on the floor.

Marcos came in. "It was just a fluke," he said. "We're perfectly safe. I can't believe those pussies ran off like that."

Marcos gestured at Kate, whose face was still pressed to her knees, and raised his eyebrows in a silent question.

Jay shook his head.

"I'm not crying," Kate said. "I'm not."

"Anyway . . . ," Marcos said. He gave a shrug. "We bribed James to clean the place up. And Mickey and I are taking these shitty margaritas to his place. You coming?"

Jay nodded across the pool. "Maybe later."

When Marcos was gone, the big tiled room seemed quieter than ever. Kate lifted up her head finally and wiped her face.

"I'm not like this usually," she said. "I don't want you to think I'm some basket case."

"It's okay."

She made a big sigh and shrugged, rolling her eyes. That mask again.

"Really, it's okay."

She locked her weird eyes on him for a while, as if testing his resolve, his trustworthiness.

"My husband left me," she said, shifting her gaze to the space over his shoulder, as if she was saying it just to hear it in this big echo chamber. "He took off. That's the thing. Vanished." Then she turned back to face him, as if she expected him to pass some judgment on her.

"Vanished?" He didn't like anybody using that word so easily.

"At first." She shrugged. "Then he called. Eventually, he

called. Like, to say he's *alive*. You know, don't *worry* or anything."

Her legs were alive with goose bumps and freckles. He laid one hand over her bare, cold foot. "People go away sometimes," he said. "They come back, too."

She stared at him for a long time, as if figuring the odds on this. Then she pulled her foot away from him abruptly. "I'm not, like, some girl you can rescue."

"I've never rescued anybody from anything."

She made a kind of rueful smirk. "I seriously doubt that."

After a long time they got up and went through the boys' locker room, then upstairs through the dark, empty school. Their clothes hung heavy from their limbs, and they left a trail of water on the floors of the halls they walked through. She carried his shirt and the letter out in front of her on her upturned palms, like an offering.

20

The second time he went in the house Walker knew enough to prepare. He got there early, parked out front and stared up at the place, breathing, taking it in. He took slow steps up onto the porch, feeling the decking sag and spring back with each step. One hard jump and he could break through the rotting wood into the crawl space below. What a hazard she had right under her nose. He stood in front of the door, touched the doorknob, which wasn't the same anymore. Even if he had his old key, it wouldn't open this.

She said, "Thanks for coming. Walker, right?" She showed him the work she wanted him to do.

He lifted his eyes and let them travel up the ravaged staircase toward the bedrooms, and then over to his left where Pops's big living room was all cut apart and hollow. A whistle slipped out of his mouth.

"It's a mess. I know. Excuse the mess."

He let her go on thinking it was her housekeeping that threw him. He tried not to see Pops there, hammering and sawing in his own time. He tried to slip into the role she expected: any old worker, here for the money, no idea where to find the bathroom or basement staircase.

"You live here long?"

She shook her head and changed the subject. They walked from room to room and she raised her arms to gesture at her various tasks and plans. Today they would be drywalling. As if drywalling all these walls would take only a day.

She was probably a decent person. She probably had no idea what she was doing to him, to his family.

She handed him a screw gun and a pouch of screws. And now he would put his gloves on and help her do it.

After a while another guy showed up, a wiry, spike-haired guy who wasn't her husband. He had dots up and down his ears from old piercings.

She stepped away from Walker, but he could hear her anyway, saying, "I was drunk last night. I'm fine now, really. I feel like an ass."

He said, "It's no problem."

"I'm under control. Really. You don't have to worry about me."

"I know," he said. "I just thought, maybe, if you wanted a hand here, I could help."

But she just stood there in the hallway, a twisted look on her face. "Why?"

The way she said it was like she had a raw open wound, where something had been ripped out. And shuddering around the wound was a clear, deep sense that she was worth nothing at all. It caught Walker's breath.

The guy just smiled and shook his head. What he felt for her, you could tell, was something way beyond. And if she didn't see that, she was really shut off cold.

His name was Jay. She introduced them. When Walker told him, "You can call me W," Jay said, "Like the president?"

then shook his head and just went on calling him Walker. Kate went in the kitchen to get a measuring tape, and Walker caught Jay shuddering as he looked around the living room, like he'd seen something. Jay said, "Place is a little spooky like this, don't you think?"

The rough brown studs were cozied in with brand-new bright pink insulation, and still he saw flashes of his mother, blood down her mouth, dripping off her chin and seeping through her yellow T-shirt, and Martin running off to hide, and that man, that man, her boyfriend, raising his hand again, and Walker couldn't stop it. "Yeah, spooky," Walker said.

The way they worked was, he and Jay wrestled up a big heavy sheet of drywall and propped it up with two wooden crutchlike contraptions that they built out of two-by-fours. When they got it tight against the floor joists above, Kate rushed in with a stepladder and a screw gun and screwed the board in place. It was tough, heavy, arms-over-your-head work, the kind that pinched up your chest and made you feel weaker than you were.

They were almost finished with the living-room ceiling when one of the crutch things—Jay's side, not Walker's—slipped out somehow, and the drywall board fell, plunking Kate hard in the head. Walker and Jay pitched forward to catch it. Kate's ladder teetered under the commotion, and they all ended up close, in a tangle, clutching each other and the ladder and the drywall board, which was dented and cracked from the fall.

"Shit," she whispered. "How many of these am I going to ruin?"

"Hey, it's okay," Jay said.

"I'm just so tired of this. What am I doing here?"

"We can still use it anyway," Walker said. "Just putty over the crack and the dent. It'll be fine."

She got down from the ladder and stood looking up at their work. "Yeah, that'll look sharp," she said. "Right here on the living-room ceiling. Nobody'll ever notice *that*."

Walker watched her.

"I'm sorry," she said quickly. "I'm sorry."

"Let's take a break," Jay said. "Let's get some air."

She got them three beers, and they went out to the backyard and sat in her lawn chairs. The sun was getting low.

"This is too much work for us, isn't it?" she said. "Can we really do this?"

"It'll just take a while," Jay said. "That's all."

"What one man can do, any man can do," Walker said.

They stared at him until he got uncomfortable. "Who said that?" Kate asked.

Walker shrugged. Pops said it. "I don't know. A movie?"

"I like it," Kate said. Her lips moved like she was committing it to memory.

"It was . . ." Walker thought for a second about the consequences and decided they would be small enough. "It was something my dad used to say."

"Smart man," Kate said.

"But just for the record?" Jay rubbed his hair back and forth, leaving it standing up. "Tomorrow let's rent one of those drywall machines that raises the board up for you and holds it in place."

"This is too much to ask," she murmured, to Jay, not Walker.

"No." Jay held his sweating beer bottle against the side of his neck. "It's okay, really. But with the machine it would be . . . It'd be *fun*."

They all laughed, then continued rubbing their arms and backs.

"So are you from Ann Arbor?" Kate asked Walker.

"I grew up here, in this neighborhood."

"Really?" She leaned forward. "What was it like back then?"

He looked around the yard, at Pops's jungle, all of his trees and plants overgrown or withering.

"Did you go to school here?" she said when he didn't answer.

"Went to Frontier." He nodded. "Was supposed to go to Michigan. Got accepted."

She gave him a curious look but kept quiet. Jay said, "What happened?"

Walker shouldn't have said anything. This was what happened. You gave somebody one little piece of info, and it connected to something else and something else, and before you knew it, they got to questions you couldn't answer at all. He shrugged. "Didn't work out." He could see it, the way she was looking at him, she didn't even believe it was true that he'd gotten in.

"Do you know who lived here before you?" Walker said.

She rolled her eyes. "Whoever it was, they had highly questionable taste."

Walker held still, just stared at her.

"It was getting rented out room by room, so it was pretty much trashed," she said.

A rooming house. Walker felt the air moving through his lungs, the rush of emotion overtaking him. He could do things; he could make her vanish. Reclaim what was his. "And before that?"

Her face flickered, then turned itself off. "I don't know." She turned away. Walker sighed, blowing out that feeling, getting rid of it. Nobody said anything for a long time. They just sat there staring through the branches at the house behind hers. It was propped up on metal I beams and blocks, its basement walls knocked out so that a giant dirt cavern yawned under the house.

"What are they doing over there?" Jay said.

"Getting a new basement," Kate said. "It's pretty intense."

Walker had seen it before when he'd come around after dark. It was lit up in the night by work lights the construction workers left hanging from the beams, probably to keep people like him from prowling in there.

"There was one bad contractor back in the twenties or teens who did a lot of these cement-block foundations," Walker said. "And now they're all failing. He was a scam."

Kate gave him an alarmed look, and Jay said, "It's true. I've heard that."

"You're lucky you got a stone foundation," Walker said, then cut himself off, inhaling. He wasn't supposed to have ever seen her basement.

She didn't seem to notice, though, just said, "It looks like a wine cellar almost. The walls are eighteen inches thick."

They sat quiet for a while longer. You could hear the kids screaming and laughing down on the corner by the ice-cream shop. That hadn't changed. When Pops was in a good mood, he used to sit on the front porch and listen to them, smiling. When he was in a bad mood or the kids got too screechy, he'd march down there and holler at them, then come home and slam the door. "Damn white kids think the whole goddamn world's made just for them." Walker closed his eyes for a second, let himself believe these were *his* guests, helping him with *his* house.

"You know what I do sometimes?" Kate said. "This time of night, at dusk, I take the dog out for a walk. People start turning their lights on, but they haven't closed their shades yet. You can see in everybody's windows, all these old houses, the furniture, the fireplaces, the dinners on the table. You can see how they live."

Walker froze up. He did the same thing.

"Peeping Tom," Jay said.

"I just walk by," Kate said. "I just mean, what you can see from the sidewalk."

"You can tell a lot about somebody by their house," Walker said.

"Exactly!" Kate said. "You *can*."

Jay gave them a skeptical look. "What can you tell about the people in this house?" He pointed at the house in the yard behind them, propped up over that big hole.

"They've got a lot of money," Walker said.

"And they want everything perfect," Kate said.

Walker went on, "Most folks just dig out a trench, replace one wall at a time. Which is a big production anyway, but this?"

"Yeah," Kate said. "They had to move out completely. All their power and plumbing and everything's disconnected. Why? Because occasionally, after a really hard rain, they'd get a little trickle of water in their basement."

Jay shrugged. "So you know them then?"

Kate's face flushed a little. She looked down and gave an embarrassed smile. "Not really."

"Ever talked to them?"

She shook her head and sipped some beer through her smile.

"So you don't know."

"We know the *house*," Walker said. "We know what the house says."

"Yeah." She laughed.

Jay shook his head, closing his eyes.

"Once I saw a great fight," Kate said, "when I was out

walking. The wife was shouting and screaming at her husband, *'Get out! Get out!'*"

"At this house?" Jay pointed at the one with no basement.

"No, over on Third Street. On the corner. And then the guy threw something across the room, made this *huge* crash. Like, not a dish." She stopped talking and got a funny look on her face, like she'd brought up a story she didn't know the ending to or didn't want to tell after all. Then she squinted out over the fence like the answer was in the air over there. "It had to be a piece of furniture or something, maybe a TV. And he stormed out the door, and I was just standing there on his sidewalk, totally dumbstruck, staring."

"Did he say anything?"

She shook her head. "He was tanked. Could hardly walk. He just sat down on the porch and waited for her to cool off. Next night, I went by, and they were out in the yard, grilling dinner together." She turned her palms up and shrugged.

"You want to do it?" Jay said. "Take the dog for a walk?"

The dog started wagging its tail and bouncing just because they all looked at him.

"Yeah. I could cook us some burgers afterward."

"I better get going," Walker said. Howard's son was taking care of him tonight, but still, Walker couldn't see eating with these people. It was bad enough he was helping her.

They worked like this for weeks, on and off, first hanging all the drywall, then mudding the seams and sanding them. The white dust settled deep into Walker's hair, making him look gray. He would lean into his mirror at home, puffing his cheeks and belly out, squinting his eyes: he looked like Pops, there was no denying it. Then he'd get out of his clothes and wash all the gray away and be Walker again.

He hated to admit it, but she was nice. She paid him on time, even tipped, treated him fine, like anybody. She had done so much already to destroy the place, strip its bones like a dead soldier, try to turn it into the kind of house her people would be proud of. When he stood inside, it got harder and harder to remember how the house had once been. It was hard to figure out how he would make it his again.

At night, after they finished working, after he went back to Howard's place and cooked dinner and got Howard into bed okay, sometimes Walker went back. He sat in Pops's garden again, in the thinking spot, just being quiet in the dark with the cricket noise and the Main Street traffic in the distance. The air was thick, humidity clung to his skin. Inside the house, his house, Kate's house, there was just the low dim glow of the downstairs bathroom light that she left on after going to bed each night. She must have been spooked in there. Her husband never came home. Walker never saw him.

It had been an hour now since all the lights but the bathroom one went out. Walker figured that was good enough and got up with his flashlight, went into the driveway, and scaled the Dumpster. He was getting better at this, getting quieter. She hadn't caught him yet, and if she came out now, he figured he'd just say he had lost something—his hammer, his tool belt—during work today, and thought maybe accidentally it had ended up in the Dumpster. Now that the neighbors had seen him come and go so often, maybe they wouldn't think twice about seeing him here.

The pickings were getting slimmer. The best things were probably the first she'd torn out—woodwork, cabinets, paneling, drapes—which also meant they were on the bottom of the Dumpster. And the bottom foot or so had become a sludge of plaster dust and rainwater, ruining everything.

Still, tonight he salvaged a bookcase he and Pops had built into the attic wall. He had almost forgotten about it, but here it was, in his hands, in his truck, a collection of one-by-sixes screwed together and painted purple by Martin. It was warped and had come apart at the joints when Kate tore it out, but it was his, solid evidence. He laid it in the truck bed as quiet as he could.

When he got home, it was the middle of the night, but the reverend was sitting at the dining-room table with his birdhouses. Walker brought him scraps of wood from time to time, and Howard glued them together and painted them. His son had started saying no when Howard offered them up, so Walker strung wire through them and hung them up all over the backyard. "Our menagerie," Howard called it. The birds were everywhere, loud and shitting on everything. But Howard liked it.

"Late night you're having," Howard said without looking up.

Walker sat down with him, put his elbows on the table. "Want some help with that?"

"You should be sleeping."

"You, too."

"What is it that you were doing? Out there?"

"I had some errands to run."

"Errands is groceries, dry cleaning, the bank. Things like that open at this hour?"

Walker rubbed his jaw. "I'm not getting in any trouble, if that's what you mean."

"That isn't what I mean, son. That's not it at all. I asked a simple honest question, in my house, with my guest and friend. Would it be too much to ask for an honest answer?"

Walker sighed. Could he be trusted? Could anyone? If he said he was with his sister, could he be sure she hadn't called?

He shrugged. "I been making some friends."

"Good. Good. It's not an answer, mind you. But it's a start."

"What do you say we go up to bed now? I'll clean this up."

Howard leaned back in his chair, crossed his arms, and looked at Walker in a penetrating way. "How are you finding life here?" he said. "Is it better?"

Walker smiled and nodded. Howard was just trying to extend the night. Sometimes he got lonely and would say anything to keep you sitting around. Sleep was hard for him.

"Sure," Walker said. "You been real kind to me."

Howard beamed a little. "Tell me about your childhood, your family."

Walker's heart stuttered. "Well. Your son said you knew my family."

"Sure did."

A flash of heat and tingles went through him. "I think maybe my pops did your gardening, at the church."

Howard squinted and nodded vaguely.

"I mean, you know our story, right? Maybe you know more than I do? Maybe you remember him? Or my mother?"

When he looked up, the reverend's eyes had glazed over. "What did you say your last name was again?"

Walker sighed. "Price. They lived on Macon Street. We did, I mean. Scofield and Loretta Price, and four kids. A whole batch of us. You remember that?"

Howard smoothed the tablecloth, lined up the pieces of scrap wood and paintbrushes. "Sometimes, the nights, I don't want to waste them sleeping." He pressed the lid of the paint can down and held it.

When Walker looked over, he caught a fearful look in the reverend's eyes, and Walker understood suddenly that he wasn't long for this world. And what would he do, Walker, when Howard was gone?

"Summer nights are like that," Walker said after a while.

The reverend pushed himself to a stand, screwed the cap back on the glue bottle.

"Naw, leave it, Howard. I'll get it." He nudged the man toward the stairs.

"Someday," the reverend said without looking back. "Some night, maybe you'll take me with you, where you go."

21

Look over here, Danny. Let's go down this way." Stuart and his brother were hiking along a dried creek bed in a forest preserve outside of Omaha. Stuart took a few steps up a smaller path that curved through some trees away from the creek. It eventually led up a ravine, he knew, and opened onto a great view of the rest of the forest. He thought Danny would like it.

They'd been coming out here for a couple of weeks. It gave their mother a little time to herself, and Stuart thought maybe with some hikes like this he could build Danny up, prepare him for a real camping trip somewhere. Nothing too far away, just a night or a weekend. But while he'd managed to get Danny this far through the new experience—an accomplishment in itself—nothing he did could get Danny to vary their route. He kept repeating the same path they'd taken on the first day, a two-hour hike along the main path, which was paved with mulch and wide enough for dog walkers and people with clunky, baby-seated bikes. This was hardly hiking. Danny wouldn't stray even a few feet: he kept to the same side of the path Stuart had used on that first day, touched the same trees and rocks Stuart had reached out to touch without thinking. He even stepped around the low spots in the dirt that had been puddles on the first day. It was like they were living inside a video that Danny played over and over.

"I'm going to go this way," Stuart tried, glancing over his shoulder to track Danny's progress secretly. Danny paused up ahead, took a few more steps forward. Then he sighed and turned around. "Stuey," he said in his deep, confused voice. The sun was filtering through the leaves up high, dancing across his face, and he blinked and swiped at it.

"I'm right here," Stuart said. He took another tentative step down the new trail. Last week Stuart had tried to take him to a different park, one that allowed camping, but Danny just scowled and wouldn't even get out of the car.

Now Danny stretched out his hands and opened and closed them in the writhing way he did when something was bothering him. He started breathing hard through his teeth.

"I'm right here. Follow me," Stuart said, reaching out a hand to him. But Danny had already started to make that low, moaning sound that preceded a fit. Stuart stepped closer to him and crouched low, looking up into Danny's eyes. "Can you do this for me? Just try it?"

Danny latched his hand onto Stuart's arm, pinching the flesh of his forearm tightly and leading him forward, back down the creek bed.

"Okay." Stuart sighed. "Okay. Calm down. You win."

Stuart had been trying to practice with him in other ways, which were failing as well. He pitched a tent in the backyard, put two sleeping bags in it, and crawled in. Danny smiled like this was crazy mischief. He moved his palms along the nylon walls for a long time, half an hour at least, enjoying the way the fabric gave, the way he could see through it. He crouched down in the tent's opening to look at Stuart in there. "Come on in," Stuart said. "It's so nice in here."

"No." Danny smiled. "Nonononononono."

"Okay," Stuart said, kicking back and making himself comfortable. "Man, I'm so comfortable in this tent. This is the best tent ever. This is all a man needs."

Danny made a delighted shriek and ran back into the house.

To try to make his case, Stuart started sleeping out there. His mom had been using his old bedroom for storage anyway, and the tent gave a little more privacy than the couch. Danny refused to go into the tent, but in the mornings, first thing, he would come outside and unzip the doorway to look in.

"Good morning," Stuart would say. "I slept so well in my tent. I'm camping. Camping is so fun." Danny would zip it back up, then down again, playing something like peekaboo. Sometimes Stuart would wake to the sound of the zipper in the middle of the night and realize Danny was out there, peeking in at him. The closest he'd come to success was a few days ago, when Stuart woke up feeling hot and crowded. He shifted in his sleeping bag and realized that Danny was lying there pressed up next to him—not inside the tent but on the damp, dewy grass outside, with just the nylon tent wall between them.

There was another trail up ahead, a pretty wide one that veered off unobtrusively. Stuart casually got himself in front of Danny and just wandered down it, without changing his pace or mentioning anything. After a few steps, though, he could hear that Danny wasn't behind him. He had continued along down their usual route.

"Danny," he said. "This way. Come on. The car is this way." Danny flared his nose.

"Come on, let's go." Stuart tried to pretend it was Danny who had veered off.

It was one try too many. Danny bared his teeth and started grinding them back and forth till they made a squeaking sound. He pulled at his shirt and paced in a small circle, swaying and working up from a low, creepy groan to restrained, intermittent half shrieks. An old man walking by with his dog glanced over at them, and Danny, who hated to be looked at in moments like this, thrust out a palm to block his face, shouting "No!" at the man. The man's little dog lunged at Danny's legs, and then Danny really lost it, pacing and screaming, slapping his palms against his thighs.

"Sorry," Stuart said. "Sorry." The man rushed away, pulling his dog along, trying to forget he had ever seen Danny, trying to make him invisible.

"It's okay, Danny," Stuart said, stepping closer but keeping his side to Danny, his gaze turned away. "We'll just head back down this way. My mistake. Let's go home now."

There was nothing to do but ride out the fits. You couldn't comfort him. Sometimes at home on the couch he would curl up next to you or hold your hand, gaze into your eyes—all the things the world thought autistic people never did. But in moments like this there was no going near him. You just had to march along in public, letting him scream out his mysterious rage until he wore himself down. This time he screamed all the way back to the car and half the drive home. Stuart was ready to blow off his own splitting head by the time they walked through the door. He went straight to the fridge for a beer, while Danny marched back to his bedroom. Their mom was curled into their deep, raggedy couch with a library book and just watched him pass.

"Well, that went well," Stuart said.

His mom laughed. "You tried."

Stuart brought her a beer and sat down with her, on top of her feet, which she liked because they were always cold.

"Why do you care so much about going camping?"

Stuart shook his head, exasperated. "It's one simple thing I thought we could do together. One little thing."

"When you think about all the stuff our brains are capable of . . . ," she said. This was the explanation his dad always used to give. Forget about language or math or trivia: the simple ability to remember the millions of different routes we've taken, or feel the difference between seventy degrees and eighty, or know with our eyes closed whether the milk jug is full or half full, and how to pour it accordingly—when you thought of it that way, ordinary life seemed a maze of uncountable, split-second calculations. It was a wonder any of us could manage it, a wonder that everyone didn't melt down like Danny.

"I know," Stuart said. "But don't you ever want . . . something more?" He wanted her to open up, confess. He wanted to hear that she felt as cheated as he did.

"I'm fine," she said quickly, in her same old tired voice.

When he didn't respond, she said, "Really. I'm over it. Wanting more . . . it just sets you up." She raised one hand to make a sort of mountaintop, then pushed it over the edge, crashing to her leg.

"Yeah. But—"

She patted his leg and got up to check the laundry.

He went down the hall to Danny's room, wanting to knock, to say something to his brother, maybe apologize for pushing him like that. He cracked the door slightly and saw Danny in there sitting at the end of his bed, in front of the TV, watching the video of Stuart throwing Kate's magazines out the window. Stuart stood looking at their old apartment, at how small and dingy it was. It was such a stupid thing to have clung to. It seemed like so long ago. "Egaw!" Danny said, throwing his fist in the air to mimic the Frisbee-throwing gesture Stuart had made with each magazine. It looked like some kind of sporting event Danny was cheering.

22

Her house was growing walls. It was like watching a rotted skeleton grow muscles, then skin, then turn into a human being and walk. She had walls. Not bumpy shells like all those she'd seen in other old houses, pickled with decades of mad wallpaper and painted-in dust—no. What she had were smooth, virgin walls reborn, waiting for fresh paint like earnest teen models, eager to reinvent, please, please reinvent.

The three of them had settled into a tight routine, Jay and Walker hanging the drywall hour after hour while Kate went around with joint compound and tape, filling and smoothing the seams between each board. It was like frosting a cake. She took to it right away. They worked well together, handing off tools and materials with a grunt or a cryptic, "Pass me the thing." She knew the different smell of each man's sweat, knew what they took on their sandwiches and pizza, knew the glazed-over look that said they'd had enough for the day.

At nightfall they would shake the dust from their hair and clothes, pass beers around, and cook dinner on the grill. Jay and Walker helped themselves, like family. Except they hadn't damaged each other yet.

Walker often took off early—taking the construction garbage with him—and Kate and Jay sat in the backyard alone, listening to the neighborhood fall asleep around them. The dog curled up on the grass between their chairs, emitting aimless groans that the night swallowed.

"I've got the hands of an eighty-year-old," Kate said, rubbing at her raw, swollen hands, which seemed to be moving too slowly.

"It still beats standing in a classroom, no?"

"I thought you liked teaching shop."

"It has its moments."

"How'd you get into it? You don't strike me as your typical shop teacher."

"Oh?" He ran his fingers up the back of his head, scratching at the gray-black bristles of his short hair.

"Well, you just seem . . ." She moved her hands through the dark air in a vague way, hoping she hadn't offended him.

"How am I supposed to seem?" He squinted at her, a bemused look on his face.

He was five or ten years older than her, she figured, maybe more. And yet he didn't have any of the trappings of a staid, older life that she expected: no paunch or jowls, no condescending gaze, no family, no closed-off, frightened mind. He had his own kind of wisdom, sure, but in so many ways he was like a teenager: taut, curious, ready to try anything.

He shrugged. "I started with art. I did metalwork for a while, welding. And gradually wandered into this."

"You're an artist?"

"I'm a shop teacher."

"So you do like it."

He made a rueful grin, and his eyes glinted in the faint light. "Yeah. My students, you know, they all come in because they want to screw around with power tools. Which,

I'll admit, is fun. They're not idiots. But they've already failed a lot of classes. They come in all jaded, closed up, ready to hate me, to do just enough work for a D. But then something happens."

"Power tools?"

He tilted back in his chair, leveling his face to the dark sky. "They start to realize that knowing how to build things, fix things, is its own kind of power. Like, if you can change even one small thing—fix a lamp, build a shelf—it carries over. You can change anything."

Kate took in a long swig of the humid night air. "Yeah, I get that."

He grinned and flashed a glance at her, then went back to studying the sky. "Yeah. You've got the bug."

They sat for a while in the shadow of the house and its strange, tall, overgrown garden. She closed her eyes, melting into the chair, feeling the keen buzz of exhaustion coursing through her.

"So, do you miss him?" Jay said.

They could go hours without talking, just sitting there, and then he would come out with these quiet, piercing questions. She groped on the ground for her beer. "I try not to think about it."

"Really?" Jay turned in his seat, an intense look on his face.

She felt his breath on her, and a thrill rushed through her. She concentrated on the dog, rubbing his side with her bare foot, the fur feeling silky in one direction, then oily and coarse on the way back.

Part of her still expected Stuart to come home any minute.

"Yeah," she said. Every time she rounded the corner of her street, she checked to see if his car was in the driveway.

It was more habit than heartache. What she was discovering was a kind of shocked liberation, as if while she was sleeping someone had sneaked in and pulled from her mouth an aching molar that had been plaguing her for years. And now her tongue kept exploring the empty space there, but the pain was dying down. The nerve, once raw and thrilling to touch, was healing. *It's gone, it's gone*, was her panicked reaction each morning when her tongue hit the spot, but then she coasted back down and stroked that new, sensitive space. How interesting it felt: gone.

The day they finished the walls was her birthday, her thirtieth birthday, but she didn't tell them. She just went up to the attic and dug through all the stored boxes until she found her camera, then came back down and took pictures of Jay and Walker in the last completed room. In their dusty hair and clothes they flexed their muscles and grinned.

"You need a picture of yourself in here." Jay took the camera. "You did it."

She spun around the big, empty living room, feeling a smile growing across her face. The floors were still just the rough, exposed wood, and they hadn't yet put up the window trim, but the drywall was finished and primed, ready for paint. There were new outlets and switches, new wiring for ceiling lights. All the hardest, scariest parts of the job were behind her.

"I never thought we'd get here," she said.

"Sure you did," Walker said.

"I know a guy who refinishes floors." Jay was collecting their tools and setting them near the door.

She laughed. "I'm a little broke for that right now. I might just try to clean them up and live with them."

"What color paint you going to use?" Walker said, wandering around with his head cocked up at the ceiling, as if trying to picture different options. There was a sadness in his voice, she thought.

She had no idea what color. She had seven rooms to paint, and the halls and foyer. And woodwork to do, but essentially, once she cleaned away the dust, the rooms were habitable again.

"It's sure a lot of house for one person," Walker said. "Or two," he added awkwardly.

She glanced at him. She had never brought up the topic of Stuart with Walker, and he'd been polite enough not to ask. But now there was this gap in the truth between them.

"Let's celebrate," Jay said.

They hitched up Ned to go for a walk and stopped at the corner for ice cream, but Walker didn't want any, didn't even want to go in. He seemed uneasy among all those kids on the sidewalk, with their shakes and ice creams and sticky, screaming bodies. "I'll wait out here with the dog," he said. Kate had started to notice this more often now: he was the only black person in sight. She and Jay went inside and got in line, but she could see Walker out there standing apart from the crowd. He wouldn't even sit down on the benches.

He was a mystery to her, but a good one. He carried himself in such a dignified, quiet way, as if he had lived three lifetimes already but was keeping them secret. And whatever he might have guessed by now about her broken-up life, her mistakes, he didn't pry, didn't ask a thing about it. He worked harder than anyone she'd ever met outside her own family. And he looked at the house the way she did, like it was alive. That he'd never been to college, that he was black, that he did odd jobs and picked up garbage for a living—that they still had things in common despite all that—made the world seem smaller, closer to the way she wanted it to be.

And he was teaching her about the neighborhood. She could point to any apartment building or condo, and he'd say what had stood there before. He knew that the strange little garage on First Street had actually been a small drugstore once, and he could describe the bins of nickel candy inside, tell her stories about the owner. When he didn't know the history of a house, they would stand in front of it and by its details come up with the owners' story: the new car and gas grill and paver-block patio that said someone had just inherited a chunk of money or refinanced; the new fence that said they were starting a family; the long wheelchair ramp up to a back entrance that said, they hoped, somebody's aging mother or father was moving in.

When she and Jay came out with the ice cream, they all walked slowly uphill along Madison Street toward the park. The houses were starting to light up for the evening, and they could see inside some of the front rooms.

"What do you make of this weird little place?" Kate asked him, pointing at a tiny little one-story house that had always mystified her. It had two shacklike additions hanging off the back wall. The place looked ready to be condemned. Aside from a few maroon patches under the eaves, the paint was almost completely worn off, so the clapboard, where it was still attached, looked like driftwood.

"Oh, this was Granny Kenny's place. She used to scare the hell out of us when I was little," Walker said.

"Granny Kenny?"

"That's what we called her. I don't remember why. She had these legs that bulged out at the ankles, like varicose veins? And she would strap them up, but the straps were always undone, dragging along behind her on the sidewalk, all filthy."

"Did you ever see inside her house?" Kate said.

"My brother did. He snuck in through the window one time on a dare, while she was walking down to the corner."

"And?"

Walker's eyes flared, and he laughed. "He came out all shaken and wouldn't ever talk about it!"

"Uh!" They all laughed, crushed. Jay started walking toward the park again, but Kate lingered.

"But think about it. So . . . Granny Kenny's long gone now, right? If she was that old when you were a kid? So who lives here now? Who bought the place and left it like this, so creepy? What does it say about them?" The yard was knee-high with weeds, but there were flowers here and there poking through—some craggy roses, some asters and black-eyed Susans—and scattered near each one was a turned-over plastic pot from when it had been planted, however long ago that was. There were dozens of them, half sunk in the dirt and covered in rotting leaves.

"It's just somebody's house," Jay said. "Why does it have to say anything?"

"It says they're lazy," Walker said.

"Poor," Jay said. "If it says anything, it says they're just trying to get by."

Walker shook his head and kept walking. "All those potted flowers? They weren't free. That's just bumble-headed laziness. Somebody maybe, I don't know, sick." He wagged one finger near his temple. "It's not right."

Jay shook his head. "I don't like this game."

"Where did you live, back then, Walker?" Kate said after a while. They were entering the park now. She unhooked Ned and watched him bound away, the flab on his sides rippling with each step.

Walker hesitated, then threw one hand up westward. "Way over, uh, way over by Murray. Yeah, Murray Street."

"I love Murray Street," Kate said. It was a narrow little downhill, dead-end street with all the houses crammed closer together, but because it was so secluded, with no traffic despite its proximity to downtown, it had become a hot address. The houses were adorable, like Key West cottages, perfectly remodeled and maintained. "Can we go over there? Will you show us your old house?"

Walker didn't say anything, just kept walking, breaking away from them.

"Walker?" Kate said again.

He spun around, eyes all jagged. It sent a flare through Kate. Even the dog drew back. "No. We can't."

They blinked at each other. "Sorry, Walk," Jay said. "It's cool."

Kate's breath vibrated through her throat. Jay touched the small of her back. "Come on," he murmured, guiding her forward again. "Come on. Let's play some Frisbee."

She kept her eyes fast on Walker's back, feeling a buzzing in her limbs. There was a pressure in the air, the feel of bad weather that wasn't quite going to hit them. The dog was oblivious. He just raced around peeing on everything, picking up scents, reading the news of the neighborhood. The three of them spread out in the flat space at the bottom of the hill to play Frisbee. Kate was grateful for the excuse not to talk. Jay was a pro, throwing and catching the disk one-handed or under his leg, but Kate and Walker were no good at it. She kept jamming her fingers and missing it, having to chase it down. Once it caught the wind and sailed past her, going higher and higher, till it landed down the hill, in the brush that outlined the park. She ran over the hump and down the hill, and saw him, their resident homeless guy. He was in his usual spot. She could only make out the outline of his body, slumped in his sleeping bag. His cell phone, cigarettes, and an empty 40 lay in the grass by his head.

She caught herself staring at him. Something was familiar. He had the same black North Face sleeping bag as Stuart. He had the same color messy hair sticking out the top, the same curled-up, hunched-over way of sleeping. She stepped closer, bending over him, reaching one hand out.

"The light's getting bad." Jay came over the little hill and called down to her. "We're thinking we should head back."

The dog came trotting down and sniffed at the man, who rolled over suddenly and opened his eyes. He gave Kate a dirty look. She stared back dumbly.

"Sorry," she said to the man. "Okay, let's go." Ned had already lost interest and was sniffing his way back up the ravine toward Jay and Walker. Kate followed him.

"What was that?" Jay said.

"Nothing. I thought, I thought maybe . . ."

"But it wasn't?"

"No." The exposed nerve flared up like that sometimes, to remind her of what she'd lost, what she'd let go to rot.

They walked slowly back down Madison Street toward home. All the neighborhood was out, walking babies and dogs, riding bikes, standing in their yards by their grills. Whole families, parties, friends celebrating, coming together and laughing.

She was so quiet the whole way home that, when they turned the corner onto Macon Street, Jay tried to humor her. He pointed at her house and said, "Okay. So what goes on in this place?"

Kate didn't laugh or answer. She felt the dog tugging her

forward but she stood still, staring at the car in her driveway, which wasn't a stranger's and wasn't Stuart's. It was her dad's. And there he was, sitting on the porch in one of her LeMar's chairs.

"Your mother asked me to drop this off for you," he said. He was holding out a beautifully wrapped shirt box with a tray of brownies on top of it. "I had a meeting in town here today."

"Oh. Thanks." She introduced him to Walker and Jay, and the four of them stood on the porch, awkwardly staring at one another.

"It's my birthday," she explained apologetically.

"Oh. You should've . . . Happy birthday," Jay said.

"Jay and Walker have been helping, uh, with the house," Kate said to her dad.

"I'd like to talk to you," her dad said, and she felt sixteen again, staring up at his insistent eyes as they glanced from her, to Walker, to Jay. In his world, this would have been a cue for them to leave now, but they were poking into the brownie tray, so at home that they didn't notice. She unlocked the front door and led her dad inside.

"What's going on?" he asked.

"Look." She raised up her eyes and pointed around the entryway. New insulated walls led up to new ceilings, and the stair treads and banister were stripped down to beautiful oak. "Look at the house."

He gave a cursory glance around. "It's nice. I see it. I'm asking about you."

She stepped into the living room. "We opened up this entrance here, see? Expanded it. Isn't that nicer?"

He ran one hand along the doorjamb, stepping from the

entryway into the living room, and on to the dining room. He took the bait. "What'd you do here?" he said. "Is this the bathroom?"

"Yeah," she said. "Look, we bumped the bathroom wall out into the dining room. It was so small before. Remember?"

He took it in, nodding. "That was a good change," he said. "People will like that."

"Do you want to see the upstairs?"

He crossed his arms over his chest and exhaled. "Where's Stuart?"

"He's out of town."

Her dad stared at her, waiting. Julia had told him. Fucking Julia, with her mouth and her need to please.

"He's out of town," she said again.

"Right," he said. "Where? For how long?"

She went into the kitchen. Thank God it was clean. "Not long. It's a work thing. You want a drink?"

"Who are these guys?" He gestured with his jaw toward the front porch, where Jay and Walker were sitting on the railing talking.

Kate got out Stuart's vodka and fixed her dad a strong drink. "They're just helping me. Walker does odd jobs. Jay teaches shop at my school. We work together."

"These are your . . . what, your friends?"

She pressed herself against the refrigerator. She'd been holding her breath for so long now, she had to suck at the air. "Yeah," she said. "Yeah."

"And there's nothing you want to tell me. Your father. But you'll tell these assholes."

His anger was filling the air; she was breathing it in. Later on, when she had cooled off, it would seem possible to her that this was his way of saying, Hey, we've heard your bad news. What's happening? Why haven't you told us? But he was not a man who formed those kinds of sentences. This was the best he could do.

"I mean, a black guy?" he said.

A tidal wave rose in her chest and surged through her. She looked through the thin, single-paned front windows, saw Walker stand up, dust off his hands, and leave.

"So there's nothing you want to tell me," her dad said. "Nothing."

She looked at the floor, carefully composing her face, stripping it blank before showing it to him again. She was not going to cry in front of him. She swallowed back all the spit that had somehow accumulated in her mouth. "Tell Mom I'll call her."

"So what was that about?" Jay asked when her dad was gone. They were in the kitchen. She had opened a beer and was guzzling it.

"What, my dad? It was nothing."

He smiled tensely. "You're not a huge fan of the truth, are you?"

"What are you, Mr. Honesty?"

He shrugged, turning his hands up. "No."

"I haven't told my parents about Stuart. I haven't told anybody. But my sister found out. And now I guess she went and screwed me."

He ran his knuckles over the stubble on his neck. "But you told me."

"Yeah." She glanced at him, then lost her nerve and looked away.

"What's wrong with other people knowing?" He reached

toward her. She thought he was going to take her hand, and she froze. But instead, he just took her beer from her and set it on the counter.

"I don't know," she said.

There was a pressure in her chest as he looked at her.

"I don't *know*."

"Why would it be different from telling me?" He was closer now. One of his hands was reaching for her jaw.

"Because you don't know me." She drew back. This was too harsh, but it would stop him. "Didn't know me."

His face showed the sting of it.

"Because you're separate," she said finally.

He sighed. "You don't have anything to be ashamed of."

"You don't know how my family is," she said, and he rolled his eyes.

"You're a grown woman."

"I know." She laughed once, realizing how surprising that truth was.

"You can do whatever you want. Look what you did here."

A smile warmed through her, and she could face him again.

Her phone started ringing. They looked over at it, watched it lighting up. She shook her head.

"Let's get out of here," Jay said. "It's your birthday."

They drove out to Dexter, along country roads that cut through low, rolling fields that glimmered under the darkening sky. They didn't say much of anything all the drive out, just sat listening to the Lucinda Williams he had in his CD player, hearing her wilting, hurt voice cut through the air. When they pulled up in his driveway, instead of going around back, where she had been before, the day they got Ned, he took her around to the front of the house. He stood for a second, looking up at the place, with the egg-shaped moon rising in the blue-black behind it.

"Well, okay. Do it to me then," he said.

"Excuse me?"

He threw one hand up toward his house. "Tell me what it says about me."

She folded her arms. "It's not fair. You're not done with it yet."

"I'll be done with it when I'm dead."

"You know what I mean."

He shrugged. "Tell me anyway."

"I already know you," she said.

"Just try. I'm curious."

The house wasn't pretty. It looked like somebody's dead grandmother's house, if the grandmother was ornery and puritanical. It was covered in scratchy gray asphalt shingles and had almost no eaves at the roofline. The window trim was missing, too, or covered by the shingles. Bleak. Poor and bleak. Its front porch was missing. You could see the dark grooves where it used to connect to the front of the house, but instead now there was just a squatty cement slab in front of the door, with a rusted two-person glider sitting crooked in the grass beside it. The only good thing she could say was that the grass was well trimmed, even around the edges of the glider.

She said, "I mean, it probably says more about the guy you got the house from than it says about you."

"Okay. Tell me about him."

She sighed. "He was practical. Too old to keep up with painting, but he didn't have enough money to do normal siding. Or didn't want to spend it, didn't care. He put on those shingles himself. I'm guessing . . . late 1970s. After that, I don't know. Something happened. Maybe he lost somebody, or his money." She thought for a while. "No. He lost somebody. And he stopped caring about the place."

That was all she had.

Jay gave her an impressed, amused look.

"That true?"

He nodded a little. "More or less. What do you expect to find inside?"

She put up her hands and smiled wryly. "Well . . . Ten to one you've got some wood paneling in there. Floors covered in nasty wall-to-wall carpet."

He grinned. "I had some of that."

He walked up and unlocked it, turned on a light. But inside, it was like nothing she'd ever imagined.

He had taken out the walls. He had torn out everything. But it wasn't "gutted," at least not anymore. It didn't look anything like her house had looked over the past month. Yes, he had stripped the floors back to the original wide pine planks, but he had painted them a glossy, twilight-blue lacquer. Every wall that wasn't structural he'd removed, so most of the first floor was as open as a city loft. On the structural wall that ran the width of the first floor, separating what should have been a dining room and living room from the kitchen and bedroom, he had removed the plaster and left only the studs, which he had painted a pale, creamy color and covered in a thin, translucent white fabric. He had just stapled it to the studs, and where there were seams in the fabric, he'd left the edges frayed. It was like being inside a framed canvas that hadn't yet been painted on. You could see through it to the kitchen and bedroom, and could make out the wires and pipes snaked between each stud. He'd made a see-through house. But when he flipped a switch the whole wall lit up like one of those fake walls in theater that changes the scene. Between each stud was a can light that shot up from the floor to illuminate each bay. It was like stepping inside somebody's mad art project or dream.

"This is incredible," she said, walking around to take it in from all angles. There was almost no furniture: just an old couch and two straight-backed chairs painted red. A big yellow door laid across two sawhorses was his dining-room table. "Your house," she said, gesturing back out to the front yard, to what she had seen from out there. "It's in disguise."

She scrutinized him in his gray T-shirt and shorts, as if all this time he'd been in disguise, too, and she was only now getting a glimpse of him.

He smiled, amused. "I guess so."

She walked over to the long wall. "Can I touch it?"

"Yeah."

She pressed her hand against the taut, silky tentlike fabric. "Are you going to paint it? I mean, like a painting, not a wall?"

"I don't know. I thought about it, at first. But I kind of like it this way."

"Me, too."

"You hungry?" It was close to eleven, but they hadn't eaten anything except the ice cream and brownies all day. She stood watching him dig a frozen pizza out of the freezer and put it on a tray in the oven, thinking, *How strange. I'm in his house, in another man's house.* One of his cats slinked up against her bare ankle, and she shivered at the intensity of the sensation.

He opened the back door to let out the cats, and they all went outside. The night was still warm.

"You have a lot more stars out here than we have in Ann Arbor," she said. Who was that *we* she referred to?

"I've got a telescope, if you want to look."

"Cool."

He went into one of the barns to bring it out and then started setting it up in the back corner of the yard, farthest from the lights of the house and road. She walked over to the big metal sculptures that she and Stuart had puzzled over the last time she was here. They were people, she realized, distorted and abstract, as if he had sketched them from funhouse mirrors: big torsos, short wobbly legs, long arms. Others had scrunched little heads and arms, enormous long legs, big feet. Some were ridiculously skinny, others just as fat. It was a menagerie of humans, each turned beautiful in its proud presence, as if saying: Here we are. She liked thinking about what kind of eye, what kind of mind would dream these up and plant them here, where they would stare back at him every day through the windows.

"Is this your studio?" she called to him as she approached the big barn door.

This was the barn he'd come out of the first time she met him. She remembered the strange screaming sounds she'd heard then, some kind of machinery.

"Yeah," he said. "The light's on the left."

She groped along the cobwebby wall until she found the switch, and the place lit up. There were big steel worktables staggered around the room, an easel in one corner, a band saw and table saw at the other end. On the wall hung a welder's arc and mask, next to shelves and shelves of tools and paints and trinkets. And along the wall, between each window, she saw them: wooden boxes. Collage boxes, housing different pictures and trinkets. Some were covered in glass, while others were left open, almost inviting you to reach in and rearrange their contents. Some were on wooden pedestals and meant to be viewed from above. Some opened and had moving parts, like cranks or pulleys; others had glass doors locked shut with ornate, old-fashioned latches. On one like that, a key hung from a chain below, but when she lifted it up to the latch, it came just far enough not to reach the keyhole. They reminded her of houses, all lined up like that, with their separate, mysterious contents.

She heard Jay behind her, coming in.

"These are beautiful," she said.

"They're pretty old. Total cliché. The requisite undergrad Joseph Cornell phase. I don't do them anymore. Come look at the stars."

"I like them," she said. One in particular drew her in: the box was painted a flat, gray-blue color like her house used to be. There were handwritten words on slips of paper crumpled up, each word alone—*dues, seeds*—none of them adding up to any clear message in particular. The pale, grayish background, she realized, had the faintest trace of faces marked into it—luminous, confused, mysterious faces that disappeared when you shifted angles. And there were photographs. These, too, were crumpled and distressed, some torn in pieces.

"This one," he said, stepping forward as if to excuse it or distract her from it. "It's not really mine. I mean, I did it, but sort of for someone else, from her idea."

Kate lingered in front of it, still staring at the grainy, black-and-white photos. One of them was of Jay, she realized suddenly, a young, skinny, pale, black-haired, angry Jay shoving his hand toward the camera, blocking out most of his face. The other was of a child's bed, a low twin bed covered in stuffed animals, standing under two old-fashioned double-hung windows. And then she figured out what she was seeing.

It was her house. It was the guest room of her house.

She leaned in, putting her face almost right into the box,

squinting, touching her fingertips to the photo: two narrow double-hung windows lined up too close together, just like hers, one hung mistakenly an inch higher than the other. The thick grooved wooden casing just like what remained of her own, with rosettes in the corners just like hers, one missing, like hers, and wide-plank pine floors bordered by the same ten-inch-tall baseboard she had found in her basement. And there, just faintly visible through one of the windows, was the flat black roof of the apartment building next door.

"That looks like . . ." It didn't make any sense. "That looks so much like my house, like our guest room." She turned and smiled at him, ready to laugh off the odd coincidence, ready for him to say, "Yeah, isn't that weird? Those houses all look alike."

Later, she thought that a different kind of man might have done that. Might have shrugged, changed the subject, or glossed over it, made up a line about how many of those West Side homes were built from the same plans, with the same carpenters, same supplies, same flaws. And the woodwork all came in the same profiles from the lumberyard four blocks away. Just across from her house, after all, were two exact, mirror-image Victorians side by side. She would have believed him, she thought. And her life would have continued under its veil of easy ignorance. None of the rest would have happened.

But Jay didn't do that. He turned to her with a calm, open face, and said, "It is your house."

She backed away from the box on the wall and bumped into another, hearing parts rattle inside.

"It's not what you think. This was way back in college. I was in your house for, like, a few hours. It's just a weird coincidence."

"What . . ." She couldn't put it together. "What for?"

He sighed and stood looking at her. He could have said, "A party." He could have said, "I had a friend who lived there." But he was Mr. Honesty in that moment, he was pure, scratchy-voiced, earnest-eyed honesty. He moved his head from side to side and said, "It was work. I worked for a cleaning crew."

"Like, housecleaning? You were a maid?"

"Sort of."

"What do you mean, sort of? What kind of cleaning?"

He grimaced and waited and finally just said, "It was, you know, like industrial cleanup. It probably would seem strange to a lot of people. But it paid well. It helped people. It wasn't as bad as you might imagine."

She stood silently, trying to piece this together, scanning his face for clues, for an explanation. It was as if someone had ripped something else out of her, something she hadn't even realized she cared about.

"When was it?" she said.

"When was what?"

She didn't like looking at his face anymore, didn't like that pure, simple expression connected with the secret he'd known all along and had kept to himself. "I know about it, okay? I know about the murder."

"Kate." He stepped toward her. "It wasn't a murder. It wasn't like that at all."

"When was it?" she said. "Just tell me when it was."

He put up his hands, giving in. "Summertime. It was hot. It would have been . . . 1987."

23

The librarian was a gangly young man with an elongated face, long ears, long nose. He looked like a caricature of a hated politician. He nodded in a bored way at Kate's question, and sent her upstairs to a little glass-enclosed room with lots of nondescript, cheaply bound gray-and-blue volumes. It looked like an interrogation room. She went inside and set down her shoulder bag. She pulled out her notebook, her pen and glasses, and also, in its Ziploc bag, the letter. What was left of it. She hated to look at it. It was the only treasure the house had offered up, and she had gone and let it fall into the Frontier High pool—before she could even get the German teacher to translate it. The dark beige paper was now warped, the tiny slanted words all blurred and missing, and tears were ripped along the seams. No one could ever make out the words now, not even whoever wrote it, if they came back to life. Not even the names or addresses were clear anymore. Still, it seemed important to bring it, to keep all her evidence together.

She wasn't sure why she had come here, what good it would do her. Last night, as Jay drove her home, he tried again to explain. "It wasn't what you think," he said. "The shooting.

It wasn't some hideous crime. If you heard the story, you might feel better about it."

Shooting. Crime. Hideous. "I don't want to hear it. Not from you," she managed to say.

"It was a long time ago," he said.

"You knew all along, Mr. Honesty." She replayed all the looks he had given her, all the ways he had chipped away at her defenses, made her vulnerable all over again.

"I didn't think you'd want to know. I went to lots of houses. I got used to it. I didn't think of it in the same way you do."

"How about your house? Did you clean up a shooting there, too? How would that feel?"

A silence settled between them. "I don't know," he said. "But those things can happen anywhere."

"So you just went around following cops and coroners, is that it? With what, little mops and spray bottles?"

He sighed. "People need to be able to go back home. We tried to make it easier for them."

"Home," she said. They were in her driveway now. "Yeah. You made it easier for them." She slammed the car door and went up on the dark porch. Her own house, meanwhile, after all the work she had done to it, suddenly felt like just a crime scene.

It was a hell of a birthday, all in all. She let out the dog and turned on all the lights, walking from one big, sterile room to the next. Which room had it happened in? Suddenly she wanted to know. In the kitchen, she collapsed on the bed, with the present from her mother wrapped up on the pillow next to her. She was stiff as a corpse, every muscle clenched. And she knew the dreams on their way would be monstrous, so she just lay there, sweating and watching the light change across the ceiling, feeling her mouth grow sour, her eyes grow bleary and dry, until finally it was dawn. She closed her eyes for a while then, waiting, but sleep wouldn't come.

Eventually she got up and showered and found a T-shirt and jeans that hadn't been ruined by all her hard work. She picked up her mother's gift from the bed, weighed it in her hands, shook it. Last year, her mom had given her a lavender nightgown, silk and lace. It was the kind of thing Julia would wear, not Kate. She couldn't bear to open it and find something like that today. Unopened, it could be anything. She set it on the counter. She fed the dog and locked the doors, and walked through the quiet, painfully bright morning streets to the library.

She had to face it. Not hear it from Jay or a neighbor or whatever random person she might meet. It was her house. She needed to know it better than any of them.

She started with the old city directories, which listed each address that existed each year, and the names and occupations of the inhabitants.

1905. Up till then there was nothing, a block of numbers along Macon Street, 540–570, that had no names or designations. And then, in 1905, the actual address popped up, 558 S. Macon, with a name after it: *Gerhard Bauer. Plumber, Schumacher & Bauer.*

Something surged in Kate's chest. These were her people. They had slept under her roof, with walls as new as hers were now. They had started it all.

1915. *Katherina M. Bauer (Widow, Wm.).* So this was Gerhard's wife, this was when he died.

1936. *Theodore H. W. Ross. Driver, Dean & Co.*

1948. *Henry Gerald Ross. Mgr., Heinrichson's Dept. Store*

She went down through the years, writing down name after name—their jobs, their spouses. There were so many of them: nine owners over one hundred years. Each of them with their own jobs and plans and dreams. Some of them with the same last names, handing the house down the line after they died, probably the biggest gift they'd ever given or received.

But none of this was really what she was looking for.

There was another book, on the shelf below the city directories, that the librarian had mentioned. Its cover was black, printed with a grainy, obviously Xeroxed photo of three rows of police officers in old uniforms, from the 1920s or so. Their chins were raised high, their faces proud and clean, with oddly shaped mustaches and haircuts, all slicked with hair cream. *A History of the Ann Arbor Police Department.* Inside were news clippings and old photos, with short explanations. At the top of each page was a year. And below the year, all the major crimes committed in it.

She read about a stolen hearse in 1952—a fraternity prank. About two convicts, on the loose in 1963, who broke into a farmhouse west of town and killed a girl. There was a season of rapes in the Arboretum, 1974, the man never caught. There were fires and thefts, drunken misdemeanors, political protests, even car accidents. In 1989, a crazy, drug-addled man barricaded himself in his house on First Street and shot at several officers, wounding two. That was just a few blocks away.

All of this made it into the book, but nothing on Macon Street. She read every page. She went back down to the info desk, where she mumbled and stammered, "What I'm really trying to research is a . . . a crime. Apparently a crime happened in a—at my address. A long time ago. Seventeen, eighteen years. Is there a way to research that? In old newspapers or something?"

The librarian said they would need to know the date, or

at least the month or year, or else he'd have no idea where to begin looking.

"I don't know the date," Kate said.

"The courthouse might be able to help you."

The courthouse. That was an awful thought. Another batch of strangers and questions, and the possibility of finding out more than she wanted, all the information framed by nothing but felonies. That wasn't a house's history; that was a rap sheet.

"I know the months. It was summer, 1987."

He shrugged. "It'll take a while. But I guess you could look at the newspapers."

So he sent her to the microfiche machines, and she settled in. She threaded each week of the summer of 1987 through the machine. It took hours. Her eyes grew itchy and blurred the facts, but still she scrolled her way around the projections of miniaturized pages from all those years ago, pages that other people had held in their hands those hot mornings, crumpled up and thrown out or burned and forgotten. She read each front page from top to bottom, then scanned the pages that followed to be sure she didn't miss anything.

Shifts in interest rates, city ordinances to create green space, and a proposed tax hike for a new high school. A deer crashed into the YMCA window. A gay pride rally drew a big crowd. The five-dollar marijuana-possession fine got debated again.

Then she scrolled to the next page, and there it was in big black letters above the fold: ANN ARBOR MAN SHOT IN DOMESTIC DISPUTE.

She took her fingers away from the machine's little joystick. She put her hands on her forehead, shielding her eyes while she tried to take this in, to decide whether she could really do this. She turned away from the screen and watched a woman across the room pulling a book from a shelf and handing it to her small daughter, who held the volume with both hands, concentrating. They walked off together out of sight, and Kate stared beyond where they'd been to the windows in the wall. She was on the second floor and couldn't see much besides the high rise of the old YMCA building, but she knew that beyond that was the city, her city, eighty thousand people or so in houses and apartments. It was midafternoon on a sunny Saturday, and there were so many of them out there, cheery and removed, shopping for trinkets, meeting for coffee, carrying Cokes and ice-cream cones down the sidewalks. And a few blocks farther west they were mowing their lawns and lighting their grills. They were taking their kids to soccer games or kicking back on the couch for a baseball nap. She had seen from the crime book that terrible things had happened in these houses, these streets, these parks where women had been raped and beaten. It was no Disneyland. In the end, no place was safe. Every place had a history.

She turned her eyes back, gave the page a quick skim, on guard to shut it all out at any second and fill in the gaps however she wanted. But all she found were five flimsy paragraphs, a skeleton of a story.

> Ann Arbor resident Donald Baker Chenille was shot three times Thursday evening in the home of his girlfriend, Loretta Price, during a domestic dispute at 558 S. Macon on the city's West Side. Paramedics transported Chenille to University of Michigan hospitals, where he was pronounced dead on arrival.
>
> Police took into custody an eighteen-year-old man. Sergeant Henry Tyson of the Ann Arbor Police Department would not release the name and could not confirm rumors that the young man had confessed to the crime.
>
> Chenille suffered bullet wounds to his neck, thigh, and

abdomen. He was 38. He was known to some Ann Arbor residents as a regular performer at the Bird of Paradise, where he played saxophone with the John Davis band.

A public hearing is scheduled for July 27.

Loretta Price is the mother of four, widow of Scofield Price.

There wasn't enough here, not enough at all. She scoured the rest of the pages, but nothing. She went to the next day, scanned the front page, and saw another SHOOTING in a headline. This time there was a picture.

She stared at this thin black boy with close-cropped hair. He looked no older than her students, but was trying so hard to look tough and in control. Defiant. She thought of what kind of boy could be capable of such an act, what kind of family could raise a child to this. What had they done to let him go this far? As she stared at him, something about his eyes drew her in, held her. She counted back the years, trying to imagine if she might have somehow seen him around town or in school. But no, she'd moved to Ann Arbor for college well after this crime. Then it hit her. The face in the picture, that boy, it was Walker. Her Walker, the man she'd been paying and feeding and telling, "Make yourself at home."

She closed herself into the phone booth on the second floor of the library. She was having trouble swallowing. Her throat seemed to be closing up. She pulled out her phone and tried to breathe. But who could she call? Not her parents, not Julia, not Jay. Who did she have left? Stuart hadn't picked up any of her calls since the night he left. She had given up calling him after that first week. But suddenly, now, he was the only one she wanted.

She dug around in her purse for change. Maybe if she called his mom's house, dialed from the pay phone, so he couldn't recognize her number, he would pick up. She had nothing to lose. She plunked the coins in and listened as it rang. Once, twice, three times. Four. And then the funny delay and the beep and the voice telling her to leave a message. She breathed in and out. She was being recorded. "I need you," she heard herself saying. "Come home. Please come home." It was true. In this moment, at least, it was true. And she couldn't see past this moment; she didn't have the strength. She went on, telling him everything, talking into his mother's machine as if this might be the last word anyone ever heard from her. "I don't even know if you're still there," she said. "I don't even know where you are or if you're okay." Maybe she was regressing; maybe she was just desperate. It didn't matter. He didn't pick up the phone.

Her change ran out, and the line went dead. She hung up and walked back to the microfiche machine, checked the screen again to be sure. It was Walker, all right. She printed out the page and folded it carefully, tucked it into her bag next to the ruined letter.

The room buzzed with the low hum of lighting and machinery. She walked downstairs, past the librarian, past all the mommies and daddies, past the two homeless guys who hung out near the front steps, past the kids going into the YMCA and the shoppers and superficials on Main Street who drove in from the Detroit suburbs on the weekends for brunches and dinners. They were loud and ostentatiously cheerful, showing off all their good fortune.

One foot moved in front of the other. It was a perfectly sunny late-summer afternoon, and just because she was alone and had all this news didn't mean she was in danger. It didn't mean anything bad was going to happen to her. She didn't need any protecting, really. She could go home and sit quietly with the doors locked, or maybe on the front porch, and none of the house's dark history could hurt her. Still, she squeezed her cell phone in her hand, wishing Stuart would do what she asked and come home.

Jay's truck was parked in her driveway when she got there. He was sitting in the cab with the windows open, but his eyes were closed and he didn't see her approach. She opened her bag and pulled out the page with the article and Walker's picture on it and held it up between him and the steering wheel.

"What's this?" he said, then his tone changed as he saw the article. "You researched it."

"Look at the picture," she said.

It took him a little while, but then it hit him. "Oh. Oh, God." He climbed out of the truck.

She gave him a sick look and sat down on the porch steps. "I don't want to go inside."

"It's so weird," he said, more to himself than to her.

She looked up at him. She was so filled with anger, at him and Walker and everyone. It seemed somehow they had both conspired against her. "He *conned* me. He worked his way in here, into my house. Like you." The nearest window of the apartment building next door slid shut with an accusing thud. They were being too loud. The whole neighborhood could hear them.

Jay gave her a wounded look. "Maybe I should talk to him."

"About what?" she hissed, trying to keep her voice down. "Who to hit next?"

He exhaled, shaking his head. "He hasn't done anything wrong, Kate."

"Oh, really."

"Has he laid a finger on you?"

"I've been in this house *alone* with him."

"And did he give you any reason to feel anything but safe?"

Kate had done this already at the library: replayed every minute she'd spent with him, trying to re-create every comment and expression he'd made, every gesture, every move. She came up empty. All he had really done was what she asked.

"I'm not a monster, Jay. This isn't about race."

"I didn't say it was."

She chewed her lower lip, working one side till it turned raw, then switching to the other. Her chest seemed to be vibrating at high frequency. She wanted to hit something to knock this buzzing from her body.

"I'm saying, he *sought out* this house, Jay." She smacked the porch railing, and the pain in her hand felt outstanding. "He came around asking if he could haul away my *garbage*. Have you seen him do that for anyone else on this block?" She paused. They both knew he hadn't. "He singled me out."

Jay released a heavy breath. "Think about it from his perspective. He singled out the *house*."

"Okay, great. He's returning to the scene of the crime. That doesn't exactly make me feel any better."

"He's returning to the house he grew up in."

"Lovely. What a life that must have been."

"It was self-defense, Kate."

She stared at him, trying to see if she could believe this. "The paper didn't say that."

"His mother was getting beaten. Okay? She was getting pulverized."

She turned away, unsettled. "The paper didn't say that."

"The papers never say anything."

She sat digging her fingernails into her ankles. Then she realized what she had done and pulled her socks up over the marks. "I don't care," she said at last. "I'm sure he's a sweet guy, heart of gold. But I sleep in this house every night, alone. And he's right here in the neighborhood, and he's angry. And he's a murderer."

"Who says he's angry?"

"The fact that he can't leave this place alone."

"He grew up here."

"You grew up in Port Huron. When's the last time you went back?"

He swallowed this. He watched the dog staring at them through the window. "People are more than what they do," he said.

"I want to find him. You can come with me, or I can do it alone."

Jay insisted they slow down, think it over. "Have you eaten anything today?" He went inside and came out with some chicken breasts, and they went around back and he built a fire in her grill. He took his time. When they finally sat down to eat, Kate pushed the food around her plate. In her mouth the chicken felt rubbery and alive. She drank a lot of beer, and they argued some more until finally he gave in. "Okay, let's get it over with," he said, jumping up, but Kate had the feeling he was going along more to protect Walker from her than the other way around.

"Why are you so intent on defending him?" she said as they got in the truck.

The muscles in Jay's face twitched a little, but he didn't answer.

It was the kind of response she used to get from Stuart. So she was making another man hate her. She was getting good at it.

"I'm not," he said, looking at her. "I'm really not."

She sat and watched the houses go by. He drove slowly up and down every street on the Old West Side, looking for Walker's pale blue pickup truck. Neither of them could remember if or where he had said he lived now.

"He promised to come work tomorrow, right?" Jay asked. "We should just wait till he shows up and talk to him then. Sleep on it. Calm down."

"I don't mind doing this alone," she said. But it was a lie. She was afraid.

Finally, they turned a corner and came upon it: his old light blue Ford pickup truck parallel-parked on Sixth Street. There were other cars parked along the street; it was impossible to say which house he was living in. They went door-to-door.

At the fourth house an old, stooped, white-haired man answered, and when they asked for Walker, he cocked his head and narrowed his eyes a little. "Why do you ask?"

"We're friends of his," Jay said. "He's been doing some work on her house."

The man thought about this for a minute, moving his body over to cover the door opening so they couldn't see inside. "What do you want?"

But Walker came up behind them, from the yard. "What's going on?"

They stood on the porch, looking down at him.

"Hey," Jay said, as if they'd dropped by for a beer.

"Hey," Walker said, giving a little wave.

An odd silence followed. Kate couldn't speak. She just stood blinking at him, trying to transpose the face in the photo over the face of this man she knew. And trying to imagine how this quiet, calm man could ever have brought himself to kill someone. Then he seemed to recognize her confusion, her fear, like he'd seen it before. He gave a slight nod.

"We know who you are," was all Kate could manage to say.

He stiffened, stretched his shoulders back. He wasn't backing down, wasn't offering an explanation.

She could feel the blood rushing to her neck and face, turning her an ugly, splotchy dark red. "I read about you in the paper, what you did in my house."

Walker kept his gaze on her. He nodded again, but he didn't apologize.

"Now, miss." The old man stepped toward her. "This is my son. And my porch."

Kate turned from the old man and rushed down the porch steps toward Walker. "I want you to stay away from my house. It's mine. It hasn't been yours for years."

"You think I don't know that?" he said.

He leaned in toward her, about to say something, and a terror flashed through her.

Before he could speak, she turned and ran back to Jay's truck, scrambled in. She'd assumed Jay would be right behind her, would open his door and start the engine and get them out of here. But when she looked up, he was back there on the lawn, shaking the old man's hand and putting one out to Walker.

24

He knew what it was like to have people see a monster in him. The way Kate looked at him, not really seeing him. The way she scolded him like a teacher talking to a little kid. Like he had to be reminded he was worth less than nothing.

It was the way his mother looked at him. And the wardens, too. He recognized it.

And her friend, Jay, Walker didn't need his pity, his pussy-whipped explanations. He turned away from both of them, pounded the ground all the way back to the reverend's garage and threw open the door. Didn't know what he'd do there, but it was dim and hot, and he could be alone. He locked the door, then watched from the window to see if Jay was telling Howard anything. But he wasn't. He just got in the truck, and he and Kate shouted at each other a little and drove off.

Walker sat down on a step stool, feeling the sweat drip down the back of his knees and the middle of his chest. Breathe in, breathe out. They couldn't do anything to him. He wasn't *guilty* of anything. They could be mad, but they couldn't send him away. He hadn't broken any law.

After a while Howard came out and knocked on the garage door.

When Walker didn't answer Howard checked the door handle. "What's this all about?" he shouted. Then his voice got quieter, and he said, "Listen, are you in trouble?"

It was Howard's garage, Howard's lock and door handle. There wasn't much of anything that Walker owned or controlled in the world. He opened the door and stood, all worthless six feet of him, draining himself out to take whatever Howard would do to him.

"What's this about?" Howard didn't sound mad. He sounded like, *understanding*, like those TV dads Walker had never met in real life. Pops was a lot of things, but he was never that. Howard just stood there quietly and waited. He didn't say or do anything.

"I'm so sick of it," Walker mumbled. Sick of being suspected all the time, having to prove himself innocent to everybody he met—and then, even if he succeeded, having the shadows catch up with him anyway. He rushed past the reverend and out to his truck, and it grumbled to life, the last bit of his dignity.

She had scraped that house's skin off and gutted it, cut away every trace of what it had been. Of course it was hers, of *course* it was fucking hers.

He got on the highway, headed east, getting passed by every car around. They were bigger and shinier, twenty years newer and twenty-five miles faster. The people inside were white, were slick, were partnered up, two by two. It was Saturday night. They were families, kids, dogs, couples leaning into each other, even kissing. They had music and phones and backseats full of pillows and bags; they had babies in seats and under window shades; they had gray hair and sunglasses, rows of hats in the back windows. And behind, in truck beds and trailers, they had lawn mowers and couches, boats and Jet Skis. They had dirt bikes; they had everything. Walker's tailpipe started chuffing out smoke. It didn't smell good, people honked at him. He got off; it was Ypsilanti anyway, as good a place as any. These were the streets he was starting to know, the streets with lowlifes and ordinary black folks, Mexicans, Vietnamese. The houses were marked with security-system signs, the shops filled with liquor and Mexican food, the college designed for dumb kids and black kids and poor kids, part-timers taking loans and working extra shifts to pay for the big charade. It was a whole other country. And maybe Tasha and Martin and Moms were right: maybe it was where they belonged. Maybe it didn't matter how hard you tried to move up; maybe there would always be somebody higher to push you back down. And maybe they all—even Walker—had some of Moms's weakness inside them.

At her house only one light was on. He sat out front for a while, wondering if Tasha was home, if she'd heard his truck, if she might just come out on her own, save him the indignity of their mother. But she didn't.

He made his way up the sidewalk, onto the stoop. He tried to see in the window. Gunshots and sirens crooned loud from the big TV set in there. He had to knock extra hard.

But it wasn't Tasha who answered as usual, it was his mom. She stood in the doorway, shoving back the little yapping white dog with one foot.

She didn't say anything at all.

He felt his brow and temples twitch. He felt how much he needed her.

"Is Tasha home?" was all that came out of his mouth.

She shook her head.

"Know where she is?"

She shrugged. "A movie, maybe."

Neither of them knew what could happen next.

He said, "Could I wait for her?"

She hesitated, then took a step back and made way for him, so he stepped into her living room again, all dark with nothing but the TV glow. The dog jumped around at his leg, yapping and scratching. On the coffee table was a lit cigarette and a bag of microwave popcorn and a two-liter bottle of red pop with lipstick marks on the mouth.

She settled back onto the couch, leaning on one elbow, putting her legs up gingerly. They looked swollen, so big that the ankles seemed deformed. He took the chair.

She gazed into the TV screen like it held the keys to the future. Two men jumped into an unmarked car and raced off after a killer, who was driving his convertible with one hand and turning around to shoot endless bullets at them with the other. Total bullshit.

"How you been?" he said, feeling his insides shriveling.

He wasn't sure if she could even hear him, and she didn't answer. So this was what he got for saving her life.

He stood up and went to the TV, found the volume button, and touched it.

She flashed her eyes at him a second, then looked back at those men.

"It was awfully loud," he said, still standing next to the screen, still staring at her.

She pushed a handful of popcorn into her mouth, opening her palm. "You don't like it here, you're free to go."

"I don't want to go."

She darkened her gaze toward him. "You get kicked out of your house?"

"No."

"You sure?" She chewed and surveyed him.

He nodded.

"Good thing. You get into trouble, you're on your own this time."

"This time?" he said, bubbling over. "This time?" He turned off the TV, not thinking about the fact that this would put them in darkness. "Oh, I'm getting pretty good at being on my own, I think. Far as getting into trouble, maybe it's you who does that."

She reached behind her and switched on a light, which lit up her face from above, showing her skin shiny and uneven, her hair all nappy with a piece of lint in it. "This the same bull you been feeding Tasha?"

"I ain't fed her nothing."

"Sure. That's why she's all questions nowadays. *'What was he like, Moms? How did you meet him? What did he think of me?'*" She spat out the words, twisting her face up and tipping it side to side.

"What do you think I'd tell her? That you shacked up with a cokehead loser not even a year after Pops died, that he blew through all our insurance money? That if you'd a had more cash, maybe he woulda stayed nice to you longer?"

She got up and headed into the kitchen in her slow waddle. "We're not gonna talk about this."

"We are," he said. "You think if I'd a told her everything, she'd have questions left for you? You think she'd still be living here, probably helping you make rent?"

"Why don't you get out of here, Walker. Before I call Martin."

Walker shouted some melted-down mixture of words. He pounded his palm against the wall. "Goddamn it," he said. "I didn't come here to fight with you."

"Huh. Good job with that." She turned away again, butted herself up to the sink, and started sorting through the dishes and running water to wash them.

"I want you to look at me," he said, trying with everything he had to sound quiet, the way Howard had sounded.

"I *am* looking at you."

"In the eyes," he said.

She made a noisy sigh and jutted her jaw out, then lifted her eyes up to look at him. It lasted just a few seconds.

"I forgive you," he said. She huffed a nasty, ugly laugh. He went on, "Damn it, I paid time for this, paid my life for this, for you, those kids, that house. And I *forgive* you."

She said nothing.

"Why can't you do the same? I mean, you had a hundred grand when he died." Why couldn't he stop this? He'd learned to take so many hits inside, to lock himself up and show nobody anything, and now this swollen, nothing of a woman, this person who brought him into the world, he hated her, hated how fast she could make him come apart like this. "You had all his things, all of us. And you couldn't hold it together, to honor that man, not even for a year."

"Honor him?" She threw up her hands and turned back to her dishes. She moved them around for a long time, clanking, running water. When she turned it off she said, real quiet, "You think D. B. Chenille was the only man to ever hit me? You think your pops was above that?"

Walker leaned over her shoulder, over the counter, trying to see her, to read her, to peel back the layers of memory. He scraped the walls of his brain for anything: a black eye, a bruise, a thump from another room after bedtime. Pounding or screaming or sulking or cops or all the extra-nice behavior afterward that D.B. showed every time.

He came up empty. Absolutely nothing. "You're lying. You're making that up."

She shrugged and walked away. "I am a fifty-six-year-old woman, Walker Price. I seen it all. It don't really matter to me what you believe." She headed for the back door, to end the conversation.

"He woulda killed you," was all Walker had left to say in his defense. And then the other thing that had burned low at the back of his mind all these years came forward.

"Go ahead, say it." She stopped before the open door, stared at the knob in her hand, then closed it. "Sometimes you wish he *would* have."

"No," he said, but it took him a long time to say it.

"Did it ever occur to you," she said real quiet, "that mighta suited me, too?"

So she had felt after D.B.'s death what she felt after Pops's. He understood then the one thing he'd always blocked himself from realizing: she loved him, D.B. Whatever little broken bit of her was left after Pops died, she sunk it all into D. B. Chenille and turned herself over to him. The punches were nothing compared to what she'd been feeling. And all that Walker had done by shooting him was turn him into a perfect memory, a thing she could go on wanting the rest of her life.

His cheeks were wet. He wiped them with the back of his hand. "You *loved* him?" he said. "You loved him."

She stood staring at her reflection in the dark window of the back door. "I never was any good at being alone."

After that he didn't know where to go. He wandered dazed out the front door, down the sidewalk to his truck. Eighteen years and one asshole's life he'd wasted just for this. Maybe even his soul, for all he knew. Don't think that hadn't occurred to him. The truck fired up, despite the smoke, and he headed back toward Ann Arbor on the surface streets, where he wouldn't have to drive so fast.

And he shouldn't have done it, he knew he shouldn't, but the truck seemed to take him right back to Macon Street. He thought it would calm him down to see it. He parked and sat in his truck a long time, trying to say good-bye to the place, trying to wash it all from his memory. There were no lights on, no TV or music, not even the back bathroom light she always left on all through the night. It was totally dark, and her car was gone. He almost worried about her. He walked around through the neighbor's yard for one last look at Pops's old garden. Come daylight he would forget it all, give it all up, he would find a way. Everyone deserved a good-bye though, and tonight he climbed the fence again as he'd been doing so many nights all summer long. He dropped one foot in and then the other, and he listened for movement, for the dog, for anything. He stood in the backyard, her backyard, where he'd sat so many times, making friends with her. Making friends like a bitch-ass suburban white boy.

He crept up to the back of the house, put his ear next to the wall by the kitchen windows, where she'd be sleeping right now if she was at home. No sound at all. He inched around the edge of the window, peered in with one eye, holding his breath. By the faint lights of the appliances, he could see that her bed had no body in it, only the dog.

He should've just been happy with that. He should've just gone to his usual corner, sat down on that log, and done whatever thinking Pops had planned for him. The night was hot and dry; the grass crunched under his feet. She never took any care of it. But right there by his knees was the great temptation. The basement window he and Jerome used to sneak in and out of all through high school.

It hadn't even been painted. It was still that same old blue. The wood was rotted out worse than ever. It was bigger than any of the other basement windows, and Pops used to say this was the coal chute from back in the days when people burned coal, not gas. They even found fist-size chunks of coal to prove it. Pops knew something about everything.

And he had to test it, had to just find out for the sake of knowing. He put one hand to the bottom of the wooden window frame and gently pulled up and out.

That stupid woman. All those stupid fuckers. Eighteen years, and none of these smart-ass Ann Arbor bastards had given a thought to the fact that this window didn't lock, didn't even stick. It was like they were asking for it.

With the window wide open he could smell that old mildewy basement. *His* mildew, right? The times he and Jerome had to go down and mop up the rainwater, the trench they had to dig along the south wall one summer, trying to waterproof the foundation. The nights when he and Lisa Stilwell used to sneak around, in high school, while the whole world was sleeping.

He could see right through the window to the washing machine and past the old black boiler to that spot on the floor by the hot-water heater where Lisa had first gone down on him. Remembered staring at the bright yellow warning labels on the side of that tall metal cylinder, how he memorized them, how he would never forget the exact five steps for lighting the pilot of an Aquastar 450 hot-water heater.

Crouching in this woman's yard this way, his ass half hanging out the window, was probably more suspicious than if he just climbed in the house and got it over with.

So he climbed in. It felt natural, too. His feet knew just where to land on the washtub, his shoulders dipped down to avoid scraping the window's edge. His head, though, damn, brushed against the floor joists above, and came away sticky with cobwebs. Well, he'd gotten taller in those years inside; he'd suspected that. Hadn't even been done growing before they found reason to lock him away. Life of a black man, guys would say inside, but they were the kind Pops would've hated. Still, sometimes he thought there was truth in it. Never mind, forget about it. Get over it. He'd been in the house many times this summer, but only upstairs, only working, only in that other role, never just as himself, alone to think his own thoughts. And now more things came back to him, all those hours he and Jerome and Martin had spent playing down here, the way the air got cooler with every step you took down the staircase. Whole days they used to kill down here in the thick of summer, to keep cool, and Moms would come down sometimes, too, sit on the bottom step with little Tasha in her lap. He could see it, Tasha's hands roaming along the cool stone wall next to the stairs, looking up and around, slack jawed in that baby way, always on the verge of drooling, trying to put together the difference between the hot of her skin and the cold, stone, eighteen-inch walls their house was built on.

It was dark now, though, in the basement. He had to stare around, blinking, waiting for his eyes to adjust. And there, on a ledge, a flashlight. He would use it just a little, he would hold the sleeve of his shirt over it to mute it. He'd heard about guys in the big house who'd been caught burgling because of careless shit like this, shining a strange light around in a dark house. He wouldn't be one of them; he *wasn't* one of them. He would just stay in the basement, just go look at those labels on that old hot-water heater, maybe see if any of Pops's old tools were down here, in a corner, maybe *that much* he would take, but it wouldn't be stealing anyway, because they were his, by rights, or would have been.

But he couldn't find any. The old shelves where Pops used to keep everything were cleared out, filled with all Kate's paint cans and brushes and tools that were definitely new. No use to him whatsoever. And the hot-water heater, damn, the stickers on it were orange. No *way* he'd been remembering it wrong, all these years. He had lived on those memories eighteen hard years, survived by them. What else did you have, inside or anywhere, if your memories went false on you?

But then, relief: the year 2000 was marked all over those orange stickers. It was a new one, not an Aquastar at all. He remembered right; she had just replaced it, or someone had. In the end she would go and replace everything, and only the studs and joists would remember his name.

From there it didn't seem like much to take the first couple of steps up the stairs, just to see if maybe Pops's tools would be hidden in the ledges and shelves that lined the staircase wall. It felt so much like high school, like those nights after he'd walked Lisa home and had to sneak back into the basement and up the staircase, up to the second floor, past Martin's open bedroom door with a *shhh* and a wink. God, it was only high school, what a kid he was, doing shit like that with somebody's daughter. But then again, why didn't he do more?

And then he was at the top of the basement stairs, facing the closed door to the kitchen. So familiar, and yet clearly a violation. The nerves started to take him, his sweat glands heated up, but the urge was there, and he felt awfully sure she wasn't home.

He stood there a long time, thinking how stupid he was, how Moms was right when she said that nothing good could ever come out of him. So *yeah*, he thought. Yeah, why not? If this was what everyone expected of him, even Kate, even his mother, even himself, what did he have left to lose?

He pushed the door open, just an inch, took a look around. It was the same, basically. Their old kitchen. With the door cracked just that little bit, he made some kissing sounds. "Hey, pooch," he whispered. "Ned. Remember me?"

The dog was still for a long time, then roused himself and rolled to his feet, crouching on the blankets and looking all around, confused. Too stupid to even find Walker, three feet away.

"Here, boy." Walker tried not to sound afraid. He was still just poking out from the cracked door, and he figured, if the thing lunged, he'd just shut the door and hightail it down the stairs and out of here. Which would probably be a good idea anyway.

But the dog climbed down and wagged its tail and pushed its snout, sniffing and wheezing, into the crack of the door. He was so happy to see a human that his whole hindquarters shimmied from side to side. Walker closed his palm over the soft, warm fur of his ears.

So it was easy to walk right in. It was like he was welcome. When he came here the first time this summer, he'd been shocked to see the place, like a wound, all gouged out. But what he saw now was all new. It was like the scab he had seen was healed over, the walls smoothed up and primed, the woodwork going in, the plaster and construction dust all washed away, the rooms just waiting empty, like an advertisement for a whole new kind of life. And he had helped build it.

While he was working he had pushed the old insides out of his memory, or at least remembered only the good days, the Christmases before Pops died, the Sunday breakfasts, the day when Moms came home with baby Tasha, her girl. But now the other memories finally came flooding back. In the dark, under just this dim flashlight, the house transformed itself. It stopped being the house at Thanksgiving dinner, the house before Pops died, and it stopped being this bare, gutted-out thing that some other lady owned. It became the house as he last saw it, that last night before they took him off. He heard his mother screaming upstairs, hysterical, and

Martin and Tasha crying somewhere, too. And little Martin poked his head up from behind the couch when Walker came in, eyes all round and teary, and put a finger to his little-boy lips. "Shhh." Martin ran over to Walker and reached up his arms, which were splattered with blue paint, for Walker to pick him up. He said, "We gotta go. We gotta hide." He was so little right then, even at seven. But just then came a thump and a scream from upstairs, and Martin clung to him, trying to drag him behind the couch, but Walker peeled himself away and headed for the stairs.

He saw Martin's face again now, saw where everything between them had gone wrong.

"Any fool with a gun," he said later that night to the cops when they brought him to the station and washed the mess off him and put him in new clothes, "woulda done what I did." He wasn't sorry. He was the man of the house. Sure, only eighteen, but still the oldest, and Pops would have done the same thing. He had relived this scene a million times in his head, and he wouldn't take back a bit of it.

But what he hadn't seen before, not in the courtroom or at parole hearings, or when the counselors tried to make him talk, talk, talk, or in all those thousands of nights with his eyes closed on that cell cot, what he hadn't remembered was the before and after. It had all been blocked out, just blacked away. He hadn't remembered Martin like that, hadn't remembered that when he ran up the stairs there were already puddles of red there, his mother's, but at the time he didn't know that, just thought Martin had spilled his paints again and maybe even sparked this outburst somehow. Like it was justified. He really considered that.

When he rounded the top of the stairs into the bedroom, he saw her, his mother, with the blood rolling down from her nose and mouth, which were smashed, and he thought of the red puddles he'd just stepped over, and he turned to his side and threw up.

It had never been this bad. A fat lip, a bruised arm. Sometimes D.B. himself came downstairs with a black eye. This was something all different. D.B. looked up and saw Walker standing there, wiping his gaping, pukey mouth. He said, "Go tell your crazy brother to get the fuck out. This is between me and her." And he slammed the bedroom door.

Walker blinked. He was frozen. Then he heard Jerome shouting like a madman up in the attic. He ran up there, two steps at a time, to find Jerome bent over and digging things out of his dresser, throwing them onto the floor. "Motherfucking, cocksucking— Ah!" Jerome shouted, and out flew a bundle of underwear and then, in his hand, a gun.

"Jesus Christ," Walker said. "Where the hell you get that?"

Jerome started loading it. "This motherfucker cannot go on living."

"Calm down," Walker said. "Give me that."

Jerome pulled it away.

Something rose up in Walker, some piece of his pops. He leaned into Jerome's face, towering over him, and heard a strange, commanding, deep voice come out of him. It was nothing at all like Walker had ever sounded. It said, "You listen to me. I will take care of this." Up until then it'd always been Jerome who bossed and shouted and fought for things. But now Jerome sat down and handed over the gun.

It was heavy and already warm and wet from Jerome's grasp. Walker had never held one. A horrible thud broke out in the bedroom below, and Jerome nodded.

"Stay here," that voice said to Jerome, and Jerome stayed. He was just seventeen.

Walker went down the stairs quietly, slowly, holding the gun out in front of him like a thing that might attack him. He felt himself growing bigger, stronger, taking the form of Pops's body, Pops's mind. He already had the voice. He put his ear against the bedroom door and listened.

All he wanted to do, really, was point it. All he wanted was D. B. Chenille to get out of their house, to stop hurting her, to stop snorting their money and go live out on the streets where he belonged. On TV people pointed a gun and everyone backed off, did what you said. This was what he expected.

Instead. Instead, the room exploded. D.B. turned around, crazy-eyed, already high and fired up, out of his head. He didn't put up his hands and back away from Moms, whose nose and mouth were still dripping red. He didn't apologize, didn't beg for his life. He lunged. And Walker's first thought was that he didn't want D.B. taking that gun from him. It seemed important. It seemed that D.B. would certainly turn around and shoot them all, every last one. So Walker clenched his hands, squeezed the heavy metal thing. It went off. Of course it did.

A gut shot, awful, blood and groaning, some kind of foreign smell in the room. And Moms screamed out and rushed in between them, but D.B. still had the strength to shove her off him. So hard she bounced against the bed frame. She fell down for the last time. Walker said, "You're done touching her." And D.B. must have been losing his strength, because he tripped a little heading toward her, and Walker did it: he shot him again.

Later, they told him, the second one went in his leg. And either of those shots might not have killed him in the end. It was the third.

It was after D.B. got stunned and started begging, finally begging and yammering, scared, but like the cocksucker that he was. He said, “Get the fuck out of here, you little shit. Put that gun down or you’ll be sorry.”

Walker said, “Say you’re sorry.”

His mother was moaning and crying, making terrible animal sounds he couldn’t understand. And D.B. had crawled into the closet. D.B. was leaving blood behind him, a lot of blood. D.B. was crying and saying, “Fuck you, fuck you, you little shit.”

The afternoon sunlight cut across the floor at a sharp angle. Anyone in the apartments next door could have looked right in and watched them. Walker said, “Say you’re sorry,” one last time. But D.B. didn’t.

And so the last one, Walker really aimed. And even then he was a bad shot, just clipped D.B. in the neck, and it sprayed. Parts of D.B. sprayed onto Walker, onto everything in the closet.

D.B. slumped to his side, and Walker stood staring, not believing this was real. He had no idea who he’d just become. Not even Jerome could do a thing like this.

Blood has a smell, when enough of it gets together. That man’s surprised eyes, his mother horrified, the blood dripping out between the fingers, everyone touching everything, his mother pressing her hand over the wounds, crying, “Jesus! Jesus! What did you do?” And Tasha’s screams curdling through every wall of the house. Where was she?

Walker stepped out of the closet, past his mother, into the bedroom. And there, in the hall by the open door, was Martin.

He had seen everything.

Really it was Martin and Moms who knew the truth, not

Jerome, not Tasha, not the cops. The truth about how that third shot went, the truth about how D.B. was only cowering, couldn't hurt anyone by then. If that truth got out, he'd have got life, not eighteen years. They had kept that secret for him, they had done that. But if they hated him, if they feared him, punished him, maybe they had good reason.

Walker went past Martin and down the stairs, out the door and down the sidewalk, where neighbors were looking through their windows at him. He walked right past them, to the corner, to the ice-cream shop. There were kids and parents inside. He opened the door and walked to the counter and put the gun down, feeling his fingers cramped up and ringing. "Call the police, please," he said. "I just shot my mother's boyfriend."

How stupid to come back to this house, to come inside. Walker wandered from room to room, all the way up to his and Jerome's old attic room and back down again. Slowly. The second floor was finished now, all white primed walls and empty rooms, no furniture, just hollow. He went in the big front bedroom. That closet had been cleared out, stripped away, every last trace. The floor though, still red, someone had *painted* it red, like they wanted that memory never to go away. He put it together: only Martin would do that.

"What a fool," he said, sitting down there, crumpling like that man's body, landing on the dusty floor and just letting go. He pushed Jerome's stupid hat off his head, threw it across the room. "What a fucking fool."

Then he thought he heard a noise just outside the house. Maybe a car door. He turned off the flashlight and ran down the stairs, remembering every step and turn. Even with her bed in the middle of the kitchen he didn't bump into anything. He made his way out the back door, off the porch, across the dark patio, and only there did he bump something—heavy and hot. The grill came crashing down onto the cement, splashing up embers around his heels. "Fuck," he gasped. He stopped and listened but didn't hear anything else. No car doors, no front door, no lights going on inside. He stooped to see about righting the grill, making sure the embers didn't light anything. But just then the neighbor's window lit up, a hand moved against the drape to look out, and he couldn't stick around like this and get caught. He ran.

25

If she hadn't left the cans of paint thinner and stripper there at the edge of the back porch, if she hadn't left the two used rags on top of them, if she hadn't neglected to seal one of the caps. If the summer hadn't been desert dry, if she hadn't failed to water anything in weeks. If the back porch hadn't been frail and rotted like ten-year-old firewood, if Jay hadn't cooked dinner on the grill, trying to calm her down, trying to drink a little beer and make peace. If she hadn't gotten spooked after nightfall and said she didn't want to go back to *that house*, if Jay hadn't driven her back to Dexter with him. If she hadn't decided not to demolish and insulate and fire-block the kitchen—the one room adjoining the back porch, the one room in the entire house she had left untouched. If she hadn't kept that forty-year-old gas oven with its leaky fittings. It might not have happened. Or at least might not have gone so far.

But it did. A cluster of those embers landed near the paint thinner, near the rag hanging down, and crawled up the fumes and into the can and ignited. And licked up the side of the back porch wall, which hadn't been painted or sealed in years and had spent the past several days soaking in those fumes. It danced up the walls and across the floor, lit onto the roll of paper towels she had left there, whispered against the stack of newspapers, flirted with and licked them, finally catching on. From there it was a short trip to the door, to the back wall of the house itself, and these barriers took longer, but they were a hundred years old and tired and ready to go.

It was as if nature had set out and planned it this way. This was how it had been happening in old neighborhoods for centuries: you could count the fires by every empty lot, every anachronistic house, incongruous apartment building, extra garage, parking lot. It had happened just next door thirty years before, where the apartments stood now. These things, they happened. Houses winked out and said good night, they had given their all. The flames moved up the back door, scratching as the dog did, begging entry, eventually making the door quiver and sweat, till the paint bubbled off on the inside and the wood weakened. Such things were not made to last. The rattan doormat was easy, the old wooden cabinets offered themselves like flowers to bees. And that brought the flames to the oven, which blew, throwing fire through the kitchen and up the staircase. The banister was slick and soaked with paint stripper, ready to go. It lit up in a flash that rose through the foyer, feeding on all that free air, climbing to the second floor. By now the heat itself could start a fire.

It moved through what had once been Tasha's room, Martin's room, what had once held Big Bird bed sets, rocket ships. It flashed its way into the front bedroom, wiping out any trace of Walker's crime, any trace of the arguments between Kate and Stuart, any trace of the nightmares they'd had. It wiped out the lousy tenants and landlords, the college parties, the restless dreams, the sex scenes, the sleepless new-baby nights, the visions of better days.

By the time the second-floor rooms were ablaze, the neighbors—who hadn't seen Walker, hadn't thought anything more about that noise and had simply gone back to bed—woke up suddenly at the sight of such a strange, bright light, coming in at an uncanny angle from the side window. It was hot. Their hearts tripped, lives flashed, mouths opened in shock and then screams. They called 911 and carried their valuables to the street. By now the firefighters were in their trucks and on the move, never seeming to drive as fast as they ought to—and the fire broke through to the attic, going up the ceilings rather than taking the staircase, and there, piled in boxes and garbage bags and file crates, it found the storehouse of Kate and Stuart's lives. Her wedding dress sealed in a box in the closet, his running shoes and old laptop, his baseball glove, her winter sweaters, the coffee tables she had bought at garage sales and restored. Their work clothes, extra sheets and towels, their books and photos, their scrapbooks and magazines. Their high-school yearbooks and college T-shirts, their sketches and bills and checkbooks, their bank statements and winter boots, their diplomas, their passports, their birth certificates.

And under the old kitchen table up there, the dog had tried to hide. He had climbed up higher and higher, fleeing the heat, alarmed and confused. He'd never seen anything like it. And the only good thing was that it wasn't the heat or the flames that got to him at last. It was just the smoke. It put him to sleep well before it choked him, well before the fire found him and kissed him. By the time the flames started singeing his fur, it was okay: he was long gone.

26

As it turned out Stuart was the first to see it. He came back to his mom's house after a day of hiking, and she was standing in the kitchen with a strange look on her face. She said, "She called."

He dropped his keys on the table. "She called? What'd she say?"

His mom pointed at the machine, and he went and stood over it, fidgeting for a second before hitting play.

He and his mom stood still, five feet apart, gazing past each other silently, listening. When it ended, he looked over at her, waiting for her to tell him something.

"She doesn't sound good," she said.

He nodded. From the back of the house they heard Danny shouting at his TV for a few seconds.

"You should go to her," his mom said.

He ran his tongue over all his teeth, as if checking to make sure they were still there. He nodded absently. "Yeah. That's right. Right?"

"I mean, you don't have to, of course." She paused, shrugging. "But I think I would."

"Yeah," he said. He was already rushing. "I'm just going to go see. Just going to find out what's wrong."

He went outside and started breaking down his tent. He rolled up his sleeping bag and the one he'd bought for Danny. He put the pillows away inside. There was a big square dead spot in the grass where he'd lived these weeks. "I'm sorry," he said to his mom, pointing at it.

She shrugged. "It'll grow back."

They nodded at each other.

Danny had come out and stood watching them, a look of concern on his round face. "Danny, I'm going to go now," Stuart said, but in the middle of that sentence Danny already started cringing away, and then he turned and headed back to his bedroom.

"He'll be okay," their mother said.

Stuart followed Danny back to his bedroom. "I'm going to miss you." His brother was leaning his shoulder into the wall, with his head tilted into it, too. He was counting something on his fingers, looking at the wall, not Stuart.

Stuart stepped closer, holding his hand out slowly. Danny shook it quickly and said, "Yeah," in a spasm, waving.

It was pretty good, as Danny's good-byes went.

So he left Omaha and drove through the night, hitting the Ann Arbor/Saline exit around dawn. He slowed down on the ramp and headed for Main Street. His mom had taken care of him. He was cleaned up, shaved, with fresh clothes and a haircut and his head on straight. His forehead had healed. He was going to go talk to Kate and figure things out. Find out what she wanted. If she never wanted to see him again, he would hear that from her own mouth, not just guess about it. He would put himself in her hands and see what she did.

It was six-thirty. She would still be sleeping. He stopped at the gas station for a cup of coffee, and he got one for her, too.

This time he wouldn't chicken out in the street or on the front porch. This time he'd go in. He looked at the cellophane-wrapped doghouse roses there in a bucket by the checkout counter, but all of them put together wouldn't be enough. He didn't know what he'd say to her. He imagined her lying in bed in that kitchen, imagined walking in and standing over her, just watching her sleep. As if he could go back to that night when he'd left her, rewind it, and do it all over.

He needed her. He didn't care anymore about love or not love, about ups and downs and betrayals and indignities. There was no perfect life. There was just *your* life.

We could do counseling, he thought he could say. *We have a history.*

He didn't think about how she had spent the summer, didn't imagine her life changing much at all. He imagined everything suspended just as he'd left it. That was crazy, and unfair. He was realizing that now as he got closer and closer.

He drove past their grocery store, then down the hill by the high school, then up again toward the stadium, and down the long decline toward their street. A dim, gray haze seemed to fill the sky.

There weren't many cars out at this hour. His eyes felt raw, his shoulders and back were kinked. The coffee was horrid, was making him nauseous. He wanted to throw it out the window but didn't want to litter.

As he got close to their neighborhood he noticed a strange smell. He'd gotten used to campfire smells and lots of other awful smells on the road, but this was different, slightly toxic, very heavy. When he rounded Madison and got to Macon, he saw the barricades blocking the street. A cop car and a lone fire truck stood near them, and he had to do a double take, because where he had expected to see his house, there was only half a house, a few melted walls drooping over a flood of mud and debris.

Is she in there? he thought. *Where is she?* He pulled the car over so fast he banged into the car parked ahead of him. He smacked his head on the steering wheel, and his nose started bleeding.

Half the roof was gone, burned off, and the skeleton of rafters and chimney, all soot-colored and wet, reached skyward. Their blue toilet from the second floor was sitting upended in the side yard. Out front the upstairs bathtub had fallen through the floor and walls and lay in plain view where the front porch should have been. His shampoo bottle, the back of their TV set, a stack of sweaters, were perched at odd angles in the rubble and on the muddy lawn, for everyone to see. A crowd of neighbors stood with crossed arms and gaping mouths, lining the perimeter of the police barricades. He scanned their faces and bodies for Kate, but she wasn't there.

A cop came over to his car. Stuart struggled to get out, wiping his dripping nose on one hand, just smearing the blood away on his shorts and shirt.

The firemen were coiling their hoses. One of them was prodding the remains of the house with a pole.

"Hold up there, buddy," the cop said, putting a hand on his chest.

"Excuse me." Stuart pushed past him, heading for the house. He had to get in there. "Kate?"

But there was a ringing in his ears, and he couldn't even hear his own words. The cop seemed to tackle him or something. He ended up in the mud, in the flooded lawn, confused and bleeding.

"This is mine," Stuart said. "This is my house. My wife."

The firemen traded glances and nodded calmly, like they'd seen this sort of thing many times before.

27

So many things happened that night that Jay forgot his usual rituals, didn't brush his teeth or let out the cats or pull the shades shut in his bedroom. And now the light was bearing in hard from the east. It was six or six-thirty; he couldn't see the clock. And the cats were mewing and scratching on the other side of the bedroom door. He held still, not wanting to break from his dreamworld, and wondered how long he could put them off.

She was here. She was in his house, asleep. There was no telling what she might think of this all when she woke up, what kind of regret she might have. Last night when he brought her home with him, she just stood in the middle of the living room, looking around dazedly, as if trying to figure out if she was still angry with him.

"I probably would have been okay at home," Kate said.

"It's no trouble." He brought out a pillow and blanket and put them on the couch for her, but she just stood there scratching her arm nervously, looking from object to object around the room, as if searching for clues.

"You like to take care of people."

"You want a beer? Some water?"

She shook her head. "I want to see those pictures again, those boxes you made."

"Okay." He got a flashlight from the back porch and led her through the dark yard out to the barn.

The lights in the barn were harsh, casting all his projects in sharp relief. "This lighting," he said. "It's like an operating room."

She turned her face up, eyes closed, under one of the lights, which washed out her face like an overexposed photo. He got out his camera. She put a hand up. "Oh, don't," she said. He put it down and just watched her. She wandered around slowly, leaning close to each shadow box she passed, absently tracing its lines in the air with her hand. She took a step back, then moved close again.

She worked her way over to the collage box with the pictures from her house, Claire's old black-and-white pictures. This project she'd wanted to make, back then, eventually he'd made it for her.

"You can open it," he said. "You can take things out if you want. You can have the whole thing. Or I mean, if you want, we could—" He wanted to say, *Destroy it*. But some part of him held back. It wasn't Claire in that box, but it was the last trace of her.

She opened the latched glass door and put her hand in slowly, as if she were reaching into a cage to pick up a rat. He photographed her doing this. He didn't know why, but he wanted a record of it. She glanced over as if to scold him but said nothing. She pulled out the two snapshots and squinted into them. "Who took these?" she said. "It doesn't look anything like you."

"It was a long time ago," he said.

"No, I mean, the expression. You look so crazed. What were you doing?"

He searched the room for something to say. "Do you want me to tell you the whole story, what happened that night, with Walker and his family?"

She thought about it for a while and shook her head slowly. "I'm sorry," she said. "Can we go inside the house?"

She headed for the door of the barn, but he just stood still.

"She was my girlfriend," he said, feeling every last thing in the barn listening. He had never told anyone. "I was hitting her."

He watched her face as he said this, and she twitched a little, but just went on standing there, waiting to see if he was going to say anything more.

And so he told her all of it, starting with the phone call from Mack that night, and Claire's desire to see the crime scene, then the scene itself and Mack blabbering on about it. He told her what he knew about Walker's family, and he watched her face to see how much she could take. Slowly, checking himself every sentence, he threaded out a description of the crime to her, and the crime scene. She nodded bravely, taking it all in. Her face softened. They sat down on the dirt floor in that harsh light, as if under interrogation, and he told her about Claire, not just the hit and the awful black stitches but how after that day she changed, got quieter, stopped showing up in the places where she belonged. Kate held the shadow box in her arms, squeezing it to her chest like a schoolgirl with her security shield of books. He told her how he could never quite shake the feeling that he had knocked her out of orbit, sent her flying into the void. He knew that didn't make sense, he knew it. He knew she wasn't that fragile. "But the thing is," he said, "people aren't as strong as they appear. You never know what might be too much for someone."

"That's true," Kate said. "That's true. They never found her?"

He shook his head. It had been eighteen years, but still her parents had never given in, never held a funeral. Like Jay, they wanted to be able to think she was flaky and cruel enough to do this on purpose, to give up everything and never come back, to reinvent herself on a commune in Arizona, or a club in Amsterdam, or a beach in Mexico.

Kate reached out one hand and set it on his, closed her fingers over his. With her other hand she still clung tight to the box.

And so, when she kissed him, it was between them, this clumsy old object, filled with his biggest mistakes, and it took a long time before she noticed it and set it down.

Her chin was tucked to her chest, her shoulder high, his dark gray sheets pulled up to her ear. Her mouth was open part-way, with the tip of her tongue jutting out. The sun was inching across the window and would be in her eyes any minute. He held up a hand to shield her when it got close.

Her breathing changed anyway. She stirred, she sucked in a sudden deep breath and opened her eyes: bright green, and bloodshot. Her hair was like a nation to itself there on the pillow. "What are you waving at?" she said.

He dropped his hand and the light blazed right at her eyes.

"Oh!" she cried, burrowing her forehead under his shoulder, like a cat.

Relief. She didn't leap up in shock and regret, throw her clothes on, and apologize. She just lay there, totally limp, no tension at all. No sign of regret. She put her palm on his chest and played with the few sparse hairs there.

"What time is it?"

"It's early. You can sleep more."

She yawned and shook her head. "The dog. I have to go home and let Ned out. He'll be bursting." He liked that, the ordinariness of this, how everything with Walker was momentarily forgotten and she was ready to go home and start a normal day. Like she was healed.

Jay leaned over her and kissed her neck, her collarbone, her shoulder, her chest.

"Mmm."

"Did you dream anything?" he murmured, scooting down.

She gasped and sat up. "Huh!" The sheet fell away and she sat there naked, laughing. "I didn't dream anything at all."

Jay saw it before she did. He was driving her home, and when they got to her corner, a cluster of people were gathered on Madison—a pair of old couples with rumpled-up hair, a wiry younger guy in running shorts. "Those are my neighbors," she said. If he had seen the barricade in time, he would have turned the car around, taken her down a different street, back to his house or out to breakfast or anywhere on Earth to spare her. But the house was already upon them and there was nothing he could do.

"Uh," she gasped. She shook her head, as if it might be a mirage, then blinked at it. It was real.

Holding her hand was completely inadequate. Trying to hug her, hold on to her, was impossible. She shifted around in her seat but didn't want to get out of the truck. "It's okay," he said feebly. "You don't have to get out. Just hold on."

They stared up at it from the street. Two cars were backed up behind him and honked, and it seemed to take an eternity to figure out how to move his truck aside.

Half of the roof was gone, and the south wall stood leaning in and melted. The glass in each window was gone, the area above each gaping hole scorched black. And through the burned-away openings you could see all the charred insides. All their work. All their work was gone.

There were piles of clothes and books, papers, lying in puddles of mud and foam in the grass. Gray clouds seeped up off them into the air. A haze hung over the neighborhood, and a few dozen people were lingering near the coffee and ice-cream shop on the other side of the barricades. They had their newspapers, their travel mugs, their curiosity. Pairs of strangers and acquaintances leaned in to each other, pulled together by fear. The invisible ties between them came to light. They forgot what to say.

A heavyset policewoman came over to the truck. Jay shook his head at the cop. Not now. But Kate just nodded her head and said, "It was mine."

So they creaked open the truck doors and stood on the sidewalk. Jay put his hand on her back, on the small of her back. She felt so thin. He could feel her spine, the two hollows down low on either side of it.

"Your husband?" the policewoman said slowly, beginning some longer question.

Kate said, "No, he's my friend."

The cop said, "I mean, they took your husband to the hospital. He's okay, though."

"The hospital?" Kate glanced around at the other cops and firefighters as if for confirmation.

"He broke his nose," the woman said. "Fender bender."

"My husband? He was in the fire?"

"No." The cop started to explain everything. But after the first few sentences Kate just wandered away, toward the rubble of the house. One of the firemen stopped her when she got too close.

"What happened?" she said. "How did this happen?"

"She's pretty dazed," the cop said to Jay. "You'll be able to take her over there?"

"Where?" Jay said.

The cop was patient. She smoothed her tight uniform shirt over her stomach, tucked it in. "To the hospital?"

Jay and the cop walked up to where Kate was clustered with the two firemen. They were explaining the source and path of the fire, the hour they'd arrived, the measures they'd taken, the number of firefighters they'd called in.

"There's a lot to be thankful for," one said, touching Kate's forearm. She squinted at him, totally baffled.

"That you weren't home sleeping, for instance. That you and your husband are safe, the neighbors are safe, it didn't spread to any other houses."

"Right," Kate said numbly.

"And insurance, for another thing," a second fireman interjected. "They'll build you right back up, better than new. All new *kitchen*, think of it." She gave the guy a zombie nod. Jay was waiting for her to break down and crumple, but she stood very erect, eyes dry and constantly scanning the rubble, as if trying to catalog it all for future reference.

"The dog?" she said, and here her voice broke, her face contorted, but she put a hand over her mouth and pressed the muscles back into place. "Ned?"

The first fireman nodded gravely. "You ought to know, it's usually painless. Probably it's like going into a deep sleep."

"He was deaf," she said. "Half deaf."

The firemen just nodded, used to non sequiturs.

"I didn't take enough pictures of him," she said.

They all stood there in an awkward silence, realizing one by one that all her photos were burned up or ruined anyway.

"I want to take some pictures," she said.

"Can you tell how it started?" Jay asked.

"Probably just accidental," one said. "Something in the back porch or kitchen, looks like. We're looking into it."

"Is there anyone who would want to hurt you?" the cop said.

"The dog," Kate said. "Ned?"

The firemen shook their heads.

But Jay wasn't thinking about the dog, he was thinking about the cop's question. He was thinking about how quick he had been to give Walker the benefit of the doubt. He was thinking of how Walker's face had twitched, how his eyes had flamed up when Kate yelled at him, and the muscles of his neck and shoulders had come to attention. He'd been *convicted*, after all. Maybe he'd never been innocent. Maybe Mack had gotten the story wrong or embellished it, or maybe Jay himself had doctored it up in the stupid, softhearted way memories went. What if Jay had been wrong about him? What if he'd been wrong to talk Kate out of her fears? What if he'd fucked up another woman's life?

He noticed something in the chain of rubbernecker cars parked farther down the street. One of them was moving, pulling out. A pale blue giant, blurring now as it got away. He'd seen it before, there weren't many around: it was Walker's old Ford truck.

28

"I don't want to do this," Kate said. Jay had excused them quickly from the cops, gave them his number, said she needed to rest and get to the hospital, and this seemed to convince them. But once they were in the car, he had a different plan. They were chasing Walker. They got glimpses of his truck in the distance, and he wasn't speeding, probably wasn't even aware of them, but he had a big head start. If it weren't for his noisy muffler and the trail of smoke and fumes, they might have lost him already.

"What would he magically be doing there, on your street?" Jay said. "It's suspicious."

Kate's heart was going at an odd, uneven clip, but other than that she felt nothing. "The smoke is all over the neighborhood," she said. "Everyone's coming to look."

She watched the houses and stores rush past, but they looked like fake TV images, passing by without meaning anything. She felt her body sitting there, but somehow she wasn't in it.

Jay passed a moving van and craned his neck to try to spot Walker's truck again in the distance. They were moving east, across town, toward Ypsilanti. They got held up at a stoplight, and Jay slapped the steering wheel and groaned.

"Really," she said in dead voice. "I don't care anymore."

He turned a quizzical gaze at her. He put a hand on her knee. "What if he's leaving town? What if he leaves for good and the cops can't find him?"

Kate turned to focus out her side window. "What would it matter?"

He sighed. "I just want to see. I just want to see where he's going."

The light changed, and he sped off the line. Kate braced herself, holding on to the seat belt. She felt as if she would disintegrate at the slightest blow.

Ned was gone. And the thought of him trapped inside, scared and looking for her. Why had she left him at home like that? What was she doing last night, hooking up with Jay like a college girl, leaving behind everything she'd owned and worked for?

What did she own now? Her stomach went queasy; her mouth started watering. She opened the window, sticking her face in the breeze. Her car. She owned a car, this change of clothes, whatever was in her purse and trunk. Whatever was in her bank account. There might be some things she could salvage from the garage.

And somehow Stuart had come home, apparently. How long ago? What would he want? All of his things were lost as well. How would she explain all this to him?

Jay was missing the point. Whoever Walker was, whatever he'd done or hadn't done, wherever he was going, he couldn't build her house again and fill it up with what she'd lost. She didn't want to be riding in a car, chasing someone. She wanted to be curled up in bed, under blankets, waiting for whatever dream might take her away from this reality. But what bed, where? Where could she even go?

They had passed through Ypsilanti now and were heading out south on country roads, following only the occasional glimpse of him or whiff of burning oil.

"After you're done with this," she said, hearing how detached and calm her voice sounded. "I want to go to the hospital."

His eyes flashed over, and he paused, then nodded. Like he was thinking about something but decided to keep quiet.

"I didn't know he was back," she said.

He just kept driving. "You're married," he said after a while. "I knew that."

She bit her lip and watched a cluster of pigs pass by.

Off in the distance they saw his truck pull off the road and down a long driveway toward a farmhouse with some barns in back.

"He's stopping," Jay said, his voice getting excited again.

Kate braced herself. She suddenly knew for certain that she didn't want to see Walker at all.

By the time Jay reached the driveway and pulled all the way down it and parked his truck next to Walker's, Walker had already disappeared. Jay got out and started looking around, calling for him. She watched him go knock on the farmhouse door and wait a while, but nobody answered. He walked around the back of the house, where a Doberman was penned up and barking at Jay. She watched the dog pacing along the fence line. When Jay walked over to him, the dog jumped up at the fence and got fierce, but it seemed all show. She got out of the truck, thinking she wanted to go over and pet the dog. Jay moved past her, heading toward the barns. She ignored him. She knelt down near the fence, sticking her fingers through. The dog got down on his front paws, his hind end up high, tail wagging. He barked a play bark. She opened the gate and went inside to him. He was out of water, and there was no grass left in his pen. She found the hose and filled his bowl, then sat down in the dry dirt next to him. Finally, she was alone, where no one could see her. She covered her face, preparing to cry, but no tears came. Nothing at all.

After a while she heard voices rising, male voices, then someone shouting. She recalled with sudden clarity that Walker really could be dangerous, just as she'd first imagined. She scrambled to her feet, rushed through the gate, past the first little barn, and then caught a glimpse of the big barn, which stopped her. It was huge, with a wide, rounded roofline that looked like the hull of a great wooden ship turned upside down. In the middle of that flat, yellowed field, it looked like an ark capsized on a dry seabed, waiting for the flood to come back. A strong wind could blow it apart. She opened the door.

Walker was standing with one arm out, gesturing and shouting. Jay was ten feet away, near a window. He was shouting, too, and pointing at Walker. But Kate couldn't even process the words from their mouths. She just stood shocked, staring at the place.

It was dim inside, but there were a couple of lamps and chandeliers set up. There was a bookcase along one wall, a little end table she'd seen somewhere before. She walked over to it, ran her hand along it, recognized it from her basement, something she had thrown out weeks ago. In front of the door he had laid out her old orange shag carpeting, and along the walls above it he had tacked up what was left of that old green paneling she had spent days tearing down. In the back corner of the barn he had set up the toilet and sink she'd removed from the first-floor bathroom. In the space that would have been her dining room, he had made a makeshift table out of plywood and two-by-fours. Hanging over it was the ugly fake brass chandelier she'd thrown out. If she squinted her eyes a little in the dim light, it was like seeing her house the day she moved in, before she demolished it, before Stuart left. To her right were the old staircase treads she'd ripped out, leaning against the wall.

Her mouth went dry, then watery; a heat flash swept over her, and her stomach began to convulse. She covered her mouth with her hand, swallowing again and again, trying to take control.

"Did you do it? Did you do it?" Jay was asking him.

Walker just stared back.

Over on the orange carpeting stood Stuart's old futon. She went over and sank into it, suddenly overwhelmed by its familiarity—the sink of the cushion, the feel of the worn-out fabric. All of it was shot through with her and Stuart's smell and hair and skin flakes and DNA.

"These were mine," she said not very loudly. "I threw them out."

The men stopped shouting and looked at her, but they hadn't calmed down at all. "They were mine first," Walker snapped. "Most of them."

"It's all gone." Her own voice sounded like it was coming from far off. "Did you see it?"

Walker nodded. His eyes were swollen. They looked wrung out, overused.

On a cinder block next to her was the old metal mailbox she had taken down and replaced. She held it in her lap now, like a pet, opening and closing its creaky lid.

"Did you do it?" Jay said again. This time, calmly.

Walker sat down on the two bottom steps of his fake staircase. "It was an accident," he said.

Kate heard Jay's sudden gasp, as if, despite all his anger and fear, he still hadn't quite believed Walker could be responsible. She put up a hand and waved it before he could say more. They waited for Kate to say something, but she just gazed at these two men in the dusty half-light, thinking of all the days they had spent working together, thinking of how they had all lost something today.

"I want to hear your story," she said to Walker.

He rubbed a hand over his short hair, over his face. "I didn't mean to hurt anything. I just went over—"

"Not that," she said. "Your whole story. From the beginning."

He stared at her in a guarded way. She nodded. She patted the couch for Jay to come over, and when he did, she curled up with her head in his lap, and they listened. They learned about Walker's moms and pops, his brothers and sister, his pops's garden, the day they first moved in. They learned about Jerome and D.B. and the gun, about the trial and prison and now his time out, about Tasha and the reverend and his crumbling memory. Kate listened and listened, her eyes blurring up. She stared through the dirty window at the warped landscape outside and felt for a second as if they were all floating, bobbing along safely in a ship big enough to hold the whole world. The more Walker talked, the more he calmed down. His shoulders relaxed away from his neck. He sounded, finally, like himself.

"See," Walker said, his face streaked and shiny. "This is what I do. I fuck things up for people."

"No." Kate shook her head. "I did it. I dreamed it from the beginning."

Walker and Jay looked from her to each other, trying to understand what she meant. She had dreamed of transforming the house a hundred different ways, but in the end it was her nightmare that came true. Her nightmare the first time she slept in the house, the first time Stuart fired up that grill: she saw in a twenty-second flash the outlines of all of this.

She said, "Could I have this couch back? For Stuart. He's going to want it."

Walker nodded.

"And this mailbox, for me?"

He smiled.

29

When the weather got a little milder in the fall, Walker took the reverend out on walks around town in the afternoons. On his good days Howard would show him the spots where old businesses had been converted, would tell him who had lived where and what their homes had been like inside. Walker tried to remember it all, to store it away. He quizzed the reverend on each walk, trying to keep his memory fit. But some days were bad, and Howard wouldn't talk at all, couldn't remember the simplest things. Other days Howard resorted to making things up, building stories about people and houses that had never been there, that were only a dream. Walker listened every time, held his doubts at bay for as long as he could, wanting to believe, to see this fantastical world where Howard knew everyone inside each and every house, where they all came together outside the same church on Sundays, not to pray but to have big pig roasts and slow dances in side yards and gardens that tumbled over with flowers.

One day they passed by the little brick church on Williams Street with the day-care center added onto the back. They had gone past it lots of times, but today Howard said, "This was my church. It used to be."

"Really?" Walker stopped and looked it over politely, then watched Howard for signs of confusion or lies. He couldn't tell. But Howard had claimed other churches, told complex stories about petty scandals inside—ministers who drank all the wine and served colored water; cleaning ladies who stole from the charity baskets.

"Was this where my dad did the gardening?" Walker asked.

Howard had never actually said he remembered for sure if Pops had been the church gardener. It was a trick Walker was playing to see what might happen.

Howard squinted at the churchyard, trying to remember. "They got a new guy now," he said. Walker didn't know if he meant a new pastor, or a new gardener. Obviously, both.

Most plants were done blooming by now for the season, but Walker could make out a cluster of deadheaded peonies by the side wall, four big hydrangea bushes up front, and a climbing rosebush along the arch that led to the day care. Pops had always liked climbing roses, but so did lots of people.

"Those mums along the fence there," Howard said. "I think he planted those."

Even the best mums wouldn't come back for twenty years straight. But Walker strolled over there with Howard and looked at them, smelling their slightly rotting scent.

"Let's pick some," Howard said, bending down.

"Howard." Walker touched his shoulder and glanced around. "I don't think it's right."

"Come on." Howard smiled. He already had a handful. He was bruising the stalks, ripping at them like this. And really they were on their last legs anyway, all splayed and drooped over under the weight of their blooms. Walker stood watch to see if anyone was coming, and when Howard had an armful they hurried back toward home, with Howard laughing like a boy.

"What was my dad like?" Walker said finally, one last time.

Howard tilted his head. "He was like anybody," he said, then stabbed his crooked finger at the air for emphasis. "Nice guy. Always on time." Walker kept waiting for more, but that was all Howard ever told him. Whatever he knew about Pops was locked inside his broken memory.

When they got home, Howard pushed his flowers at Walker. "If I were you and still had a mother, I'd take these over to her."

"Nah." Walker shook his head.

"You only go around once," Howard said. "Trust me on that."

Walker thought about it a while. He took the flowers in the kitchen and trimmed them up, threw out the sorry ones, put the rest in a cup with a drop of bleach and a teaspoon of sugar, like Pops always did when he brought home flowers he'd cut at work for Moms. Walker remembered it now, how she would lean her head back and smile at him, hold the blooms to her nose. Were those doghouse flowers, apologies? Had his moms told the truth about him?

One thing he knew about her was, for all her problems, she really never was a liar.

He poured a quart of oil in his truck and started the engine and drove across town, keeping his speed down, trying to think of what he'd say when he got there.

Tasha was out on the stoop reading a magazine when he came up. "Hey," she said. "Did you come to buy me dinner?"

Walker shrugged. "Sure." He could take them both out, somewhere decent. He had saved up a lot. Maybe they could go by and see if Martin would come.

Inside, his moms was folding laundry. He held the flowers out to her. They were yellow and orange, small, and wilting, and stolen. He said, "Me and the reverend picked these," but he decided not to tell her about Pops's garden. He decided he wouldn't bring up anything like that again.

She gave him a guarded smile. He nodded and smiled. Harmless, see?

"What'll I do with these?" she said in a pleased sort of way.

"Whatever you want."

She gave him another puzzled look and he stared back, trying to open himself up. "You want to go to dinner?"

She cocked her head slightly, made an odd expression with her mouth. But he stood there and waited and waited, and after a while she went and got her jacket.

30

Julia's wedding came on a cool, gray Saturday in early October. Kate was upstairs in her old room at her parents' house, getting dressed. In the next room, Julia was drinking champagne with her bridesmaids as they got their hair done. Kate could hear them giggling and shrieking, like girls at a slumber party. When she finished her makeup, she'd go over and join them for a while.

She stood in front of the mirror, checking her dress from different angles. It was a simple, butter-colored thing with a plunging neckline, and she moved around in many poses to see if the edge of her bra would show. It did, so she contorted herself a little to pin it to the fabric. There. It was fine. She had laid out all her new makeup; Julia had taken her to the mall for makeovers last weekend and bought her all this, these brushes and compacts and tubes. People were brimming over with nice gestures toward her these days. She ran her fingers over the little compacts, trying to remember which colors went where.

She was starting to accumulate things. She had been staying here over a month. New clothes, a new stock of underwear, a swimsuit, this dress, two pairs of shoes. Having nothing worn out or ill-fitting or faded made her feel slick and put together, almost like Julia. Though it felt like a charade to Kate, there wasn't much she could do about it; in time her things would fall apart again and look like her. She did like not having boxes of junk and bills, files waiting in purgatory to see whether they were needed; she liked not having anything to fix or take care of. What she had could fit in her car and be whisked away at any minute.

The other thing she lost was her nightmares. It was as if, having lived through a real nightmare, she was no longer so frightened by the world. She had survived. Whatever the world could do to her now, she could take it.

Her dad had given her two books of house plans, and she liked to look through them, though she wasn't sure yet if she wanted to rebuild. Men had come and bulldozed the remains of the house for safety's sake, so now when people drove down the street there was a gap where number 558 should have been. Probably for a few weeks it made a conversation piece around the neighborhood. But already now people's eyes had adjusted, didn't find the absence shocking anymore. The family in the house behind her had asked her how much it would take to buy the lot. She couldn't say.

"Kate," she heard her mother calling from downstairs. She stepped out into the hall and looked down over the railing. Her mother was dressed up in a lemony, satin dress that fit close to her body and showed off her strong, slender arms. "Your friend's here," she said, pointing through the big windows on either side of the oversize front door.

There on the driveway was Jay in a green thrift-store suit, shaking her dad's hand. Other people would be saying what a beautiful house it was, though she secretly hoped Jay didn't. Beyond them she could see the sharp, white-coated caterers moving into and out of the big tent they'd set up on the lawn. There were dozens of round tables and chairs standing on the grass and under the tent, and tall outdoor heaters placed at intervals. There were two big, fully stocked bars and a string quartet tuning up on the terrace. It looked pretty much like Kate's wedding had looked, but this time inside the tent was a cake Kate had made, a big white simple cake with almost no decorations. As Julia said, it was elegant. And it was easy.

She leaned on the railing and watched Jay talking to her father, not caring at all what her parents thought or whether they liked him. She had moved past being frightened by them, and they could smell it. After the fire, she didn't notice whether anyone judged her anymore. No one seemed to expect anything of her. They just cast frightened glances her way and tried to stay off all the subjects that might pain her. She was delicate and dangerous in their eyes. In her own, she was free.

Stuart had settled into an apartment in Ypsilanti, and in it he had his couch and some new CDs and what few clothes were left after his trip. He, too, was buying things. The insurance check had come through, and they split it. He had gotten another job that even paid better. He had a small scar on his bumped forehead, but his broken nose had healed fine. They got together from time to time; they went for walks. Last week they went out to the Humane Society, where Stuart said he'd been volunteering and looking for a new dog. They walked three different mutts around the yard, but none of them seemed quite right. They sat on a picnic bench under a tree, watching other people trying out other dogs, putting some back and taking some away.

"They're like surrogate kids, these dogs," she said.

He nodded quietly.

It was not the same between them. They were polite together, often speechless, careful not to open any wounds.

"Do you think we might ever . . . ," he said.

She said, "Who knows?"

"You're not ruling it out?" He smiled, watching her closely. She didn't answer. She didn't look at him.

"I thought that if I went away, maybe, I don't know. You'd realize how much you needed me." He laughed a little. "It was a gamble," he went on. "Pretty stupid."

She shook her head quickly. "I think it was brave. I think it was the bravest thing you've ever done."

He held her gaze for a while, then glanced away nervously, petting the dog they had with them. It was a boxer mix with a smooth, tiger-striped coat and a smashed-in face. His name was Sam.

"He snorts too much," Kate said. "He'll keep you up at night."

"I don't sleep that much anyway."

"Don't get pathetic," she said, grinning at him.

"Yeah." He got up to lead the dog back to its kennel. "I'll keep looking."

Kate went back into her room now to finish her makeup before going downstairs. But looking at the jars and tubes, she didn't feel like it. She opened the big empty drawer on the bureau and swept them in. She would look how she looked. Next to the mirror hung the only real possessions she had left from inside the house: Jay's shadow box, its frame warped and as dinged up as the old house had been. Inside it were the photos from Claire, and behind them, the letter Kate had found. She had left it in its Ziploc bag in Jay's car that night when he drove her out to his house. He had put it in this box for her, given her the whole thing. She opened the glass door and reached in, pulling out the letter. Warped and stiffened by the dried water, it felt like burned skin. It was nearly blank, except for the red wax seal and a few spots where the black ink had bled into a blur of indecipherable language. At night, before falling asleep, she imagined what things the letter might have contained. From someone in Erie, Pennsylvania, to someone in Hanau, Germany, in 1828. That much she remembered, as well as the delicate, curving penmanship that made her believe it belonged to a woman. Kate thought of her as a new arrival in the States, a settler, a pioneer, reporting home on what she had found in the New World. She imagined it told of a journey by ship across rough seas, and of families moving westward across plains and forests, what little baggage they had being both a burden and a comfort. It told of strangers swindling them, of thin, steaming horses, of log-filled rivers and disease and rumors of savages. Of strange sounds in the night, of dwindling rations, of landscapes that seemed both barren and rich with potential. Which way did she see it?

It told about the struggle to hold lives together, to make shelter and lose it, to hope, to endure, to be lonely, to be lost, to injure, to remember. The author of the letter lost things along the way like everyone else: a bag tipped over at a river crossing, an heirloom chair swept up in a fire, a hair comb stolen from her pocket by some stranger. On the night she sat down to write this letter she was heartsick, regretting she'd ever left home. She was missing the comforts she'd once found insufficient—including her receding language, which she struggled with, blurring her penmanship when the correct spellings eluded her. She was trying to sound brave and strong, optimistic, trying to tell the people who knew her back home that she'd be all settled soon, and ready for visitors, and they'd all be amazed to see what she had built here.

ACKNOWLEDGMENTS

Were it not for the support of so many people, I probably would have given up on this book many years ago. For their astonishing generosity and wisdom, I want to thank all my writing teachers at the University of Michigan, in order of appearance: Joshua Henkin, Nicholas Delbanco, Eileen Pollack, Charles Baxter, Peter Ho Davies, and Nancy Reisman. My classmates and friends in Ann Arbor—too many to name—were a dream team of writers and accomplices, the likes of which I can't imagine duplicating anywhere, ever. For their help with this novel, I am particularly indebted to Nick Arvin, Mary Jean Babic, Margaret Lazarus Dean, Francesca Delbanco, Nicholas Allen Harp, Sara Houghteling, Scott Hutchins, Donald Lystra, Patrick O'Keeffe, Sharon Pomerantz, Emily Tedrowe, and Ami Walsh. Many thanks to Tom Harp for his help with my research on criminal justice, to Michael Logghe for his *True Crimes and the History of the Ann Arbor Police Department*, and to Jonathan Marwil for his *A History of Ann Arbor.* Dozens of friends let me appropriate for these pages their homes, dogs, cars, yards, and haircuts, which made me feel less alone during the long slog of writing this book. You know who you are. Thank you.

For their support during the writing of this novel, I am grateful to the Avery and Jule Hopwood Awards, the Ragdale Foundation, and Carthage College. Big thanks to Don Lee at *Ploughshares* for giving me my first break, on which all others depended. Thanks to Claire Wachtel and everyone at HarperCollins for getting behind this book early on, when I really needed it. And enormous thanks to Dorian Karchmar, whose guidance and encouragement at every stage have been invaluable.

Most of all I am grateful to my parents and family, and to Rodney, for enduring and indulging me, and to Donna and Russ, who are better writers and readers than I'll ever be.